With Best Wishes!!

Mildred and the Kat Chamber

K.S. Horak

First published in the United Kingdom in 2024 by Wolf House Publishing Ltd.

Copyright © K. S. Horak 2024
FIRST EDITION
The moral right of K. S. Horak to be identified as the author
of this work has been asserted in accordance with the
Copyright, Designs and Patents Act 1988.

All rights reserved. No part of this publication may be reproduced, stored in a retrieval system, or transmitted in any form or by any means, electronic, mechanical, photocopying, recording, or otherwise, without the prior permission of both the copyright owner and publisher of this book.

A catalogue record for this book is available from the British Library.

ISBN: 978-0-9557769-2-2

Wolf House Publishing Ltd
8 Shoplatch, Shrewbury, Shropshire,
SY1 1HF
United Kingdom

Further information is available at
k.s.horak.com wolfhousepublishing.com
katchamber.com

Cover art by Lyndon White who has granted exclusive license
for perpetuity to K. S. Horak or nominated assignees.
This is a work of fiction, any references to historical events, places
and incidents are used fictitiously, any resemblance to actual persons living
or dead is entirely coincidental.

Printed in Great Britain by Bell and Bain Ltd, Glasgow

Contents

Chapter One:	North Of Ballater	7
Chapter Two:	No Place For Drones	38
Chapter Three:	The Thaumaturge	54
Chapter Four:	Dragon Bones	63
Chapter Five:	Chainmail And Masks	80
Chapter Six:	Faded Headstones	96
Chapter Seven:	Sleepwatching	112
Chapter Eight:	The Rightful Guardian	127
Chapter Nine:	The Harbourage	146
Chapter Ten:	The Armourer	162
Chapter Eleven:	Eight Of Nine Lives	176
Chapter Twelve:	Stealth Mode	188
Chapter Thirteen:	Darwin's Gate	204
Chapter Fourteen:	Grope Lane	224
Chapter Fifteen:	A Hotel For Elders	240
Chapter Sixteen:	Audible Demolition	258
Chapter Seventeen:	Much Wenlock	279
Chapter Eighteen:	Knights Of Old	303
Chapter Nineteen:	Lapis Lazuli	327
Chapter Twenty:	Tame The Rejects	346
Chapter Twenty-One:	Illuminated Wolves	365
Chapter Twenty-Two:	Swallows Have Flown	377
Chapter Twenty-Three:	The House In The Corner	395
Chapter Twenty-Four:	Recover The Fallen	422
Appendix One:	Late For Surgery	450
Appendix Two:	Cabinet Office Briefing Room Alpha	457

Chapter One:
NORTH OF BALLATER

TWENTY-FOUR HOURS AFTER THE LOXLEY INCIDENT.

JUST OUTSIDE THE VILLAGE OF BALLATER, ABERDEENSHIRE, SCOTLAND.

The lack of speed was frustrating but necessary. The chauffeur-driven car wound around what felt like a hundred bends, consistently beneath the speed limit for the whole trip. Avoiding attention was one matter; the other was having much-needed time to think. Leaving Loxley early in the morning, they had travelled for over four hundred miles, with the last twenty or so through the ups and downs of the winding mountain road, passing through the stunning mountains of Glenshee.

Even in August, there had been occasional snow patches on the highest peaks. Turning right at the village of Braemar, thousands of trees lined the road on either side. There was no traffic, just peace; there wasn't a soul in sight. Lady Safiya took a deep breath as she rubbed her temple and looked out of the window at the unblemished Scottish landscape. They were now approximately fifty miles to the west of Aberdeen, in the heart of the Cairngorm mountains. It had been a long time since she had been here, but she knew the village of Ballater was rapidly approaching. From there, they were only minutes away.

Safiya faced a daunting task ahead, knowing the challenges she was about to confront were substantial and unprecedented. She felt the weight of recent events bearing down on her as she rubbed her temple and closed her eyes in concern. A Gatekeeper had crossed over, leaving their UK headquarters in ruins and resulting in the loss of lives. All their clocks had stopped. This halt in time was not confined to Loxley; it affected the entire Order, serving as a clear message that they hadn't got long. The long-feared prophecy of old had finally come to pass as every timepiece froze at two minutes past midnight.

The Order bore the solemn duty of preserving balance and warding off the Gatekeepers and their malevolence – the clandestine force that upheld equilibrium. The prophecy was a source of dread for all members of the Order, none wishing to witness such an event in their lifetime. Next to Safiya sat Nubia, their leader of anxiety and pessimism, carrying the burden of worry, apprehensive of what was to come. Safiya opened her eyes and glanced at Nubia, surveying the passenger she had invited along. Nubia, their Curator, was visibly tense, her hands clenched over her knee, discernibly trembling.

Safiya glanced back out of the window; the view of thousands of pristine trees was a moment of blissful distraction. Her eye was caught by a wild rabbit sitting tall on its hind legs, sniffing the air, and then a sense of dread enveloped her. She knew she was about to face an inquisition; she had been summoned, after all. The Grand Council was likely already waiting for her, and she did not want to face them alone. Nubia might be able to offer words of support or share insights from her deep memories of the past.

Safiya noticed the sign for Ballater as it quickly passed by the window.

"Ma'am, we are almost there," the driver announced.

Safiya met the driver's eyes in the rear-view mirror and offered a nod. Anxious, she swallowed hard, fully aware that they were just minutes away from their destination. She turned to Nubia, attempting a small smile, but it was not reciprocated.

The car veered sharply up a narrow track and then turned onto a lane to the right. A prominent sign at the entrance instructed 'No Entry' in bold, oversized letters. The car bumped over a cattle grid and then its suspension faced the challenge of navigating a dirt track riddled with potholes. At the end of the track, a modest farmhouse stood, surrounded by tall trees. The farmhouse, like many in the area, was unassuming. Its heavy stone walls were painted white, with small leaded windows to both the ground and first floor and wooden supports flanking the front door. These supports upheld a small canopy, providing protection from the elements to anyone standing on the smooth, grey stone doorstep. Smoke rose from a single chimney.

Although it was mid-summer and the mountains were several miles away, it still got cold at night in this exposed area. In the unlikely event of a tourist or hillwalker passing by, it was important that the property looked lived in and appeared to be a working farm to the untrained eye. There were sheep meandering on the adjacent land, the occasional highland cow, and plenty of rabbits. To the right of the supposed farmhouse was a garage along with other farm buildings. As their car slowed near the garage area, they noticed rusty farm machinery in the surrounding buildings and alcoves.

Their driver, a dedicated soldier of the Escarrabin, leaned forward in her seat and pressed a button on her car door. The window slid open, allowing a cool breeze to enter the car. As she looked ahead, she noticed a patch of nettles with formidable spines standing about ten meters in front of the garage. Amid the tangled foliage, a concealed metal post caught her eye. She edged the car level with the post and, with a determined tug, she unravelled the fake ivy that veiled its top, revealing the illuminated crest of the Kat Chamber. Leaning further out of the window, the driver carefully lifted the lapel of her jacket towards the post. Her pin badge made contact and the garage door began to slowly open.

"Are you okay, Nubia?" Safiya asked, her voice filled with concern.

Nubia gazed directly at Safiya, her eyes bloodshot from a lack of sleep and occasional tears.

"It's been a long time since I've been here, my Lady," she replied softly.

"I feel the same way, my friend, I really do," Safiya responded, her voice tinged with emotion.

The silence of the farmyard was broken by the sound of the garage door creaking as it rolled upwards. At the Order's properties, birdsong was conspicuously absent, driven away by the presence of cats. The eerie stillness of the surrounding landscape amplified every noise, making every movement seem intensified and ominous. Their driver, clearly uneasy, anxiously scanned the area, her eyes darting left and right as if searching for potential onlookers who might be watching them.

After the car entered the garage, the driver cut the engine and the old garage door rasped closed behind them, plunging them into darkness. Safiya felt vulnerable in the cold, damp environment. Despite the engine being off, the dashboard lights emitted a low glow. In the dim light, Safiya noticed the driver's nervous fingers tapping on the steering wheel. The vehicle shook as it started to descend, accompanied by the sound of metal parts crunching. Nubia took a deep breath as they sank slowly into the dark place below.

A deafening bang echoed through the car as it landed heavily at the bottom of the abyss. Safiya heard Nubia's relieved exhale as lights on either side of the car illuminated the expansive tunnel ahead. The car's navigator automatically took control, restarting the car and accelerating them swiftly into the bleak, damp tunnel.

The cold white light from the tubes lining the tunnel's walls caused all three of them to squint. Glancing at the dashboard, Safiya saw they were travelling at sixty miles per hour. Despite the speed, the short journey felt oppressively claustrophobic and uncomfortable. She couldn't help but marvel at the enormity and time-consuming effort that must have gone into excavating this tunnel, trying to distract herself from the feeling of being trapped in this unwelcoming, subterranean place.

The tunnel began to incline and the car advanced steadily towards a perfect circle of natural light. Safiya felt a sense of relief at the sight of the approaching light, knowing that their Curator, Nubia, was uncomfortable in dark places.

As they neared the end of the tunnel, the driver reached for a pair of sunglasses, anticipating the sudden transition from artificial to natural light. With precision, the car burst out of the tunnel, and the navigator swiftly applied the brakes, gradually decelerating to twenty miles per hour. Safiya squinted and shielded her eyes from the sudden brightness as their secret meeting place emerged in the distance – an enigmatic castle concealed from public records a long time ago.

Nubia blinked and focused intently. "I'd almost forgotten how beautiful this place is," she said, shaking her head.

Safiya looked at her, "I thought you always remembered everything!"

They both smiled briefly.

A low buzzing sound filled the air and, as they drew away from the tunnel, multiple armoured drones swooped down from behind them and surrounded the car. The drones flew aggressively close on either side, their weapons trained upon them, filming the passengers and scanning for any others or hidden devices in the car.

Nubia pressed a hand against Lady Safiya's leg in concern, noticing a drone's weapons pointing directly at her. "My Lady..."

"They are nervous, Nubia, understandably so. They will not take chances; they need to be sure it really is us. We will be fine, I promise."

Safiya looked at the drones, knowing full well their pictures were being taken and their life readings being scanned. Safiya knew their images were now on screens in the security office of Castle Macdui.

Nubia swallowed hard and nodded at their airborne escort.

"I suspect we may need to get used to this."

Nubia's eyebrows rose in a panic, "What do you mean, my Lady?"

"We don't have drones like this at Loxley, do we."

Nubia's eyes flared with worry.

"I suspect our beautiful home will end up becoming like this after what's happened. We will have to adjust and implement strict security measures; it will be beyond our control," Safiya said, shaking her head as she considered 'Fortress Loxley.'

Nubia looked out of the window at the armed drone filming her and muttered, "I hate technology."

There was no response to Nubia's comment as the swarm of drones massed together and headed back towards the castle. In the distance, a helicopter landed. Castle Macdui had its own private runway. Two private jets sat idle on the tarmac, with their pilots outside refuelling them for their long-haul return journey.

"It would have been much quicker if we had flown, my Lady."

Safiya nodded as she gazed at the Escarrabin scattered in every direction. They were abundant along the route they had taken. It was evident that news of the Gatekeeper crossing over had reached this place, as ground-level gun mounts had been added, and an intricate weapons system loomed over one of the turrets above, with its barrels all pointing skyward.

Leaning in towards Nubia, Safiya placed a hand over her mouth so their driver couldn't hear and whispered, "It would have been quicker to fly, but to be honest, I was not in a rush to get here."

Nubia gazed into the eyes of the most senior member of the Order in the UK, excluding the Grand Council members. Loxley Manor didn't have its own runway, but they did own a private airstrip twenty-five miles away from the base.

Safiya continued to whisper, "I needed time to think. I'm still unsure how to answer some of the questions that will be put to me."

"Well, that would explain the silence throughout this drive, my Lady," Nubia whispered. Then, resuming at a normal volume, she said, "The security here is much more advanced, my Lady."

"The Reeves make these decisions, Nubia. I suspect it won't be long before Loxley becomes like this."

The Curator looked horrified.

Safiya nodded. "I suspect it's only a matter of time, my friend."

Nubia let out a sigh as both of them stared out of the car windows. The grounds of the ancient castle were expansive. They drove past statues of previous members of the Order, their stone figures weathered by years of harsh wind and inclement weather. The most prominent statue, that of Lady Salma, was visible in the distance. Similar to the one at Loxley, her arm was extended forward as a symbol of resistance against the Watchers. Here, the statue was positioned high on the hills, overseeing the beautiful black loch below.

Nubia couldn't help but feel a sense of unease as she looked out, the driveway slowly coming to an end. The turrets and small windows were typical of a Scottish castle, but what stood out were the numerous satellite dishes and antennae. There was a stark contrast of old and new, and Nubia's disappointment was evident as she sank back into her seat. This was far from progress; the beautiful building had been transformed into a modern monstrosity.

A row of luxurious executive cars lined up outside the castle, indicating the arrival of some of the most senior members of the Order. Safiya noticed their presence and realised that it wasn't just the Grand Council in attendance; other high-ranking Elders were also present. It was becoming clear to her that her summoning in front of the Grand Council was going to be a significant event, with many important figures present to witness it.

As their car circled a fountain, they noticed a significant centrepiece sculpture depicting an old battle scene. The stone figures in the sculpture were eroded and worn from the constant splashing of cold water over the years. Today, the fountain was silent, with the water lying still at its base. The security personnel had other priorities; turning on the fountain's pumps was not a concern. A meeting like this had not taken place for many generations.

As the car approached the main entrance, Nubia slowly undid her seatbelt and extended her legs, massaging her toes to alleviate the stiffness that had set in during the long drive. Feeling weary from the journey, she anticipated the relief of stepping out of the car and stretching her back. The faint sound of gravel crunching under the tyres signalled the vehicle coming to a gradual stop.

The three occupants of the car noticed the amount of Escarrabin soldiers constantly patrolling and felt the many trained eyes upon them. Safiya noted a significant change since her last visit. This time, their Scatterblades were openly carried rather than being secured to their backs as a ceremonial item. Tension was palpable, especially after the news of the Loxley incident had spread worldwide throughout the Order. It would only be a matter of time before the rumour mill reached the lower ranks and younger Elders. This day was crucial for several reasons, including the need for all members of the higher echelons of the Order to align their stories. A slip of the tongue from a junior member could potentially lead to public scrutiny, which would be disastrous. Nobody wanted law enforcement, journalists, or amateur detectives poking around.

Safiya grabbed her cane as the engine switched off. A flashing message on the navigator appeared, saying, 'arrived at destination.' Their driver got out of the car and opened Safiya's door. "Do you need help, my Lady?" she offered her hand forward. "No, I'm fine, thank you," Safiya said as she placed her cane on the ground and slowly exited the vehicle.

"I'm fine as well, thank you!" Nubia exclaimed as she put on her shoes. Their driver lowered herself to look into the car and glanced over at Nubia, who was shuffling across her seat and opening the door for herself. "I can help you if you need, Madam Curator."

Nubia swiftly gestured, fully aware of Safiya's higher rank. While their driver had appropriately followed Safiya's instructions, Nubia couldn't help but desire some respect for herself. The new Reeve at Loxley was sorely lacking, in Nubia's opinion. There was an urgent need for a renewed emphasis on discipline and protocols.

"Officer of the Escarrabin, I apologise for my rudeness, but I must admit that I do not know your name. I'm sorry that we've travelled this far without exchanging introductions."

The security officer smiled and said, "I believe you had much to contemplate, Madam. My name is Jazmin."

"Thank you, Jazmin, for chauffeuring us for the past eight hours. You must be fatigued. Please go and rest. It seems we will be here for quite a while."

"Yes, Madam. I have been advised that I can leave the vehicle here; I just need to park it in line with the other cars. Kindly notify me via your navigator when you wish to be transported back to Loxley."

"If we are transported back," Nubia interjected, "Who knows where we will end up with this predicament!"

"Nubia, composure is necessary at this juncture. This is just the beginning."

Nubia looked down at the gravel, conceding to this point.

"Yes, Madam, I will leave you both to it. I know you are familiar with the route."

"We are. Thank you, Jazmin."

The Escarrabin officer closed the car door and slowly walked away, nodding to her fellow soldiers guarding the main entrance. Silence fell as the helicopter's propellers came to a stop. Lady Safiya and Nubia looked over and recognised Lady Dina as she stepped out of the helicopter. Nubia shook her head, "I haven't seen her for a while."

The Grand Council had recently convened, as is their tradition before any gathering. It was remarkable to contemplate that a mere forty-eight hours had passed since their last assembly, considering the momentous events that had since transpired, events that could greatly influence their own destiny and that of all beyond their Order. The primary focus of the Council's latest meeting, as always, was to determine advancements in rank as needed and to address other matters of great importance. They held authority not only over the

United Kingdom and Ireland's Kat Chamber but also over the global Kat Chambers, or to use their truer name, The League of Light. However, at this earlier meeting, the passing of Lady Tempest not only commanded their attention and deliberation but also their deep concern. Now, the ancient prophecy had been fulfilled. Everything was about to change.

"I'd say that Lady Dina is not pleased to be here, none of us are. We have been friends for a long time." Safiya slowed her pace, tapping the end of her cane on the gravel as she pondered. "However, I must remind you that what is about to happen will be uncomfortable. Please try to remain calm, my friend."

"What exactly do you mean, my Lady?" Nubia inquired.

Safiya smiled. "You know precisely what I mean, Nubia."

Nubia shrugged her shoulders, uncertain of how to interpret Safiya's statement.

"As far as I know, your now not-so-private conversations with Lady Ebonee have not yet come to the attention of the Grand Council. If I were you, I would keep that information to yourself and refrain from drawing attention to yourself or Ebonee. I suspect she will have much to say about the events of the last twenty-four hours."

"My Lady, I believe she will have an important voice here. She has predicted this and has had insight into these matters for some time."

"Perhaps, but she can be unpredictable. You know what the Keeper and other seniors think of her. They do respect her, but her views can be unconventional at times."

"But this is her home."

"It is, and she will certainly express her opinions. She won't appreciate this place being disrupted by all of us, just like you, Nubia, when others come to our home."

Nubia shrugged her shoulders again, acknowledging that Lady Safiya was right.

They continued walking toward the historic oak entrance doors.

"Good afternoon, Ma'am," the soldier to the right of the doors greeted them with a bow. She had secured her Scatterblade across her back as they approached.

Safiya noticed the two soldiers on either side of her had not. She looked at the member of the Escarrabin who had spoken to her, noticing the blue sash across the breastplate of her body armour, indicating a senior rank. "Well, it's not a good afternoon, but thank you all the same."

"The last member of the Grand Council has just arrived Ma'am. They await you in the usual place."

"Am I also expected?" Nubia felt she was being overlooked again.

"I do not know, Lady Curator," the soldier replied with a fleeting smile, took two paces backwards, and pressed a hidden button within her body armour as the old wooden doors moaned and started to open.

As Safiya and Nubia walked past the guards, the senior among them unclipped her Scatterblade from her back and held it forward again.

As they entered the castle, the temperature plummeted immediately; the feeble warmth of the Scottish sun was non-existent in this place. The sturdy stone construction contributed to a cool ambience regardless of the season.

Glancing at the upper floors, Nubia noticed the logo of the Kat Chamber hanging on a banner to the left and the logo of the Reeves on the right – a testament to the merging of their two Orders many years ago. The central banner, rarely displayed in the castle, was proudly presented today, signifying the presence of the Grand Council. Nubia held her breath as she looked up at the detailed image of Bastet, the goddess of cats.

Safiya's cane made a scraping sound as it dragged along the floor while they made their way towards the lifts. Despite the castle's ancient age, unlike Loxley, the lifts were capable of moving both up and down. The walls surrounding them were adorned with portraits of Elders who had passed on, their expressions always serious and sometimes scowling. A few of the artworks featured a favoured cat. The Elders in the portraits wore heavy-looking robes and multiple gold chains, emanating an intimidating presence as they stared down at the onlookers as if passing judgment. Nubia's steps faltered briefly as she recognised one of the Elders whom she had known from some time ago.

"Nubia, we need to keep moving," Lady Safiya urged.

Sadness passed through Nubia as she focused on the familiar eyes of her former friend. She read the inscription below the portrait (Lady Aya,1812 – 1894).

"Nubia!"

"Yes, my Lady, I'm coming," Nubia replied, picking up her pace to regain her place next to Lady Safiya.

"Did you know her, Nubia?"

"Yes, Ma'am, she was a great lady. Feels like a couple of lifetimes ago."

"Your memory and longevity are unique, Nubia. That is why you are important to us, that is why you hold the position you do."

"Yes, my Lady, but with every Lady that passes over, it doesn't get any easier. I'm guessing that Lady Tempest will have her portrait here soon, as well as in the long walk back home."

Safiya looked at Nubia with sadness and nodded with acknowledgement. "I'm trying not to think about it."

A member of the Escarrabin discreetly pressed a button on her lapel as the lift door opened.

"Ma'am," the Escarrabin nodded as they passed her by and entered the lift. "Are you ready, Ma'am?"

"Yes, thank you."

Despite her *'importance'* of rank, Nubia realised that she had been ignored yet again.

The Escarrabin pressed her lapel for the second time as the lift door closed.

In the confined space, Nubia trembled a little. "I don't like this part."

"What's to like, Nubia," Safiya replied confidently, lifting her right hand and pulling at her hair to release a hairpin with a crest in the centre. Ignoring the various buttons in the lift, she inserted her pin into a slot next to the main panel. A screen lit up in front of them, immediately displaying Safiya's face. She leaned forward towards the screen.

A computerised voice announced, "Retinal scanning activated."

Nubia observed as a sensor moved over Safiya's left eye on the screen, capturing her retinal pattern. A crosshair flashed briefly on the screen, indicating the scanning process. "Identity confirmed. Safiya. Level One. Access permitted," the voice declared. The screen then went dark, and a small console with three differently coloured buttons appeared. Safiya pressed the blue button, and the lift began its descent.

Curious, Nubia inquired, "I've never asked my Lady, but what are the other two buttons for?"

"Another time, my friend, another time," Safiya replied cryptically, aware that all conversations within the lift were recorded. As the lift accelerated, they descended deeper underground.

Nubia's trembling persisted as she steadied herself against the side of the lift.

"Security bunker. Level 15 below," they both instinctively looked up towards the speaker as the lift shuddered to a halt. As the doors opened, two Escarrabin turned around, their Scatterblades reflecting against the low light. Nubia was eager to step out of the confined space of the lift. As they exited, the two Escarrabin approached them. One clipped her weapon into her breastplate and removed a scanner attached to her body armour. "If you could step towards me, Ma'am."

"Why?" Nubia asked assertively.

"Security checks, Madam Curator."

"We've been through enough of those, thank you! If you are acknowledging the Lady of Loxley as Ma'am, you already know who she is."

"Nubia, they are just doing their job, although at some point common sense must prevail," she said, looking at the member of the security team who glanced at her colleague and nodded. "Sorry, Ma'am. With everything that has happened," the security team member replied.

"Yes, we know, we were there!" Nubia's voice had risen somewhat.

"Yes, Madam Curator," they both took a couple of steps back. The security team member replaced her security scanner and unclipped her Scatterblade, holding it prominently again.

Safiya smiled at them as she dragged her cane across the stone floor, heading towards an enormous set of double doors. She tried not to use the cane in front of others. "Remember Nubia, keep calm here, please."

They were caught off guard by a sleek black cat sauntering past them. The cat wore an array of glittering jewels around her neck. Nubia knelt down, her voice soft with curiosity. "Hello there, come over and say hello." The cat paused, meeting Nubia's eyes before deciding against it and strolling away. Nubia straightened up, brushing off her clothes with a touch of embarrassment. "A bit rude. I must be losing my touch." She shook her head.

As the Curator, it occasionally upset her that, unlike other ladies of the Order, she was not a protector of cats. Nubia's bloodline was incredibly rare, allowing her to live all nine of her lives as one. As such, her life was dedicated to the administration of the Order. Her long service had granted her the title of Lady.

They approached the imposing set of double doors in front of them. Safiya took a deep breath; these doors were the only barrier between them and the Grand Council. Nubia turned her neck to the left until it cracked. As she turned it back to the right, she could see Lady Safiya swallowing nervously as she brushed at her gown and straightened her back.

"Do I look okay, Nubia?"

"You always look immaculate, my Lady; you are as you should be."

"And what is that?"

"A Level One Elder and the Head of Loxley."

Safiya's slight, albeit nervous, smile didn't falter as the huge doors parted. The enormous weight of the reinforced armoured doors groaned as they opened across the immaculate black marble floor. As the doors parted further, staring faces came into view, their eyes focused upon Safiya and Nubia. With unwavering confidence, Safiya stepped forward, purposefully banging her cane onto the marble flooring with every step. She was determined to make her presence felt and refused to be intimidated by the Council she knew of old. The noise from Safiya's cane reverberated around the huge chamber as they stepped forward, one of them clearly exuding more confidence than the other.

In the heart of the vast semi-circular chamber, the crest of the Kat Chamber shone in gold on the dark marble floor. Aligned with the dome above, it symbolised light over darkness. The room was dimly lit, surrounded by marble and dark walls. Nubia gazed up at the beautifully lit dome with wonder. Below the dome, she estimated there to be ten levels each supported by huge marble pillars. Each level ran in perfect circles to the top. Being underground, the dome was artificially lit by projectors. Nubia watched the projection as the occasional cloud moved overhead, the blue sky resembling a perfect summer's day. Her brief smile reflected the tranquillity of what she was seeing before being interrupted by a voice at *'ground level'*. She quickly focused on the sea of eyes in front of her.

"Presenting Lady Safiya, Degree Level One, Lady of the Manor of Loxley, and her assistant, the Curator of the United Kingdom of Great Britain and Ireland."

Nubia scowled upon being referred to as just 'the assistant' and not as a Lady, a title which she felt she had earned in the eyes of the Council. She glared at the Senior Elder who announced them into the room and made a mental note to address her on this point another time.

The darkness of the room was unnerving, and the temperature was cold. Safiya glanced around her, feeling trapped in the semi-circle of imposing pressure. She knew the exit doors behind would have automatically locked. Eight of the nine members of the Grand Council were directly in front of them, seated twenty feet above. This ceremonial practice was designed to be as intimidating as possible, ensuring those being interrogated knew the power of those addressing them. Other senior members and consultants were scattered on either side. Safiya swallowed again, feeling the atmosphere evolve quickly from intimidating to hostile.

"Safiya!"

Startled by the hostile tone, Safiya looked up at Lady Seraphina, a senior member of the Grand Council from Italy.

"Yes, my Lady."

"We'll start momentarily. Lady Mariangela has misplaced her cat."

"We just saw a black cat outside the door, my Lady," Nubia casually pointed a thumb at the door behind them. Safiya glanced at her without saying anything.

"Cats always find their way, Curator, as well you know."

Nubia coughed slightly under her breath, "Yes, my Lady."

"Her cat can't go anywhere anyway; this is a secure bunker! Her cat will come to her if she chooses and when she's ready. There are more pressing issues to deal with!"

"Thank you for your observation, Lady Dina. It's evident that matters are pressing, and I am eager to hear Safiya's input as well." Lady Dina, who lived on the Isle of Man, arrived last in the helicopter that Safiya and Nubia had seen. It was widely recognised within the Order that patience was not one of her virtues.

Nubia glanced to her left and saw Lady Ebonee openly grinning at her. Nubia was surprised to see her displaying such a blatant sign that they were friends or even conspirators. Nubia tried to signal Ebonee to be discreet, but Ebonee continued grinning as if she had seen a long-lost friend. Feeling awkward, Nubia focused her attention on the three main ladies sitting directly in front of them. These seats were occupied by the most senior ranking members of the Grand Council. They sat in their elaborate 'thrones', two of them slouching with one tapping her fingernails on an armrest, clearly irritated and eager to start proceedings. The third lady sat straight-backed, looking focused but agitated. Her name was Lady Lucretia, and she exuded an air of elegance and grace, much like the other distinguished members of the Council. All three esteemed members of the Council fixed a piercing gaze upon the two guests standing below them on the emblem of the Kat Chamber.

Each member of the Grand Council was attended to by their own Clerics, who meticulously managed their schedules, appointments, and even their ceremonial attire. For special occasions, other senior members of the Order would assist the senior ladies with their intricate dressing and adornments, a process that could take several hours.

The three distinguished senior members of the Grand Council were resplendent in their attire, each wearing a unique, vibrant gown adorned with a dazzling array of jewels and precious stones. Their regal ensembles featured jewels adorning their necks, intricately woven into their immaculately groomed hair, and sparkling on their fingers. Completing their appearance, each of them wore a striking diamond-encrusted brooch that radiated a captivating brilliance even in the dim light. Nubia recognised their brooches; they were crafted during the formation of the Order in ancient Egypt. The emblem of old defined the necessity of the Order's existence. A symbol split in two displayed their more common emblem, the head of the Sphinx cat, along with the older symbol associated with evil - the serpent.

The extravagant exhibition of jewels was a symbol of valour, representing countless years of defiance against the renegade bloodline of the Watchers. These jewels bore witness to battles won and lost, the most recent of any significance occurring centuries ago. Today their ostentatious display of wealth and power seemed strangely inadequate.

Nubia fixed her gaze on Lady Lucretia with an intensity that bordered on inappropriate. She couldn't help but cover her mouth with her hand and lean in to whisper to Lady Safiya, "My Lady, have you noticed? She seems untouched by the passage of time."

"Shush, Nubia, please," Safiya whispered, gently covering Nubia's mouth. "It's called surgery."

Nubia looked perplexed by this statement, her eyes lingering on Lady Lucretia who noticed her gaze and leaned forward. "Can I help you with something, Curator?" Her tone was sharp and unwelcoming. Nubia couldn't discern if she were frowning, but her forehead seemed to glow in the dim light.

"Oh no, Ma'am, I'm just fine, thank you."

"I didn't ask how you are."

From her years of disciplined service, Nubia grimaced, unimpressed by the rudeness of the tone. "Yes, my Lady. It's just..."

The atmosphere in the Grand Council chamber was tense as the members waited. Suddenly, the sound of a door creaking open behind them brought a welcome distraction.

"Oh good, Mariangela, you are here," Lady Seraphina, the master of ceremonies, stated in a curt manner.

"Sorry, Seraphina, regrettably Mina, relieved herself next to the door outside," Mariangela responded apologetically.

"We have more pressing issues to discuss than your habit of mislaying your cats or their toiletry functions!" Lady Seraphina retorted.

"I'm well aware of the history of my cats; they have earned their right to roam and seek. Do you know yours?" Mariangela replied, standing her ground.

Lady Seraphina expressed her frustration with a subtle shake of her head. It was a rare occurrence for members of the Grand Council to bicker. The strain from the events of the last few days was becoming evident. Safiya and Nubia exchanged knowing looks as they observed the absence of jewels around the neck of Lady Mariangela's black cat.

It was clear to them that another cat search would soon be underway. Taking her seat, Lady Mariangela placed the jewel-less cat on her lap.

"Now that we are all present," Lady Seraphina began, "the time has come for this extraordinary meeting to commence."

Nubia glanced sharply to her left and caught sight of the scribe diligently making notes. Records like this were always meticulously recorded, yet they remained securely hidden away within the archives. Despite her extensive years of service, Nubia had never been entrusted with the knowledge of the location of this special place. Lady Seraphina leaned forward; her intense stare fixed directly on Lady Safiya. "You know exactly why you are here, Safiya. You have some explaining to do. Let's start with our national headquarters being partially destroyed."

Safiya coughed slightly under her breath in an attempt to clear her throat. "Yes, my Lady, well..."

"Then you can tell us about the tragic incident involving the loss of a Cleric, who seemed to be under the control of a Watcher, if indeed that's what happened."

"Yes, to start..."

"You don't have to go into detail about the losses suffered by the Escarrabin order. From what I understand, your new Reeve has already been summoned to Spain to meet with the senior Lady of the Reeves. There she will be questioned about those matters and the numerous security failures at our UK headquarters!" Lady Seraphina leaned even further forward, successfully exuding an intimidating aura. "Your Reeve hasn't been at Loxley for very long. I'm certain she will be made to feel most uncomfortable." Lady Seraphina's sinister partial grin perfectly showcased the lingering animosity between some of the highest-ranking members of the Order and the Reeves.

"I don't trust her!"

Safiya's eyes widened in horror, she immediately looked at Nubia with some disgust at her outburst.

Nubia's unwelcome insertion into the questioning had put Safiya immediately on the backfoot. "You were not being questioned,

Curator. In fact, I'm not fully sure why you are here. Safiya, care to clarify?"

"I invited our Curator as she has memories of old and experience in these matters. She also has knowledge of the ancient prophecy," Safiya explained.

"As Do I!"

Lady Seraphina reclined in her grandiose chair, letting out a heavy sigh as she recognised the unmistakable voice of Lady Ebonee, with her broad Scottish accent. Gripping the sides of her throne-like chair, Seraphina braced herself for the forthcoming 'points of view' she was about to hear, her knuckles turning white. Meanwhile, Lady Charmeine, the third senior member of the Grand Council, leaned forward and assured Lady Ebonee, "We will come to you if necessary."

"If necessary! This is my home and you are guests here."

Lady Charmeine sat back in her seat, her fingers tightening around the intricately carved wooden armrests. "Your home heralds from Dundee, Ebonee," she said, her voice laced with tension. "And this is not your home, Ebonee. It belongs to the Order. All of our homes belong to the Order."

Ebonee shifted in her seat, asserting, "I will be consulted, and I will ensure my opinion is heard!"

"Oh, trust me, we are all aware of your interpretations of the prophecy, Ebonee," Lady Tien's tone was patronising as she glanced around, receiving smirks from the ladies on either side of her. "Being 'heard' has never been your problem, Ebonee."

"It has not escaped my attention that many of you make fun of me, but I am right. What has happened over the last couple of days has been foretold in the writings of old. It is taking place right now as we speak. A great change is upon us, and we, as proven by events at Loxley, will not be strong enough to stop it!" Ebonee pointed a finger randomly at the ladies present.

As the atmosphere grew tense, Lady Evangelina, hailing from Peru, finally broke her silence with an air of authority. "Oh, stop it, Ebonee.

Your wayward commentary on events is not necessary," she remarked. As she spoke, the members of the Grand Council turned their attention to Lady Evangelina, who, with crossed arms, exuded a palpable sense of annoyance.

"Your arrogance will be your undoing!" Ebonee focused her pointing at Lady Evangelina "as well as the rest of you!"

"Come on, Ebonee, are you implying that we need to turn to the world of men for help?" Laughter and patronising snorts filled the chamber, but Ebonne, Safiya, and Nubia remained composed. "This is not a laughing matter," Safiya's assertive voice conveyed her frustration, immediately commanding everyone's attention. The Council's laughter was a defence mechanism rather than genuine amusement.

Lady Seraphina firmly acknowledged Safiya and rose to her feet, raising her hands for calm. "That's enough! Ladies, please. This bickering will not solve a thing! We are Ladies of the Order and we must behave as such. We will set an example, especially during testing times such as these. Scribe, do not add my last words to the record. Ladies, we WILL have order here." Lady Seraphina took a deep breath, resumed her seat, and looked across at Ebonee. "You will be heard, my friend, as we all will be. Decisions will be made here today! Safiya, please proceed. We need to know more about this supposed Watcher."

"Thank you, my Lady," Safiya said with a tremor in her voice, her eyes darting around the room. She took a deep breath, swallowed and nervously dampened her dry lips with her tongue. "It was brought to my attention by the new Reeve that there may be problems with a Watcher whose behaviour was attracting attention. Now, that's not the first time a Watcher has been somewhat unruly or rogue, but there was also the mention of an ancient creature somehow risen from thousands of years of sleep in the area below Loxley. Truth be told..."

There were audible gasps around the secured bunker, the weight of her words was palpable in the air.

"What? An ancient creature, you say?" The disbelief and fear in the voices of those present echoed off the bunker's walls.

Safiya met Lady Seraphina's eyes, realising that this fact from Loxley had not reached the Grand Council or Lady Seraphina herself. "Yes, my Lady," Safiya stammered, her hand nervously running through her hair. "It concerns the Hydra, specifically." Lady Seraphina's expression turned to one of horror, causing Safiya to struggle to maintain eye contact with the leader of the Grand Council. Eventually, it was easier to look at the floor. Lady Seraphina's gaze then shifted to the senior members of the Grand Council, all of whom appeared equally uneasy.

"Vile creature should have been killed off years ago, during the time of the ancients; in fact, I thought it had been! Did you destroy it or fire it back to Greece, Safiya?"

Lady Angelisa, who lived in Greece, looked with some disdain at Lady Dina's outburst.

"Well, it never escaped," Safiya said as she unconsciously scratched her head. "It seems that there's an iron wall in the below that none of us knew about. Even our new Reeve was unaware of it. It's suspected that the Reeve's built it a very long time ago. The creature had been lying in peace for hundreds or maybe thousands of years behind this iron wall, and suddenly it came back to life."

Lady Seraphina's voice trembled with disbelief as she uttered, "So, you are saying this beast was there all along, at Loxley! This is madness, Safiya. How did it live for so long? Did you see it?" Her words were filled with a sense of urgency and disbelief. Pausing briefly to gather her thoughts, she continued, "Wait a second... Safiya, are you saying it's still there, it's still alive?" Lady Seraphina's eyes darted to the other members of the Grand Council, reflecting her growing alarm.

Safiya stood with her hands placed firmly on her hips and nodded solemnly. "Apparently so, and no, I didn't get to see it. None of us did. Only the Reeve and the Escarrabin went below."

"Safiya, how did the Hydra live down there? How on earth did it get there?"

"I don't know Lady Dina. The Reeve is still looking into it, and I understand that she is as perplexed as the rest of us. Events escalated in a matter of hours, and everyone had to act quickly. All I can say is that they suspect that it is protecting something, but they are unsure of what that could possibly be. The creature has never been heard until recently. In fact, it was heard not long after the arrival of this so-called Watcher who was found outside our gates."

"This same Watcher the Reeve had raised concerns about?" Lady Lucretia looked around the room to observe the other faces to see if she was the only one not really understanding a great deal thus far.

"Yes, my Lady, the very same one. It's unsettling to learn that he knew of our location at Loxley as well. When you put all of this together, it's highly alarming."

"Put together, Safiya! We still do not understand the first thing that is going on! All we do know is that all our clocks have stopped, and the prophecy seems to be unfolding. It's a prophecy that will test us and could potentially lead to our downfall." Lady Evangelina pointed at Lady Ebonee, "We do not need your interjection at this stage, Ebonee. Thank you."

Lady Ebonee was visibly shaking, eager to express her viewpoint.

"And the Watcher called himself Duat!"

Lady Safiya closed her eyes upon hearing the words from Nubia's mouth. There were gasps around the room as Safiya looked down at Nubia, questioning herself - why *had she brought the Curator with her?*

"Safiya, I implore you to confirm this is not true! A Watcher has appeared outside Loxley using the name of the ancient Underworld, the Duat, a place of unfathomable darkness and horror, filled with serpents, trees of turquoise, and lakes of fire..."

"Thank you, Mariangela," Lady Seraphina raised her hand for order. "We do not need a reminder of the horror of the Duat. There are enough funerary texts in this very castle detailing the terrifying nature of that place. May I remind you all, we were established to ensure the dark world does not enter this realm." Lady Seraphina lowered her head and ran her fingers over her eyebrows. She then looked to her left and right, whispering words to her most senior members of the Council. She nodded as she heard their thoughts.

"Safiya, a Watcher has appeared out of nowhere, adopting the name of Duat. Are you not alarmed by this?" Lady Charmaine's head shook as she spoke.

"My esteemed Lady, as you are aware, security matters do not fall under my jurisdiction. I was completely unaware of the arrival of the Watcher at Loxley until the Reeve brought it to my attention. Let us be candid, esteemed members of the Grand Council, the truth of the matter is that we are unaware of the exact number of Watchers present at Loxley. The below has remained unexplored for years, serving solely as a containment area for Watchers. No one has ventured all the way to the bottom, which explains our lack of knowledge regarding the iron wall."

"It wasn't a Watcher, was it, Safiya!"

Safiya raised her eyes to meet Lady Tien's, nervously chewing on her lower lip. "No, my Lady, it was not. I believe it was a Gatekeeper."

Heavy sighs reverberated throughout the room. Each member of the Council was well-versed in the lore and the prophecies surrounding Gatekeepers and harboured a deep fear of their existence. Within the Order it was told that there were twelve Gatekeepers in total, but these were rumours only. These enigmatic beings resided in the realms of the Duat, standing as guardians over restless spirits and evil. The mere notion of one manifesting in the present timeline invoked a sense of unease. Moreover, if Safiya's account indeed described a Gatekeeper, it would not be of a senior rank. Gatekeepers adhered to a hierarchical order, and the possibility of a more senior and destructive entity arriving remained. Safiya's apprehensions and words gradually resonated with the Council, casting a palpable chill over all that listened.

Lady Seraphina leaned in to address her two closest advisors in hushed tones, their whispers were the only sound in the vast underground chamber.

Safiya nervously wiped at her dry lips and glanced at Nubia. Nubia shrugged her shoulders; both were unsure of what would come next.

After their private discussion, the three senior council members concluded their conversation.

"Safiya," Lady Charmaine began, "I, too, possess some knowledge of the so-called prophecy. It is essential for women of our standing to be informed, even if a prophecy is merely speculation and not a proven fact."

Lady Ebonee appeared agitated by this statement.

"We are well aware of the malevolent forces at play. This Order endures to combat them until they are vanquished for good. However, it is an undeniable truth that Gatekeepers cannot simply materialise. They can only traverse realms when the alignment is precise, resulting in the temporary opening of a portal between their world and ours."

"Lady Lucretia just told me about a recent planetary alignment, so we will proceed with that assumption. Which Gatekeeper do you believe you saw?"

"Well, I am not an expert, my Lady. I can only recount what I witnessed. It transformed from the appearance of a Watcher into something entirely different. The singular eye we associate with Watchers separated into two. The creature developed a snout, its body mass increased significantly, and its talons grew to an enormous size. The creature's back cracked, and wings emerged, unfolding, alive with pulsating veins running through them."

Lady Dina grimaced. "Alive with poison, I think you mean Safiya!"

"Yes, my Lady."

"It had a long tail as well!" Nubia, having not been heard for at least a couple of minutes, felt the need to elaborate further, "it transformed right in front of us, its tail nearly took off all of our heads when it swooped over and took to the sky!"

"My ladies, Nubia is absolutely correct. It had a long, dark tail and its scales looked armoured, making it difficult to defeat, I suspect."

The only sound in the room was the whispering from the three most senior ladies. They huddled together, partially covering their mouths as they spoke. Lady Seraphina started nodding and then looked to her left and right for support. She nodded further and the words "settled then" could be heard. Leaning forward, she asserted, "Safiya, if the scriptures in the archives are accurate in their interpretations, worryingly it sounds like it may well be a Keeper of the Gate. Tell me, Safiya, was there a turquoise colour from its palm?"

Safiya nodded thoughtfully, her eyes reflecting the weight of her words. "Turquoise was seen, although that is not unusual for Watchers. They all bear some resemblance to the underworld and the awfulness of that colour in some way."

"Your observation is astute, Safiya," Lady Seraphina interjected, her voice tinged with concern. "Even with a possible planetary or star alignment, there must have been a portal or gateway that allowed it to pass through into this domain. If so, what does it want and why target Loxley?" A heavy silence hung in the air before Lady Seraphina continued, her furrowed brow betraying her unease. "There are so many questions that need answering, ladies, including the fact that none of us knew about the wall of iron in the below at Loxley," she shook her head with disbelief, "and the serpent creature that was lying behind that wall."

She paused, the weight of her words hanging in the air. "As this creature has remained unseen by any of us, I urge members of the Council to maintain an open mind. If the return of the Hydra holds truth, then the Gatekeeper must possess some extraordinary ability to allow it to resurrect and breathe life back into this creature. That alone is a major concern. Right now, he will be looking for others to help him, as we do not believe he has completed his objective. From what we have heard, it sounds like he is alone and no one else crossed over with him. If this were not the case, I suspect we would already know by now. The portal must have been open for a very short time. As for its purpose, I don't think any of us know. Let me be unequivocally clear, ladies. They yearn to be here; they strive to be here. I'm sure none of you will deny this," declared Seraphina with a sense of urgency.

The members of the Grand Council remained in a solemn silence. Even Ebonee had nothing further to add at this point. Worry and apprehension filled the room.

"How could none of us have foreseen this?" Lady Mariangela shook her head in disbelief. "Curator, you're the one with the answers. The prophecy speaks of an imminent arrival, one who could bring either great fortune or unfathomable malice. Nonetheless, this individual will bear a distinguishing mark. Has such a figure made themselves known?"

Despite the blunt and assertive tone, Nubia was gratified to be consulted. "Yes, my Lady. A newborn arrived the very next day in a turquoise carrier if you can believe it. This occurrence was quite unlike our usual processes, and it left the Keeper deeply concerned."

Lady Mariangela nodded thoughtfully, her eyes reflecting concern. "Indeed. I know she won't like it, but as private as our esteemed friend the Keeper is, we may need to ask her some questions about how this cat was delivered."

There were murmurs around the room. They all knew that the Keeper's practices were shrouded in mystery. No one ever inquired about how the cats were brought to her; it was a tradition upheld for thousands of years by her predecessors.

"Where is the prophesied cat now, Nubia? I trust she is safe?"

Safiya turned her head to Nubia, her eyes conveying urgency, and she gently put a hand over her mouth. "Choose your words carefully," she whispered.

Nubia coughed slightly to clear her throat, her gaze meeting each lady's eyes in turn. "My ladies, I'm pleased to inform you that the prophesied cat is being protected by one of us."

Nubia believed in upholding tradition and protocol, yet she couldn't help but disagree that such a weighty responsibility should fall upon a newly appointed Elder. Nubia sighed and placed her hands on her hips, her stance reflecting unease. "She is with a newly made Level Eight Elder."

There was an audible gasp of panic around the room. Lady Seraphina, in a fluster, banged on her throne-like chair with a gavel to silence everyone. "Safiya, is this true? Is the responsibility of all of this and our fate in the hands of a lower-ranked Elder?"

Although it was hardly her fault, Safiya looked somewhat embarrassed. "Yes, my Lady, I'm afraid that is the case. She is a relatively new intake. The Keeper said that tradition needs to be followed. Nubia has already expressed her views on this matter; however, the Keeper's view and her knowledge needs to be respected. As I understand it, the prophesied cat is currently with one of our ladies, who, for the time being, is called Mildred. She lives in Shrewsbury, Shropshire, in the middle part of England."

Lady Seraphina lifted her right palm to silence Safiya, noticing how red Lady Ebonee had become and the continued unease in her body language.

"Ebonee, you have been quiet throughout, but you look very uncomfortable to say the least. Do you know something about this?"

"Well, I...um..." Lady Ebonee scratched her head and ruffled her already untidy hair. She closed her eyes, unsure of what to say next.

"Ebonee, what do you know?" Lady Seraphina leaned forward, attempting to make direct eye contact with Ebonee. "Or more importantly, what have you done?"

There was no response.

"Ebonee!" Lady Seraphina hit the gavel on her chair so hard it made the occupants of the room jump to attention.

"Well... my friends... as you know... I... um... like to investigate certain... um... things and..."

Lady Seraphina looked to her left and right with some impatience. She received similar looks of disapproval. "Will you just spit it out, please, Ebonee!"

"Well...erm...yes...right, a few years ago," Nubia's eyes flared with worry as she glanced up at Lady Ebonee, silently pleading for her to stop talking. She recalled the time she was outside Mildred's house, speaking to Ebonee on the phone. She whispered, "Please don't say anything," as she shifted uncomfortably, feeling like she urgently needed the toilet. However, it was all in vain as Lady Ebonee continued.

"In fact, it's been almost three years to the day, now that I think about it," Ebonee said, shaking her head as she tried to gather her thoughts on what she should disclose. "I requested Mildred to be kept under surveillance because something seemed off in her timeline. I couldn't quite put my finger on it, but I had a feeling she was going to be fast-tracked. The Keeper let something slip to me about her bloodline, so I started my investigation from there."

The room fell silent, but Safiya couldn't help but notice Nubia's sudden discomfort. Nubia's body rocked back and forth, drawing Safiya's attention.

Lady Dina shook her head and asked, "What happened next, Ebonee?"

"Well, I asked Nubia to keep an eye on her," Ebonee said.

Nubia's eyes closed in an instant, and her head fell. With her eyes still closed, she could hear Safiya taking a couple of steps away from her. She opened her eyes, ran her hands down her blazer, straightened her pin badge, and looked up to see every member of the Grand Council staring at her.

"There you go Nubia, that wasn't so bad now, was it?" Hearing Lady Ebonee's words, she couldn't help but look at the ground. No doubt, Ebonee was grinning again. Nubia knew that looking at Safiya would not be a sensible option.

The gavel was practically slammed against the old throne-like chair. "Curator of the United Kingdom and Ireland; what exactly have you done?"

Nubia looked directly at Lady Seraphina. "My Lady, I was just following Lady Ebonee's instructions, just to keep an eye on this particular Mildred."

"Clearly, Ebonee was not in a position to do this, so she recruited you, but pray tell, how did you go about it?"

"I just attended her house, my Lady, and followed her a little. I did have to use one of our modified cameras to stun a police officer, now that I think about it, but other than that, not much to report. It was a few years ago."

There was silence. Nubia looked across the ranks of the Grand Council, witnessing mixed reactions from heads buried in hands to others shaking their heads in disbelief.

"Safiya, did you have any knowledge of this?" Lady Tien enquired.

Safiya chewed at her lips in annoyance and looked down at Nubia. "No, my Lady, I didn't," she shook her head. "Honestly, is there no end to your mischief," she whispered her statement at the Curator.

Nubia shook her head and stepped forward in an attempt to smooth things over. "The truth be told, my ladies, is that other than that, nothing much has happened with Mildred over the last three years, well, until the last few days, that is. But she has the prophesied scarred cat, I don't know much more than that." Nubia stepped back again.

"Well, other than poor Lady Tempest being involved, do you know about that, Nubia?" Ebonee said.

"My Lady," she looked up at Ebonee, "it was not me that appointed poor Lady Tempest to keep an eye on Mildred, it was you."

"I was right to be suspicious. I sensed something was wrong around Mildred and the area she lives in. Something was bound to happen."

"And it cost Lady Tempest her life!"

"Yes, it did. One of her lives, indeed. I'm sorry about that, but these things must be investigated. Look at where we are now. Clocks have stopped, and events are unfolding. You should have listened to me!"

Lady Lucretia pointed at Ebonee. "You played with the safety of one of our own, involving someone who was not trained for security."

"I believed it was best to keep it in-house. Like Nubia, I don't trust the modern-day Reeves' and their security gadgetry. They have too many secrets, they hide too much from us. You can't deny it, ladies. The fact that they knew of this hidden wall in the below is further proof of this. What else are they hiding?"

Ebonee's words briefly silenced the room for a moment's contemplation.

"She won't be happy." The Council all looked at Lady Mariangela. "She won't be happy at all. Tempest will want vengeance for what befell her. Safiya has already reported that she thinks Tempest was intentionally killed."

"Days have passed. She will no longer be in the void. Tempest will have already returned; where and to whom is bound to be revealed in time." Lady Dina paused and turned her eyes towards her fellow Council member. "However, this does not excuse your wayward actions in any way, Ebonee!"

"You say that my friend, but it was as I was told. I needed to do something!" Ebonee snapped her eyes shut and gritted her teeth at the slip of the tongue. She knew that everyone was bound to be focused on her.

"You were told what, by whom, Ebonee?"

"Oh, it was nothing, just a rumour. I just wanted to be sure." Her lack of eye contact with anyone suggested she was not being entirely honest.

Lady Seraphina rose to her feet and pulled her gown together as she took a few steps in Ebonee's direction. Ebonee opened her eyes and swallowed seeing the most senior member of the Grand Council heading towards her. Ebonee scratched at the table in front of her with her long nails and closed her eyes again feeling the presence of Lady Seraphina over her.

"Who have you spoken to, Ebonee? What have you done now?"

Chapter Two:
NO PLACE FOR DRONES

"Wow-wee!" Mildred exclaimed as she pinched her nose and kicked her fridge door closed. A burst of laughter escaped her as she made her way over to the kettle and switched on the gas. "Anyone want a fish paste sandwich?" she chuckled to herself, thinking about her inedible and over-ripe sandwiches. Glancing up at her unmoving clock, she reached up, taking it off the wall and removing the batteries. "I must replace these later, Missy," she muttered, grimacing slightly as she looked over at the couch in the front room.

She still found it strange calling her cat Nahla, but this was apparently her real name. Nahla was perched on the cat pillow, observing the newborn rolling around on the carpet below her. "Everything okay, Nahla?" Mildred asked. Her black cat with the white-tipped tail turned her head towards Mildred, indicating her understanding of the question. However, Mildred wondered why Nahla's tail was rolling inwards and then outwards repeatedly. Mildred watched with puzzlement as Nahla studied the newborn that Mildred had decided to name Comet.

Mildred was aware that Comet would have to be a temporary name. The Order had explained that kitten names are temporary until their real name is revealed. Apparently, one had to earn the right to know the real name or something nonsensical like that.

"Are you playing, or is something bothering you?" If Nahla had understood this question, she didn't show it. Mildred was struggling to comprehend a lot about the recent goings on. She blinked a few times, her thoughts distracted by the whistling of her kettle. She took her eyes off Nahla and Comet to switch the gas off. *Maybe it was jealousy or something, Mildred considered.* She had read in *Cats Quarterly* that when a new cat is brought into the house, it can be tricky at the outset, not always, but sometimes. She dropped a teabag into her mug, and with the addition of the hot water from the kettle, the smiling face of a cat instantly appeared on the side of the mug. She smiled back at the cat. With the arrival of Comet into her life, she had plenty to be happy about. She was not so pleased about the other newborn, the one she apparently was not allowed to keep. Mildred glanced behind her to see the unnamed kitten staring back at her. "Why are you not playing with the other two?"

Mildred placed her foot on the pedal bin to keep the lid open. She dropped the used teabag into it, kicked the bin so it closed and moved to the front room. The unnamed kitten followed her. In addition to having to *'give the other kitten away,'* there was something else that required her attention. She set her mug down on the side and picked up her new certificate.

'Member of the United Kingdom Kat Chamber.'

Shaking her head and letting out a sigh, she walked over to the other certificate that had hung on the wall for the last three years. She held up the new one to compare them. At the top of the certificates, the emblem of the Egyptian-looking Sphinx cat was the same. The emblem was in gold leaf, and the layout was completely uniform on both. Both certificates had a border the colour of turquoise. Her name was printed on both certificates, but there was no mention of either cat that had been 'given to her.' It was strange when apparently, she was their protector.

Mildred found it amusing that she was considered the *'great protector'* of Nahla and Comet. The certificates did not mention the length of her membership, were undated, and did not contain any other notable information. Aware of the organisation's penchant for codes and puzzles, she turned the new certificate over and shook it a few times to check for any hidden details. If there were any, they weren't obvious. "Why would you frame two identical certificates on a wall?" She didn't take her eyes away from the Sphinx cat on the certificate, "you know anything about this Nahla?" she asked her eldest cat. Nahla blinked in response, and Mildred interpreted it as a cat version of a shrug. If cat blinking was a code, Mildred thought the Order's eccentric veterinarian, Dr Fennaway, might have some knowledge about it. However, inviting Dr Fennaway into her house was the last thing she wanted to do right now. She turned to Comet, "How about you? Do you know what to make of all of this?" The newborn didn't show any interest, more preoccupied with rolling on her back and clawing at the old carpet. "Of course, you don't understand my question, Comet," Mildred said, placing her hands on her hips. "I don't even know your real name!" Mildred giggled to herself, waving her hands and the certificate in amusement. She paused in thought, *Well, she may understand my question, but she's not listening to me because I don't know her name!* Mildred shook her head, surprised at herself for starting to believe some of this nonsense. She blinked a few times and snapped her thoughts back to the real world. "You want to go outside, Miss..." Mildred coughed slightly under her breath, "You want to go outside, Nahla?" In an instant, Nahla's head sprung upwards, and the rolling and curling of her tail stopped. "I guess that's a yes then." Mildred dropped the certificate on the side and headed towards the cat flap. Since the arrival of Comet and the unnamed paws, Mildred had secured the cat flap to prevent the kittens from getting out and to help the cat sisters get to know each other. "Now then, Nahla, before I open this, please come home on time for tea later. I don't want to be yelling in the street for any longer than I must, the youths at the bus stop make fun of me! Also, Bang Goes Your Money is on later, and I'm not missing it. Do you understand?" Nahla looked into Mildred's eyes, but nothing was exchanged between them. "Do I need to call that lunatic vet Fennaway every time I need to get a message through to you, Nahla?" Mildred smiled, bent down, and removed the old phone book from the flap. "Off you go then."

Nahla shot out of the flap as Mildred watched her from the kitchen window, bouncing at speed down Rocke Road. "Where are you off to in such a rush?" She had never seen her cat move so fast. The phone book was quickly returned to the flap, and her tea drinking would now commence.

The back of the Futility pub was usually quiet at this time of day. The cobbled area next to the car park, affectionately known by locals as 'the Sway,' drew closer as Nahla hurried. She felt drawn to her secret den, even though it was where she had first experienced the pain of her temporary illness. She had no idea why this had happened to her or what any of it meant, but something inside her told her that answers were coming. It had been a couple of days since she regained consciousness, and some pain in her chest remained. The muscles around her heart were sore, perhaps from overuse. At times, she thought she felt the presence of another in her heart, but it was unclear. The draw of the den seemed to be somehow connected to all of this. When she had collapsed into an unconscious state, her mind was filled with a battle of darkness against her will. Although she had endured pain throughout, some of the disturbing thoughts remained. Her dreams during this period were dark and, at times, scary. Something bad was coming, and she knew Mildred was involved in some way. The arrival of the newborn and the change in Mildred's usually peaceful demeanour told Nahla that changes were already underway; she could sense it.

Nahla's mind was filled with vivid recollections of a surreal place. In her visions, she found herself surrounded by eerie chambers, dark caverns, and trees that shimmered with a surreal turquoise colour. In this otherworldly realm, she encountered creatures devoid of empathy. One of these beings ominously warned her that change was inevitable and unstoppable, their laughter echoing through the strange landscape. When these creatures made contact with Nahla, their plans and desires were inexplicably transferred directly into her mind. These enigmatic creatures, who control mystical gates, yearned to escape their entrapment and find a new existence amidst green fertile lands and the realm of the living. These unsettling visions evoked a sense of déjà vu, as if she had lived through similar experiences in another time.

Despite the relentless ache in her heart, Nahla swiftly made her way to the Sway. With nimble agility, she leapt onto the bonnet of a van, then gracefully traversed the wall until she reached the kitchen area. Peering down over the wall, she surveyed the usual debris that littered the ground below. Navigating through the treacherous terrain, she carefully descended amidst shards of broken glass, weaving her way around discarded beer glasses and sidestepping an old fire extinguisher. Upon reaching the concealed entrance, she forcefully parted the thick strands of ivy, determined to make her way into the den.

As she entered, the ivy fell back across the entrance, blocking out the light. Despite her strange attraction to the den, she immediately felt the chill of the place. She glanced to her right and recognised that the scratching on the wall held some significance. Though she didn't understand its meaning, she cautiously approached the wall and focused on the etching of the Egyptian-looking cat. When she touched the symbol with her left paw, she was startled by a sudden jolt in her heart. She was certain that the scratching on the wall was made by another cat, not by human hands. The symbol was now faded but obviously etched a long time ago, leading her to believe that finding this place was not a coincidence. As she looked into the eyes of the Egyptian-looking cat, she had a strong feeling that the arrival of the new kitten at home was not a random event. Something was wrong, and darkness was swiftly approaching.

"Okay, hold position. Are your sights locked?" Kassia asked, her gaze fixed intensely through the binoculars as she adjusted the focal ring.

"Yep, got it," Yara confirmed, her finger poised on the trigger of her Scatterblade.

"Fire if you have it."

Yara pulled the trigger, releasing a brilliant white pulse of light that streaked across the gardens from the rooftop of Loxley Manor. The drone was struck, erupting into a small ball of flame before the remaining debris fell onto the grass below.

Lowering her Scatterblade, Yara and Kassia rose from their position next to the dome, situated five floors directly above the central lobby. As they moved to the edge of the roof, their elevated vantage point offered a clear view across the once beautiful gardens, all the way to the entrance gates about a mile in the distance. The devastation was apparent, even from directly above, where the main entrance doors had been blown open. Stone, wood, and glass were strewn across the lawns and gravel.

"Third drone in the last twenty-four hours," Kassia sighed, tucking the binoculars into her pocket.

Securing her Scatterblade across her back, Yara remarked, "I suspect there will be more."

"Yep, ever since that comet or whatever it was crashed in the distance, they've been buzzing us. Probably the Government or someone trying to spy on us. We are not on the map after all. The area is listed as farmer's fields or something, so I was told."

"Or nosy individuals trying to pry into things that don't concern them."

"Their interference is not welcome here. The more they send, the more we'll remove. Eventually, they'll understand."

"Or they might come in numbers."

Kassia glanced at Yara.

"Especially if they are government or law enforcement drones."

They contemplated their words when they were suddenly interrupted by a noise in the distance.

"Do you see that?"

They looked towards the end of the driveway, where the trees were shaking in the distance. Kassia grabbed her binoculars. After the trees settled, they heard the familiar sound of moving metal. The gates were opening.

"Do you know of any visitors? I wasn't informed of any," Kassia asked.

Yara shook her head.

They waited to see who it was as Yara unclipped the Scatterblade from across her back.

"I have a bad feeling about this," Kassia said, adjusting the focal ring of her binoculars. Unhappy with what she saw, she put them away and unclipped her own Scatterblade. They both raised their weapons in anticipation of whoever or whatever was about to appear at the top of the driveway.

"I don't believe that Gatekeeper creature will be making an entrance through the front gate, Kass!"

Kassia calmly lowered her weapon and securely re-clipped it into her body armour. With determination, she retrieved her binoculars from her pocket. "I can't see anything... oh, wait." A smile spread across her face as she lowered the binoculars. "Only one of us rides something like that!"

In the distance, a sleek black motorcycle could be seen speeding down the driveway. Yara nodded knowingly and smiled. "Kalara!"

As the powerful motorbike was skilfully navigated around the debris scattered across the driveway, the two Escarrabin vigilantly kept watch from the roof, the sunlight reflecting off the engine's glistening chrome. "We should go down and see her!"

With their weapons securely fastened across their backs, they sprinted past the dome towards the stairwell. Kassia placed her palm against the security scanner to unlock the door leading to the stairs.

"Come on, if we move quickly, we can catch her."

"I'm doing my best. I'm sure she knows something!"

"I heard that Raysmau assigned her a mission."

"I'm sure of it. She always gets the most important tasks, and her presence here after what just happened cannot be a coincidence."

They hurried down the stairs. "At times like this, I truly wish there was a lift in this place!"

Kalara decided not to use the Escarrabin's entrance to the Manor after seeing the main doors had been destroyed. She carefully secured the kickstand of her motorcycle, removed her jet-black helmet, and placed it gently on the gravel next to the front wheel. After taking off her leather gloves and unzipping her padded leather jacket, she straightened her ponytail and stood still, surveying the damage to their home. With a shake of her head and a deep sigh, she placed her gloves on the bike and headed towards what was left of the front entrance. She nodded at a couple of the Escarrabin guards, noticing that they were holding Scatterblades, something she had never seen before at any property owned by the Order.

As Kalara stepped over the remains of one of the heavy wooden entrance doors and made her way into the central lobby, she noticed Kassia and Yara running down the stairs, somewhat out of breath by the time they reached her.

"Hello, girls," she nodded at them and pulled at her hair tie to free her hair. "I'd heard what happened, but I never expected it to be as bad as this."

"You should have seen it, Kalara, major firefight," Kassia exclaimed.

"There's a demon below as well," Yara excitedly interjected.

Kalara shook her head. "Demons are messengers. From what I hear, what you have is something quite different."

Kalara seemed more distracted by the singed walls and darkened picture frames that were missing their canvases. "I liked that old picture that hung up there," she said, nodding towards an area to the right of Raysmau's destroyed security doors.

"So, tell us, what did you find on the outside?" Yara asked.

"Did you go into a pub and have a pint?" Kassia quickly added.

Kalara turned to them, looking uninterested. "Did I what?"

"Did you…"

"Is Raysmau in her office? I need to see her right away," Kalara interrupted.

"She is. We are keeping out of her way. Not surprisingly, she's not in the best of moods. Why, what do you know?" Kassia asked.

"Calm down, the pair of you. Remember, I outrank you both. It's for her ears only," Kalara stated firmly.

She walked towards Raysmau's quarters, leaving the others behind. "And no, I didn't go for a pint," she said, pausing and turning back to them, "but I did play a game of golf." She shook her head. "Pointless endeavour, no idea why they bother with it."

Kalara turned back and made her way to Raysmau's quarters, stepping through puddles of water as she went. The old security gate was detached and buckled, now propped against the wall outside the entrance. Stepping into the corridor leading to Raysmau's private quarters, she encountered mounds of rubble swept into corners, resembling stone chippings, likely remnants from the pulse blasts that had scarred the walls. Undeterred, she continued towards Raysmau's door.

"What's wrong with her?" Kassia asked.

"I have no idea. Nobody seems to be themselves right now," Yara replied.

They turned and walked towards the two Escarrabin guarding the lift shaft to see if they had any new gossip.

Before reaching Raysmau's door, Kalara glanced to the left into the security control room. Lotfia, a member of the Escarrabin, immediately jumped to her feet.

"Kalara, it's good to see you. It's a shame you weren't here. We could have used someone with your skills," Lotfia said with a hint of regret.

Kalara looked at the security controls and the disused Scatterblade that lay next to them. "I was busy elsewhere," she replied softly. She took a deep breath and shook her head. "So, this is where it happened, where the Cleric killed Layla and Amera."

Lotfia nodded, understanding the weight of the situation.

Kalara acknowledged the nod and chewed at her lip; there were no words she could suggest that would soothe things. She nodded her head towards Raysmau's door. "Is she in?"

"Yes, she may be out the back. Would you like me to call her?" Lotfia offered.

"No, don't worry, I'll find her," Kalara reassured.

"Kalara, I should warn you, she's somewhat tetchy," Lotfia cautioned with concern.

Kalara nodded, showing the slightest of smiles. "She usually is."

Kalara left the room and knocked a couple of times on the heavy door in front of her. She waited a few seconds, but when she received no response, she knocked again. With no reply, she pushed the door open and let herself in. Inside, she noticed the huge chair behind the enormous oak desk. The usual paperwork and work orders were absent, making the desk look vacant. It was rare for Kalara to be in this room alone, so she took the opportunity to inspect the historic artwork on the walls. Each frame depicted a battle, there were no pictures of Elders of the Order as featured in most rooms throughout Loxley. These artworks were of a different age, and all depicted battle victories. Her eyes were drawn to a flag that bore a red cross, and the flag bearer rode a horse. She frowned, not recognising the flag as belonging to the Order she had been involved with for some years.

Instinctively, she checked her non-ticking watch, reminding herself to focus on why she was there. Making her way behind the desk, Kalara knocked at the door that led to Raysmau's quarters. Still receiving no response, she turned the old metal handle and let herself through. Inside, she saw Raysmau's Scatterblade on a desk and her chain mail thrown across a huge oak chair.

After spending some time away from the manor, Kalara's senses had acclimated to the fresh outdoor air. Stepping into Raysmau's quarters, a musty smell enveloped her, catching her off guard. The wooden panels that lined the walls and ceiling added to the mysterious atmosphere of the room. A massive, time-worn shield displaying the traditional emblem of the Escarrabin adorned the furthest wall. A glass case, standing about eight feet tall, drew her attention. Its open door revealing an unclothed mannequin, devoid of its uniform.

Glancing back at the door she had entered through, Kalara noticed the walls on either side were adorned with a collection of old weaponry and defensive armour. Swords, helmets, breastplates, and gloves with spikes of various sizes embedded in them spoke of a violent and tumultuous past. Suddenly, a noise from beyond the far door startled her, prompting her to cough loudly to alert Raysmau of her presence.

As the door creaked open, Raysmau emerged, her dishevelled appearance and barefoot state a stark contrast to her usual commanding presence. It was evident that she hadn't heard Kalara's warning cough.

"Ma'am."

Raysmau's head sprang upwards, startled by the member of the Escarrabin in her quarters, dressed in biker leathers.

"Kalara!" she pulled at her dressing gown to ensure she was covered, feeling a little embarrassed by the way she was dressed. "How did you get in here?" The sternness of her tone made Kalara flinch a little.

"I made my way through, Ma'am. I did knock."

Raysmau brushed her hair away from her eyes. "Did you now! You'll be finding a lot of changes regarding security will be taking place around here."

From what she had heard from other Escarrabin, Kalara nodded with acceptance that change was inevitable.

"Why are you here and in my quarters no less?"

"As you know, Ma'am, on behalf of the Reeve and yourself, I have been investigating what happened to Lady Tempest."

"Yes, have you found something out?"

"Yes, Ma'am, shall we take a seat."

"No, thank you, Kalara, I'm fine where I am." She pulled at her dressing gown again.

"Yes, Ma'am." Kalara nodded, put a hand into the pocket of her leather trousers, and removed a phone. "I have something to show you, Ma'am. May I?"

Raysmau nodded, her face a picture of concern. "Yes, of course."

Kalara walked towards Raysmau, tapping at the phone as she went. "I think you should see this, Ma'am." She passed the phone to Raysmau.

Frowning, Raysmau took the phone from her.

"Please press the play button in the centre. I should warn you that it's uncomfortable viewing, Ma'am."

"Everything is uncomfortable right now." She pressed the green arrow as the picture came to life.

"It's CCTV footage, Ma'am."

Raysmau nodded, keeping her eyes fixed on the screen as she observed two dark-suited individuals harassing a woman near a busy road. She was certain she recognised her. "Is this Tempest?"

"Yes, Ma'am."

She noticed a red bus approaching in the distance. She didn't need to see what was about to happen; she had been informed. She looked away from the screen momentarily and then glanced back to see the lifeless body of Lady Tempest next to the bus wheels. The picture quality was grainy, but she was sure she saw a flash of colour in the palm of one of the suited individuals. She shook her head in disgust. "Duat!" she said as she lowered the phone with anger.

"Duat, Ma'am?"

"The name of the Watcher, or what we thought was a Watcher. That creature in this footage has been in this very office," she said, rubbing her eyebrow. "Let's take that seat after all," Raysmau nodded toward the desk covered in body armour.

Kalara pulled the smaller of the two chairs, watching Raysmau gently place the phone on the desk and gather up her chainmail. "Tell me what you know, Kalara."

Kalara noticed Raysmau's shoulders straining from the weight of the chainmail as she walked over to her glass cabinet and started to redress the mannequin.

"As you are aware, Ma'am, we were suspicious of Lady Tempest's passing, especially since she was in Shropshire, which is not her usual operating area. It turns out our suspicions were justified. In the footage, you can see that Duat, the person you mentioned, was collaborating with someone else. It's clear from the strange steampunk-style glasses they were wearing that they are both Watchers. One of the lenses was much larger than the other, indicating that the other lens was fake."

"Steampunk... what does that mean?" Her voice quivered a little from the physical exertion.

"Oh," Kalara smiled a little, "it's a fashion and lifestyle choice outside of here."

Raysmau shook her head, not understanding any of it. She dropped the main body of the chainmail on the mannequin, glad to be free of the weight, and walked towards her desk. She gently placed her Scatterblade to the side and took her seat.

Kalara instantly recognised the familiar pattern of Raysmau lost in thought as she watched her superior move a thumb around her index finger.

"So, he was working with another."

"Yes, Ma'am, there can be no doubt."

"Strange. He showed up here alone." Raysmau's thumb kept moving in circles. "That means the other one is still out there somewhere."

"Yes, Ma'am, that's correct. In other footage that I haven't shown you, they both had hold of her," she swallowed, "it looked like they were torturing her in some way, definitely making her talk. There is no sound on the CCTV footage, but it looks like they got what they wanted from her and then... well."

Raysmau lifted a hand and took a deep breath. "It's okay, Kalara. You don't need to finish that sentence." Raysmau's voice had lowered considerably. "Has anyone else seen this?"

"Yes, Ma'am."

Raysmau's eyes widened in shock. "Who?"

The footage was captured from a camera on Benbow Street in Shrewsbury. The camera was outside one of the strangest types of convenience shops that I've ever seen. The footage was presented to the civilian police, so some police officers will have seen it. However, I was able to prevent it from going any further. I have already reported this to the Reeve, so she is aware of this. There was also a camera inside the bus. That footage was much clearer and quite disturbing, I'm afraid. It captures events just outside one of the windows. In that footage, you can see the bus driver quickly getting out of the bus, concerned that he had hit someone. His bus is passenger-less. It's out of view, but as he bends down towards where Lady Tempest fell, you can see a turquoise flash from the palm of one of the Watchers. You can't see what happens next, but the driver gets back to his feet, gets back in the bus and drives off. The internal bus footage shows him driving erratically as if something was wrong with him. It's strange, almost as if this Watcher had the power to control him somehow.

"That does sound possible from what we have seen here."

"I was able to crack the hard drives and backup systems of the bus company. I thought it prudent to destroy all the footage. The civilian police or anyone else will never get to see it; it just remains in my mind, and that's where it will stay."

Raysmau nodded, "But what about the footage on the phone? Who has that?"

"It's complicated, Ma'am, but I wiped it from all the police databases and backup storage. So, although some police officers have seen it, there are no copies remaining in their possession, so the chain of evidence has evaporated. The footage you have seen now only exists on the dark web."

Raysmau nodded, although her thumb had stopped moving. She was deep in thought. The frown across her forehead gave it away.

"The dark web is a storage system, Ma'am, shall we say, away from normal eyes."

"Yes, I knew that!" Raysmau nodded and shifted uncomfortably in her seat.

"Yes, Ma'am, of course."

"So, is it safe in this dark web place you mention?"

"Of sorts, Ma'am. The dark web is often used by criminals and those who want to hide away from the prying eyes and ears of others. The police nip in and out of there looking for criminal activity, but I've hidden it well. It shouldn't be found."

"I see." The thumb had started turning again.

"Would you like me to access the files on the dark web and destroy them?"

"I'm not sure, Kalara. I'll need to speak with the Reeve. Given your expertise on this matter and this dark web thing, you may need to be present to explain."

"Yes, Ma'am, but as long as that footage is on that phone, it does represent a risk."

Raysmau nodded. "Do you know why Lady Tempest was in that area? Have you been able to establish why she was there?"

Kalara shifted her eyes from Raysmau and looked at the floor. Kalara swallowed and softened her voice, "She was speaking with someone, Ma'am. I tracked the records and listened to some of the calls." Kalara swallowed and bit at her lip. "It's a little awkward."

Raysmau leaned forward on her desk. "Tell me, Escarrabin, what do you know?"

"Erm...well," Kalara took a deep breath and looked up. "I know that she was speaking with a member of the Grand Council."

Raysmau flinched, taken aback by the comment. "Are you sure of this?"

"Yes, Ma'am. In fact, I think it was a member of the Grand Council that sent Lady Tempest over there in the first place."

Raysmau scratched her head and blinked a few times.

"It is also worth mentioning that there is something very suspicious about one of our own members in that area."

"In the area of Shrewsbury?"

"Yes, Ma'am. I can't put my finger on it yet, but I will in time if you wish me to continue my investigation."

"In truth, Kalara, the rest of this conversation may have to be with the Reeve."

"Yes, Ma'am, I understand."

Raysmau slumped in her seat, pondering this new information. Her thumb started to circle around her finger again when she suddenly paused. "What is the name of the member who lives in that area?"

"She's a lower-level lady, so her name is temporary, of course, Ma'am. But for now, she is known as Mildred."

Chapter Three:
THE THAUMATURGE

Ebonee swallowed and reopened her eyes. She wished she hadn't, seeing the shocked faces staring at her. Glancing down, Lady Safiya looked very concerned, and Nubia's mouth hung open with worry.

Ebonee raised her hand slightly to appeal for calm and then shrugged her shoulders, "Well, okay... I did meet with a Thaumaturge."

There were gasps around the room, and even Nubia raised a hand to her mouth in disbelief at what she was hearing.

"You met with a wonder worker, Ebonee; you can't be serious!" Lady Seraphina's words were spoken with disgust as she snatched at her gown, heading back towards her seat.

"You all dismiss the magic world, but I'm telling you they have insight as well!" Ebonee was pointing again in a bid to defend herself. "Just because you don't like them does not mean they are uneducated!"

Lady Seraphina shook her head with dismay and resumed her seat. "Tell us exactly what happened, Ebonee, and why you are communicating with the magic world."

"I wasn't. They communicated with me!"

"Strange how it's you they communicate with, don't you think, Ebonee?"

"Because they know I will listen, unlike the rest of you all clinging to the past." She paused for breath, gathered her thoughts, and regained composure. "I was contacted by a Thaumaturge called Solange-Cher. She said that she must meet with me as only I would listen to her. This organisation has shown great disdain towards the magic world for hundreds of years. So, I agreed to meet with her in Shropshire, not far from where the Mildred in question lives, Shrewsbury specifically." Judging by the number of perplexed faces looking at her, Ebonee knew a couple of Grand Council members from other countries were not sure of where she was referring to. "It was mentioned before, it's in the middle part of England, my Ladies, close to the Welsh border. The magical world has a concealed sanctuary located at the heart of Shrewsbury, known as one of their houses of life. I accepted the invitation and visited the location where Solange-Cher explained her anticipation of an imminent portal opening."

Ebonee observed members of the Council rolling their eyes and expressing disapproval. She reminded them, "Let's not overlook that this is our prophecy, not theirs. It was considerate of them to forewarn us!" Ebonee was not impressed by her peers on the Council, as usual her contributions were not appreciated. "The meeting occurred just over three years ago. Due to our concerns, I tasked Lady Tempest to assist with my investigations. Solange-Cher mentioned the significance of the area where we convened, suggesting that someone, possibly affiliated with us or soon to be, could disrupt our stability. Not long after, a new Elder emerged, residing exactly in the forewarned area! Ladies, this is not a mere coincidence; please consider this!" Ebonee nodded with satisfaction, capturing the attention of every Council member and putting a stop to the eye-rolling and disapproval.

"I was urgently summoned by Solange-Cher a few weeks ago, and she emphasised the need for a private discussion. Subsequently, events began to intensify, including the demise of Lady Tempest. Solange-Cher suspected an incursion from the dark realm!" Ebonee straightened her back and crossed her arms. "She and others of her kind were aware of the planetary alignment. It wasn't a secret, the public also monitors such occurrences. However, it was a matter detected by the magic order in Paris that raised the most concern."

"Paris, Ebonee," Lady Charmeine shook her head. "What happened in Paris?"

"Have you heard of the Barriere D'Enfer, my friend?"

Lady Charmeine shook her head.

"Have any of you?" Ebonee raised her voice to address the whole room.

There were no responses, just the occasional shake of the head or a shrug of the shoulders.

"Well, I have heard of it! On the eastern side of the Barriere D'Enfer, in the catacombs below. A sombre and ghastly place, a place not of the living," Ebonee shook her head with concern. "It has happened, ladies," Ebonee pointed skywards, "as above, so below." She started wagging her index finger and slammed her palm on her chair. "The timing and alignment were right. The magic world monitors these things: movements, vibrations, alignments, as well as seismic events. Such seismic activity was detected in Paris a few weeks ago. Solange-Cher believes it could possibly have indicated the opening of a portal, meaning that something could have crossed over." Ebonee nodded to emphasise the importance of her point.

"So, Ebonee, did the wand-wavers inspect this so-called portal you speak of? Did the public detect such vibrations or seismic tremors?"

Ebonee frowned at Lady Mariangela's rudeness and the occasional snigger in the room. "No, apparently, the activity only lasted a matter of seconds. They suspect it closed almost immediately, but it was enough time to allow a creature to pass through. As far as they know, this event was not detected by others. Due to the history of the catacombs, the magic world keeps a close eye on this area of Paris."

"Well, can't they find the answer in their tea leaves!" Lady Angelisa smirked and looked around the room for supporting laughter but found little.

Running a hand through her hair, Lady Seraphina raised her hand. "That's enough, please, ladies," her tone was solemn. It was evident to everyone in the room that Lady Seraphina was giving some serious thought to what Ebonee was saying. "So, are you saying they didn't inspect it?"

"No, my Lady. Why would they? Security is supposed to be our domain, not theirs. They monitor things. The magic world has lived in peace for a very long time. If that overriding peace is about to be disrupted, that will also concern them. As we all know, they, like us, must live in the shadows."

"If this escalates, there will be no more anonymity for any of us!" Lady Lucretia exclaimed.

"That is a possibility, my Lady. From what we now know, there can be no doubt that something has come through, as our friends from Loxley will testify."

"We have to consider that we will need help, and uniting with the magic world may have to happen!"

"Oh really, Ebonee? Shall we pick up the phone and call the world of men next while we're at it!" This comment from Lady Tien received a couple of muted snorts and laughs.

Lady Seraphina raised her hands. "Ladies, we note Lady Ebonee's comments. But that is it for now. We will not rush into things, and we need more facts." Lady Seraphina turned to look at Ebonee as she made her point. "Ebonee, I do not speak French. Tell me, what does Barriere D'Enfer mean in English?"

Ebonee swallowed and ground her teeth with worry. "My Lady, it means the gate of hell."

Safiya and Nubia both looked at each other with worry. There were audible sighs of concern in the room.

Lady Seraphina whispered in turn on either side of her.

"With all that we have considered here today, there can be no doubt this Gatekeeper will return. To what end, we are not sure. Safiya, what is to become of the Watchers you have secured at Loxley?"

Safiya looked at Nubia again and received another shoulder shrug in response. "I don't know, my Lady. I believe Raysmau, our head of security and leader of the Escarrabin at Loxley, is making changes. But of course, she consults and takes instructions from the Reeve. I have already made my views clear. There needs to be more transparency between our organisations. I will do all that I can to ensure this happens." Safiya looked around the room and received nods as she did.

Lady Lucretia spoke, " I believe it's crucial to acknowledge the necessity of having one of our own members assist with security matters at Loxley. We need someone who will report directly to us and whom we can rely on completely. I sense that we are being kept in the dark about certain critical aspects."

The Council turned their attention towards Lady Lucretia.

"Lucretia, who do you have in mind for this role?"

"Charmeine. It's been quite some time since I last spoke with her and even longer since I've seen her, especially after her last unfortunate accident. She may be a bit unconventional, but she is trustworthy. She is one of us and has no association with the Reeves'. We could involve the Armourer in our plans."

"What?" Nubia placed her hands on her hips and chuckled nervously.

Safiya glanced around, observing the concern on multiple faces; even Lady Ebonee raised an eyebrow.

"Lady Lucretia, this is a challenging time. You can't…"

"Can't I? It is indeed a challenge, ladies." They all watched Lady Lucretia rise to her feet, the weighty stones and mass of jewels around her neck glistening in the dim light. "This cannot continue. Our security arm of the Reeves is not sufficiently transparent, our clocks have stopped, and a Gatekeeper is out there at this very moment! We need all the assistance we can get."

"Lucretia, with all due respect, the role of the Armourer is more symbolic. It hails from a bygone age. That's why, over time, the role has become obsolete; no one ever hears from her," Lady Seraphina said.

"We will all become obsolete if we don't take action! We will need to fight, ladies. We will require her expertise and her knowledge. Her exceptional mathematical skills and expertise in physics might well save us from having to rely on the wand wavers of this world!"

"Does anyone know where she is? Has anyone spoken to her recently?"

There were shaking heads around the room.

"Last I heard, she had accidentally blown herself up along with a tower block. It took a long time to cover that one up!"

Lady Lucretia sighed, "Yes, it's true, Evangelina. She has blown herself up on occasion, along with other things. However, innovation can take time. We will need her expertise. She may have created more visionary products now, after all, she is a weapons expert. We have become far too reliant on the Reeve's for such innovations."

"Are you going to be standing next to her when her 'expertise' is needed, Lady Lucretia?"

Lady Lucretia frowned at Lady Dina.

"If she is even still alive, does anyone know?"

There was a moment of silence after Lady Seraphina's question.

"She must be. Her details will be here, in our archives. If anything to the contrary were the case, we would have heard. She's one of us, after all," they all looked at Lady Ebonee. "But I'm telling all of you, we need to stop holding on to the past. We need to make friends again and build bridges," Ebonee leaned forward on her chair. "I'm telling you all, if we get this wrong, it will not just be the end of us. It will be the end of everything. That Gatekeeper needs to be destroyed or sent back to where it came from. If he achieves his goals, the others will come, and an era of dark rule will be upon us all!"

Grimacing, he rubbed at the wounds of his singed skin; the pain was not easing. Burns across his arms, left shoulder, and upper back caused him to grimace and grind at the remainder of his mishappen and rotting teeth.

The unusual glasses he had been given provided some protection from the sunlight, but they were uncomfortable, and he needed to be in the shade, not in the bright August sun. Years spent in the darkness below, alongside his brothers, had made him sensitive to the light. As Bellator rubbed at his shoulder, he glanced at his new master, who stood alone near the edge of the Welsh mountains. His Master was deep in thought, presumably about their failure at the Loxley mansion house. Bellator didn't really understand what their failure was. He was only aware of a beast in the below, which was protecting a portal. Although he had been told what the portal led to, he didn't really understand. Those were all the facts he had been given, along with being told that he and his brothers were failures as well.

Bellator winced in excruciating pain as he reluctantly stopped tending to his wounds. He knew he needed urgent treatment for his injuries. He felt the weight of his age as his wounds were not healing as swiftly as they used to. The black cloak had fused into his thin skin in several places, a painful reminder of the blast from the Scatterblade weapon that had unleashed a devastating wall of fire upon them.

Struggling to his feet, Bellator grimaced. His toenails were chipped, his feet covered with dirt, and his sandals barely clung to his feet. He and his brothers at Loxley had bestowed the title of Master upon Duat, who had promised them a safe passage and escape from the clutches of the Order and their security arm, the Escarrabin. However, the promised escape had not happened, and here they were in the rugged Welsh landscape of Snowdonia. Uncertain of their next move and what lay ahead, Bellator was left without answers as Duat, his new master, had concealed any plans from him.

Following their escape from Loxley, Bellator witnessed Duat's transformation back to one of his kind – a Watcher. Duat had revealed his true identity as a Gatekeeper and told him about an afterlife and a time when he had a distinct 'purpose'. Standing on the mountaintop, Bellator adjusted his glasses to protect his all-seeing eye. He pondered the elusive nature of this 'purpose', apparently the Escarrabin and the Order they were made to serve had stripped him of his identity and memories.

Pulling at his cloak, he winced as he stumbled towards Duat. "Master," he coughed, "Master."

The Gatekeeper in the black cloak turned around to him. Duat wiped the drool from his chin. "What do you want? Why do you bother me?"

Bellator looked down before he spoke, "I'm sorry to disturb you, Master, but I'm in pain. These burns are not improving."

Bellator glanced up; Duat was staring at him. Right now, he looked every inch a Watcher, not the Gatekeeper creature he had been only hours before. Duat, as was the case with all Watchers, had a distinctive vein that fed his one eye. Even with slightly blurred vision, trying to focus through the unusual glasses, Bellator could see Duat's central facial vein pulsing. Bellator knew he was angry. Bellator listened to Duat's deep and very audible breathing. Watchers typically sounded like they were heavy breathers, to the point that they sounded very ill, but what Bellator was hearing in front of him was exceptional.

"If you were not so weak, so frail, your blood would already be repairing your wounds!"

The impatience and anger in his new Master's voice sent shivers down Bellator's spine, causing him to take a few steps back instinctively. The menacing snarl on his Master's face revealed the jagged, discoloured remnants of his teeth, creating a chilling sight. As Duat raised his right palm in frustration, vibrant turquoise patterns on his skin burst into life across his palm. Overwhelmed with fear, Bellator stumbled backwards, nearly losing his balance in the process.

"I need time to think, and I do not wish to be disturbed by you!" Duat's voice boomed, commanding attention and obedience.

"Yes, Master. I apologise, Master," Bellator stammered, bowing repeatedly in a display of utmost deference.

As Duat lowered his hand, the turquoise patterns slowly receded. Bellator could hear the steady rhythm of his Master's breathing once more and cautiously dared to glance up, only to find Duat turning away to stare at the mountains in the distance.

"We move after dark. There is another who will help us. He is not far from here," Duat declared, turning his neck until it cracked. He knew it would be a thirty-minute flight to reach the other Watcher who would help them. Flying meant transforming again, and transformation hurt. Taking a deep breath, he realised the pain he had suffered when he had been poisoned by the noxious gas in the chamber had passed. "When we arrive at our destination, we will find you help, as your blood is so useless," Duat stated firmly, turning to look at the cowering Watcher. "Until that time, you speak no further of it. Once you were a warrior, now look at you!"

Bellator nodded obediently, his voice trembling as he uttered, "Yes, Master, thank you, Master." Duat turned back around and took a few paces towards the edge of the cliff. In the August sun, he could see humans trekking up hills in the distance. Luckily there were none heading towards where he currently stood. Further irritation he did not need. The thought of having to explain his failure to his own Master added to his mounting frustration.

Bellator's frayed nerves slowly began to settle. Duat's presence was a constant source of unease for him. The Gatekeeper, whom he now addressed as Master, had only materialised a few days prior. There was an overwhelming amount to absorb from the recent events, but Bellator harboured a deep distrust for Duat. He had willingly sacrificed one of the other Watchers to facilitate their 'escape'. As he absentmindedly rubbed his left arm, a sharp pang of pain shot through him. He remained puzzled as to why Duat had given him the name Bellator and had never inquired about his real name.

Chapter Four:
DRAGON BONES

"You know, I have absolutely no idea what to feed you!" Mildred bent down and gathered Comet into her chest. "How can you be away from your mother at such a young age?" Comet was smaller than Missy had been when she was delivered. Mildred fluttered her eyes; *oh no, correction, when Nahla was delivered, she thought to herself.* Mildred smiled, having just apologised to her own brain for the name error. "So, you will have a real name as well then, Comet." Mildred shook her head at the craziness of how her life had changed in the last week or so. She placed Comet gently on the cat pillow on the couch. "Weird, just weird." Mildred put her hands on her hips. "At least I don't need to see any of the cult of cat crazies again for another year. I'll make excuses when the monthly meetings come up," she nodded at Comet and giggled away to herself at her newfound anarchy and strength. Mildred looked around her front room, surveying the masses of piles of paper and receipts scattered everywhere. She knew she would have to go and see Mr Franks later, so that meant leaving Comet alone with the other kitten. She would need to tidy up the place and move anything chewable or destroyable out of the way from inquisitive claws. "We can't have you hurting yourself, can we? I'd never forgive myself. I know what Missy was like when she arrived, chew this and chew that." She tapped herself on the head at calling her cat Missy again. Mildred was deep in her own thoughts as the other unnamed kitten ran into the room. With the absence of both of their mothers, she would have to feed both kittens soon. When Nahla had been brought to her, she had put her straight on milk and tinned fish. It never did her any harm, Mildred considered. "Are you too small for solids, the pair of you?"

The question was asked, but she received zero acknowledgement in return. The kitten, of no name, kept watch as Mildred bent down over Comet. "You are so cute. Come here!" She picked up Comet again for the umpteenth time and, on autopilot, commenced brisk stroking. The mark on Comet's flank bothered her; it looked unnatural, like a painful burn, not a birthmark like the sheriff woman had said it was. "Ok, I'll get you some milk and... OUCH!!!" Mildred immediately jumped, recoiling her fingers from Comet in an instant. She shook her fingers in shock and instinctively put them in her mouth as if she had been burnt. She removed her fingers from her mouth but couldn't see any marks, although the burning sensation at the tips of her fingers remained. Mildred looked down at Comet and blinked a few times in shock; she felt sure she had seen something move across the scar on her new cat.

As the heavy doors closed behind them, the thud reverberated throughout the chamber, creating an echo so powerful it felt as though the very foundations of the castle were being shaken. Nubia meticulously adjusted her pin badge, ensuring that it was perfectly straight and smoothed her hands against her jacket, despite the absence of any visible creases. She then glanced up at Lady Safiya and offered a nonchalant shrug. "Well, that wasn't so bad, my Lady."

Safiya looked somewhat perplexed and stared at Nubia with a mixture of disbelief and amusement. "Oh really, you think so! It's not you they will be directing further actions at."

The cat adorned with jewels around her neck appeared again, settling herself in front of the two ladies. The pair from Loxley returned the cat's gaze, but as before, she displayed complete disinterest before gracefully strutting away.

"How odd. You'd think she would show some concern. Your cats at Loxley sense what is happening, my Lady; it's in their blood," Nubia remarked.

Safiya nodded in agreement, acknowledging Nubia's observation. "It will be in her blood as well, my friend. Perhaps something from one of her past lives is the reason for her calm."

The Escarrabin in the lobby area remained in reverent silence, their Scatterblades held prominently in front of them.

"What do you think, my Lady?" Nubia inquired, quickening her pace to keep up with Safiya. She sensed that Lady Safiya desired to exit the castle as swiftly as possible.

"Let's go upstairs," Safiya announced, bending down and covering her mouth slightly as she whispered, "Walls have ears; we'll talk outside." As they approached the lifts, a member of the Escarrabin took a step forward. "Would you like to go up or down, my Ladies?"

Nubia furrowed her brow, realising that they were not at the very bottom of the castle as she had assumed. "Up, please!" Nubia's tone was blunt as if she was giving an order rather than a request.

"Yes, Ma'am," the member of the Escarrabin pressed a button to request the lift.

"Would you like a coffee before we leave, Nubia?"

"Given our location, I'd much prefer a decent Scotch, my Lady."

The doors opened, and they entered the lift; Safiya pressed a button on the console for the ground level.

"I do worry about your drinking, Nubia."

"We all have our vices, my Lady, and given the circumstances, I think I can be excused. Besides, it's just to occasionally steady my nerves." There was a slight shudder as the lift ascended.

"All the same, my friend, we must focus right now. We'll talk later."

"Central lobby," the robotic voice announced. They both heard the ping of the lift as it ground to a halt. As the lift doors opened, they could see a couple of senior members of the Order who were already in the main central lobby, staring over at them. "It feels distinctly chilly in here, my Lady."

Safiya nodded, "It does, my friend. I don't feel especially welcome here today."

"NUBIA! NUBIA!!!"

Nubia closed her eyes, recognising the voice immediately. "Keep walking, my Lady, keep walking!!" Nubia's words were anxious. It was futile as Lady Ebonee drew up behind them in an instant.

"How on earth did she get up here so quickly?" Nubia whispered as best as she could. They both turned around and froze.

"Well, now, ladies." Ebonee stepped off a motor scooter and put her hands on her hips. Close up, her appearance, as usual, was somewhat dishevelled compared to the other immaculately presented members of the Grand Council. Old jewels were prominent, but her tartan blazer looked like it could do with a good clean; along with her hair and the rest of her, if truth be told.

"We should talk, yes!"

Safiya and Nubia were somewhat surprised to see how gleeful she looked. "My Lady, I think we should only speak when the Grand Council is present."

"Nonsense Safiya, we'll never get anything done like that. Let's go upstairs to my quarters and have a coffee; it's rare I get visitors after all."

Nubia spoke for them, "To be honest, my Lady, I think we are going to get back to Loxley; it's probably for the best."

Ebonee was still beaming and looked down at Nubia. "What harm can a chat do, eh?"

"My Lady, I..."

"You shouldn't go back this evening anyway; your driver will be shattered. I've got some good Scotch, Nubia, rare batch."

This new information halted Nubia's words. She paused and looked up at Lady Safiya. "Well, I guess a quick chat couldn't hurt, my Lady?"

Safiya shook her head with dismay. "Sometimes you are so transparent, Curator." Safiya looked around the lobby to assess who was watching. Given the reputation that Ebonee had with the Grand Council, coupled with the stares they were receiving from others, this may not be the smart play.

"I have insights, Safiya. There is more to know."

Safiya sighed. Unlike Loxley, Macdui Castle had lifts that went in both directions from the main lobby. Safiya tapped her cane on the floor and conceded with a brief nod; she would have Nubia complaining for eight hours in the car on the way back if she didn't. Safiya nodded again in the direction of the lift. "Will your motor scooter fit in the lift, Lady Ebonee?"

"No idea, I didn't need it, I just knew both of you would take some catching, so I took a different way up. There are many secret passages in this old castle, you know!"

Safiya gave a brief smile and, with some reluctance, started moving in the direction of the lift. *Let's hear what the wayward member of the Council has to say.*

✢✢✢✢

Bellator sat patiently waiting for daylight to fade. Despite his efforts, his pain persisted, and he eagerly awaited some guidance from his Master. He longed to seek assistance for his wounds. For hours, an uneasy silence hung between them, broken only by the occasional presence of hikers straying from the paths. Each time they approached,

Bellator and Duat took cover behind the boulders without exchanging a single word. Bellator couldn't help but notice Duat's unwavering focus on maintaining the blood circulation in his right hand, the vivid turquoise hue of his palm standing out against the surrounding landscape. Bellator was certain that if the hikers had come any closer, their journey would have met an abrupt and final end.

As the last traces of the summer sun slipped away, Bellator felt a sense of relief as he removed his protective glasses. He rose to his feet, silently urging Duat to act so they could escape their desolate surroundings. Wincing, he picked at the remnants of his cloak that had become seared into the thin skin of his left arm. Being high up in the Welsh mountains, he knew that the temperature would soon plummet, enveloping them in dampness. He tugged at his cloak, feeling the first chill of the evening air. Their need for warm clothing was becoming increasingly urgent.

Duat lowered his head, removed his protective glasses, and turned to face Bellator. "Carry these, and make sure you don't lose them," he instructed, tossing the glasses to Bellator, who carefully stowed them away in a pocket within his damaged cloak. Without a word, Duat then discarded his own cloak, throwing it towards Bellator. As he flexed his fingers and turned his back, there was an unspoken understanding between them.

Duat collapsed to his knees, hissing in agony and placed his left palm over his midsection for support. With an enormous roar, he fell forward, his right palm on the ground. The roars of pain must have echoed over the mountain range for miles. Bellator retreated a few paces in terror, having witnessed this transformation only once before. A couple of lights come on in the distance, hikers camping for the evening, no doubt rethinking their plans having heard the most terrifying of screams.

Duat threw his head back, his snout protruding across his skull and his all-seeing eye splitting down the middle to form two eyes. Bellator winced as he heard the bones moving and shattering; the metamorphosis process appeared to be incredibly painful.

Duat kept howling in agony, saliva dribbling from his growing, pointed teeth. Huge claws formed and grew, enabling Duat to push himself upward onto his knees. His wailing persisted as a ridge that ran the length of his back began to form; it pulsed before splitting open. The Gatekeeper materialised as two massive bone fissures accompanied the appearance of his enormous thickly veined wings. Bellator had only recently learned that this was the Gatekeeper's true appearance.

Duat's breathing became less laboured, the howling had begun to lessen, but the agony of his transformation was still unbearable. Clearing his throat, he let out one last enormous roar. The volume of pain was so great that Bellator had to raise his burned hands to cover the holes on either side of this skull. Unlike his captors at Loxley, he had never had ears that were visible from the outside.

"Master!" Bellator lowered his hands. All he could hear was Duat's pained breathing. For what felt like an eternity, Bellator stood nervously, waiting for Duat's strained breaths to return to some semblance of normality. As the temperature dropped rapidly, he noticed steam billowing from his own mouth, and he began to tremble as the damp cold seeped into his bones.

"It is time," the Gatekeeper spoke.

Bellator took a couple of hesitant steps towards the Gatekeeper. Once transformed, the Gatekeeper's voice was deeper in tone, its sound uncompromising and devoid of empathy. As Bellator looked into the Gatekeeper's deep red eyes, a shiver of fear went down his spine. Duat had described his transformed true self as a 'thing of beauty'. Bellator clutched Duat's robe to his chest, ensuring both pairs of glasses were secure in his pocket as a massive claw wrapped around him, its talons digging into his damaged torso. Bellator winced in pain but gritted his teeth together, willing himself to endure as he closed his eye. Suddenly, a rush of air enveloped him as he was lifted upwards and carried across the mountainous terrain. Duat had mentioned earlier that this flight would last about thirty minutes, but where to and in what direction Bellator had no clue.

✠✠✠✠

It was Nubia's first time in Lady Ebonee's quarters. The room was windowless and cold. She gulped, seeing the amount of taxidermy displayed around the room.

Ebonee noticed Nubia's discomfort, "they were collected from the side of the road, not protected in any way. They are my constant companions and a reminder. We never really die, do we."

Nubia felt uneasy and looked to Safiya for support.

"I've only been in here once before; it's a somewhat acquired taste," Safiya whispered to Nubia.

Nubia nodded, her eyes wide open in surprise as she absorbed the room's contents. There were multiple shelves, most of them bowed in the centre from the weight of books and scrolls. Old-looking paintings hung on the walls, crooked and featuring creatures or scenes from history that Nubia didn't recognise. She wondered to herself if these creatures and scenes had ever existed at all.

"Come, both of you, follow me; we can sit through here." Ebonee extended her arm towards a heavy wooden door at the far end of the room. "Nice and private in there!" She beamed as she removed a considerable bunch of keys from a pocket inside her robe.

Safiya and Nubia stood behind her as she flicked her way through multiple keys, "ah-ha!" She turned and smiled again selecting what would be the first of many keys to release locks and bolts securing the door. "No security scanners and gadgetry wizardry in here, ladies." Hearing the final lock release, she waved the keys at them. "Sometimes tradition, such as old keys, is just as good."

Nubia, usually welcoming of discussions about tradition, found herself feeling differently today as she stared into the darkness while Ebonee pushed open the creaking wooden door. Ebonee stepped inside the room and reached over to her right to untie a rope attached to the wall. "Bear with me a moment, ladies," she said. They both observed as she walked forward with the rope in hand. In the dim light, they could discern an old chandelier descending from the ceiling. Taking what seemed to be a piece of flint or stone from her pocket, she leaned forward and flicked a fingernail, instantly igniting a flame in the room. She proceeded to light the nine candles around the circle of the chandelier. As each candle was lit, more of the room was unveiled to them, exposing the circular and windowless space. "Almost there," she said as she walked back to the wall with the rope, pulling it as the chandelier ascended back to the ceiling. Ebonee secured the rope and headed toward a cluttered desk covered with handwritten notes. She clumsily kicked at a chair, sending dust into the air, "There you go, Safiya, take this one. Nubia, there is one over there that you can use; drag it over to us." Safiya glanced down at her immaculately presented robe; a dust-covered chair didn't appeal to her. Nubia went to the side of the room and pulled at an old red-backed chair. "Would you care for some tea, Safiya?" Ebonee asked as she removed a bottle of Scotch from her desk and slammed it down to indicate where Nubia would be sitting. Judging by the mustiness of the room and the fact that the antiques and furniture were covered in thick dust, Lady Safiya declined the tea with a wave of her hand. She placed her cane on the desk and sat down as gently as she could, pulling at her robe to cover as much of her body as possible.

Nubia dragged the chair across the wooden floor, causing the old floorboards to creak, much to Safiya's annoyance. Sensing her displeasure, Nubia apologised, "Sorry, my Lady, it's heavier than it looks."

"That's because the legs are made of dragon bones!"

Nubia froze dragging the chair immediately as Safiya looked at Ebonee in shock.

Ebonee grinned, "Only joking, it's just old. Come, Nubia, pull it in front of the desk."

Safiya watched as Ebonee lit a couple of candles perched precariously on the desk, making the room look like one big fire hazard. Ebonee then pulled out some old-looking crystal tumblers from a drawer and poured a decent measure for Nubia, who accepted it immediately.

"You fancy?" Ebonee asked Safiya, waving the glass that rattled against the multiple rings she wore.

"No, thank you," Safiya replied curtly, watching Nubia swallow nearly the whole measure in one go. "Suit yourself. It's distilled not far from here, thirty-two years old." Ebonee poured a measure for herself and flopped onto her chair, sending a cloud of dust into the air.

Enjoying the taste, Nubia leaned across the desk and picked up the bottle to read the label. "This is a good one, Lady Ebonee!"

Ebonee frowned momentarily. "Well, of course it is, it's Scottish."

Safiya coughed under her breath. "I must say, my Lady, you are somewhat buoyant given the recent events."

Nubia swallowed the rest of the contents of her glass and looked at Safiya. Nubia agreed with Safiya's words. Given Ebonee's constant interpretations of the prophecy, they had both expected to see a very negative and scared member of the Grand Council, not the one who sat in front of them now.

"I've always planned for these things; it's been a long time coming, after all." Ebonee's voice filled the dimly lit room as she reached for the bottle of Scotch, offering Nubia a refill with a gesture. Nubia eagerly slid her tumbler across the desk for a top-up, not needing a second invitation.

Surveying the walls, Nubia noticed symbols drawn by hand in thick black ink, clumsily scrawled upon the dirty and discoloured stone white walls. Their meaning eluded her, but she suspected that Ebonee's connection to the magical world might provide some insight. She decided she may inquire about this after receiving her refill.

Ebonee handed the refilled tumbler back to Nubia, her tone filled with pride as she leaned back in her chair. "So then, here we are. Who would have thought that just over three years ago, I was right all along!" Ebonee's triumphant expression lingered as Safiya and Nubia smiled but remained silent.

"Three years ago, Nubia, I told you it was coming and something was going to be amiss with the Mildred woman in Shrewsbury," Ebonee continued.

"Lady, you mean Lady Ebonee; she is a Lady and one of us," Safiya corrected.

"Is she now, Safiya? I'm glad you are confident of this point because I'm not so sure! She will gain power and find her own way, but let's hope it's not at the detriment of all of us," Ebonee replied before snatching the whisky glass. "She will evolve quickly now that she has the prophesied cat by her side," Ebonee added, watching Nubia take another large mouthful from her tumbler. "Just become a Level Eight, hasn't she, Nubia?"

Nubia swallowed too much in one go, the peaty Scotch making her cough slightly despite her enjoyment of it. "Yes, my Lady, that is the case," Nubia confirmed.

"Mmm, she'll need watching, you know, along with the three-year-old cat that is already with her. How her cat will bond with the new one could be tricky." Ebonee took a mouthful of her Scotch. "Damn shame that we can't talk to cats like Fennaway can. It would be so much easier if we could all understand what they are saying or thinking – don't you think?"

Ebonee's guests smiled without comment.

Safiya watched Ebonee drain the rest of the tumbler.

"My Lady, how did you know there was something unique with this particular Mildred?"

"I found something in the archives, Safiya. That's how! Like your home of Loxley, there are many secrets and storerooms here as well. I research, and I try to understand our place in all of this. My home is not just a convenient meeting place for the Council when they feel like it." They watched Ebonee shift uncomfortably in her seat as she scowled.

Safiya chose not to remind Ebonee that it wasn't her home and that it belonged to the Order.

"Ladies, in what is regarded as recent history, compared to the longstanding overall history of this great Order, the prophecy has only shown itself on two occasions." Ebonee looked at her guests. She knew they didn't need a history lesson, but all the same. "What was called by the world outside of our Order as the Black Death was the one that really cost us." She pointed at both of them and, in contemplation, tried to take a sip from her empty glass. Realising it was empty, she took a deep breath and placed the tumbler back onto the desk. "Thousands perished within our Order. Even our superior bloodlines were powerless to stop it. Those who persecuted cats because of their 'so-called' association with witchery and magic have a lot to answer for."

She paused and gathered her thoughts.

"The persecutors unwittingly served the dark place and the dark masters. The terrible disease spread uncontrollably because our cats and other cats worldwide were culled en masse, and it couldn't be stopped. The rats and serpents thrived, and the rats spread the disease far and wide. That's why we, in this Order, still fear those creatures today. Never forget that both of you." Ebonee pointed at Safiya and Nubia in turn. "Let's hope this Gatekeeper is not planning to take the same course of action as before. We can only assume not, as resilience to such diseases is much higher now, and of course, there are many more cats to fight the vermin. Our sisters are not persecuted as they were in the past."

"You say that my Lady, but the resilience of the world outside is not flawless. They have had their own pandemic issues in recent years."

"True," Ebonee paused for thought. "I'm not convinced those events were connected to the dark places, though."

"During the period when the Black Death was prevalent, the magic world lost many as well, my Lady."

"They did, Safiya, and they do not forget. It is for reasons like that they like to keep an eye on events. You and the rest of the Order may not talk to them, but I do."

"Their world is intertwined with the world of men. That's why we do not associate, my Lady."

"And do you know why we do not associate with the world of men, Safiya?"

Nubia looked at the Head of Loxley to see how she would answer this.

Safiya shook her head, reluctantly mumbling, "I don't, my Lady."

Nubia looked back at her Scotch, knowing full well that she didn't know the answer either.

Ebonee smiled and leaned forward on her desk. "It's incredible, isn't it? For all our knowledge, history, and insights, none of us know the answer to this simple question. It's ingrained into us to think that way as soon as the Order has its clutches on us. I bet most members of the Grand Council do not know the answer to that question either if you were to ask them. I'm sure of this! All I know is this." She leaned forward even further and whispered to them, "The Reeves have something to do with it." Then, she nodded at each of them and sat back in her chair. "I can find nothing else to explain this point. I don't trust them."

Nubia smiled in response to Ebonee's words. Her own distrust of them was well known across the Order, and the arrival of the new and more modern Reeve had not improved her opinion. The disappearance of the former Reeve at Loxley was still a subject of speculation.

They sat in silence for a minute or so. Safiya began to fidget in her chair, wondering about the purpose of the meeting. "You did find something, presumably, my Lady?"

"I did, Safiya. I found something disturbing in the archives. It was cryptic and open to interpretation, but due to my open-mindedness and unique insights, I was able to figure it all out!" She smiled while grabbing for her tumbler again; this time, she added a measure.

It was no wonder the Grand Council worried about Ebonee, Safiya considered.

"What I found attracted my curiosity. That curiosity quickly developed into worry, and well, from there…" Ebonee was waving her hands in the air. Nubia frowned, watching some of the expensive Scotch tipple over the sides of the tumbler.

Ebonee slammed the tumbler down on the desk. "What I found centred around the area in question, in Shropshire, rather than the person. It was only when I discovered that a lady within that particular area of Shropshire was about to become one of us that the penny dropped, and I knew straight away that change was underway." She leaned back in her chair again, content that she had made her point clear *(she hadn't)*.

"Are you saying that the area around Shrewsbury is of special interest, my Lady?"

"Yes, that's correct, Nubia. The ley lines in that area are clearly identifiable with a little research. I have discovered that a portal once opened there. I found an imprint from a member of the Order dating back to that time."

Safiya and Nubia exchanged surprised looks. When Safiya turned her gaze back to Ebonee, Nubia tilted her tumbler and raised her eyebrows to get Ebonee's attention.

"Yes, yes, Nubia, help yourself," Ebonee said, leaning over the desk, moving her handwritten notes to the side, and sliding the bottle in Nubia's direction. Safiya glanced at Nubia disapprovingly.

"Sorry, my lady, I appear to have one of those evaporating glasses."

Safiya shook her head and sighed.

"Ladies, before the age of computers and other modern irritations, people used pen and paper, quills, and the like," Ebonee said with a smile, making an obvious statement. "They would write down their thoughts, and some of our members kept diaries. This was not encouraged, and it still isn't, as we don't want outsiders to learn about us and our secrets. We also didn't want to be associated with the magic world, given the persecution and accusations of witchcraft at that time. Nonetheless, some of our senior members did keep records for future generations of the Order. Due to the ruthless persecution and mass murder of witches and their associates, these records were taken and hidden away. Some of them ended up here. The Grand Council is unaware of this; they don't know what is stored here. I was born in Dundee, but this is now my home, and I choose not to tell them. I interpret and assess. This makes them and others in the Order think I'm wayward, along with other such words they use to describe me," Ebonee said, crossing her arms. "Don't think that I'm not aware of the things you all say about me!"

Her guests looked uncomfortable, conceding guilt.

"But I assure you both, I'm far from wayward, and my knowledge is considerable. It's just misunderstood by all of you!"

Safiya and Nubia looked towards the floor as they were being addressed once again.

"A prominent Elder named Usha extensively investigated the area around the county town of Shrewsbury and its surroundings for months. She sensed a disturbance that she believed would lead to a significant presence. Like me, she had the unique gift of insight."

Ebonee emphatically hit the table, "She knew that something was approaching. The prophecy warns us of such events. Those from the dark place will always seek to rule here. With many bad and wicked souls cast into damnation, they need a new realm to dwell in."

Safiya raised her eyebrows and glanced at Nubia to gauge her reaction. The conversation was quickly becoming surreal. Nubia, however, was fully engrossed in what she was hearing.

"There was either a crossover or a surge from the planet's core or a physical event in space, something, I don't know, the records do not detail, but something caused an opening. There is something in that area, presumably a cave system, something buried deep and hidden. I haven't been able to pinpoint the exact location, but the Elder did discover something." Ebonee nodded as her guests absorbed her words.

"What did she find, my Lady?" Nubia asked softly, her mouth slightly agape.

"Like me, she was ridiculed by other Elders. Aware of this, she had to encode her findings. You need an exact cypher to read those findings. She left clues on how to find and use that cypher for those who were interested. I am interested in studying such things for the good of the Order. It took time, but I managed to crack it. Once deciphered, the code revealed a significant area in Shrewsbury. I've been there a couple of times, but I'm yet to find the code Usha left behind. I've narrowed down the area to approximately two square miles. The entrance to the probable cave system has been marked. A scratching with our own symbol, the head of the sphinx cat, was etched into a wall. The cave system or possibly a portal lies beyond."

You must remember, ladies, that in those days they didn't have Scatterblades and other weapon technologies to fight with. They were reliant on insight, resilience and swords, of course, when needed. This time, the Gatekeeper will be prepared. That is not to say that he won't try to communicate with serpents or rats in some way, especially if eradication is his goal, as opposed to a stand-up fight. Lady Ebonee shrugged her shoulders, "I expect he will summon assistance now that his being here is exposed, also if he suspects the magic world knows as well. And I tell you this, ladies, you can bet your nine lives that others will be lurking in the shadows waiting to join him."

"But last time a Gatekeeper crossed over, their objective was not successful if you consider their overall agenda, Lady Ebonee."

"I personally wouldn't be so dismissive, Safiya. They eradicated millions before we were able to counter..."

"I didn't for a second, my Lady...I..."

"Don't be thinking we have earned the right to stop this again. If it were not for Lady Salma and her blood being used as a vaccine, eradication of life as we know it during the Black Death was a distinct possibility!"

Nubia looked at the worried face of Lady Safiya. She was not used to hearing the Lady of the House of Loxley be spoken to in this way. Ebonee, for all her possible faults, knew her place, and that ranked over them both.

"I believe you may have seen the pathogen if what I've been told is correct?"

Puzzled, Lady Ebonee's guests looked at each other.

"I'm not sure..."

"He held it up to you, Safiya, didn't he? The turquoise blood flow?"

"We saw turquoise movements within his palm, but of course, we are always careful of Watcher's palms. Any…" Safiya abruptly stopped speaking, deep in thought. She closed her eyes. She needed to remind herself that it wasn't a Watcher they had seen but a keeper of the Gate.

"Some Watchers can yield turquoise within their right palm, but not to the magnitude that you both witnessed. What you saw was a living pestilence right in front of you. That blood is highly toxic. Only time will tell what the Gatekeepers want and what their overall plan is. Do they wish to eradicate, or do they wish to convert, and in doing so, mankind as we know it becomes their slaves."

The only sound in the room was Nubia swallowing another mouthful of peaty Scotch.

"We will need all the help we can get." Ebonee was nodding slightly. "Nubia, keep in touch with me of any developments you hear."

Safiya turned to look at Nubia, considering this to not be the wisest idea.

Ebonee pushed herself to her feet and swiped at the tumbler of Scotch; she finished it and banged the glass down hard on the table. "Come, both of you; before you leave in the morning, you will need contact details for the Armourer."

Chapter Five:
CHAINMAIL AND MASKS

The Reeve patiently waited until the coast was clear, observing as a few tourists passed by. People travelled great distances to visit this area, drawn by the allure of the old architecture. Once the last of the stragglers had disappeared, she reached beneath the stone bench where she sat. With her left hand, she located a hidden recess in the stone and pressed a concealed button, triggering a green flashing light on her watch, signalling that she had ten seconds to react.

Rising from the bench, she briskly approached a ten-foot-high wall draped with thick vines. After ensuring that no one was in sight, she parted the vines and located a camouflaged protective cover. Pressing her right palm onto the scanner concealed beneath, she anxiously watched as the red lasers scanned her palm. She couldn't help but ponder whether security measures would need to be revised, especially at Loxley, their home base. The events she had recently witnessed would undoubtedly impact everyone in the Order.

Finally, the flashing on her watch ceased, and the screen next to the scanner displayed a few words in Spanish, a language she didn't speak. However, she recognised her own image alongside her name, Kiya, and the words 'Class Uno' and 'Loxley,' Reino Unido de Gran Bretaña. Presuming the final words meant "Great Britain," she replaced the protective cover and pushed against it, revealing a small passageway as she heard the shifting of heavy stone behind the vines. After checking one last time to ensure no one was watching, she stepped into the vines and the narrow, pitch-black passageway. As the entrance closed behind her, a light flickered on, illuminating her path forward.

The Reeve advanced and raised the pin badge on her jacket's lapel, pressing it against the red-illuminated crest of the Reeves. The crest shifted from red to green, and the metal door in front of her slid open with a clicking noise. The light above her went out and the summer sun flooded the passageway, prompting the Reeve to wince and put on her sunglasses. Stepping into the daylight, she made her way toward a centuries-old white stone archway, where the Reeves' prominent crest adorned the central keystone. Although faded now, in the tranquillity of this private place, it would have once proudly stood out, visible only to a select few.

Wearing her polarised glasses, the Reeve looked up at the cloudless sky, knowing that if she had her tactical security glasses on, she would be able to see the network of lasers above, always prepared to detect any unwelcome presence from above.

Her senses alert, the Reeve noticed two armed officers approaching her, likely potential Reeves in training. Despite her higher rank, their stern expressions indicated their displeasure at her presence. Clearly, news of the events at Loxley had reached even this secret location, the residence of her senior Elder, Lady Berenike. The presence of their Scatterblades strapped to their backs did not escape the Reeve's notice. Unlike at Loxley, where weapons carried by the Escarrabin were now held prominently.

As she navigated the beautiful walled garden, the Reeve heard a fountain gushing into a small pond in the distance, the only sound in the serene surroundings. Nervous but determined not to show it, she braced herself as the officers approached.

"You are Reeve of Loxley?" The Reeve quickly discerned the Spanish accent and broken English. She was aware that the two junior Reeves knew exactly who she was, making her wonder if their question was merely a formality if they had been forewarned about her limited proficiency in their language.

"I am," she said as she stepped towards them and looked one of them in the eyes. "I think you already know that, and if you don't, you should." Given their obvious knowledge of recent events, it was best to show zero weakness and take the high ground when possible. She could see the security officer grimace slightly. If they knew about recent events, they would be aware that members of the Escarrabin and a Cleric had been killed. The Reeve glanced over her shoulder, hearing the doors to the road outside close behind.

"You have meeting with Dama Berenike, Lady Reeve."

"Yes, that is why I have travelled here."

Truth be told, she didn't know if other senior members of her Order would also be here. This could be an ambush, and she could be facing a full-on inquisition. Other country headquarters the world over were no doubt very nervous. After all, security was the responsibility of the Order of the Reeves, and the Escarrabin followed the Reeve's orders. That is how it had been since both organisations joined forces.

"Wait here, Lady Reeve, por favor."

As the officer in training walked away, she could feel the eyes of the other recruit bearing down upon her. Choosing not to meet her gaze, she decided to refresh herself with some of the surroundings of the beautiful gardens. It was here where her Head of Order lived in peace and contemplation. She headed towards the domed canopy. The stone supports had begun to crumble in places, with shards of stone lying at their base. It had been some time since the Reeve had been here. As she glanced up, she remembered the inside of the dome was covered in an incredible fresco dating back to the thirteenth century. She knew this, having been told about it when she was here during a phase of her initiation training. The fresco was the creation of one of the most senior Elders of that period. Apparently, she immersed herself in art after retiring from the field of battle. The Elder believed that some stories from the past needed to be recreated and brought back to life in the form of art and should never be forgotten. The art also served as a warning of the ticking of time and that history will always repeat itself.

The Reeve had never delved into the mysteries of some of the other artworks and sculptures concealed within the main house. Among them, she remembered, were a couple of battle scenes. One appeared to depict Escarrabin fighting alongside men with a Reeve commanding them. The male-looking figures in the artwork wore chainmail and facial masks, attires that clearly did not belong to the earlier times of the Reeves or the Escarrabin. It was evident that these uniforms were from the world of men. The dark hoods of the Watchers they were in battle with were also unmistakable. She recalled the raging storm and the battle fought during a torrential downpour. Atop a stone-covered hill stood a figure that appeared to be a more senior Watcher, wielding a trident-shaped weapon. The Watcher was huge in stature and exuded power, the weapon he held was acting as a lightning conductor, as if he had control over and was harnessing the lightning for his own purposes. What became of him and who he may have been was a mystery. The Reeve knew that answers would eventually be revealed to her over time once trust was established. While curiosity was a valuable trait, she understood that it had its place and time.

A voice spoke from behind, "Lady Berenike will see you, Reeve of Laxley."

With her back still turned, the Reeve smiled slightly, amused by the mispronunciation of the UK headquarters.

She turned to face the serious-looking security officer and nodded in acknowledgement. "Thank you," she replied.

Familiar with the way, the Reeve proceeded through an arch into the main building, her 'bodyguards' accompanying her as she went.

The door she needed to enter stood ajar. With a confident stride, she stepped into the dazzling semi-circular room. Sunlight flooded in through the open windows that encircled the space, bringing with it a gentle afternoon breeze. As she crossed the pristine white marble floor towards the centre of the room, she found herself enveloped in a sense of tranquillity. The room exuded an aura of purity, its white walls and ceiling devoid of any artwork. It was a stark contrast to the dark wood and carpets of Loxley. Seated behind the desk was her senior Elder. A white sheet adorned with the crest of the Reeves concealed the desk. The sight of her Elder made her swallow nervously.

Lady Berenike, a senior Elder of the Reeves and 'retired' from active service, was draped in a flowing, plain white robe that exuded an air of timeless authority. As the Reeve entered the room, her attention was immediately captivated by the imposing collection of ancient, heavy-looking scrolls neatly arranged on Lady Berenike's desk. Upon hearing the Reeve's arrival, Lady Berenike looked up, releasing the scroll she had been perusing. Without uttering a word, she delicately turned the centre pin of the ancient scroll, winding up the secrets it held. With meticulous care, she removed her white gloves, folded them, and placed them gently on the desk. As she looked up once more, she allowed her monocle to fall naturally from her left eye, its chain swinging momentarily above her chest.

"Buenos tardis, Reeve of Loxley."

"Good afternoon, my Lady," the Reeve reverently bowed, though unbeknownst to her, her face had paled.

"I'm not surprised you are uncomfortable being here, Reeve."

The Reeve managed a faint, forced smile, acknowledging her Elder's insight and her own reluctance to be in this position.

Lady Berenike's words, as always, were measured and softly spoken. "The League of Light has relied on us for centuries, ever since our alliance was forged. For generations, the League has battled with the Watchers, their servants, and their blood kin. There were victories and tragedies. They needed us and our unique talents. Our responsibility for security has not only protected them but also shielded those outside our Orders, those who remain unaware of what is really happening around them."

Lady Berenike rose from her seat, her eyes filled with a mix of disappointment and frustration. "They are too preoccupied with politics, celebrity, and greed," she began, her voice tinged with disdain. "It's no surprise that the League strategically places its own members among these so-called decision-makers, who are elected to power by the public. However, recent events have changed the dynamics." Her tone became condescending as she walked around her desk, her pristine white gown trailing behind her. "You have been entrusted with a monumental responsibility. Loxley is not just the UK and Irish home of the League; it holds immense historical significance. The security and preservation of this place are now in your hands for safekeeping."

Pausing in front of the Reeve, she continued, "You have not held this crucial position for long, and now we have a potential Gatekeeper loose, right under your nose! This is unacceptable, Reeve of Loxley!"

The Reeve bowed her head in acknowledgement, "Yes, my Lady, I have no excuse."

"Look at me," Lady Berenike demanded, "Leaders must lead by example. You must take responsibility for both success and failure. The Grand Council is convening as we speak. Changes will be made because of this breach. They will demand more involvement in security matters, risking the exposure of our treasures and wealth that fund everything. It's not just beneath the statue of Salma where our treasures are kept; there are many other locations. I won't disclose them to you, not when you have failed to protect Loxley!"

Lady Berenike stood tall; her piercing stare fixed upon the Reeve.

"My Lady, if I may," the Reeve began tentatively.

Lady Berenike's expression remained stern as she inquired, "What can you possibly say that changes anything, Reeve?" A tense silence hung in the air as they locked eyes.

"I can't. All we can do is harden and counteract where and when necessary. Respectfully, my Lady, I had no knowledge of what was hidden in the below at Loxley. What was the Hydra doing there? In fact, my Lady, I'll reword that. What is it still doing there?" The Reeve's words were measured, filled with a sense of urgency.

Lady Berenike lowered her arms to her sides and propped herself against her desk, deep in thought. "I still do not know. These scrolls I'm studying have some of the details. It is peculiar indeed. My best guess is that it's there to protect something. I suspect that when the Gatekeeper crossed over, some form of event happened in the below that brought it back to being. Our foremothers would have chosen that beast for a reason. A multiple-headed serpent creature is the perfect deterrent to keep us and others away. We have always feared serpents and rats. Do not forget it was the rats that carried that awful disease in the past. It nearly wiped us all out and killed millions of others in the process. It will not surprise me, Reeve, if the League try to bring in someone else, one of their own who may claim to have some knowledge of security matters."

The Reeve nodded; the idea of collaborating with someone outside of the Reeve's secretive Order did not bring her comfort.

"We will know in time; the Council have an obligation to report to my superiors if changes are being considered. We, of course, cannot deny them or force them in any way; we can only advise. We are supposed to work together after all," Lady Berenike stated with authority.

The Reeve nodded, but she was itching to know why she was there. So far, this conversation could have happened without her travelling. "My Lady, events are worrying; there is no doubt of that. The Gatekeeper escaped, and my feeling is he will return. I still do not know what his objective is and why he was there. He clearly didn't achieve it so far, but I must ask you why I am here?"

"You are here because there are important matters that I need to discuss with you. If the League requests changes, they may ask for the iron wall to be opened and the Hydra to be killed. The wall is there for a reason, and it has been there for hundreds of years. As far as I understand, you have not heard anything since the events?"

"No, my Lady. Since the Gatekeeper left, there has been complete silence below."

Lady Berenike nodded. "The silence would suggest that it has returned to its former state and that it is resting again. However, you will need to check the wall to ensure it is sealed and there is no structural damage. You cannot risk trying to open it while that Gatekeeper is still in this realm. Keep it sealed. You can investigate when the Gatekeeper is no more. Do you understand me, Reeve? Not until then!"

"Yes, my Lady, I understand. But respectfully, we still could have had this conversation remotely."

Berenike offered the faintest of smiles. "Not for what I'm about to tell you." Lady Berenike stopped leaning on her desk and pushed herself upright. "Follow me."

✣✣✣✣

The door was pushed open with such force that Mr Franks jumped from reading his newspaper; the tinkling of the shop bell was almost an afterthought. "Wow, are you okay, Mildred? That was a determined entry!" He chuckled to himself, adjusting his belt to allow his belly some room.

"Sorry, Mr Franks," Mildred pushed the door closed. "You know when you have slightly too much energy!"

Having been absent from physical exercise for several years, Mr Franks put his hands on his hips and shook his head. "I don't, to be honest, Mildred."

"Oh, right. Well, anyway... exciting news!" Mildred clapped her hands together with zero interest in the state of Mr Franks' physical health. "I have a new cat!" Mildred was ecstatic, her smile beaming from ear to ear.

"Well, do you now." Genuinely happy for his most loyal customer, Mr Franks rocked backwards and forwards. "That's amazing news, Mildred. I know you've been a little unhappy the last couple of times I've seen you, what with the local boys and all that fish paste you've been buying for the church." Hands still on hips, he continued to rock as he thought. "I hope they appreciated your sandwiches, although the fete isn't for a little while yet, Mildred."

Mildred froze, having dropped a clanger recently when questioned by Mr Franks about the need for so much fish paste. "Um... yes, it was for something else."

"Oh, right you are then." His rocking recommenced, his breathing audible as usual.

"So, what is the name of the new addition then, Mildred?"

"Comet!" Mildred beamed with pride. "After the comet that flew over recently. Did you see it, Mr Franks?"

"I did not. A bit late in the evening for me, Mildred, when it happened, or so I read. However, I'm aware of it, and I hate to correct you, Mildred, but it was a satellite collision. It was a falling satellite that you saw."

"Oh, really..."

"Indeed. However, Comet is a better name. You can't be calling your cat Satellite now, can you? That would be a bit weird!" Mr Franks started rocking backwards and forwards, rasping for breath between his laughter.

"Yes, well, there's been a few weird things going on of late."

"What was that, Mildred?" He stopped laughing.

"Oh, nothing, just thinking out loud."

"Right, you are." Mr Franks smiled. "So, where did you get your cat? Was it from the local adoption shelter?"

Mildred froze, her eyes widening as she realised her mistake. This was a matter for the Kat Chamber, and secrecy was crucial. "Erm... no, although I know the place you mean. They do very important work. Erm... a friend gave her to me."

"So, it's a she then, Mildred?"

"Oh yes, they only ever have females."

Mr Franks immediately stopped rocking and looked reasonably perplexed by the oddity of Mildred's words.

Mildred quickly averted his eyes. "Well, I guess I better get my supplies."

Mr Franks nodded, watching Mildred bend down to pick up a basket and shuffle off to the other end of the shop.

Confident that her face couldn't be seen, Mildred closed her eyes and screwed up her face at her lack of preparedness for yet another Franks inquisition. *Never mind, what does he know,* she thought to herself as she approached where the cat food was displayed. She recalled needing batteries again; the clock in her kitchen had stopped working, and for some reason, her old clock in her bedroom had given up the ghost as well. Only the television displayed the correct time if she had the news channel on. Having stopped at the cashpoint on the way to Mr Franks' shop, it turned out what Jessica had said to her was true (although she was now called Suzanna after some bizarre sword-waving ceremony). There was an extra £500 in her account, in recognition of her 'promotion' up the ranks, presumably, or whatever it was that they called it to be a higher member of the mysterious Kat Chamber. Apparently, she was 'pre-determined' to join.

She had been lost in her thoughts and was worried that she had been staring at the shelves for too long. Glancing over her shoulder, she saw Mr Franks reading his newspaper. It seemed like he hadn't dwelled on their previous conversation, as news of world events seemed to be his only distraction.

She picked up a couple of tins of the usual food for Nahla and added them to the basket. She also noticed kitten food on the shelf and decided to try it, considering she had no idea if the kittens were old enough for that type of food.

Next, she walked over to the old humming fridge unit. Placing her hand in between the heavy plastic strips that barely contained the cold, she took out a two-litre bottle of milk and placed it on top of the tins in the basket. She grabbed an oven-baked pie for herself and a couple of packs of batteries before heading to the till.

"Hey, Mildred, take a look at this. It's weird. You rarely see this," Mr Franks said, turning the newspaper around to show Mildred the headline *'Police admit puzzlement over missing CCTV'*.

"The police rarely admit when they are wrong, Mildred. Something very odd is going on here. There is a camera outside belonging to the shop next door, and I guess that's the footage that has gone missing," Mr Franks continued.

Mildred skimmed through the story, already aware of the accident that had happened outside the shop recently. "It is odd, Mr Franks," she nodded at the shopkeeper, but she seemed generally disinterested.

"No witnesses either. How can that be on a busy street? That poor lady was knocked down right outside here, Mildred. Apparently, the bus driver has little memory of it as well. Very odd," Mr Franks remarked as he watched Mildred place the basket onto the counter. "More batteries, Mildred? What on earth are you up to? You only bought some the other day!" Mr Franks chuckled to himself.

"Your batteries appear to be somewhat useless; my clock keeps stopping."

"I've not heard anyone else say that, Mildred. They are the ones you see advertised on TV," Mr Franks added.

"Well, we'll see. I'll try them again. Although I'll return them if they stop working right away," Mildred replied.

"You do that, Mildred. I always want my favourite customer to be happy," Mr Franks said with a smile as he bagged Mildred's purchases. "I'll have to charge you for the bag, I'm afraid. Not everything in life is progress."

Mildred closed her eyes at the thought of yet another 'Franks' carrier bag to add to the collection. Why she never remembered to reuse the bags instead of hoarding them at home was anyone's guess.

Mr Franks' eyes were distracted as he noticed a black shape passing by through the glass door. "Say, isn't that your Missy, Mildred?"

Mildred spun around, seeing her black cat with the white-tipped tail passing by the door. "Yes, it is. I wonder what she is up to?" She took her purse, bulging with receipts, from her pocket, not taking her eyes off her cat. "Can I pay, please?"

Having paid Mr Franks, she grabbed the carrier bag from the side and quickly made her way out of the shop. She looked around, wondering why her cat was prowling the way she was. Nahla's tail swung back and forth in a rhythmic action, clearly focused on something. "Nahla," she whispered. Although the shop door was closed, she did not want Mr Franks to hear the recent name change of her cat. "Nahla!"

Her cat stopped moving, her body rigid.

She placed her bag down and walked up behind her. "Nahla," she said. Her cat jumped, feeling Mildred's hand across her back. She looked into Nahla's eyes. She seemed to be scared.

Something was sorely amiss

Holding on for dear life, Bellator supported himself inside Duat's claw as best as he could. The warmth from the August sun had passed. Uncomfortable and in pain, he shook as he nestled against the cold torso of the Gatekeeper.

Having taken flight from the Welsh mountains, he had no idea how far they had travelled. During their flight, there were many periods of silence as they flew over what he guessed to be agricultural lands with sparse populations. He had seen occasional lights from what he presumed were farmhouses sitting on many acres of grounds.

They only passed over one area that had plenty of activity; a small town's lights were visible from the altitude at which they flew. Other than that, it was unremarkable.

Now, they were heading in the direction of a well-lit place, much bigger than the last town they had flown over. This was a heavily populated area. Even in the low light, multiple church steeples were silhouetted across the horizon. Now that the sun had dipped, probably a hundred or more car lights weaved their way around the local streets.

He felt the claw tighten around him, he flinched as the long talons dug into his ribs, one of many areas of his body already in pain. Bellator closed his eye and screwed his rotten teeth together in pain; he placed a hand as close to his ribs as he could to try and ease the pain. As they plunged suddenly at speed, he struggled to hold Duat's cloak and their glasses. In a panic, he opened his eye as the town drew closer. From their rapidly descending height, the illuminated town almost looked like an island completely encircled by a river. It felt like their speed increased as drool shot from his mouth into the night. He heard Duat snort as the Gatekeeper's wings tilted to the right, and their trajectory changed; they were now in a full-on plummet.

Bellator felt the wind pushing against his upper lip, his shattered and malformed teeth feeling as though they were in a vacuum. He winced in total dread as the ground rushed quickly in their direction. The Gatekeeper extended his legs, and Bellator felt the massive claw supporting him tighten even more. He tried, instinctively, to pull his knees toward his chest. As the Gatekeeper got ready to land, his talons glittered against the moon. They slid farther to the right to avoid a collision with the rapidly approaching car lights. As they prepared for impact, Bellator heard two cracking noises, which were probably coming from the Gatekeeper's legs. Bellator was suddenly freed from the claw, falling a short distance and striking the ground, bouncing across someone's garden.

He cried out in agony, clutching his right shoulder, which had borne the brunt of the fall in addition to his pre-existing injuries. A tear ran from his eye; the agony was excruciating. He forced himself to his knees in anguish, and as his cry faded to a whimper, a deafening roar instantly hushed him. Bellator halted at the sight of the Gatekeeper's piercing red eyes, virtually frothing at the mouth, not far from where he knelt. Bellator took a seat on his knees, gripped his side, and ground his teeth. He took slow breaths and focused, attempting to numb the ache.

The Gatekeeper raised his right claw to his nose while perched on his talons. A slight flash of turquoise emerged from inside the right claw as the piercing red eyes fixed themselves on its hand. The Gatekeeper fell forward, writhing in agony as his legs buckled. With an energetic flap, his wings pulsated with a turquoise colour that flashed through the veins. The Gatekeeper roared, and the wings gave way with a crack and a recoil as the colour reached the tips.

Kneeling in someone's garden, Bellator was immediately distracted when he noticed a light coming on in the house next to where he was. As the figure of Duat started to reappear, the pained noises of the Gatekeeper's transformation continued. Bellator dropped the robe and glasses and started waving his arms to try and get Duat's attention, but his actions were not noticed. Still holding his midsection, Bellator pushed himself to his feet and moved behind some bushes to hide.

A figure appeared at the upstairs window. The window flew open abruptly as the man inside the house leaned out.

"Who's there?" he shouted aggressively.

Even in pain, Bellator thought the question to be somewhat odd. Given all the man would have heard was a couple of huge roars, most people would probably not want to inquire.

"Who's there, I say?"

A short distance away, Bellator could hear the laboured breathing of Duat. Thankfully, he was out of sight from where the man was looking.

Having spent the last couple of days in predominant fear, Bellator peered from behind the bush to see Duat on all fours. Bellator could see that Duat's midsection was quickly rising up and down as he struggled to regain his breath. He could see turquoise flashing from Duat's right palm. With confidence, Bellator waved, this time catching Duat's attention. Bellator raised his index finger over his mouth. Duat looked at him and acknowledged the signal, hearing the man shout out of the window again.

"Damn kids!" was the last thing that both Watchers heard, other than the window being slammed closed in a temper. As the curtains were snatched together, Bellator moved from his hiding place. He held his midsection, grimaced, and shuffled towards Duat.

"Master, are you okay?" The stupidity of the question was not lost on the transformed Gatekeeper; he growled in response. Bellator took a step backwards and bowed slightly, holding up Duat's robe in front of him.

With some contrition, Duat stepped forward and snatched at the robe.

They were startled, hearing a sudden cough to their right. They both turned immediately, seeing a man staring at them over a low garden fence with a lead in hand. His unseen dog started to growl. The stranger froze upon seeing Duat and Bellator, his face somewhat panicked.

"What do you want!" The words were spat aggressively in a deep and hostile tone by Duat as he pulled the robe over himself. Bellator noticed Duat's palm started to flash in the low light of the evening. The stranger, observing the two skeletal figures with only one eye, was rigid in fear. Duat's central vein that delivered blood to his eye pulsed heavily. The man's dog hopped its front legs up on the fence. Hearing Duat hiss at it, the dog whimpered and fled immediately, dragging its owner away with him.

Knowing full well that anyone not associated with the Order would never have seen Watcher's before, Duat removed his worn sandals from the pocket of his robe. It didn't take long for him to speak. "I think we better go," Duat's words had regained composure, along with his breathing.

"Yes, Master," Bellator swallowed and anxiously looked around. He couldn't remember the last time he was outside of Loxley. With no influence over what was happening, he felt panicked, just like the human who had just been dragged away by his dog, "but where are we heading to, Master?"

"Not far. There has been another here for some time. He is wiser than you, not that that is difficult," Duat lifted his hand and concentrated. "He has never been captured by the Order; he's not been incarcerated like you. He understands how things work here, in this primitive place." As the fading palm started to glow again, he stepped over the low fence and looked up and down the street. He could see people in the distance and there were lights on in houses, but no one paid them attention. He placed his palm on the ground, closed his eye, and concentrated.

It didn't take long. He opened his eye and removed his palm from the ground. As the turquoise colour faded, he stood up. "We go this way."

Chapter Six:
FADED HEADSTONES

As they walked down the street, Bellator noticed the different architectural styles of the houses. Across the street was a contemporary house with large glass windows, while others had dramatic black timber patterns against white walls. Glancing up, he saw the year 1807 carved into the stone of one of the bigger black and white houses. Not sure what year it was, he noticed 2011 carved into a keystone across the street, suggesting some of these houses had been here for a long time.

The adjacent roads were narrow and lined with uneven cobblestones, eroded over many years by passing cars. Whenever someone approached, they crossed the street, taking care to avoid any oncoming pedestrians. They kept their heads bowed and covered their faces with their robes to avoid drawing attention.

"We should change our clothes," Duat mumbled from beneath his hood. Bellator, still nursing his midsection, remained silent, his pain a constant, sometimes unbearable presence.

Noticing that no one was approaching, Duat stopped abruptly in the middle of the pavement. He turned to look behind him. The street they were in was quiet. He flexed the fingers of his right hand, crouched down, and waited. When the familiar glow appeared, he placed his palm on the pavement and waited. Conscious of their appearance compared to everyone else, Bellator turned to ensure they were not being watched.

Duat nodded to himself and removed his palm; the turquoise glow dissipated immediately. "Two streets away, there is a church called St. Alkmund's. He will meet us there; he is already waiting for us."

"Who are we meeting, Master? Who is in this place who can help us?" Bellator asked.

Duat flexed the fingers of his right hand and gave it a shake. "I have already told you; he is one that has not been polluted as you have. His blood is purer and not corrupted with ignorance such as yours."

In shame, Bellator bowed his head. The abusive comments from Duat were never-ending.

"Is he a Watcher, Master?"

"Yes, although it is only the Order that call you 'Watchers'. He is a Sefali, like you were once." They resumed their pace.

As they reached the end of the road, they stopped at a junction. Cars passed by, their occupants casting curious glances at their unusual attire. When there was a break in the traffic, they carefully crossed the road and made their way towards the church steeple, which loomed not too far ahead.

The speed and the noise of the passing vehicles unnerved Bellator, having only ever seen his captor's vehicles at Loxley. Bellator cautiously edged along the pavement, constantly looking out for danger.

"I've been informed that there's a large graveyard at the back of the church. No one should be about at this hour, so we'll meet there," Duat instructed. Bellator nodded in response, his pulse racing and his skin clammy. Despite what he had been told about Watchers not feeling fear, since leaving Loxley, fear and anxiety were all that consumed his mind.

Dimly illuminated by streetlights, the church of St. Alkmund's stood before them. Duat pushed open the creaky, weathered wooden gate, granting them access to the church grounds. The gate's rusty metal fixings squeaked and squealed as the bottom dragged along the weed-covered concrete path. Above the gate, a weathered shelter in the shape of an upside-down V had shielded it from the elements for generations, its roof tiles adorned with a layer of moss. It was a testament to the passage of time and history that had unfolded within these grounds.

The darkness had descended swiftly, shrouding the graveyard in an eerie cloak of shadows. The moonlight struggled to penetrate the dense canopy of trees, leaving much of the burial ground enveloped in pitch-black darkness. As they ventured deeper, Duat and Bellator realised that the graveyard extended far beyond the rear of the towering church, stretching out into the distance with ancient, weathered headstones lining the path.

Stepping off the path, Duat made his way through the overgrown grass towards the older graves. The graveyard exuded an unsettling stillness, broken only by the hoots of an owl, a reminder that they were not alone in this desolate place. As they continued, they passed rows of headstones, some crumbling and others lying in disarray on the ground, their inscriptions worn away by time or obscured by a thick blanket of moss.

The further they ventured, they noticed newer headstones, some adorned with remnants of decaying flowers. Pushing deeper into the darkness at the rear of the cemetery, they passed older graves reclaimed by nature, overgrown with brambles and forgotten, while the newer ones stood as meticulously maintained memorials.

Disregarding the sanctity of the graves, Duat strode purposefully over the burial plots, leading Bellator towards the overgrown end of the cemetery. Suddenly, a cracking of twigs pierced the silence, drawing their attention to an outline of someone standing in front of them.

As the Watcher approached, his presence was barely visible in the dim light. Suddenly, a fox darted past in a panic, rustling the bushes nearby. As Bellator looked up, a loud hooting filled the air as an owl took flight, disappearing into the distance. Then, a new sound emerged – the unmistakable grunt and heavy breathing of a Watcher.

As the Watcher drew closer, his imposing figure came into full view. It was the first time Bellator had seen one of his own kind like this. The Watcher wore a sleek black suit with a matching shirt and tie. A hand with fingernails much shorter than his own pressed a button on the glasses he was wearing. Bellator could hear mechanical parts moving, and in the low light, what looked to be an emerald colour screen folded over to reveal the solitary eye of the Watcher.

Duat acknowledged the Watcher with a nod before turning to Bellator. "This is what you look like out here, not as a robed slave. His name is Aazar."

Bellator moved closer, curious. The Watcher's facial features appeared different from his own – his skin thicker, the feeding vein of his all-seeing-eye not as prominent as his own, and his teeth were in better condition. There was drool, but not as much as his. He had more bodyweight, his overall build being far stockier and broader. He looked strong.

Aazar shook his head, his expression a mix of disappointment and disdain. He removed a handkerchief from his jacket pocket and delicately dabbed at his mouth to remove spittle before speaking. "You present yourself in the robes of a slave," he said in a dismissive tone, his voice filled with disgust, unimpressed with Bellator's appearance. "So, it is true then, Sire," Aazar turned to Duat. "Those of us who live freely have heard what happens when the Order gets their claws in." He stepped closer to Bellator, invading his personal space, the presence of the suited and confident Watcher unnerving Bellator in an instant. "It's difficult to know what you are or what you have become."

Bellator swallowed nervously. He had little knowledge of what Aazar was referring to, only the words he had heard from Duat about what he really should be. "Bellator stays with us all the same," Aazar continued to stare at Bellator as if fascinated with a new toy to play with. "Yes, Sire," he grunted in disapproval and stepped backwards. "Bellator has injuries from an Escarrabin pulse blast. He needs some form of medical assistance."

Aazar quietly growled under his breath, clearly irritated by the prospect of assisting Bellator. This he considered to be an inconvenience and a deviation from what needed to be done.

"Somewhere that will not attract too much attention."

"Out here, we attract attention wherever we go, Sire. Until all are slaves to us, our appearance is disturbing to them," he stepped forward to Bellator again. "They have no idea of what is to come." Duat expressed his approval with a snort, pleased there was another who shared his vision of the future. "Until then, we need to attend to this outcast," he declared.

Bellator, feeling embarrassed and still gripping his wounds, looked at the ground as Aazar contemplated the situation. After a moment of thought, Aazar suggested, "There's a veterinarian not far from here. They could examine him; we can't take him to a hospital. The humans who are yet to be enslaved would panic, and some of their police are armed. It's best to avoid drawing attention until the time is right, Sire."

Bellator looked up, shaking his head, and asked, "What is a veterinarian?"

Stepping forward, Aazar bent down to meet Bellator's eye, "It's someone who takes care of animals."

"An animal worker?" Bellator panicked, "But I have serious burns!"

Duat nodded at Aazar, "he's right. You can't go to a hospital." Addressing Aazar, he added, "Show us the way. You have much to explain about this area. Have you learned more about the one they called Tempest and her activities here?"

Growling under his breath, Aazar responded, "Yes, Master. I've discovered that she had conversations with others. I spotted what I believe was a senior Elder and I suspect that the magic world played a role in some way."

Duat shook his head slightly and snorted with amusement. "Magic," he grinned, "all that wand-waving and spell-casting nonsense won't help them. They'll learn when the time is right."

Aazar returned the grin and continued, "There's also a cat in the area, Master. A black cat with a white tip at the end of its tail. I sensed its significance immediately. I believe it may be connected to their bloodline. I know where the cat resides. The Tempest woman had some involvement with either the cat or the person the cat lives with. I also suspect there's a hidden magical house in the centre of this town that serves as a meeting place for the supposed wonder workers."

Duat nodded, pleased with the information he was receiving.

"Their magic house is hidden in plain sight, Sire. Very few know about the magic types and they do not know of its existence, but with my abilities, I have been able to smell their lair. I have not flushed them out yet as I waited for your arrival. We need to interrogate whoever the Tempest woman was talking with. In their meeting house, I am sure we will find answers."

"So be it," Duat said, looking at Bellator. "Let's get his wounds treated first."

Aazar looked at Bellator and grunted. "Follow me, Sire. I do not know if anyone will be at the animal worker's place at this time of night, but it is not far from here. Until you have new clothes, we need to keep you concealed from people. Even though you will not need the glasses after sunset, covering up our solitary eye stops unwanted attention, so I keep them on for the most part. This way."

Duat nodded and followed.

In pain and feeling every bit the outcast, Bellator clutched at his robe and followed them to the animal workers.

"Castle Hollow Veterinary Practice," Duat sneered, wiping drool from his mouth, as he glanced at the sign next to the main entrance, which listed the names of the individual vets. The main gate was open, and the three of them stood outside, taking in the sight of the reasonably new-looking single-story building. Only one car was parked outside, displaying the name of the vets on its doors. A single light illuminated the interior, indicating that maybe someone was inside.

As they observed their surroundings, they noticed the green mesh fencing that encircled most of the compound, except for the rear area. The recently cut grass led to a steep bank that dropped away behind the building.

Aazar leaned towards Duat, "There are security cameras, Sire." He nodded in the direction of two cameras fixed above the main entrance doors, there were more along the sides of the building.

Duat murmured in acknowledgement and pulled his hood up, "Bellator, pull your hood up and do not look at the cameras."

They paused watching a tabby cat mooching around the front of the building.

"Vermin!" Aazar muttered under his breath.

"Is it one of theirs?"

"No Sire, that is not the one. Here kitty, here kitty." Aazar gesticulated for the cat to come over.

Bellator looked somewhat surprised, "What are you doing?"

The tabby started moving towards them as Aazar bent down and held his hand out. Just a couple of meters away, the cat suddenly stopped. It sensed something was wrong. Its hackles went up as it hissed. Aazar sneered in response and hissed back aggressively. The tabby cat immediately took flight and ran as fast as it could back towards the cover of the building.

Aazar removed his glasses from his pocket, unfolded them, placed them on his face to cover his single eye, looked at Duat and shrugged. They collectively walked towards the entrance doors, being careful not to look up at the cameras with their heads slightly bowed. Duat pushed against the door, but it wasn't moving. He tried again with the same result. "The door is locked."

"Look, Master, there is some sort of speaking device," Aazar said.

Duat looked at the red push button, unsure of what would happen next, and pressed it. They heard a buzzing noise inside the building. Removing his finger, they waited. A few seconds passed by, and Duat raised his finger again, freezing when he heard an approaching police siren. The noise reminded him of when the Escarrabin had come for him, choking on poison gas and his incarceration in the below at Loxley.

Aazar and Duat looked at each other with concern.

Bellator turned his head towards the approaching noise. "What is that?"

"That is unwanted," Aazar replied sternly. "It's their enforcers; they have rules out here."

"The Escarrabin, Master?"

Aazar snorted with no attempt to conceal his amusement.

Duat sighed. "No, Bellator, the soldiers of the Order are not here. What you hear are different enforcers called the police."

"Should we be worried about them Master?"

"No, they are irrelevant, if they get in the way, we will dispose of them accordingly."

Duat flexed the fingers of his right hand as the turquoise colour came to the surface of his skin. Suddenly, he stopped flexing as they heard a male voice through the intercom.

"Yes, hello, Castle Hollow Vets," someone said.

The three of them looked at each other, clueless about what to do next. The road outside started to light up in a flashing blue colour as the police siren got louder. Duat pushed the red button and tried to speak as softly as he could.

"I'm here for... my cat," he said, looking at Aazar and shrugging his shoulders.

"Oh, yes, Mr Muddles," the voice on the intercom replied.

They looked at each other in confusion. The police car passed by as they heard the door locks parting.

"Yes, come in, you're a little early," the voice on the intercom said. There was an immediate buzzing sound overhead. Aazar guessed the meaning of the sound and lightly pushed the door.

Bellator followed them inside. "Master, who is Mr Muddles? Should we be worried about him?"

The waiting area of the veterinary practice was meticulously organised. Plump pillows adorned the seats, neatly stacked magazines awaited perusal, and an array of posters adorned the walls. Above the main reception counter were displayed individual portraits of the veterinarians, along with their names. Duat's attention was drawn to a life-size cardboard cut-out of a cat on the counter, advertising a brand name and a slogan about 'happy cats do not have fleas.' Disgusted, he snatched it up, allowing drool to fall from his mouth onto the cardboard. He tossed it to the floor, hearing footsteps approaching from the corridor behind a heavy looking door. Duat prepared to confront the newcomer, his turquoise-tinged palm ready to unleash his abilities if necessary. All three of them bowed their heads as the face of a man appeared at the glass panel in the door. There was a loud click as the door opened.

"Well, I'm pleased to say that it's not as bad as we first thought. He will make a full recovery..." The man, removing a pair of disposable gloves, immediately stopped in shock, looking at the two figures with bowed heads dressed in filthy black robes and a tall, black-suited figure wearing the strangest of glasses. From behind the counter, he shook his head with concern and swallowed. "Mrs Fisher?" his words sounded frail, his eyes wide, acknowledging he had let people in again without checking the security camera. He swallowed further. "I am expecting Mrs Fisher."

Duat slowly looked up, the hood of his cloak falling back to reveal his intense stare. With a low growl, he removed his glasses, and Bellator, sensing the tension, did the same, hoping the frightened man before them would be of assistance. The man, visibly panicked, brought a trembling hand up towards his chest before nervously clutching at the counter. His breathing was loud and erratic as he frantically looked around for help, but there was no one in sight.

"What do you want... in fact... what are you!" he exclaimed, his voice trembling as he looked at them with fear. "God..." With sudden resolve, he turned to make a dash for the secured door behind him.

"Stop where you are!" Duat's commanding voice filled the room.

The man hesitated, his hand hovering over the door entry system as he was about to enter his passcode. He glanced back over his shoulder, his eyes filled with panic and tears. "Are you going to hurt me?"

Duat stepped forward, the vein running to his solitary eye pulsing with intensity.

"I believe you know; I always knew this day would come; how long did it take you to learn English?" the man said, his words causing confusion for both Aazar and Duat.

Duat addressed the man firmly. "Our colleague has burns; you will fix them!"

The man nodded in a mixture of fear and excitement. "My name is David, I'm the senior partner here." His words tumbled out awkwardly as he smiled, still shaking like a leaf. "You need to come through here, my Lords." He input his door code and pushed the door to its fullest extent, revealing a corridor beyond.

David stepped into the corridor, swallowing as he watched the three accidentally invited guests make their way towards him. Starting to sweat profusely, he kept his distance from them as best as he could; it was evident that the alien who hadn't spoken yet was badly injured.

"Come, come," David beckoned them forward, bowing repeatedly as he spoke. "Your shipmate looks hurt."

Aazar leaned towards Duat, voicing his unease. "This is unusual, Sire; they are usually scared of us."

"He is scared, I can sense it, but something else is on his mind. Be ready, just in case he tries something," Duat replied in a low, cautious tone.

"Yes, Master," Aazar was confident of his own fighting abilities. If he needed to prove them to his Master on this human, then so be it.

Bellator was at the rear, still clutching at his wounds. The only humans he could remember being near had wanted to hurt him and, if not, demanded he perform chores for them. He needed help but would have preferred it from one of his own kind.

David stopped outside of his office. "You can come in here."

The three of them filed into David's office. The sound of the three Watchers' heavy breathing filled the room as they all stared at the nervous and excitable man. The sweat across his brow was obvious to them.

"You are right to fear us," Aazar said with a growl.

David swallowed, "but why? Have you not come in peace?" He looked at them with anguish and confusion.

His confusion was met by theirs as David pointed at a poster on the wall. The three strangers looked at the poster, it depicted some form of craft with an accompanying statement saying, 'I Want To Believe.' Duat stepped forward, the man stepped backwards. "What is this?"

David watched Duat lift his hand as the extended long fingernail pointed at the poster.

David smiled, albeit nervously. "It's a spaceship. Where is yours? May I see it?"

The two Watchers and the Gatekeeper in disguise looked at each other with confusion.

"Well, you must have got here somehow. Can you go into the future as well?"

"Silence!" Saliva shot from Duat's mouth in anger.

David was instantly terrified, the deep tone of Duat's voice filled him with fear as his shaking and sweating continued.

Duat pointed at David and then pointed at Bellator. "Fix him and stop talking now!"

David nodded repetitively. He was as white as a sheet, his pulse racing uncontrollably. This was not like the friendly alien visitors he had heard about in a recent podcast.

"Please step forward to me, you can lie down over here," he said awkwardly, bowing. "You do know I'm not a doctor."

Aazar leaned towards him, and David could smell him. He flinched as a growl came from the suited alien.

Why would an alien be wearing a suit? David briefly considered. He would dwell on that later if he got out of this. He was surprised this was the first thing that came to his mind.

As Bellator lay on the bed meant for smaller animal surgery, David couldn't help but grip his own nose. The smell was overwhelming. The alien smelled of decay, his robe seared into his thin skin in multiple places.

"Can you remove the robe to expose the upper part of your body?"

Wincing, Bellator removed the robe as best as he could. In places, he had to pull to the extent that he lifted skin with it. Bellator howled in pain.

David flinched; the other two guests did not take their eyes away from him.

David made a mental note to ask about their one eye later.

David was amazed at what he was seeing during this first contact. He visually assessed the creature, wanting to ask many questions but feeling hesitant. The body, although thin, looked similar to his own form. The arms were slightly longer, and the fingernails were very long, although damaged. The alien looked malnourished, with muscular definition present due to hardly any body fat. The torso was covered in veins of varying sizes. At one point, David thought he saw a turquoise colour move quickly through the veins of the patient, but he couldn't be sure. The most significant differences were in the skull.

The alien had a large head with a thin neck, holes for ears but no ear lobes, a small, almost flat nose, and teeth in terrible condition, causing saliva to constantly fall from its mouth. One of the most unsettling features was the huge vein that fed the single oversized eye, which was centrally located on the skull. The eyelid would occasionally blink, but it seemed to serve little purpose in sunlight, indicating that the creature may have evolved in the dark. The pupil was black and the eye appeared bloodshot. David suspected that the creature's pale, thin skin was an adaptation to living in the dark.

They were not sun worshippers, David thought to himself, along with wondering how he could capture this moment on film. David reached over to a scalpel to assist the creature with removing the fused garment. *If I can film this, it will be amazing for business, TV interviews, the lot!* David, still fearful of his guests, from whatever planet they came from, secretly smiled on the inside. He knew all three of them looked nothing like the usual grey aliens that featured in most of the documentaries he watched.

As David lifted the scalpel, he felt the immediate presence of the other two creatures.

"Be careful animal doctor, your life depends on it!"

The alien who had spoken seemed to be the leader of the three of them, and David nodded at him as he approached. He was dressed in the same kind of robe as the injured one. "Do you have acid for blood?" David asked.

"What?" Bellator's eye moistened from the pain and he appeared bewildered.

"Never mind, it was just a film I..." With a shaking hand, David held up the scalpel and glanced at his one-eyed patient, coughing under his breath, "Anyway, this may hurt."

David glanced at the clock hanging on the wall and realised that over an hour had slipped away since he had begun treating the burns on the alien's body. He carefully wrapped the alien's injuries in gauze and bandaged the more severe wounds, doing his best to ease the creature's pain. The alien emitted haunting howls as David applied protective ointments, causing the atmosphere to tense with discomfort.

As he worked, the alien wearing the black suit leaned in so close to David that he had to brush drool off his shoulder. The intense, noisy breathing of the alien, so close to David's own ears, sent shivers of fear down his spine. Despite his unease, David treated the alien to the best of his abilities.

Satisfied with his first time operating on an alien body, David moved to his desk and perched on the end of it. He took a deep breath. "I've done the best I can, I do not know how long wounds take to heal with your species." He shuffled his bottom across the desk, knowing that he had a camera in the drawer below. "Say, would you be able to tell me how you got here and where are you from?"

He was met with three vacant expressions.

"Where is your ship?"

"Ship?" Duat responded, "What stupidity are you talking about, human?"

"Well, how did you get here, how long did it…"

"Silence!! My knowledge goes far beyond your primitive existence."

David's curiosity had now caused him to panic again. He swallowed, his hands shaking uncontrollably, "I don't mean to upset you, I want to understand."

Duat sneered, "You know nothing!"

"It's just…it's just strange…us…we humans always want to learn."

Duat sneered, "You are incapable of learning. You make war with your own kind; you are a warring species that needs leadership and control."

David didn't know, but his face had turned as white as a sheet again. "Are you going to invade?"

The suited alien almost choked on his own laughter as he looked at his Master. "We are already here, human," Duat stepped closer to David. "Change is already underway."

David shook his head. "Change... seriously... what is going on?" He folded his arms. "Maybe I should have checked that cat properly after all." He shook his head at the absurdness of it all.

David's guests immediately looked at each other. "WHAT DID YOU SAY?" The tone of the alien leader's raised voice made David jump. David discreetly slid his hand down the side of the desk, reaching for the drawer. There needed to be photographic evidence of this, there was only CCTV outside. "What do you mean?" David nervously questioned, his shaking obvious to all of them.

"What did you just say?" Duat was now in arms reach of David. "Tell me now!" Spit flew out of his mouth over the terrified veterinarian.

"Erm... oh... it was nothing. I was just thinking out loud, strange phenomena and all that." David shook his shoulders and smiled nervously. He could feel the sweat running down his forehead at an increasing rate as he wiped the spittle off his face. "Phenomena is never strange, human. Even your meaning of the word is perplexing to those with insight. You mock your own kind when they see what is really happening around them. I will ask you again and for the final time, what did you just say about a cat?"

David was perplexed by the alien's question and shook his head, "The cat... it was nothing really?" In fear, he avoided Duat's huge solitary eye, noticing that the vein feeding it was pulsing faster and faster. "A cat was brought in here a couple of days ago like I say, nothing really," David shrugged his shoulders, "one of our vets thought it had two heartbeats." David chuckled to himself, but his amusement was short-lived.

Duat stepped back and looked directly at Aazar.

"What did you just say?" Aazar demanded and moved closer to David.

David shook his head in concern, "What do you mean... I told you it was nothing."

The alien leader's eye took on a more sinister appearance as it filled with blood and started to redden in colour. David watched as the creature flexed the fingers of its right hand.

"I don't understand, what is going on? What is happening?" David could sense the volatility in the air, "what have I done?"

The alien leader lifted his right hand, the palm pulsing with the colour of turquoise. He placed his right hand over the terrified vet's head and reached out with his left hand, grabbing the vet by his white gown. He drew David towards him as he placed his right pulsing palm directly over his eyes.

David's eyes watered in fear as he screamed.

"Tell me everything about the cat with two heartbeats!"

Chapter Seven:
SLEEPWATCHING

The Franks' carrier bag and its contents were unceremoniously dropped onto the kitchen floor. Mildred quickly pulled Nahla away from her chest, her worry evident as she looked over her cat. "Don't tell me we've got to ring Fennaway again!" The thought of the odd 'I can talk to your cat' veterinarian coming to her house again filled her with dread.

Mildred abruptly shook her feet, sending her worn-out shoes skidding across the discoloured floor before slumping into one of the chairs at her kitchen table. "What on earth is the matter now? You haven't been back long."

She pulled Nahla into her chest again. Nahla's pulse was fast but nothing like it had been a few days ago. That had been an awful experience. "The other vet said you are okay, Nahla, but you look like you are scared of something – are you?"

Nahla turned her head to look in the direction of her water bowl. Mildred had to concede, since being informed of her cat's 'real name', she found they could communicate with each other a little better.

Mildred sighed, but there were no answers coming. "Okay, water it is." Mildred carried the shorthair cat over to her bowl. Placing her gently on the floor, she put her hands on her hips in surprise at the amount of water Nahla was drinking. "Well, that's not natural."

Nahla immediately lifted her head from her bowl, sensing the presence of another in the kitchen.

"Oh, look Nahla, your sister is here!" Mildred rubbed her hands together with glee, the new addition filling her with much-needed happiness. She frowned, noticing Nahla's tail straighten and her body becoming rigid. "Oh, come now, Missy," Mildred shook her head. "I'm sorry, I meant to say Nahla. Don't be jealous of your sister." She wagged her finger at her three-year-old cat. Nahla was obviously unimpressed with the newcomer. Mildred went over to Comet and picked her up. "We are all friends here!" She stroked the kitten down her flank, and as her fingers moved over the kitten's scar, Mildred immediately recoiled her hand. "Ouch!!!" Mildred's high-pitched yell made Nahla move away from her water bowl in shock. Mildred shook her hand and flexed her fingers. The pain was like a collection of needle pricks, it hurt but was short-lived. She continued to shake her hand and flex her fingers. She immediately froze, thinking she saw a brief flash of turquoise in her palm.

"Understood, Ma'am," Raysmau nodded. "Do you have an idea of when you'll be back?" She nodded again. "I see. Yes, Ma'am, Kalara is here as well. I think she'll want to see you when you return, regarding Lady Tempest."

After exchanging further pleasantries, Raysmau hung up the phone. She sat back in her large chair, resting her right elbow on its arm, and started turning her index finger around her thumb. Kalara, standing next to Raysmau's desk, had seen this before. Raysmau always turned her thumb around her finger when she was thinking.

"Kalara, the Reeve will be returning tomorrow. Without any word from the Lady of the House following her meeting with the Grand

Council, it's difficult to know what steps to take. However, the Reeve wants us to take the initiative with the remaining Watchers."

"What does the Reeve have in mind, Ma'am?" Kalara inquired.

"Search and detain. They will need to be taken from the below and moved elsewhere. Apparently, the Reeve and Lady Berenike are assessing old plans and schematics of Loxley. They are trying to assess how many floors, caverns, and other rooms are down there," Raysmau said, flicking her hand dismissively and shaking her head. She quickly resumed thumb-turning and frowned. "As I recall, some of the walls below looked very rough, not carved with the precision you would expect from our ancient architects. I suspect the Watchers have made many changes. It would not surprise me if some of the old plans are now redundant."

"No word, Ma'am, on why the serpent creature is down there?" Kalara asked.

Raysmau shook her head and paused briefly. "No, that seems to be eluding everyone at the moment. It's not been heard again, but there must be no chances taken. Full protective gear, Scatterblades, and trackers will be needed."

"Where can the Watchers be housed, Ma'am? The Escarrabin security wing is secured, but the girls won't be happy having Watchers in there with them," Kalara expressed her concern.

"That's as may be, but it's not their decision to make, Kalara!"

"I know, Ma'am, but I thought I'd mention it all the same."

Raysmau took a deep breath considering her options. The thumb and index finger resumed turning. "We will have to use the Cleric's wing; it's secured as well as windowless, of course."

Raysmau leaned forward and pressed her intercom.

"Yes, Ma'am?"

"Control, send a couple of the Escarrabin into the Clerics wing to assess that it is still properly secured. Check all doors, locks, and alarm sensors. Also, establish whether there is enough space to move the Cleric's temporarily into the security wing."

There was a brief pause as the instructions were considered. "Yes, Ma'am, I'll arrange that now."

Raysmau let go of the intercom. "Kalara, I'm going to need your thoughts on security. The lift down has been destroyed as well as the security door allowing entry to the below. This is not simply a case of carrying out repairs. We need to learn, adapt, and improve. At some point, we will need to know exactly what is down there in the below, and I mean everything. Every room, every cavern, and what lies behind every locked door." Raysmau took a deep breath and shook her head at Kalara. "Let alone how a multi-headed serpent creature can just suddenly come back to life." Raysmau slumped back into her chair, hearing the absurdity of her own words.

"Yes, Ma'am, I will look into it," Kalara replied.

"Do so, make your investigations, and only report to me. There is too much that we don't know. It worries me."

✝✝✝✝

Lady Berenike closed her eyes, feeling the weight of the Grand Council's decisions. With a sigh, she rubbed at her temple and pressed the intercom, speaking in Spanish to request a security officer to summon the British Reeve to her office.

Glancing at her clock, which still read two minutes past one, she rose to her feet and walked to the other side of her room, where a warm breeze from the open windows greeted her.

Taking a deep breath, she had spoken with other senior Reeves around the world. She pondered the unusual event of the clocks all stopping at the same time, two minutes past midnight, British Summer Time, where it had all begun.

The mystery of the buried Hydra at Loxley and its resurrection troubled her thoughts. What force had roused it from centuries of slumber? If this was indeed the fulfilment of the great prophecy, she knew they might need to seek assistance. As it stood, they could face a Gatekeeper and rogue Watchers, but the possibility of more Gatekeepers crossing over posed a daunting threat. Their malevolence and hunger for darkness would spread uncontrollably, causing chaos and panic among the public and potentially inciting global turmoil. The Order of the Reeves, the Escarrabin, and the League of Light would be exposed. So, too, would the magic world. It would be impossible to contain.

As she stepped into the sunlight, she closed her eyes, feeling the warmth of the sun and contemplating the potential consequences. The last thing they needed was public interference and ignorance, triggering a reaction against an unknown enemy. Unaware of the secret Orders, the prophecy, and the existence of Watchers and a restless Underworld, the public's perception of history was limited and distorted. The world was already in disarray, constantly embroiled in conflict, without adding this hidden reality into the mix.

Her contemplation was interrupted by a knock at her door. "Come in," she called, her back still turned to the door as she admired the serene view outside her windows.

"The Reeve of Loxley, my Lady," the Escarrabin announced in English, ensuring the non-Spanish-speaking Reeve understood.

Turning to face the Reeve as she entered, Lady Berenike acknowledged her, and as the doors closed, she observed the Reeve's dishevelled appearance, her hair down, and dressed in casual gym attire.

The Reeve glanced around to ensure she was alone with her senior.

"You called, my Lady," the Reeve said.

Nodding, Lady Berenike replied, "I heard you had been exercising. I have my spies, Kiya."

It was the first time that her senior had addressed her by her real name.

Kiya smiled slightly, not surprised by this statement but unsure where all of this was leading.

"The Grand Council has not formally reported to me, but they will in time," Lady Berenike gathered her thoughts. "I have someone who reports back to me; she was present at the earlier meeting that took place in Scotland. Your own Safiya and that irritating Curator were summoned."

The Reeves both found some solace in the thought of Nubia being summoned. "The Council is not happy, not happy at all. Words such as 'losing confidence in us' were used. They do not feel as safe as they did, Reeve of Loxley," Lady Berenike said in a controlled and soft tone. However, the Reeve sensed that something else was coming.

"It was always going to happen, but the Council wants more transparency, they want to be involved more in security processes, and that, in turn, will also mean financial matters. Reeve, our storage area below the statue of Salma is far from our only one; we have other secretive spaces located across the globe, entrusted to the selected ones, such as you."

The Reeve nodded her head. This was clearly a rebuttal hidden in calmness.

"At least for now. There are treasures below the statue of Salma that do not concern the Order; they are the property of the Reeves. In time, some of those treasures will need to be rehoused and possibly used. You will be supported when the time is right. However, for now, their poking around in security matters does concern me when we have our own Order to support." Berenike moved to face the Reeve directly. "A long time ago, the joining of the League of Light with us was of simple convenience. They needed us and our security arm; in return, their knowledge, insights, and bloodlines were of great importance to us. We became united in defeating the Watchers and their masters – the Gatekeepers. It suited both Orders, so we cooperated and worked alongside each other. However, we were never really fused as a joint venture. That is why we have our secrets. Reeve, there is much about us they do not know. It worries me that things may change." Lady Berenike swallowed and looked Kiya directly in the eyes, "they are bringing in another."

The Reeve put her hands on her hips and started shaking her head. She smirked with amusement or possibly bemusement. "Another, my Lady?"

"Yes, and you won't like it as she will be loyal to them, to the League, to their Order. Her loyalty will always be to them, and she will not take instructions from you. She will report back to the Grand Council on everything and most certainly will report back about you!"

The Reeve continued to shake her head and shrugged her shoulders. "I don't answer to anyone, my Lady, other than you, senior Reeves, and others of your rank. Who is it you are referring to, my Lady?"

"I've never met her, but I'm aware of her. She is unorthodox, ill-disciplined, and clumsy; her techniques are somewhat dangerous. She considers herself as an inventor, more like a pioneer of chaos."

"Who is it, my Lady?"

"They call her the Armourer, and she is not to be trusted."

5:45 AM, ROCKE ROAD

Mildred's heart raced as she placed a trembling hand over her chest, trying to slow her pulse with deep breaths. She blinked rapidly, focusing on the cobwebs that adorned her bedroom ceiling. Pushing herself up on her bed, she drew her knees close to her chest, bewildered and wiping the sweat from her brow. These disconcerting dreams had become a nightly occurrence. With an elbow resting on her knee, her left hand remained pressed against her forehead as she contemplated the vivid and bewildering images that her mind conjured. Each night, it was the same unsettling sequence: a lake engulfed in flames, flashes like lightning, deafening noises, hooded figures, and a menacing beast with a tail and piercing red eyes. It all seemed utterly nonsensical, and she couldn't fathom how or why her sleep was besieged by these distressing thoughts. The dreams were in a place of chaos, entirely removed from the safety and familiarity of Rocke Road. Although her pulse gradually began to calm, she couldn't shake the apprehension that if these dreams persisted, the fear of sleeping would become a constant companion.

Mildred rubbed her tired eyes and was startled as she glanced towards the foot of her bed. Her pulse quickened once more as a shiver ran through her, causing her to clutch the bed covers tightly. On the duvet, Comet, took a few steps towards her, emitting an unusual noise. Her tail swayed rhythmically as she stared intently into Mildred's eyes.

Mildred scanned the room. Nahla was nowhere to be seen.

Mildred pulled the duvet over her knees. The piercing stare of Comet sent an unexpected shiver down her spine. She took deep breaths, trying to comprehend how she could feel afraid of a tiny kitten.

Comet, with her peculiar mark, continued to lock eyes with her, but Mildred noticed the intensity of her stare beginning to wane. The kitten's tail stopped its back-and-forth motion as it settled down.

Feeling unsettled, Mildred kept her knees drawn close to her chest and pulled the duvet up even higher, inadvertently bringing Comet closer to her. This behaviour was far from normal, even for the most inquisitive of cats. She was certain that the kitten's eyes had been completely black at one point, but now they had returned to her normal colour, her pupils distinctly visible. "What is it, Comet?" Mildred's voice quivered slightly. "Why are you staring at me, and what was that strange noise you were making all about?"

Comet's unwavering gaze remained fixed on Mildred.

Shaking off her nervousness and regaining her composure, she pondered Comet's lack of sleep. It wasn't the first time she had noticed the kitten staring at her. "Did you even get any sleep?" The question felt futile.

Recently learning that Missy's real name was Nahla, Mildred now found understanding and communication with her so much easier. However, she couldn't establish any such communication with this new arrival, suspecting that even the peculiar Dr Fennaway wouldn't be able to either. Something was amiss.

Mildred grimaced; surely a kitten needed its rest. Comet seemed wide awake. Judging by the light filtering through the window, she knew it was earlier than her usual waking time. Glancing at her clock, she realised it still displayed the same time as it had for the past few days. The clock downstairs was no better, and she resolved to return her new batteries to Mr Franks later, seeking replacements or a refund.

Throwing the duvet aside, Mildred got out of bed and made her way to the open window. The birds were chirping their morning songs, and she spotted a woodpigeon perched in the tree by her front gate. As she raised her right hand to stifle a yawn and rub the sleep from her eyes, she noticed something peculiar. Her palm and fingers were strangely sore for reasons she couldn't fathom.

✢✢✢✢

"Wow, she's up early," Ana observed.

"Mmm," Soad mumbled from under the duvet. "You what?"

"She's already out of bed," Ana remarked.

Soad pulled the duvet back over her head, Ana could hear a yawn and muffled words from under the duvet, "What time is it?"

"I have no idea. My watch, like yours, hasn't worked for the last few days," Ana replied.

Ana continued to keep watch from the upstairs window at number 51 Rocke Road.

Soad, still under the covers, asked, "How do you know it's early then?"

Ana shook her head in frustration. "It's obvious from the height of the sun and all the birds chirping. They're trying to tell everyone in the area to get up, including you. Haven't you been on surveillance before?" Ana was unimpressed by Soad's lack of commitment, but there was no response from her fellow member of the Escarrabin.

"I wonder what's got her up so early," Ana mused, turning around and hearing a snore from the bed. "Oi!" she kicked at the bed. "I've been here for the last few hours listening to your snoring. Go and take a shower, and then it's your turn."

"Alright, alright," Soad grumbled as she pushed herself up.

Ana chuckled. "Look at the state of you. Your hair looks like a Scatterblades gone off in it."

Soad responded with a sarcastic smile.

"I've never known anyone to sleep so heavily, especially when out on assignment," Ana remarked.

Soad threw the covers all the way over, got to her feet, and joined Ana at the window. "Where is she now?"

"I guess she's in the bathroom," Ana replied.

"How long do you think we'll be here?" Soad asked, leaning on the windowsill.

"Are you serious? After what happened at Loxley and knowing this Lady of the Order has something to do with it, I think we could be here for months," Ana said.

Soad sighed. "Ana, we can't fight from here in this suburban place of anti-fun. I want to be involved!"

"That's if you can stay awake, of course," Ana teased, and they both smirked.

"Do you really think Mildred over the road has something to do with this? Have you been watching the same person that I have? She doesn't strike me as a possible great Elder or a future soldier. She couldn't hurt a fly. She can't even get her cat in for feeding on time, imagine her with a Scatterblade," Soad questioned.

Soad had a point, and Ana nodded in concession. "All I know is that the Reeve seems to think so. It was lucky this house was empty and available to buy immediately. No idea how much money must have been paid to arrange it so quickly. In any event, it's 24/7, and we can't risk getting burnt. We'll drone her later if we need to, when she goes to the shop. She may have already seen us outside."

Soad yawned and stretched her arms. "Let's hope today has more excitement than yesterday."

"I hope so too. I suspect something is going to happen around here soon," Ana said.

✢✢✢✢

An hour had passed since Mildred's abrupt awakening, the remnants of her unsettling dream still lingered in her mind. The persistent sleep disruption was wearing her down, evident in the heavy yawn that escaped her lips as she gazed at the boiling kettle. Puzzled by the recurring pattern of distressing dreams, she stretched her arms and turned off the gas, silencing the whistling kettle. As she poured hot water onto the tea bag, the image of a smiling cat on her mug greeted her, and the latest issue of *Cats Quarterly* lay ready on the kitchen table, though she had already perused it three times.

"Cup of tea, a little reading, and then to find Nahla," she murmured, her attention caught by Comet, weaving in and out between her legs. "You are quite the affectionate cat, but I could do without you staring at me while I'm sleeping."

Bending down to pick up Comet, Mildred mused, "I don't even know when you are allowed outside. Although I wouldn't mind a house cat; it would save me from having to call out down the street twice a day."

As she considered her options, she brought Comet close to her chest and retrieved a spoon from a drawer. Pausing as the kitten without a name appeared at the kitchen doorway, she smiled to herself, knowing that the unnamed kitten would soon need to be given to the new owner. "I have no idea how I'm going to do that."

Dabbing at the tea bag with the spoon, Mildred realised she hadn't fully thought through the process. "How am I going to manage this?"

She placed Comet on her chair, freeing her hands to remove the tea bag and add milk. "Okay!" Picking up Comet, she sat down and made sure the smiling cat on the mug was facing her, allowing her to multitask in a different way: sipping tea, reading the magazine, stroking the cat, sipping tea, reading the magazine, stroking the cat... "Waaaa!!" Mildred jumped and recoiled her right hand, immediately shaking her fingers. "What on earth?"

"Oww!" It felt incredibly strange, she thought, as she continued to shake her fingers. Her hand didn't hurt, and her fingers felt fine; it was almost like an electric shock. Frowning, she examined her hand, but nothing seemed out of the ordinary. She had seen a vision, only a flash, but someone had tried to speak to her. It was the face of a lady she didn't recognise; she was trying to warn her of something. Mildred lifted Comet towards her face, for the second time in as many days, she felt sure she saw something inside her scar move.

✝✝✝✝

Just after 7 a.m. Ana walked into the bedroom, wide awake following a cold morning shower. Soad grabbed her surveillance camera and both peered through the small holes they had cut in the net curtain, their line of observation nearly opposite Mildred's house. Soad brought the camera up to her eye and asked, "How long do you think this will take today?"

Ana replied, "If it's anything like yesterday, I'm mentally preparing myself for up to ten minutes of ear abuse!" Soad laughed to herself and switched the camera on. From their hidden position, they looked across the street at number one Rocke Road. The unsuspecting Mildred was standing outside her front door dressed the same as the previous morning, in worn fluffy slippers, an old dressing gown, and a knitted blouse. Even from their distance, her hair looked like a tangled maze of misery.

They watched Mildred head to her overflowing recycling bin and take an empty tin out. She already had a dessert spoon in hand, and that's when the shrill started.

"Nahla!!!!!"

Not appreciating the morning's disturbance, the racket sent the woodpigeon into immediate flight. The observing security officers rolled their eyes as the clanging of the spoon on the empty cat food tin started.

"Nahla!!!"

Soad placed her fingers over the microphone on the camera so her voice was not recorded and asked Ana, "Wasn't she yelling Missy yesterday?"

Ana replied, "She did to start with, but the cat didn't respond until she called out Nahla. I'm guessing she was told the cat's real name at the recent gathering. She probably doesn't know the name of the new kitten she has, along with the one she's supposed to be delivering to the new Level Nine Elder any time now."

With her fingers still over the microphone, Soad fiddled with the focus on the camera and said, "Well, I wish I knew what all the fuss is about with this particular Elder. It's strange to be surveying an Elder anyway, especially one as young as Mildred."

Ana replied, "Well, she's not a complete youngster, early middle age I would guess. But no, I have no idea what's going on, Kassia mentioned something about a special bloodline, but you know what a gossip she is." Soad laughed and removed her fingers from over the microphone.

"Nahla!!!" The tin was struck multiple times, producing a resounding clang. Mildred noticed the curtains in the bedroom window opposite were twitching again as a disapproving face appeared. Undeterred, Mildred continued to call out for her cat. She pondered the neighbour's evident annoyance but carried on banging the tin, unfazed. The neighbouring house with the net curtains had been empty for some time, so Mildred was not disturbing anyone there.

As she walked down her path, opened her front gate, and stepped onto the pavement, Mildred paused, hands on her hips, glancing left and right. The peaceful road was eerily quiet, with the bus stop standing empty. Mildred found solace in the tranquil morning birdsong but couldn't shake off the memory of the rude boys who had teased her a few days ago. She had resolved not to tolerate such behaviour anymore and vowed to stand up for herself. However, for now, she had a missing cat to find.

"Nahla!" she called out, pausing after banging the tin. Suddenly, she heard a noise from her own house and fear gripped her. Rushing up the pathway in a panic, she dropped the tin and spoon into the grass, her heart racing. Comet, her other cat, was peering at her from outside the cat flap. "Comet, I don't think you are allowed out yet!" she exclaimed as she crouched down, her hands trembling, beckoning the kitten to come to her. Despite her pleas, Comet remained unmoved, fixated on Mildred. As she made her way towards the kitten, Comet seemed poised to flee. Mildred lunged toward the mischievous kitten, and to her relief, she succeeded in catching her.

She managed to secure both hands around Comet just as she fell backwards into a large bramble bush. With a loud shriek, Mildred quickly sprung back up from the brambles, holding Comet at arm's length so the kitten didn't get pricked by the awful stabbing plant. Releasing one hand from her hold on Comet, Mildred shook her arm to try to shake off the brambles now embedded in her dressing gown.

"Comet, look what you've done, I've hurt myself!" She pulled the kitten towards her chest, cradling her with both hands. Unintentionally, Mildred's hand came into contact with the cat's scar. "Ouch!" she yelled, feeling a searing sensation through her right hand, making her take a few steps backwards in shock. "Ouch, that really hurts, Comet," she shook her hand in pain and stepped back further, slipping on the empty cat food tin and landing straight onto her backside.

As she fell, she instinctively lifted her left arm, proudly holding the kitten high above the overgrown grass. Mildred pushed herself up, amazed that Comet was still safely held in her left hand. Mildred looked in shock at the kitten and started flexing her right hand; the pain immediately faded.

"What is wrong with you? I keep getting shocks from you!"

With grass entangled in her hair and brambles in her dressing gown, Mildred heard a rustle to her left. Nahla was staring at her, and Mildred had to admit that her oldest cat seemed quite perplexed. Mildred shook her head. "Come on, let's get you both in." She made a mental note to secure the cat flap in the future.

The two Escarrabin across the way exchanged shocked glances from behind the privacy of the net curtains. "Tell me you got that on film?" Soad nodded and swallowed, her face a mixture of astonishment and amusement.

"Well, that's a unique bloodline that she's got! If she's meant to be the chosen one, I think we are in a spot of bother!"

Chapter Eight:
THE RIGHTFUL GUARDIAN

Blocking the cat flap with one of her kitchen chairs, it was now time for serious contemplation.

From the kitchen, Mildred kept her eyes on both of her cats, along with the one that apparently was not meant for her. She had observed that Nahla didn't really spend much time with her new sister – surely that was odd. Comet seemed to be keeping her distance from both cats as well. Mildred knew that she wasn't an expert on these things, but you didn't need to be when something was clearly amiss. It was bound to be tricky with new arrivals in the house, but at least they were not fighting. The kitten of no name would snuggle up to Nahla on occasion, but as for Comet, well, there didn't seem to be any bond forming at all. Nahla and Comet remained independent of each other.

Mildred cast her mind back to a few days ago, the intimidating sheriff woman from the Kat Chamber or was it the Order…or the League of whatever it was. Anyway, the scary-looking suited woman had explained that Comet was important, very important. Mildred shrugged her shoulders, deep in her own thoughts, *I have absolutely no idea what that means,* she considered as she sat on her other kitchen chair. *All cats are important after all, what was so different about this one that required this clear distinction?* She locked eyes with Comet, *the special one*. Mildred shook her head and folded her arms; the kitten never looked away from her. "Why are you staring at me, Comet? You do that a lot. In fact, every time I look for you, you are already staring at me." Mildred continued to shake her head. "I wonder what your real name is, I bet that would shine some light on things?" Mildred broke away from the stare and glanced over to her sofa in the front room. Nahla was sat upright on the cat cushion, wide awake watching her every move. The unnamed kitten was playing below her, chewing one of the many bits of discarded paper. Mildred frowned. "Now you see, Nahla, that's not like you either." Usually, the cat cushion was a place for sleeping, which was always after breakfast, but Nahla had shown no interest in her breakfast whatsoever. "You are worrying me Nahla, you must eat. I don't want you to be unwell again!" She waved her finger at her cat, a pointless gesture that Nahla ignored.

The magazine that usually gave her a smile was still on the kitchen table. Mildred glanced at the cover *of Cat's Quarterly*; she suspected it didn't contain answers for a cat that gave you some form of body shock when you picked it up. She was waving her finger again, "You know Comet, as I think about it, it was only a few days before you arrived that my bad dreams started." Mildred stood up and walked over to the scarred kitten. She crouched down as Comet lifted a paw. "Are you wanting to play or are you going to give me some form of electric shock again?" She picked up her new cat being mindful not to touch the so-called birthmark on her flank. It looks more like a scar or a burn to me, Mildred considered.

She settled back into her chair, gently drawing Comet into her lap. Her fingers traced the unusual marking on Comet's fur, she wanted to study it in more detail. As she lifted Comet, a peculiar sensation struck her. A nagging feeling that the cat had grown heavier since the last time she held her. The mark itself seemed unchanged in size, but she couldn't shake off the notion that Comet had somehow grown larger. Dismissing the thought as absurd, Mildred ran her hand down Comet's flank, pausing at the distinctive brown mark that contrasted against her coat. The texture of the skin where the mark was felt coarse and uneven, unlike the smoothness typical of a newborn.

Lost in contemplation, Mildred pondered her next steps. Comet, despite the peculiarity of the mark, displayed no signs of illness, devouring her food and lapping up milk with ease, unlike Nahla. Mildred hovered her hand over the mark, she felt foolish as she hesitantly dabbed with her index finger on the 'birthmark'. Comet didn't move, and nothing happened. Mildred smiled to herself, thinking that all this Kat Chamber craziness was getting to her.

Convinced that her mind was simply playing tricks on her, she brushed her palm over the mark. Suddenly, a sharp, piercing pain shot through her, causing her to cry out in agony. Clutching her head with her left hand, she found her right hand inexplicably stuck to Comet's scar as if glued in place. A vivid vision flashed before her eyes—a woman in distress, wearing a familiar pin badge, struggling to communicate something urgent. Mildred's right hand shook as she finally pulled it free from Comet's scar. The vision was gone in an instant. Mildred took a deep breath and shook her right hand, noticing a fleeting turquoise colour pulsating through a vein in her palm. Overwhelmed with pain and confusion, she heard a noise from the living room. She glanced over, her eyes watering, the new kitten, still awaiting delivery, had taken refuge beneath the sofa, while Nahla bristled with fear and hostility. She looked terrified, hissing at Mildred to the point of spitting.

It was an unusual time of the day for the post, but hearing the letterbox snapping closed caught Suzanna's attention. Earlier in the day, her Elder, Lady Abrielle, had delivered her a new kitten, Suzanna was thrilled to see it was a sphinx cat. The main insignia for the Kat Chamber was the head of the sphinx, harking back to the earliest of times and the creation of their organisation in Egypt. With Suzanna being Daphne's Elder, Lady Abrielle had also delivered a new kitten for her as well, following Daphne's promotion at the Gathering a few days ago. With three fully grown cats and her new kitten, as well as Daphne's, the house was now a sanctuary for cats. Suzanna smiled to herself and rose to her feet, heading towards the front door, where a bulky envelope was waiting for her on the doormat. She recognised the neat handwriting in an instant. As usual, only her first name was written on the front. Surnames were not used in formal communications for reasons that had not been explained to her yet. Presumably, it was a security procedure.

Walking back into her kitchen, she tore the brown envelope open and turned it upside down; the contents fell onto the kitchen table. She sorted through a variety of new identification cards, all bearing the name Suzanna; her previous name of Jessica was being erased from history.

She momentarily gave it some thought. Her former name was all she knew, but in terms of the Order, she had officially 'come of age.' She picked up her passport, wanting to see what picture had been used inside. She certainly hadn't posed for one in some time. The vet she had 'crashed' into recently had taken her picture, but this was not it. Her hairstyle told her it had been taken not too long ago. She studied the picture further; she was wearing a black dress. Seeing her exposed shoulders and the plunging neckline, she recognised the dress in an instant. She had worn it at the gathering last week. She closed the passport and shook her head, considering how this was possible. She couldn't help but open it again for another inspection; the angle of her face was not completely straight, and she could see a tree behind her in the distance. She shook her head with a little wry smile; the security officers must have taken it when Mildred was looking for her invitation.

"That's sneaky!" she exclaimed, dropping the passport onto the table. As she hastily grabbed at the other documents, her eyes fell on the same image printed on her new driving license. A letter related to her car insurance and her name changed on the electricity bill, the water bill, and various other documents confirmed that everything had been meticulously altered. Flicking through the papers, she realised there was no birth certificate, but she couldn't recall ever having one anyway. She remembered reading about something called a birth certificate in a magazine, a subject she had never discussed with anyone and no one had ever raised it with her.

She knew that she would have to deliver Daphne's kitten soon. Daphne, now a Level Seven Elder, already had two cats, so she was accustomed to the process by now. There was no need to rush the new kitten to her. Suzanna loved playing with her cats, so selfishly holding on to Daphne's kitten for an extra day was okay. She mentally justified it and was satisfied with her decision.

Suzanna rattled her pristine fingernails on the kitchen table in deep thought. Lady Nubia had asked—well, more like told—her that she needed to keep an eye on Mildred. However, Daphne was Mildred's direct Elder. Before she delivered Daphne's new kitten, she would need to contemplate and decide what questions she could put to Daphne about Mildred. The rattling of the fingernails abruptly stopped, and she pondered, *Lady Nubia said I can go to Loxley anytime I want, now that I am a Level Six Elder.* She thought about it further. *She definitely said it was okay, so I could go there unannounced and have a proper look around!*

She rubbed at her chin and pulled at her hair. Walking over to the mirror in her kitchen, she took a good look at herself. She nodded, observing that her hair needed styling and a little bit of makeup couldn't hurt. Judging by the rudeness of Nubia when they met, as well as when they spoke on the phone, she felt she had not made a good impression. Suzanna inspected the jogging bottoms she was wearing. "Let's see if she likes me this time around." And with that, she headed upstairs to get changed.

Mildred looked down into her lap, relieved that Nahla was finally at rest. Though her eyes were open, the hissing and panic had stopped. Peace had resumed in the house, but it felt far from a place of feline tranquillity, more like an oddity. With shaky knees, Mildred sat back on her sofa. Her eyes were fixed on the kittens, unable to tear away from the new cat addition to the household. Mildred held Nahla tightly; it pained her to see her cat so upset, especially after all they had been through in the last week. Mildred leaned to the right and glanced at the floor, where the unnamed kitten was curled up in a ball, asleep. Mildred knew that the kitten had been scared; both cats had sensed that something was wrong. Mildred looked down at Nahla, and they both glanced over at the kitchen chair, where the cat with the strange mark was asleep. "Nahla, what do we do?" They momentarily looked at each other and then back at the unnerving kitten. "I didn't imagine it, Nahla," Mildred shook her head. "I saw the same face again. I don't know her, I don't recognise her, but I feel like she is trying to tell me something!" Mildred brought her left hand up to her forehead; she didn't have a headache but wanted to check before she gave herself one. Earlier, for the second time, she had seen a foreign colour flash in her right palm, it had no worldly place being there. Struggling with her thoughts, Mildred tried to recall if the colour turquoise had ever appeared in her hand before the arrival of Comet. She gave it ten seconds or so and couldn't recall a single occasion when it had happened before. She shook her head, knowing it was a ridiculous notion. She jumped as the unnamed cat woke up and brushed against her legs. She had wanted to have a new cat for some time, but all of this was becoming a bit too much.

With no idea what time it was and how long she had been lost in her thoughts, something needed to be done. Expert opinion was required. "I think we need help!" Mildred stood up to look for the number for Castle Hollow Vets. Dr Sarah Belloch will have a view on this, she thought. With Nahla still clutched firmly to her chest, the unnamed kitten followed them as Mildred walked over to her phone, surrounded by an ever-increasing mound of paper. "You know, Nahla, I still don't know why they gave you that cat collar, weird!" Mildred shook her head. It was strange. If the vet's practice name had been on the collar, that might make some sense, simple advertising, but it wasn't. It was plain and looked new as if it had just come from a shop.

Placing Nahla on the floor, the two cats nosed at each other but kept their distance from the sleeping kitten in the kitchen. "Okay, so where is it now?" Mildred shuffled through bits of paper, tossing what she didn't need to the side. "Sarah's business card is here somewhere; she gave me her personal mobile phone number!" Mildred smiled proudly at her cats, feeling a sense of importance. As she sorted through the papers, a photograph caught her eye. It was the flyer she had taken from the café, *'I'm Doctor Bethany Birks'*...oh yes, *the lady who understands animals!* The phone number for the animal psychiatrist was printed on the rear, next to the photograph of the lady in question. Mildred put the flyer down next to the phone and placed her hands on her hips. *Now this lady might have an interesting point of view on all of this!* She turned to look at Comet asleep in the kitchen. Mildred chewed at her lips in contemplation. She knew she had been warned. She was not supposed to call other vets, only Dr Fennaway, as apparently, she *'understands cats'*, as well as being able to talk to them! Mildred shook her head abruptly, struggling with the madness of it all. She looked at the flyer again. Dr Bethany Birks was not advertised as a vet; she was an animal psychiatrist. Is that breaking the rules? If she were honest with herself, she knew it probably was and she didn't want the sheriff woman showing up here again. She looked down at the two cats who gazed back at her. She shrugged her shoulders with some contrition. "Ok, I'll call Fennaway, but any fun and games, I'm calling the animal psychiatrist!" The decision was made as both cats exchanged a glance.

Mildred was lounging on her worn-out sofa when she heard three distinct knocks on her front door. The bangs were so loud that Mildred and the three cats jumped to attention.

"Well, who can that be, Dr Fennaway shouldn't be here yet?" Mildred heard her letterbox close with a snap. Mildred made her way to the front door. A white envelope was waiting for her on the doormat. She didn't notice it and opened the door and stepped outside. The street was peaceful, except for a neighbour mowing the lawn. Mildred leaned on the gate, observing the deserted surroundings. A woodpigeon cooed above her, "Did you see who it was?" Mildred asked glancing towards the bus stop. She noticed a couple of the youths who had been unpleasant to her, but they couldn't have run back there so quickly. The last time this happened, it was someone from the cat club delivering her invitation to the gathering. She turned around shaking her head and noticed the white envelope on her doormat. She glanced up at the woodpigeon, "Why do they always scarper!" She returned to pick it up. The envelope was addressed to 'Mildred, Rocke Road, Shrewsbury,' with no postcode or surname. Recognising the neat handwriting, Mildred knew it was from the peculiar Kat Chamber. "And I wonder what delights are in store for me today!" Her tone was patronising, but she felt it needed to be. *Bloodlines, Watchers, cat guardians* were just a few words that shot into her mind as she considered the odd women from the Kat Chamber.

Backheeling her front door closed, she headed into the kitchen, opening the envelope as she went:

MILDRED – LEVEL 8 ELDER
1 ROCKE ROAD, SHREWSBURY, SHROPSHIRE, UNITED KINGDOM.

You are hereby instructed to present the unnamed kitten, recently delivered to you to its rightful guardian. You are to do this within the next forty-eight hours, along with introducing yourself to:

DAPHNE – LEVEL 9 ELDER
18 CROSSHOUSES ROAD, MUCH WENLOCK,
SHROPSHIRE, UNITED KINGDOM.

You are to present this important kitten to this new Lady of the Order. Failure to do so will be met by a formal reprimand and other serious action taken against you. Such action could include the removal of a cat from your guardianship and a reduction in your Elder status within the Order. This could also mean wage forfeiture.

Do not say anything untoward about the Order to Daphne. Inform her about the Kat Chamber only what she needs to know; this includes meetings. Remember you are now her Elder, please set a good example.

Always remember to inform your own Elder if you see any strange figures wearing peculiar glasses.

End of Message…

Please destroy this card after delivery, remember, we are always watching.

Mildred double-blinked and tossed the neatly handwritten card onto the kitchen table. She took a seat, glancing at the now wide-awake scarred kitten. She brought a hand up to her mouth and started picking at her teeth. *I wasn't aware I am an employee!* She considered at the clear indication of being told what to do. *A formal reprimand!* She shook her head and kicked her shoes off across the kitchen floor. Folding her arms, she considered her next move. The thought of her money being stopped was a worry. Every month for the last three years, money was paid into her account; it was only recently that she found out it came from the Kat Chamber. The money came into her account without a name or reference, and she had always kept quiet about it. It was not a subject she had ever wanted to discuss with the bank. She never asked questions, didn't want to cause a fuss, and it allowed her to look after Nahla full-time. Not having another job suited her just fine.

However, it did occur to her that not having a car was a presumption on the Chamber's part that she could get to this other address. She knew Much Wenlock was only twenty miles away or so, but all the same. If a bus didn't go there, she faced the prospect of a taxi ride with a stranger. She shuddered at the thought of it, knowing all the uncomfortable questions that may come her way. And if it weren't that, then there would have to be small talk!

Maybe she should keep the cat after all to avoid all of this. She swallowed, and her grip tightened against her folded arms. The sheriff woman and the security ladies at the gatherings were not the nicest of people. I don't want them showing up here. I still don't know what they want! This Order, this Chamber, this League, did they have any other names? *'We are always watching!' What on earth did that mean?* Mildred considered at what had she got herself caught up in?

Dr Fennaway was quick to answer the phone, and within moments, she was on her way to Mildred's house in Shrewsbury. Mildred, feeling drained from sleepless nights and unsettling dreams, stirred her tea absentmindedly, lost in thought.

Hooded, unnerving figures featured throughout her dreams, with one figure in particular standing out – a menacing drooling figure that left her feeling unsettled. Mildred stopped stirring her tea and looked at her right palm. In her dreams, this prominent figure often held his right hand forward. She frowned and flexed her own right hand. She couldn't be sure, but was the colour she had seen recently in her palm the same colour as the palm of the stranger in her dreams? She recognised the colour; she saw it every day. The border of the certificate framed and hung on her wall was turquoise. The one she was presented at the recent gathering by the Kat Chamber also had a turquoise border. It was all very confusing. Turquoise was not her colour of choice.

She jumped upon hearing a knock at the door. Mildred looked out of her kitchen window and saw that her gate was open. Having been lost in her thoughts, she hadn't heard someone come up her path. She leaned closer, bumping her temple on the glass, and glanced to her right. The strange cat doctor was standing at her door. Mildred took a deep breath, wondering what weirdness was about to unfold next.

"Hello, Dr Fennaway," Mildred said, holding open the front door, her tone not the most welcoming. The lack of politeness in Mildred's tone was not lost on the doctor who was responsible for the health of the Order's cats.

"Hello, Mildred," Kamilah Fennaway frowned as she pushed her way into the house before being invited. "This cat is very special, Mildred." Fennaway showed herself into the kitchen and started turning around in circles. She crouched down to look under the kitchen table. "Pray tell, where is she, my dear?"

Frowning, Mildred pushed her front door closed and walked into her front room. "She is in here, Kamilah." Given the vet's rudeness, Mildred chose to address her by her first name rather than her title. "Maybe someone would be good enough to explain to me why this cat is so special that when I run my hand over the marking on her side, it keeps giving me some form of electric shock?"

"Mmm, yes, dear, we'll get to that. Have you been taking your meds?" Kamilah walked into the front room, looking at the cat in question asleep on the couch.

"Are you talking to me or Comet?" Mildred's hands were back on her hips, as they had been a few times so far on this day.

Kamilah placed her bag down and noticed the black cat. "Mmm, what, Mildred?"

"Meds, Kamilah, are you talking to me or Comet because I don't take any?"

"Oh, sorry, I must have been thinking of someone else..." Kamilah shook her head. "It has been a long few days." Kamilah's words were absent of any thought. It was a messy attempt at conversation. She never took her eyes away from the sleeping cat as she spoke. Kamilah crouched down, and as she did, Comet's eyes opened. "Ah, there you are, little one." Kamilah reached for her medical bag. "Could I trouble you for a cup of tea, Mildred, and a fish paste sandwich if you have one? I've had a bit of a drive."

"I'm sure I can spare one as well as the tea. You can have those when you've finished your diagnosis. Last time you were here, you were being somewhat shifty with some form of flashing device. The other vet I spoke with had no clue what that was either, so I think I'll watch you throughout this time, Kamilah."

The vet swallowed. "Okay, my dear, as you wish. There's nothing untoward going on, I assure you." Kamilah knew that Mildred was not convinced and she needed to get things back on track. "So, you are saying that when you touch her, you get some form of shock?" The vet turned her attention to Mildred. Even with Kamilah's knowledge of the Order and their special cats, this was somewhat puzzling.

"Yes, that's right, over that burn-type thing that is on her side," Mildred pointed quite abruptly.

Kamilah was reasonably well-versed in the prophecy; she knew what had happened at Loxley and that the Order's prophecy had been realised. However, throughout their history and when the prophecy had taken place previously, she had never heard of a cat that could do such a thing. This was new on every level. Kamilah rubbed her chin and laughed. The laugh sounded fake to even the most casual of observers. "It's just a birthmark, Mildred," she continued to smile, although she averted Mildred's eyes as she told this complete lie.

"Well, whatever it is, I don't like it, and I don't think Comet enjoys it either. I think it hurts her as much as me!" Mildred decided not to mention the visions of the lady who kept trying to talk to her.

"Comet, Mildred. Is that what you've called her?"

"Yes, after the comet thingy that flew overhead recently."

Kamilah smiled, fully aware of what Mildred was referencing. "Now, Mildred, I think you'll find that was a satellite crash."

"Well, if you say so."

"It was, Mildred. It crashed not far from the Loxley Headquarters."

"What's the Loxley Headquarters?"

Kamilah froze at her slip of the tongue. "Yes, well... anyway... I'm sure it's nothing. What's going on then Comet? What are you doing to poor Mildred?"

Mildred lowered herself to look Kamilah directly in the eyes. "What is the Loxley Headquarters, Dr Fennaway?"

Annoyed with her own error, Kamilah sighed, realising she was cornered. She scratched her head and awkwardly ran a hand through her hair. "Look, Mildred, you're still new to this organisation. There's much you do not know."

Mildred leaned in closer. "So, I keep being told. So, tell me."

Kamilah swallowed. Something had changed in Mildred; she was not so mild-mannered this time. She spoke with more determination and confidence, as if she had become empowered.

"It's a place, Mildred. A place that you may get to see in time. But at your rank in the Order, it's not appropriate yet. Maybe in a few years or so." The cat doctor averted her eyes. Mildred was being far too inquisitive for her liking. Kamilah knew she should not speak of these things to a Level Eight Elder.

Mildred recoiled back with a giggle. "Rank, honestly, what are you all like! Like some sort of secret base, I guess!" She laughed to herself with the absurdity of it all.

"Yes, that's right."

Mildred stopped laughing, looking at the vet with seriousness. She straightened herself up and folded her arms. "Let me guess, I need some form of ceremony. Now then, what could that possibly be... I guess I need to wear a robe, a crown, and stand on one foot or something like that and then..."

"Stop being ridiculous, Mildred," the cat doctor cut her off. "That's an absurdity from the world of men."

Mildred looked into Kamilah's eyes; she could sense that the vet was not impressed. Q and A was over for now, but Mildred would be asking more questions at the earliest opportunity.

"Now then, Mildred, shall we see what is wrong with Comet?"

Mildred coughed under her breath, looking slightly embarrassed. "Yes, please," she said. She wanted her new kitten to be okay and for the pains to stop for them both. She also wished the visions would cease and that she could get an explanation of what they meant.

Kamilah rummaged inside her bag and pulled out her Signapher, choosing not to conceal it from Mildred this time. Kamilah pressed various buttons, and the display on the device came to life. "Now then, Comet, relax. You will not feel a thing," Kamilah said as she stroked the cat. She was somewhat surprised that the kitten had appeared to have grown already. The vet watched Comet's eyes as the device moved over the scar. The cat's eyes narrowed and looked angry, but there didn't appear to be any pain or instant bodily reaction, just anger at the violation. Kamilah looked away from Comet's eyes and focused on the Signapher. The display told her the same as when she last looked at the prophesied cat at Loxley. There were two heartbeats.

The vet looked away from the flashing lights, switched off the device, and took a deep breath. In thought, she clicked her teeth together, unsure of what to do next and what to say to Mildred; this was not fixable. Kamilah glanced at the cat's eyes; they had calmed, but the stare had not deviated. Comet watched her intently; the kitten may be young, but her brain was evolving quickly. Kamilah, who prided herself on being exceptional with cats, felt troubled as Comet's tail twitched back and forth. It almost appeared that the kitten was amused.

"So?" Mildred could see that she didn't have the attention of her house guest. "So!" She prodded Kamilah in the shoulder, causing her to jump; she had been miles away.

The vet turned to Mildred, and for the first time in this meeting, Mildred noticed the cat doctor looked concerned.

"So, what did the flashing thingy tell you?" Mildred asked.

Kamilah knew she had to think quickly. If she left Mildred's home without providing answers, she risked Mildred calling the other vet, the one who had no knowledge about the prophecy and the Order.

"Well, Mildred," Kamilah began, "the flashing thingy, as you called it, is a sophisticated piece of equipment. It tells me if everything is okay, and that is what it does. It tells me that Comet is okay." Kamilah raised a hand. "However, I sense that you are not happy, and I want to help." Kamilah gathered her thoughts. "Has Comet been outside, eaten something that she shouldn't have?"

Mildred sighed. "Yes, she scooted out of the cat flap for a moment, but I grabbed her. This is not about that; this is about the mark on her side and if it has some sort of power or something!" Mildred waved her arms in the air, clueless as to what was going on. She wasn't the only one.

Kamilah's fake laugh rang out again, hearing Mildred's words. "Now, let me tell you something about the Order, Mildred."

Mildred did not look impressed by Kamilah's laughter.

Kamilah gestured emphatically to Mildred, her index finger wagging in the air to capture her attention. "We all have powers of some description. They become more pronounced the longer you are involved in the Order. You are still new; you've only been a member for a few years, my dear. As such, you will not know yours yet."

Mildred's eyebrows raised; she had heard this said before.

"Usually, most ladies who are part of the Order are members for many years longer than you before they discover what their gift is."

Mildred shook her head, hearing words of further absurdity from the vet. "Like yours is talking to cats – right!"

"That's correct, Mildred," Kamilah proudly beamed.

Mildred shook her head. "If I had been allowed a cat or any pet as a youngster, I would have spoken to them as well, as you probably did!"

Kamilah shook her head. "No, I wasn't allowed pets when I was young, Mildred." Her words were solemn, the vet's face distracted.

Mildred was momentarily silenced; she had not been allowed pets either. Her parents, especially her father, had been very strict on this point.

Kamilah looked at the scar with worry; she knew she had to do something to soothe Mildred's concerns; no other vet could be involved at all costs. "Electric shock, you say, most peculiar." Kamilah knew that she'd need to mention this veterinary visit to Nubia, but what could any of them do about the prophesied cat? She doubted even the Keeper had any answers. "Tell you what, dear, why don't you touch the birthmark, and we'll see what happens."

This was a certain risk, but Kamilah was out of options. If there were a reaction, Kamilah would be clueless as to what to do next. She needed to hope for the best, but in her heart of hearts, she knew that Mildred was telling the truth.

"Looks more like a burn to me than a birthmark, doctor, but yes, I'll give it a go."

Kamilah shuffled her knees along the worn carpet to allow Mildred to squeeze in next to her.

Having knelt, Mildred leaned over the troublesome and scarred kitten; the young cat's eyes now watched Mildred's every move.

Mildred licked her lips and extended her right hand. Kamilah noticed Mildred's hand was shaking slightly as it hovered over the unusual mark. Mildred screwed up her eyes in anticipation as she gently placed her palm down on the mark.

Kamilah looked at Mildred. The lowly ranked Elder had her eyes closed, and her breathing was audible. Mildred looked nervous; they both were, for entirely different reasons.

A few seconds passed, and Mildred opened one eye. She looked down at Comet, who blinked but maintained her gaze.

Kamilah looked at the kitten, then back at Mildred. "So?"

Mildred opened her other eye, shook her head, and looked at the vet. "I don't understand. Nothing happened."

"Well, of course it didn't, Mildred. Let's face it; you've been through a lot over the last few days, what with Missy being unwell also."

Mildred removed her hand and brought it up to rub her forehead. "I've been told her name is Nahla." Her words were quietly spoken as Mildred rubbed at her forehead. There was no headache, just confusion.

Kamilah immediately gasped, bringing her hands up to her mouth to silence herself. The vet, still on her knees, shuffled across to be out of arm's reach from Mildred. She watched Mildred try to run her right hand through the tangled mess of her auburn hair.

Mildred stopped, hearing the vet's gasp. "What was that?"

"What was what, Mildred?"

"You gasped, what's the matter?" Mildred noticed the vet was not looking her in the eyes, her focus seemed to be following her hand instead.

Kamilah shook her head, her lips pinched tight together, her eyes as wide as saucers.

"Whatever is the matter?"

Kamilah kept shaking her head. "No, no, it's nothing." Her voice pitch had increased enormously; she sounded terrified.

Mildred heard her do the fake laugh again and knew that something was bothering her.

"Dr Fennaway?"

"Mmm, erm...do you mind if I make a quick phone call, Mildred?"

Mildred crossed her arms. The vet seemed to be watching her hands again. "Let me guess, do you want to make a call outside, or would you like to use my phone?"

The vet rummaged quickly through her bag. Mildred couldn't help but notice how panicked and impatient her hand movements were as the vet searched for her phone.

Kamilah cast the bag to the side and pressed her hands quickly against her jacket pockets. With some relief, she brought out her phone. "I'll do this outside, Mildred, just a second opinion."

This wasn't a question; the vet was being decisive and wanted to be out of the room.

Kamilah got to her feet and headed towards the front door at some speed. Mildred shook her head with worry and looked down at Comet. Nothing looked untoward; Comet lay casually on her side. Nahla and the other kitten were sat upright next to each other. They appeared to be keen on watching proceedings as well. "Nahla, what's going on?" Her eldest cat stared at her and only shifted her gaze on hearing the front door close.

Kamilah walked briskly down the path and propped herself against the gate. She turned towards the front door to ensure Mildred wasn't following. She couldn't see her silhouette behind the discoloured net curtains watching what she was doing. Swallowing hard, Kamilah pressed at her phone; her hands were shaking as she brought the phone up to her ear. She glanced back at the door again. "Come on...come on."

"Yes, who is..."

"Nubia, things have taken a serious turn for the worst." The noise in the background suggested to Kamilah that the Curator was likely travelling in a car.

"How can things possibly be worse, Kamilah? Why, what's happened?"

Kamilah froze briefly, thinking she may have seen the net curtains twitch slightly at a bedroom window of one of the houses opposite.

"Well, what is it, Kamilah?"

The curtains were still; she may have imagined it. "I'm at Mildred's, and I've just seen a sign of the dark realm."

The Curator's response was panicked and instant, "What do you possibly mean!"

"I saw it...Nubia...it's happening! I saw a flash of turquoise across Mildred's right hand."

Travelling back from Scotland, Nubia looked at Safiya in panic.

"Nubia...Nubia?"

"Oh no," were the only words Kamilah could discern before the phone was hung up.

Chapter Nine:
THE HARBOURAGE

"What do you think we should do, my Lady?" Lady Safiya brought a hand up to her mouth and looked out of the car window. She could see in the reflection that Nubia had leaned forward, clearly shaken by the call from their vet. Having left Scotland earlier in the morning, other cars passed by them as they headed down the M6 motorway. Traffic notwithstanding, if they had a good drive, they were only a couple of hours away from Loxley.

After a moment of contemplation, Lady Safiya leaned forward and discreetly activated the privacy divider in the car, shielding their conversation from the driver. She turned to Nubia, her expression solemn reflecting the gravity of the situation.

"I have never been in a position like this before, my friend. It's difficult to know where to start," Lady Safiya began, her voice tinged with uncertainty. "The Reeve is responsible for security, but we can't be certain if she's truly keeping watch over Mildred as she promised. The Grand Council has clarified that we are out of the loop on security matters, and they intend to change that. The prophesied cat could hold the key to great power or great danger. If something is being transferred to Mildred, we cannot know the consequences. Will Mildred, one of our own, be a force for good or for evil? Could she lead to our success or our downfall?"

As the car continued down the M6 motorway, the weight of their responsibility hung heavy in the air, and Lady Safiya knew that the decisions they made in the coming hours would have far-reaching consequences for their Order.

"The last time this happened, we had Lady Salma, my Lady. Her bloodline led to the development of the vaccine that ultimately eradicated the Black Death. Before that, the vile rats proliferated, spreading their filth and the plague." Nubia's words were quick and spoken in panic. "They wrongly blamed witches, my Lady," Nubia continued, her voice urgent.

"I'm well aware, Nubia…"

Nubia's distress was palpable as she continued, "Unjustly accused of witchcraft, many with precious bloodlines were murdered, along with their cats. Our bloodline suffered immeasurably. Removing the cats allowed the vermin rats to flourish, and then…"

"Nubia! I do not need to be reminded." Safiya interjected, her tone firm.

Safiya stared out of the window, watching the passing cars, their occupants oblivious to the recent events and the potential situation that could unfold.

"We do not have a Lady Salma this time, my Lady. We have a scarred kitten and a lower-ranked Elder, who, according to Lady Suzanna, likes fish paste sandwiches and game shows!" Nubia immediately crossed her arms in worry.

Safiya shivered at the thought of fish paste and nodded her head a few times as she thought. "Wait," she wagged a finger, "but there would have been a scarred kitten last time around if the prophecy is to be played out according to records."

"There was my Lady, Lady Salma's kitten, I remember it. I think sometimes you forget my age; my nine lives roll into one."

Safiya nodded and offered the faintest of smiles, "I know, my friend. So, what happened last time, Nubia?"

"The kitten was scarred, its markings were the same as those we saw on the new kitten at Loxley recently. The kitten grew quickly. I suspect the kitten now with Mildred will as well. The kitten was white last time, not dark like Mildred's. Both were shorthair cats, but the dark mark is what they had in common. Salma communicated to the then Grand Council that she felt the kitten had given her power. She felt strong, the kitten was for good, and she was positive about that. What happened next was ultimately the dark realm's undoing, the scarred kitten had changed Salma's blood. Her blood contained the antidote. This transformation and the action performed by one of our ladies was considerably more powerful and greater than anything the Order of Reeves accomplished.

They wanted to battle, but the plague travelled far and wide because of the rats, especially because people transmitted it among themselves. No Gatekeepers had crossed over, or nothing was recorded about it, so there was nothing to battle against. Something created that virus, that plague. There were all the signs of the dark realm at the time when the prophecy took place. And lo and behold, a scarred kitten was brought to us instantly and then presented to Lady Salma."

"You know, Nubia, outside our organisations, they have their own interpretations of what happened. Their scientists claim other things."

"Pwah! Scientists with their computing wizardry. They are wrong." Nubia paused for breath and reached for a bottle of water. "I know you are aware of this, my Lady, but people died in their millions until the vaccine was created, thanks to Lady Salma. The Grand Council of the time decided to use this to strengthen our relationship with the Reeves. The Reeves had to concede that we endured, we, the League of Light, and that fighting is not always the answer. Without us, rather without Lady Salma, to be specific, and of course the prophecy, there would have been mass eradication. If that had happened, you bet the Gatekeepers would have come. They failed. This time they've sent one ahead to oversee whatever it is they are planning; they don't want to make the same mistake again." Nubia lowered her hand, realising she was pointing at Lady Safiya.

"Nubia, why have they waited for so long if that is the case?"

"Well, if Lady Ebonee and her purported wand-waving friends are to be believed, something to do with planetary alignment," Nubia shrugged. "I'm afraid it's outside of my expertise."

"Nor mine Nubia, nor mine."

"The previous kitten transferred something to Lady Salma, my Lady, and I tell you this, it was not turquoise-coloured blood!" With a severe expression on her face, Nubia crossed her arms once more and asked, "Those Reeves couldn't help before; what can they possibly do now? We should get rid of them because they keep far too many secrets."

The sight in Safiya's eyes was enough for Nubia to recognise she was listening. Safiya turned again to look out of the car window and gaze as people passed them by.

"The Grand Council is worried, I am worried. We need to have direct involvement and take a grip on what is happening with our security," she said, taking a long breath and turning to face Nubia. "Do you still possess the number that Lady Ebonee provided you with?" Nubia gave a nod.

"Good, call the Armourer."

The peace of Porthill Crescent was abruptly shattered by crashing and yelling, a familiar but unwelcome sound. Suzanna, known locally as the cat lady, had hurriedly changed her clothes, but whilst doing so, her adult cats slipped out from the house. "Come on, please!" she called out, hitting a spoon against a metal tin in a quick and repetitive rhythm. Her heels were subtle, like her earrings, immaculate yet unobtrusive. Suzanna placed the empty tin in the recycling box as her cats approached her and carefully rested the spoon on the side wall. "Come on, please, I need to pop out," she urged, running her hands down her pencil skirt and adjusting her waistcoat. Her three cats obediently headed down the path towards her. "Well now, that's very well-behaved of all of you," she remarked, impressed with her cat recall skills. "Come on, the front door is open. I want you to watch your new sister and Daphne's kitten. I won't be gone for long. You can go back out when I get back."

She closed the cat flap. Satisfied that her home and cats were secure she entered her front room. The noise of the door opening disturbed the unnamed kittens from their sleep. "All of you, go and say hello," she instructed. Both kittens yawned as Neith and Tabby jumped onto the sofa to join them. "Kherpri, you are in charge. Tabby, I should be told your real name soon!" she stated. Kherpri looked at her, and for a moment, Suzanna thought she saw Kherpri nod. Suzanna double blinked. Unlike their veterinarian, she knew she didn't have the gift of speaking 'cat'; she must have imagined it.

Assessing herself in the full-length mirror, she turned to one side and then to the other. She hadn't endeared herself to the Curator when they met, she was certain of that. In consideration, banging the car horn at a Watcher certainly hadn't helped, but then, what did she know about them anyway? How could she possibly have known what he or it was? At some point, she would like to see them a bit more closely; plenty of rumours were circulating about their existence.

Trust appeared to be the key, and it went a long way. She knew she would only be entrusted with more information by earning the trust of her Elders and her increased promotion up the ranks. Now that she had her real name, surely, she had earned their trust. Loxley Manor was a curious place, a huge mansion with many locked doors. But something had caught her attention on her first visit, it had played on her mind. She was certain she had recognised a face in one of the paintings along the 'long walk' corridor. Grabbing a hair tie off the side, she fixed her hair into a ponytail and checked herself over again.

How could she possibly have recognised a face at Loxley? She had never been there before. A date had been inscribed underneath the painting, but with Nubia in such a rush, she hadn't had the chance to read it properly.

Satisfied with her appearance, she turned to her cats and crouched down to stroke the new addition that she was now the protector of. "I'll need a name for you, little one. Until I'm told your real name, I'll think about that while I'm out," she said. The kitten playfully bit one of her fingers. "Ouch, you little so and so," Suzanna laughed and stood up. "Well, if you are going to be nasty, I'll call you Nubia!"

She giggled to herself at this brief and private rebellion. Her navigator was on the kitchen table, and her tartan jacket with her 'access all areas' pin badge was hanging on the back of a chair. Clutching both, she locked the front door and pressed the remote for her car door.

Without Nubia remotely entering directions to the navigator, this was the first time Suzanna was trying the system for herself. Placing her jacket on the passenger seat, she switched the navigator on. Immediately, the driver console turned around, revealing the dock where she could place the navigator. Suzanna rattled her teeth a little, unsure of what to do next. She pressed the button for the car to start. She couldn't remember the way there, so the navigator was a much-needed aid. The cursor flashed on the screen of the navigator: "Erm…Loxley…Loxley Manor…please?" The flashing cursor disappeared as auto-drive appeared on the screen along with first gear. "Wow, is it really that easy!" Suzanna clapped her hands together, hearing the engine trying to accelerate. The car shook as the engine tried to pull away, but they were not moving. She sat patiently, the noise of the car trying to accelerate distracted a couple of the neighbours talking on the opposite side of the road. One put her hands on her hips; Suzanna knew she was the subject of gossip again. "What can I…Oh…" she noticed the handbrake light was still lit on the dashboard. Rolling her eyes, she released the brake as the car hurtled immediately down the drive at speed. Passing by them, Suzanna could see the neighbours shaking their heads, looking in her direction.

It didn't matter; she was off to Wales.

MADRID

"By the time you return to Loxley, I suspect a new scroll will be waiting for you; an attaché of the Keeper should have delivered it by now. It will detail the new Elder being brought into the ranks. This is to do with the Mildred you visited in Rocke Road."

"Yes, my Lady, Mildred will be the Elder for this new lady. The new lady's details were read out when the Keeper arrived last Saturday with the four caskets, including the one containing the prophesied kitten."

"Secure the scroll in the usual way, Reeve."

The Reeve nodded.

"Walk with me before you return to the UK; there are matters I need to discuss with you."

The Reeve swallowed. "So, I'm not being fired then?"

Lady Berenike tilted her head, indicating the direction they were to head. "Not yet, Reeve, not yet. I still need to confer further with our own Council. But let me be very clear about this." Lady Berenike turned to the Reeve, "Any more incidents akin to the severity of a Gatekeeper breaching your security and the subsequent destruction and loss of life will be met with severe consequences. It is purely by some good fortune that you are new in post; no one else is prepared for such a responsibility. We need you there, at least for now. Any more incidents though, our Council will act, and furthermore, I will support them. You will become an outcast, stripped of everything you know, silenced, and your memory wiped; no one outside of this Order must know what you know."

The Reeve swallowed harder; the expression on her superior's face conveyed the gravity of every single word.

Lady Berenike took a deep breath; she needed to compose herself before her guest departed. "Let's sit outside."

The Reeve nodded, her mind swirling with a mix of uncertainty and apprehension. There were always consequences for failure, but this was the first time it had been conveyed to her with such stark clarity.

"Let's sit here," Lady Berenike said as they entered an area surrounded by a circular white wall. The pristine white marble floor featured the emblem of the Reeves prominently displayed at its centre. The garden was adorned with beautiful flower arrangements under a clear blue sky. They sought refuge from the sun in a shaded area. This garden area was known as 'off-limits', and only ladies of high authority, such as Lady Berenike, could use it.

Lady Berenike gracefully perched upon the semi-circle marble seat, the only seat in the garden, with just enough room for two people.

"Sit, Kiya," she beckoned.

"Yes, my Lady," Kiya replied.

Lady Berenike gazed at the cloudless sky, "Our ancestors revered the sun as a deity, a symbol of light triumphing over darkness. It signifies the eternal struggle between good and evil, a balance reflected in nature's predator-prey relationships. As events unfold and uncertainty looms, I fear that we will become the prey."

Kiya sat down, just about squeezing into the narrow gap on the seat.

"This garden is where I come to contemplate," Lady Berenike continued. "I reflect on our Order, those who have departed, and those who have returned."

Lady Berenike tapped her fingers on her knees as she considered her next words. "Something has troubled me about Loxley, starting around six months before your appointment. As you know, you replaced the former Reeve, Lady Tawaret. You are also aware that she was in place for years."

"Yes, although I never met her, my Lady, I have been told about these things," Kiya replied.

Lady Berenike nodded, "Quite. But something had changed in her. That is why you were summoned here. I did not want to discuss these things over the phone or over the net. Upon replacing Tawaret, we needed someone fresh, of a lesser age, whose bloodline was historically unblemished. That is you, Reeve. Your heritage speaks for itself. Your upbringing was principled, your mother was a former Reeve. She made the conscious decision to raise you to be a Reeve. Despite you only being in your thirties in this lifetime, I, along with other members of our Council, voted unanimously for you to take this huge responsibility. Alongside the other Order, we try to lead good lives, doing good, ensuring balance and harmony. We all have nine lives to ensure this. This is our major gift as we alternate between the human and feline form with each passing. In essence, we have been here for a long time. Take nothing, I say as a sign of weakness. Irrespective of your ancestry, if you fail, there will be repercussions. We cannot let the dark world in."

"What happened to the former Reeve, my Lady, and what concerns you?" Kiya asked.

"I shouldn't have to say this, but I will. This conversation never leaves this garden."

"Yes, my Lady, I understand."

"Lady Tawaret kept a diary, although we were unaware of this. Many of our former ladies kept diaries to inform future Reeves about the Order and the way of things. It's not something that we encourage. However, there was a noticeable change in her communications, not just with me but with other members of the Reeve's Order. Her tone changed, and her words lacked clarity and became unbalanced. This went on for a few months and her words sounded more confused as time passed. She drew attention to herself, and we needed to investigate. It would have made her suspicious if I went to Loxley or sent another Reeve. She would have been on her guard and careful of what she did and said. That's exactly what we didn't want. We needed to be sure that our Reeve was okay and stable. So, I took the course of action and spoke to Raysmau to keep an eye on her discretely."

"Raysmau, my Lady!"

"Yes, she is a good soldier, older than you by a few years, still a potential Reeve, maybe. Her bloodline just isn't as pure as yours; it lacks the pedigree. That's why she was placed into the Escarrabin order."

"I see. What did she find out, my Lady?"

"Nothing for some time. However, she noticed that a Scatterblade was missing from the weapons store one evening. She checked the log of the Sergeant-at-Arms, and no Scatterblade was registered as being out. She searched the grounds high and low. Raysmau could not find her for some hours until she saw her around the base of the great statue of Salma. Now, of course, Raysmau is not aware of our vault being underneath, but in any event, if Lady Tawaret were inspecting or checking something in the vault, she would not need a Scatterblade. She must be in fear of something." Lady Berenike looked up to take a pause. "Something was wrong with her, Kiya. Raysmau saw this happen on two further occasions, Tawaret was seen around the statue late at night. We did not know this was happening at first, as Raysmau is loyal and did not want to report on Lady Tawaret unless she was sure something was wrong. Raysmau had also sensed a change in her; she became snappy in tone, her appearance and rooms unkempt, not the behaviour of a Reeve."

Lady Berenike kept tapping away with her fingers. "On the third occasion, in the middle of the night, Raysmau saw Tawaret appear again around the statue. From what she told me, I suspect she had been below the statue into the vault again. Raysmau reported that Tawaret was holding what she believed to be keys. In the moonlight, she was not positive but could hear them rattling together. She followed Tawaret, maintaining some distance from her, all the way to the front gates."

Tawaret opened the gates, walked across the road, and disappeared into the undergrowth around the trees on the other side. Raysmau thought it best not to follow further as Tawaret might see her. Raysmau returned to security control and watched the outside cameras. Tawaret was gone for over two hours. Upon her return, even in the low light, the cameras showed she was covered in dirt as if she had been on her knees, digging with her hands.

The Reeve frowned, "This is incredible, my Lady. What on earth was she doing?"

"Well, I didn't know then but given what has happened over the last few days, I think I've put it together. Raysmau continued her observations and took the opportunity to search the Reeve's office while the former Reeve carried out inspections of the in-house Escarrabin. It didn't take her long; she found the diary."

Lady Berenike turned toward the Reeve with a troubled expression on her face. "Lady Tawaret had been in the below and now I suspect far down, who knows where she ended up. Those caverns have not been searched in years."

The Reeve, clearly intrigued, inquired, "Why did she go below, my Lady?" Lady Berenike sighed and replied, "We do not know. Her diary entries do not provide a clear reason. It could have been initial curiosity or perhaps the influence of a Watcher that led her there. We know that it was during daylight hours when she ventured below, so the Watchers were above ground. Something drew her to those depths, like an addiction she couldn't resist."

Taking a moment to gather her thoughts, Lady Berenike continued, "It was then that Raysmau contacted me."

The Reeve, now fully engrossed in the conversation, asked, "Because Raysmau discovered she had been in the below?" Lady Berenike shook her head and explained, "No, Tawaret was furious with Raysmau. With all the changes she was experiencing, paranoia had crept in. She suspected she was being watched, perhaps even before it was true. She had set up a hidden camera in her room and caught Raysmau going through what is now your desk. Tawaret became increasingly paranoid, questioning everything, and their argument was the tipping point. We had to get her out."

The Reeve, now wide-eyed with surprise, remarked, "Because of an argument, my Lady?" Lady Berenike's expression turned grave as she replied, "No, it wasn't because of that at all. The turquoise flashing that Raysmau saw in Lady Tawaret's right palm led to her removal." The Reeve, visibly alarmed, questioned, "She had been turned or something like that?"

Lady Berenike nodded. "Yes, I suspect so. The colour of evil was in her veins."

The Reeve, struggling to comprehend the gravity of the situation, expressed, "Raysmau has never said anything to me about this."

Lady Berenike explained, "She wouldn't, out of loyalty. She respected Tawaret. They had worked together for years. See it from Raysmau's perspective, she wouldn't want you to know that she spied on the former Reeve."

As the weight of the conversation settled in, the Reeve asked, "What became of her, my Lady? Where is Lady Tawaret now?"

Lady Berenike revealed with a heavy heart, "She is now in recovery if you can call it that. She's at the Harbourage, a secure care facility away from public eyes. Her condition has worsened, and she is under constant monitoring." In disbelief, Lady Berenike shook her head, "She was so loyal for so many years. That's one of the reasons that the Curator doesn't like you. In her diary, she had befriended Nubia, wanting her onside for something."

"And that is why you were rushed in so quickly. But as things are becoming more apparent, I'm greatly worried." Lady Berenike ensured she had eye contact with the Reeve. "She screamed at Raysmau words to the effect of 'he's coming, he's on the way,' something like that. And I'm told that Lady Ebonee has been speaking with the magic world at the Grand Council's recent meeting in Scotland."

The Reeve raised her eyebrows. "Why on earth would she do that?"

"Well, Ebonee is wayward on the best of days, so who can say? However, as I understand it, the magic world had sensed a possible portal opening in Paris, providing the opportunity for something to have crossed over. Don't you see, if that were true, Tawaret knew about it and not just that, I think she may have been involved."

"How so, my Lady?"

"Well, if Raysmau is right, keys were missing, weren't they? I think she may have given away our secret Loxley location to the Gatekeeper and not just that, provided him with the opportunity to attempt to open the wall of iron in the below!"

The Reeve lifted her hand in shock. "I thought that Duat had somehow used my handprint on the scanner to gain access."

"No, I don't think so. There is still the security process before the scanner to get into the stairwell before the vault. I think it's possible he may have had the keys before he allowed himself to be caught and that he carried them in right before your very eyes. He knew he would be taken and imprisoned in the below, it's all he needed!"

There was a brief silence as the Reeve considered how Duat brought the keys in.

"Kiya, I suspect it's not just the Hydra down there. There must be another reason why Duat was trying to open that wall. I will continue to conduct my research, but we already know something changed, something happened to our former Reeve. You must round up the remaining Watchers as soon as you return and remove them from the below."

"Yes, my Lady, it will be done."

"And Reeve?"

"Yes, my Lady."

"Take no chances. Always be on your guard, there is something unnatural down there."

"Are you sure you want to stop here, there's nothing around here other than trees?" The car stopped next to a narrow road bordered by dense foliage. A semi-circle marked the end of the road, but there seemed to be nothing else in sight. The taxi driver squinted through the windshield searching for any recognisable landmarks. His satellite navigation system provided no assistance.

"I always know where I am, and this is where I'm to be. I'll walk from here."

"I'm glad you do, I've never been over this way at all." The driver turned around in his chair, observing the strangely dressed lady sitting on the back seat, clutching what looked to be an old medicine bag. "It's up to you, but what with all of your bags an' all," he trailed off, trying not to stare at her for too long.

There was no response as she let herself out of the taxi.

The taxi driver raised his eyebrows. "Well, okay, then…" With the engine still running, he exited the car and opened the back to unload her bags. He took out two large sealed brown leather bags, one old-looking military backpack, and one heavy trunk. Dropping the trunk down with a thud, he grimaced and straightened his back. "Don't know how you carry that."

"I'm strong! You take cash, I presume, many don't these days."

"Cash is king," the driver smiled. He smiled even more seeing the wedge of notes being pulled out before him.

"Is this enough?"

The amount passed to him was more than plenty. "Thank you. Look, are you sure? I don't like leaving a lady out here, wherever we are." He looked around, the semi-circular road looked like a dead-end.

She stepped forward. "I can take care of myself."

He shrugged. "Well, okay, if you are sure."

She watched on as the driver did a U-turn and drove back in the direction he had come from. He stared at his former passenger as he went past.

The backpack went on first, the two heavy bags went over one shoulder, her medicine bag over the other, and the trunk was dragged on its wheels down the lane.

With a few puffs, she dropped the bags next to the grass semi-circle and waited. With everything she had been told only an hour or so before, her arrival would be unexpected. Looking around, she could see two CCTV cameras nestled into the trees, there was a discrete post that bore the Egyptian sphinx logo. She hadn't been here for years and preferred it that way. A scientist requires peace and quiet. Nevertheless, she was surprised to get the call. Her old pin badge may work, but that wasn't the point. She was here to check on things, so she would wait to see what happened.

Only a minute had passed when there was a buzzing overhead. She looked up at the drone as it descended for a closer look at her. She removed her hat so she could be clearly seen; the scars around her left eye and forehead were quite distinctive.

"Ma'am!" there was a quick succession of knocks on the door.

Raysmau looked up, hearing the noise. "Come." She watched the security officer enter her room. "What is it?"

"Ma'am, I think you need to see this."

Raysmau frowned, got to her feet, and followed the security officer to the monitors. On one of the screens, there was an image of a very old identification card. The screen flashed red with the words 'attention.' From the images the drone had taken, the database had recognised the visitor. Raysmau flinched immediately, seeing on the other screen the smiling face of the lady outside the gates, someone she hadn't seen in years. Her scarring was unique, and her attitude was memorable.

"Ma'am, the system knows her and says she's been redlined."

Raysmau bowed her head with dismay. "Yes, she was booted a long time ago. This is all I need; she has the right bloodline but was redlined by the Reeves a long time ago." Raysmau rubbed at her forehead. "I didn't even know she was still alive."

"Ma'am, the drone is equipped with a stun weapon, do you wish me to deploy?"

Raysmau looked back at the screen knowing this was a problem. "Bring back the drone and open the gates."

"Yes Ma'am, as she's redlined, do we need to intercept? May I ask who it is?"

"A problem is what she is. A serious problem." Raysmau shook her head. "That's the Armourer."

Chapter Ten:
THE ARMOURER

Being dressed in a black Loxley robe was certain to attract local attention. Having only found garments suitable for a veterinary doctor, Duat pushed open the front door to the clinic wearing a white gown and blue trousers. The other two Watchers followed closely behind. Bellator's former robe had been cut away during his operation. He was also dressed as an animal doctor. Still recovering from his surgery, he clutched his and Duat's glasses. His movements were slow and pained, and he supported his torso as much as he could. Not used to witnessing what he had just seen, for a fleeting moment, he considered the veterinarian's pain; the doctor was now permanently silenced.

They made their way towards the car park. Hearing Aazar jingle a set of car keys, Duat held his hand out, the turquoise patterns had faded away, "I'll drive the automobile."

Aazar looked at Duat with surprise. Unlike Bellator and his polluted mind, he knew the full significance of Duat and what he really was. "Master, respectfully, can you drive?"

Duat stopped walking instantly. "The temporary inhabitants of this place only use about a third of their brain; the rest of their headspace is redundant. I can travel between worlds and speak hundreds of languages." He almost growled as he spoke, "I think I can master their feeble transportation devices."

Aazar looked towards the ground with embarrassment. "Yes, Sire, of course," he humbly passed the car keys to Duat.

They headed towards the only car in the compound. The compact car only had one door on either side; it would be a tight squeeze for all three of them. Duat stopped next to the driver's door, considering what to do next. He pulled at the door handle, but the car door would not open. He pulled again with more force and shook the handle, he immediately recoiled as the car alarm sounded. All three of them looked around to see if they were being watched. In the evening silence, the noise of the alarm echoed and could probably be heard far and wide.

"What is this thing doing? How do you stop that noise!" Duat kicked the side of the car. It was somewhat ill-thought as he was still wearing open-toed sandals. He growled under his breath, "Aazar, what is wrong with this device?"

"Press the button on the key, Sire, it's a remote control!"

Duat did as he was told, and the alarm immediately stopped, bringing peace back to the area. They looked around one more time. Except for an owl hooting close by, it appeared they were alone. Duat pulled at the door handle, and this time, it opened.

Aazar pulled back the passenger seat and gestured towards Bellator, "You sit in the back." Bellator, clutching his midsection in pain, squeezed into the cramped back seat of the very small car as Aazar adjusted the passenger seat and settled in. Duat closed his door and Aazar fixed his own seatbelt. The three of them sat silently as Duat held the steering wheel, shaking it with annoyance.

After a moment, Aazar spoke up, "Sire, you need to press the flashing button and put your foot on the brake pedal." Aazar pointed at the dashboard. "I had to learn these things a long time ago. I had to bury three driving instructors before I finally learnt how to drive."

With some contrition, Duat growled under his breath and followed Aazar's instructions. The car started, but it didn't move. Aazar knew that Duat had no clue what he was doing, so he chose his words carefully. "Sire, you must pull that handle towards you, and the car will move. You also press the pedal by your right foot for speed."

Frowning, Duat turned to his left and glared at Aazar, saying, "I already knew that!"

"Yes, Master. I was explaining more for Bellator," Aazar lied.

Duat pulled the gear shift towards him, and the car lurched forward. Duat pressed the pedal to the floor as the car sped off, wheels spinning on the gravel. Duat turned the wheel to the left, passing the surgery at speed they shot straight over the curb onto the grassed area. With speed increasing, the drop at the end of the bank drew closer.

Aazar shouted, "Sire, the brake is the pedal next to the accelerator!!!" but his warning went unheard as the car shot over the bank, sliding down the hill on the other side. Bellator was yelling, an alarm was sounding inside the car as not all of them were wearing seatbelts. There was a scraping noise as they hit the remnants of an old wall, immediately flipping the car onto its side.

The driver's airbag detonated with a loud bang, striking Duat in the face as they continued to slide down the slope. Bellator continued to yell as they slid onto some high tree roots, flipping the car upside down. The car was slowing but was now spinning on its roof as it approached the bottom of the bank. Duat's fingernails ruptured the airbag, causing a second bang as they came to a stop. Bellator's face hit the back windshield as Duat fell against the roof.

Duat pressed the start/stop button to stop the engine running. The only one secured in his seat was Aazar. The only sound was the saliva dripping from his mouth onto the windscreen below, they remained upside down and were silent.

"Sire, would you like me to find another car?" he asked, breaking the stillness while still strapped in by his seatbelt and upside down.

Bellator tried to push himself the other way around, holding a palm to his face to check whether any more teeth were broken.

"Sire?"

"I have decided that we will walk."

✣✣✣✣

"Ma'am, should we go to meet her?"

Raysmau rubbed her chin, unsure of what to do. *Why is she here? What could she possibly want? Something must have happened at the meeting of the Grand Council.*

"Yes, we should go. It's important to show hospitality but be cautious."

"I don't wish to speak out of turn, Ma'am, but how much of a problem is this?"

Raysmau murmured to herself under her breath.

"Ma'am?"

"Send a car to pick her up. Go to the front and inform the driver to be exceptionally careful of what she says."

"Yes, Ma'am."

"I suspect anything seen and anything said will be reported back. If she's anything like how she used to be. You can bet she's not here to assist us. She'll have her own agenda. Am I clear?"

"Yes, Ma'am. I'll issue the instruction and make my way to the front."

Raysmau quickly returned to her quarters, grabbed her mask and ceremonial sword, and clipped her sword to her leggings. She made her way to the main entrance. As she entered the central lobby, she went over to the four clerics sitting at their desk. Addressing the one on the right, she placed her hand on the desk for attention. "Cleric, can you tell me the location of Kalara?"

The pale-faced cleric looked up. "I can check for you, Ma'am."

"Thank you. Can you try the security wing first, please? When you find her, can you ask her to meet me out the front? We have an unexpected visitor."

"Yes, Ma'am."

Raysmau could hear a car pulling up outside the main entrance. The damaged front doors bore witness to the recent turmoil, remaining open from the Scatterblade blast. As she walked, Raysmau fixed her ceremonial mask that covered the lower half of her face and tied her hair into a ponytail. The long dark mane, secured to the mask, fell between her shoulder blades, resembling a tail of sorts. This ceremonial dress was usually only reserved for when the Keeper visited. Their visitor was unexpected and not nearly as high ranking as the Keeper, but given the circumstances, Raysmau thought an effort should be made. The visit was suspicious and would be reported on, so some formality should be shown.

As Raysmau stepped outside, the car was moving away, and the member of the Escarrabin was making her way back towards her. "Did you tell her what I asked?"

"Yes, Ma'am. She's on her guard."

Raysmau nodded, seeing the unwanted guest appear at the end of the long driveway. As the car made its way to the front, Raysmau took the opportunity to look at the surrounding mess. The portcullis was badly damaged, with blockwork, glass, and wood strewn across the lawns. *I'm sure she'll have plenty to say about this,* Raysmau thought. Four other Escarrabin were on duty outside, their Scatterblades fixed to their backs.

"Najla."

"Yes, Ma'am."

"Once a decision is made about the Watchers below and the serpent creature, I want this entire area cleared. Where are our architects right now?"

"As far as I know, Ma'am, they are on their way. They have been dispatched from Bulgaria."

"Good, what about these doors and the portcullis..." Raysmau blinked twice, "What is that car doing?"

Najla walked down the steps and saw that the car was on its way back, minus the unexpected guest. Dust clouds from the gravel driveway briefly obstructed the view of the guest slowly approaching them. As the car returned to them, Najla moved forward to speak to the driver and find out what was happening.

Raysmau put her hands on her hips, puzzled, and shook her head as Najla spoke to the driver.

The car pulled away and headed towards the security wing.

Still shaking her head, she said, "Well?"

"Um, I'm sorry, Ma'am, but she refused the lift. Apparently, she wants to see the failings of the Reeve and the Escarrabin and would rather walk."

Raysmau snatched off her mask and tucked it under her arm, "How dare she!"

"Somewhat rude, Ma'am."

"So, what, do we stand here like a pair of lemons until she gets here?"

There was a slight cough from behind. "Ma'am, I heard you call for me."

Raysmau turned to see Kalara standing by her side.

"The Cleric mentioned an unexpected guest."

"You could say that the Armourer is here."

Kalara looked down the driveway at the figure in the distance heading in their direction. "The Armourer, Ma'am? What's an Armourer? I've never heard of that title before."

"I'm not surprised, Kalara. It's from before your time, but you are looking at her right now."

The three of them focused on the approaching figure.

"The Armourer had a crucial role in the League of Light before its union with the Reeves. We became responsible for security roles and the handling and use of weapons. Her role in the League of Light became somewhat redundant, or rather her predecessors' role. Although the position still exists, to my knowledge, there has been no involvement from an Armourer for generations. I only recognise her from my early days when performing security detail for a gathering. I remember her clearly; she was experimenting with mixing red wine and other concoctions she brought along with her because she was bored! She's not a protector of cats, you see. That's why Armourers are rogue; they don't like being told what to do. They are almost outcasts."

Kalara and Najla looked at Raysmau with concern.

"Judging by the close-up on the CCTV, she has acquired a few more scars since I last saw her all those years ago."

"Do you know why she is here, Ma'am?"

"I don't, Najla, and I don't like it. I don't like it at all."

✠✠✠✠

Mildred heard the front door close. Concerned, she picked up Nahla and clutched her tightly. From worry, her hug was a little stronger than she realised. Nahla lifted a paw and patted Mildred on the hand, "Oh, sorry, Nahla, I'm just a little concerned. There always seems to be something going on at the moment."

Kamilah walked into the front room; her face was difficult to read. "Mildred, may I take a seat?"

Mildred nodded with concern, "Of course, Kamilah."

The cat doctor sat down, the dust scattering into the air from the seat making her sneeze. Pulling a very discoloured handkerchief from her pocket, she squeezed her nostrils together and made the most awful racket as she blew her nose. Mildred grimaced, hearing phlegm expelling from the nose of the woman who could talk to cats. Glancing down at Nahla, Mildred noticed Nahla looking straight back at her. They were both puzzled.

"So, Kam…"

The vet blew her nose again, the sound and aftereffects making Mildred feel quite nauseous. "Sorry Mildred, it's strange that someone such as I can be affected by dust sometimes."

Mildred looked around considering that the vet may be suggesting her house wasn't tidy. "So, what's going on Kamilah? You are here for the second time this week, and a variety of things you have said and done concern me."

"Oh, come now, dear, there's nothing to worry about." Mildred looked at Kamilah, the vet's smile was forced, she wasn't the best of liars, considering she was involved in an organisation that is supposed to keep secrets. Sitting down with Nahla on her lap, Mildred crossed her arms and took a deep breath.

"I know you want answers, Mildred, we all do. That's what we do in this great organisation, we seek and find!"

The frown on Mildred's face spoke for itself.

"Cats, dear, cats, it's all about cats and protecting them."

Mildred's facial expression was unchanged.

"Well, we…" Kamilah stopped talking as Mildred raised a hand.

"Dr Fennaway, I have no clue what you are talking about! Now please stop stalling for time and tell me what is going on here."

Kamilah swallowed, considering how she could word things. "I must ask you something, Mildred. Have you changed in any way since your new kitten was delivered?"

"Which one, Dr? Comet, you mean?"

"Yes, the other one is not for you."

Mildred crossed her arms again. "I know, so I keep being told."

"It's important, Mildred. Has anything changed? Is there anything unusual going on?"

Mildred shook her head quickly in amazement. "Besides a kitten giving me electric shocks, you mean?"

Kamilah gave a nervous laugh. "Well, yes, that's one thing, but have you noticed anything else?"

"Isn't that enough?"

Kamilah remained silent, sensing Mildred wanted to speak. "Well, I'm having strange dreams, but in truth, they've been happening for a couple of weeks or so. It's nothing to do with Comet arriving. Why would a kitten arrive change me in any way? Do you know how strange your question sounds?"

Kamilah nodded. "I do, Mildred, but Comet is a special kitten." Kamilah noticed Mildred lifting a hand. "And yes, my dear, I know that all kittens are special before you say. It's just that your kitten maybe... a little different."

"Besides having a strange burn-looking mark on her side?"

They both turned, hearing Comet walking in from the kitchen. She sat down in front of them as if she was party to the conversation.

"It's a birthmark, Mildred. I have told you this."

Without the sound of the ticking clock, there was silence in the room.

"Look, Mildred. I noticed when I came here last time that you have your certificate framed over there on the wall."

"Yes, it's been there for a few years now. Why would you mention it?"

"What is your observation of that certificate?"

Finding the question odd, Mildred placed Nahla to the side and stood up. Instead of going over to the framed certificate, Mildred started rifling through the mounds of paper on her sideboard.

Kamilah leaned back in her seat to see what Mildred was up to. "What are you looking for, Mildred?"

"Well, I have..." Mildred stopped what she was doing as she was interrupted by the meowing from her cat phone. "Excuse me, Kamilah." Mildred picked up the receiver, placing the cat's bottom next to her mouth. "Number one Rocke Road, Mildred speaking."

"Hello, Mildred, it's Daphne. I was just checking in on you and..."

"Hello, Lady Daphne." Mildred moved the phone away from her face and looked at Kamilah. "It's my Elder."

Kamilah smiled and nodded, suggesting she take the call.

"Lady Daphne, can't talk now, got the vet here. I'll call you back."

In shock, Daphne instantly responded, "Again, Mildred, what is going on now?"

Daphne didn't get an answer as the phone was put down. "Oh, here we go." Finding what she was looking for, Mildred sat back down and held her new certificate aloft. "It looks the same as the other one on the wall."

"It won't be, but that's not what I'm asking. What is the colour on the border of both certificates?"

Mildred studied the certificate in her hands and then looked at the one on the wall. Other than a casual glance, she hadn't really paid a great deal of attention to her new certificate. Now that it had been pointed out, she could see they were the same colour. "I don't know, like a bluey kinda green or something?"

"That's right."

"Turquoise, I think."

"Right again, Mildred."

"So?"

"It goes back to our origins, dear, from when we were formed as a cat club."

Mildred noticed that Kamilah didn't look her in the eyes when she said, *'cat club.'*

"Turquoise is a powerful colour, once sought after by many, it holds a powerful allure from ancient times. Its colour adorned jewels and objects of significance. Yet, for some, including us, it carries a much darker connotation. A forewarning, a colour entwined with ominous realms."

Mildred's face showed her state of confusion. "I fail to see the relevance and what that has to do with me. When Daphne arrived, she gave

Missy to me under the condition I join the cat club. No further explanation was provided, nor other actions taken. We meet up and talk about cats... well, some of us do. Some of the older ladies seem somewhat aloof."

"Perhaps they grapple with more weighty matters, dear. I understand this is perplexing but trust me when I say that's why your certificates bear a turquoise border. It serves as a cautionary symbol, a colour we steer clear of, a reminder of our purpose."

Mildred lifted Nahla and settled her on her lap while the unnamed kitten clawed its way up the sofa to join them.

"I'm sure Comet appears larger already; don't you agree, dear?"

"Mmm, please don't change the subject, Kamilah. What is our purpose?"

"Look, Mildred, I cannot divulge beyond my place. Many of these things are above your level. With two cats, you have ascended to an Elder of Level Eight. Your Elder, Daphne, with three cats, holds a Level Seven status. Even she is unaware of much that I'm saying. You are being entrusted with Comet because she is very special. It's quite a responsibility." Kamilah observed Mildred stroking Nahla enthusiastically. "You mentioned distressing dreams; would you care to share them?"

"Well, it's always the same. A lake is on fire, a blazing lake of sorts, there are creatures in the fire, the surface ablaze. I can't tell what they are or how many of them. Behind, a grand palace is burning. There are figures, but I cannot see them, they wear dark robes of some kind. One of them gets closer to me with every dream like he wants to say or do something. It's all very weird. And...are you okay, Kamilah? You've gone as white as a sheet."

Kamilah swallowed hard. Her hands were visibly shaking. "Are there trees in your dreams, Mildred? Are there trees?"

Mildred bobbed her head back in surprise at the strange question. "Is that relevant or something? Many people have trees in their dreams, although odd that you should mention it, though, as they are the same colour as the border on the certificates!"

"Oh my, oh my." Kamilah placed a hand to her mouth and looked to the floor. "You're telling me that you can see lakes of fire and trees of turquoise, Mildred?"

"I think it's just the one lake."

Panicked, Kamilah leapt to her feet and began to pace the room. She didn't stop until she was staring straight at Comet. "Who are you? Who are you?"

"You know exactly who I am, Kamilah, and I don't care for the tone of your voice!"

Kamilah bent down looking Comet in the eyes. "I wasn't talking to you, Mildred."

The vet began making the oddest sounds, and Mildred froze. Comet rose up right away, raising the hackles on her back.

"What are you doing, Kamilah?" Mildred felt Nahla moving uncomfortably on her. The unnamed kitten immediately jumped onto her lap in fear.

Mildred let out a huge gasp as the vet turned to her. Her pupils had transformed into arcs, the colour of her eyes was changing.

"Oh my God, what are you doing?" Terrified, Mildred picked up both cats, got to her feet, and quickly moved behind the couch. Mildred was visibly trembling as she stared fearfully into the veterinarian's cat's eyes. The veterinarian turned back to Comet and continued making the most bizarre noises.

"Enough already, go! Leave Comet alone. What's wrong with you?"

With a fierce hiss, Comet lashed out, scratching the veterinarian's hand before bolting from the room.

Mildred nearly fell over the sofa in panic, unsure of where to go next. Both cats were wrestling with her, desperate to get away. "Okay, okay," she placed the cats on the ground as Nahla gently bit around the neck of the kitten and dragged her out of harm's way. Placing a hand on her chest, Mildred stabilised herself against the sofa, her eyes watery with fear. She watched Kamilah take a deep breath as she put a hand to her face and stood back up. She turned to Mildred, her eyes changing back to normal as she did. Without words, Kamilah sat down, her hands shaking as she looked up to see Mildred brushing a tear from her eye. "I'm sorry you had to see that, Mildred. I couldn't help it. It was very unprofessional of me."

Mildred shook her head in panic, she was without words.

"Oh my, oh my indeed."

"Oh my, really! Oh my, is that all you have to say! You just changed into a cat or something, where are you from? Please leave my house now!"

"Mildred, I'm so sorry. I didn't mean to do that. As I say, some things are above your level."

"Level! You're not even human!"

Kamilah rubbed at her face and ran her hands through her hair. "It's complicated, but believe me when I say, we are all good, all of us involved in the Kat Chamber are good."

Mildred dabbed away another tear. "I want no part of this. I'm calling the police."

"And tell them what, Mildred? I just changed into a cat, mmm? They'll be locking you up. Look, I can see you are distressed, so I'll leave."

"Please do right now and leave my cats alone."

"But they are not your cats now, are they, dear?"

Mildred put her shaking hands on her hips.

Kamilah grabbed her bag, knowing that she would have to explain all of this to Nubia.

As Kamilah headed to the front door, Mildred kept her distance but wanted to ensure the cat 'doctor' left.

Kamilah pulled at the front door and turned to Mildred with concern. "I saw it, the colour of the dark place. I saw it in your palm, Mildred."

Mildred could see that Kamilah was visibly upset.

"Please be careful, dear." Kamilah started to pull the door closed behind her and stopped. "Oh, and be careful of strange figures wearing peculiar glasses."

The door was closed. Mildred could see the vet moving away through the dirt-stained glass. Rubbing at her eyes, Mildred noticed the kitten and Nahla moving back into the room, rejoining her at her feet. Breathing heavily, she looked down at them. "It's okay, she's gone." Both cats looked nervous like they had seen a ghost. Mildred shook her head and glanced up; she instantly felt a chill. Comet was on the kitchen table, staring at her.

Chapter Eleven:
EIGHT OF NINE LIVES

Having removed their robes, they blended in more with their surroundings. A man in a suit walking with two uniformed vets did catch curious glances from late-night stragglers and dog walkers. The dogs were a hindrance, their sensitive noses picked up the strange scent of the three Watchers. To avoid causing alarm, they all donned their protective glasses to shield their solitary eye.

"I can't stand wearing these glasses anymore."

"I know we don't need them for vision at this hour, Sire. However, our appearance will still attract attention. We can visit a dress-up shop in town later."

"Dress-up? What is that?"

"I'm not sure what they call it, Sire, dress-up, costume shop, something like that, but it allows them to dress and appear as something else."

"Such as what?"

"Well, I don't know, but it allows the face to be covered. It may make it easier for us to move around in daylight. I usually travel in a car. I don't get close to humans unless I require something from them."

"What could you possibly need from them?"

"A mechanic if the car stops working, a tailor if I need a new suit, things like that. Despite the crudeness of their human bloodlines, they have someone for everything."

"Someone who can breach a wall of iron?"

"Wall of iron, Sire? They possess cutting tools, yes."

"It's inconsequential; I'll revisit the iron wall another time when their guard drops again. It's only a matter of time. They'll be fortifying right now."

They had walked some distance and had finally reached the outskirts of the town called Shrewsbury. In this town resided the cat with two heartbeats.

"Let's rest for a while until it's light. We need to plan our next move."

"Yes, Sire, there is a passageway between those buildings. It's covered so our eyes will not be affected by direct sunlight later," Aazar pointed directly in front of them.

Duat nodded, "So be it."

Bellator, who had been struggling with pain during the journey, felt a wave of relief at the prospect of a rest. The effects of the pain medication given by the vet were starting to wear off, and he was finding it increasingly difficult to keep up with the others.

"I'll go ahead, Sire, to make sure it's clear of anyone else."

"Good. Wait here, Bellator." Duat instructed.

"Yes, Master."

They stood at the side of the street while Aazar went ahead. A fox appeared from around the corner, sniffing its way around the various doorways. Aazar beckoned them to follow as the fox darted away, disturbed by the unexpected presence of strangers at this time of night.

After crossing the road and entering the passageway, they disappeared from sight and could remain unseen by any unwelcome passersby.

The passageway, a hidden path that linked two roads together, ran beside two houses and was constructed of solid brick. In the darkness of the night, it was eerie and pitch black in the centre.

They all removed their glasses. Duat passed his to Bellator. Aazar placed his in his suit pocket.

"So, we now know where the cat resides," Duat remarked, a sense of anticipation and determination in his voice.

"Yes, Sire, I believe the vet was telling the truth. I've been to that house before. I suspected the occupant was part of the Order. I could smell the foulness of the cat's bloodline from a mile away, which led me to her. However, I was not aware of the cat's uniqueness."

"Good. I want to attract as little attention as possible. They have foreseen my coming here in their prophecy, so it's no surprise they have a cat or a cat guardian to assist them. It's their way of trying to maintain balance – an equal fight."

"Could this cat or guardian be powerful, then, Master?"

They both turned to face Bellator and saw the shadows reflected in his eye.

"It needn't concern you, Bellator. According to their prophecy, the cat or guardian could be the great protector of their Order, but they could also be the destroyer of it." Duat nodded. "We will discover more in due course. Aazar, tell me more about this so-called 'magic' place, where you think someone from the Order may have visited?"

"It's not far from here, Sire, a narrow passageway between overhanging buildings. I'm positive of it. Like the cat vermin, I can smell the lairs of the so-called wonder workers."

Duat hissed with satisfaction, "I have no doubt, my friend, they are pathetic individuals dabbling with their wands, trying to create potions, feebly attempting to delve into matters they cannot possibly understand."

Bellator was at a loss for words to contribute to the discussion. There was much he didn't know, or if Duat was to be believed, his mind had been wiped of all memories.

"If a member of the Order has been there, I want to know why and challenge the one she was speaking to!"

The dust from the driveway had long settled, and patience was wearing thin. Raysmau, standing at the top of the steps, chose not to descend to greet the guest due to her rude demeanour. The Armourer, a formidable figure clad in a long black trench coat, heavy boots, and gloves, appeared visibly affected by the scorching sun as she dropped her trunk onto the gravel with a resounding thud. "Raysmau! I heard you were still here; I can see you've been eating well," she remarked with a hint of sarcasm.

Raysmau, visibly annoyed, rolled her eyes. The Armourer released her other bags and carefully set her backpack down before stretching her limbs with a confident smile, seemingly unfazed by the tense atmosphere.

"Why are you here, Armourer?" Raysmau asked, her tone betraying her irritation.

Bending over to try and touch her toes, she got nowhere near. "Honestly, I'm like a stiff brick these days." As she stretched, she glanced briefly at Raysmau. "Well, didn't they tell you! Look at all this mess; someone needs to be here who knows what they are doing."

Raysmau glanced at Najla and Kalara. They were not impressed.

"So, I don't know who you are?" The Armourer ascended the steps. Najla extended her right hand for a handshake, "I'm Najla, my Lady."

"She's not a Lady," Raysmau quickly interjected.

The Armourer smiled mischievously. "Are you sure you want to shake hands with me? I wouldn't if I were you." Grinning, the Armourer and Najla stood face to face as the visitor removed her gloves, revealing a chrome, robotic-looking hand. "It goes all the way up, right up to the shoulder." The Armourer shed her coat and gloves, tossing them on top of her luggage. "Look, now this is science!" She rolled up her sleeve to reveal her almost bionic arm. "Shoulder is still mine, but this is special, watch on." She descended the steps and effortlessly lifted a piece of scattered brickwork, crushing it easily, the stone granules falling to the floor. Returning up the steps, she brushed off her hands, displaying a self-satisfied smile. Najla lowered her arm, wanting no part of a handshake. "My own creation," she smiled. "Would you care to shake hands with me, Raysmau?"

Raysmau emitted a short, patronising snort, observing the scarring on the Armourer's face and the bloodshot right eye. "So, what happened to your arm?"

"Science is never perfect, Raysmau. It takes dedication, perseverance, and above all, commitment."

"That's as maybe, but you didn't answer the question."

"Oh, well, I blew myself up. My arm was torn right off; it's still in the freezer at home, I may be able to use it for something else."

The Escarrabin looked at each other with bemusement.

"Scars heal; sacrifice comes with the territory." The Armourer put her hands on her hips. "Innovation, you see."

"Yes, well…"

"And innovation, you clearly lack, ladies." The Armourer stepped forward to Raysmau. "Don't think I don't know what you've done."

Towering over the Armourer, Raysmau stepped into their guest's personal space. "And what is that?"

The Armourer smiled, looking Raysmau in the eyes. "Our removal, my kind being put out to pasture. The League of Light didn't need you; they didn't need the Reeves or the foot soldiers of the Escarrabin because that's what you are, Raysmau, a foot soldier!"

Their eyes locked as the atmosphere soured.

"We are very capable of looking after our own, Armourer."

"Are you now? Not judging by the state of this place. I understand this is now a hotel for Gatekeepers." Her smile was a patronising one.

"I don't care for your tone and you will address Raysmau with respect."

"Oh, the other one speaks, and you are?"

"Kalara."

"I notice you didn't address me as Ma'am."

Kalara stepped forward. "I don't need to if you are not a Lady."

"Mmm, it's true I'm catless, but then I have other priorities. And while you're at it, sorry, did you say your name is Calamity?"

Kalara rolled her eyes. "I'll address respect where it is due, and it's not in this present company." The other four Escarrabin on duty sensed tension in the air and moved closer.

Aware of their presence, the Armourer looked around at the numbers surrounding her. "Well then, girls, show me to my quarters, please."

"This is not a hotel, as you just mentioned."

"I should think not, Calamity. Judging by the state of the place, I'd be asking for my money back. All the same, I'm a member of the Order. Would you like to check my coat for my pin badge?" Kalara looked at Raysmau.

"It's not Raysmau's decision to make," she had a grin across her face, "tell you what, I'll go and speak to the Clerics, I'm sure we'll work it out."

Raysmau nodded as Kalara stepped to the side.

"Say, bring my bags, would you, Calamity? The trunk is heavy, and please be very careful with the backpack, wouldn't want you to lose an arm as well now, would we!" The continued grin from the Armourer suggested she was enjoying every minute of their confrontation.

Kalara moved next to Raysmau with a concerned look on her face. They watched the Armourer confidently stride through the smashed entrance doors.

"Oh," the Armourer turned to them, "always a pleasure, girls. I'm sure we'll be catching up very soon."

Observing the Armourer walking in the direction of the Clerics, Raysmau shook her head and crossed her arms with frustration, "Pity it was just her arm she blew off."

✢✢✢✢

"My ladies, we're not far away now, I would think twenty minutes or so, traffic permitting," the driver announced. The security screen in the centre of the car had been lowered earlier in the journey.

"Thank you," Safiya responded.

Nubia fiddled with her jacket pocket, retrieving her phone. Reading the message, she nodded to herself, "The Armourer has arrived, my Lady. She says she's introduced herself to Raysmau and a couple of the others."

"Good, I'm sure they'll get along fine," Lady Safiya replied.

"Let's hope so, my Lady. It's been a long time since we have called the Armourer. I'm amazed she got there so quickly," Nubia remarked.

"Ebonee said she lived not far away, in the middle part of England. In a quiet hamlet apparently. Away from prying eyes, I guess. I don't suppose she had much on," Lady Safiya said, staring out of the window deep in thought.

"She would have had her suspicions though, my lady," Nubia pointed out.

Safiya took a deep breath, her thoughts elsewhere, "Mmm, what was that?"

"Suspicions, my Lady. She's still a member of the Order, her clocks would have also stopped, presumably," Nubia clarified.

Safiya nodded, looking at the passing cars, "I guess so. The prophecy affects us all."

Safiya leaned forward and pressed the button to raise the shield again for privacy. Satisfied when it was closed, she moved across the seat to be closer to Nubia. "You know that the Armourer will not be the only addition. The Council will now be deep in thought, and changes will be made. They are of no doubt that the Gatekeeper is here. Word of change will spread to the Reeves, I hope it does not cause division, we need them."

"My Lady do not forget; they also need us. They have battle skills and courage, yes, but we have other gifts they do not. Mine is my constant longevity, to witness time through the ages and yours is…" Nubia was interrupted.

"Remind me, please, my friend, where are you in your transitionary period? How many lives have you seen so far?" Safiya asked.

Nubia turned to look away from her superior, "I'm nearing the end, my Lady. I'm on my eighth cycle, I only have one more left."

Safiya nodded and placed a hand on her friend's leg.

Recognising the surrounding roads, Nubia knew they were nearly back at their headquarters. She turned to the Lady of the House, "And before my time is up, my Lady, we must see this through, one way or another."

✤✤✤✤

Mildred stepped into the kitchen, unsure of what to do next. Considering what she had just witnessed, if she were to describe herself, alarmed would be a worthy word. She slumped into one of the kitchen chairs and kicked her shoes off. Squishing her feet into balls to try and calm herself, she placed her head into her hands.

"So, the vet turned into a cat," Mildred looked across at the sofa. Nahla and the kitten looked wide awake, monitoring her every move. "The vet turned into a cat," she repeated her words, speaking very quietly and slowly. Her attempt to laugh at her own words came out as nothing more than a mumble.

Placing her head into her hands again, Mildred started nodding away to herself. "She spoke to Comet and scared her." The nodding of the head became a shaking of the head. "It's not possible! It's not possible!"

But she knew what she had seen. Mildred rubbed her eyes; she was tired, but getting some sleep was unlikely. "Turquoise this, turquoise that, how about…" she immediately jumped. Comet was on the table staring at her. "When did you jump up here? I never heard you!"

Comet stepped towards her, "Why was she asking you what you were? How can you be anything else other than a cat?"

Comet sat down, looking Mildred directly in the eyes. Her tail stopped waving. "She scared you; I know she did, but she looked worried as well; how can this be?"

Comet's eyes narrowed; her focus was intense.

"What are you trying to tell me, are you trying to tell me something?"

Mildred leaned forward; she couldn't help it. The intensity of Comet's focus was like a magnet drawing her in. Mildred's eyes turned bloodshot in an instant, her words deliberate, although later, she would have no recollection. "What are you, who are you?" Now just in front of Comet's whiskers, Comet's eyes narrowed as a flash of turquoise shot across them.

Mildred let out the tiniest of screams and instantly threw herself back in her chair. Placing a hand over her heart, she was breathing heavily and quickly. She immediately looked away from the eyes of the quickly growing kitten. If the cat-talking vet was to be believed, she knew this was a warning. In anguish, she looked across at the sofa. The unnamed kitten was hiding behind Nahla. She flicked her eyes back to Comet, and for the second time that day, she felt scared in her own house.

✣✣✣✣

Bellator woke up suddenly and saw Aazar removing his foot from his ribs. The kick had been harder than necessary, and Bellator winced, realising that the pain relief medication had worn off.

"You didn't need to kick me that hard!" Bellator protested.

"You needed to be woken. Our kind doesn't usually sleep at night," Aazar replied.

"I'm still recovering from my wounds!"

"We need to keep moving. Randoms could come through this passageway at any moment, and we don't want to be seen up close."

In the dim light of the passageway, Bellator could see Aazar clearly, realising that he had been asleep for quite some time.

"Put your glasses on," Aazar instructed.

Struggling with his veterinary trouser pockets, Bellator eventually retrieved his and Duat's oversized glasses. As he put his glasses on, he noticed Duat walking toward them from the end of the passageway.

"Give me those," Duat said, taking the glasses from Bellator. "My eye is starting to hurt. How much farther do we have to go from here?"

Aazar pulled out a phone from his pocket. "Not far, Sire. I'll just check."

Duat looked surprised. "You have a portable communication device."

"Yes, Sire. Although people rarely seem to speak to each other using them. They just message or use the internet."

Still clutching his midsection, Bellator inspected the object in Aazar's hand. "What's an internet?"

Duat, not understanding, looked at Aazar.

"It's an information highway. I read about it in a newspaper someone had thrown away. You can find out anything. I've been here for a very long time, so I thought it would be useful to learn more about the humans and their surroundings."

"But how did you get that device?"

"It was painful, Sire," Aazar said with a pained expression, shaking his head. "I had read that criminals use these devices to communicate in secret using something called a clone. It's not registered anywhere. I read that you can buy them in pubs from what their police call undesirables. Not far from the magic people's lair is a pub with motorcycles outside, but they dress strangely inside. I observed the place for a couple of nights, knowing that I needed to blend in to find an undesirable I could get one from."

"That doesn't sound painful!" Bellator remarked.

Aazar immediately hissed at Bellator, making him take several steps backwards. "What would you know about anything out here, slave!"

Bellator looked at Duat, but he didn't receive any support.

"The humans are easy to manipulate and control. So, I seized one of them after the pub had closed. This one decided to fight back, so I disposed of his body in one of the outside bins, took his clothes and returned the following night."

"I see. Was the body discovered?"

"I don't know, Sire. I've not heard anything. The place was open as normal the following night. They have the strangest of sounds in there. It's called music, but it's unlike anything I've ever heard. They scream, Sire."

"Scream?"

"Yes, the guitars are very noisy as well. After carrying out some observations, I spotted a man with phones and managed to obtain a cloned version from him. I mentioned the music, and he said, 'You clearly don't like hard rock then,' or words to that effect. It was an unpleasant experience, but I did get the phone. I paid for it with the money I found in the clothes from the man I had put in the bin. I do not care to return there. My glasses were attracting attention; one person pointed at me, shouting, 'Cool shades, dude.'"

"What does that mean?"

"I've no idea, Sire. It wasn't cold at the time either."

Duat nodded, "Bellator, these are examples of why we need to lead. They are without master's and classless. We will dominate them."

"If they are still here, Sire."

"What does that mean, Aazar?"

"I read a lot on the information highway on the phone. They have nuclear devices."

"What is that?" asked Bellator.

"The biggest explosions your little mind can picture," Aazar said, glancing at Bellator. "Sire, if they use these devices on each other, there will be nothing left; it will destroy everything," Aazar said, turning to face Duat.

Duat's expression was confused, as Aazar could tell.

"They war with each other; they always have; why would they want to destroy everything?" Duat said. "Because of their weakness, fighting over land. In any case, Sire, it wouldn't be a complete eradication because, from what I've read, the rats seem to be resilient. Aazar began to push buttons on the cloned phone.

"Well, I guess that's something," Duat shook his head at the ignorance he was hearing.

"While I am aware of the location of the magic door, I am not entirely familiar with this town. They have a navigation system on their phones as well, it will show us the way." Aazar entered the road name into the phone and waited. "There, it is showing me. We are going to Grope Lane."

Chapter Twelve:
STEALTH MODE

"Number one Rocke Road, Mildred speaking."

"Are you okay, Mildred? Your voice sounds distant; is there something wrong with Nahla again?"

"Oh, hello again, Lady Daphne. Sorry, I was going to call you back, but my mind seems to have been elsewhere."

"Well, you've had a trying time, Mildred. You mentioned on the phone earlier that you had called a vet again, pray tell, it wasn't a vet from the outside, was it?"

Mildred knew instantly that this was the real reason for such a quick return call. "No, Daphne, Fennaway was here."

Daphne, also having an astute mind, noticed she hadn't been addressed as *'Lady'* this time; Mildred twigged she was fishing. "Well, I'm pleased to hear you called our own vet, but why was she there? Is Nahla suffering again?"

"I'm clueless as to what is going on, Nahla has been acting strangely, the kitten that I can't have is being distant, and as for Comet. That's why I called her, there's something quite unnerving about her. I can't quite put my finger on it; well, if I do, it's painful, she's got a weird mark on her, and it makes me jolt. And you know what, I'm sure she's bigger already, I think she's going to be a huge cat!"

Daphne stared down the phone, her eyebrows raised with concern. Mildred, the lady she was responsible for, was talking a load of gobbledygook. "Okay, wait, please slow down, Mildred; let's deal with one thing at a time. Let's start with the strange mark on her and that she hurts you or something. I've never heard of a cat doing that before. Did I hear you correctly?"

"Your hearing is just fine, Daphne! Given the comments you made to me at the gathering, I'm telling you something weird is going on here."

"It's a lot of information for you, Mildred, in a short space of time. I know there is a lot to take in, but you didn't answer the question. What exactly happens to you when you touch this mark that you refer to?" Daphne's concerned expression was evident as she awaited Mildred's response.

"It's like a burn on her flank, and if I run my hand over it, my body jolts, and it's painful," Mildred explained, her voice filled with distress.

Mildred wouldn't have known it, but if she could see Daphne's face right now, there was deep concern etched all over it. "Mildred, my friend, I've never heard of anything of the sort."

"I'm telling you the truth; that's why I called Fennaway," Mildred insisted.

"I see. And what did she say? Was there a diagnosis?"

"No, nothing of the sort! She had to make a phone call outside again, and then she decided to change into a talking cat. I mean, seriously, where do you even start!"

Daphne was staring at the phone again, her mind racing with thoughts.

"Your silence speaks volumes, Daphne, do you know something about all of this?"

Truthfully, Daphne had never heard of the things that Mildred was claiming. Rubbing at her forehead, she knew she had to say something, but she was actually wondering about Mildred's suitability for being a member of the Order.

"Erm, you said that Comet has gained weight already. Just bear in mind, Mildred, that I did not present Comet to you, so I've not seen her yet," Daphne pointed out.

"No, I know. The high sheriff woman brought her."

Daphne was still rubbing her forehead with confusion.

"But, yes, I'm positive Comet's put on some weight already," Mildred insisted.

"Are you sure, Mildred? That hardly sounds possible. What are you feeding her?"

"Well, fish paste sandwiches. I have plenty. Other than that, the tins and bits I buy at Mr Frank's shop, and milk of course,"

Daphne scratched at her head with confusion. "Maybe you should try something else, Mildred," her words were mumbled, unsure of what else she could possibly say. "Maybe I'll pop down to the shop in a bit. I need to get more batteries for my clocks anyway. My clocks seem to have stopped working."

Daphne frowned. "That's odd. I have a few clocks and none of them are working."

This time Mildred looked confused. She pondered to herself, *how could that be?*

"So, Mildred, what happened next? What did Fennaway have to say?"

Mildred hesitated before responding, "Well, after her cat shenanigans, she appeared to become agitated about something, so I asked her to leave."

"Agitated? What on earth could have caused her to act like that, Mildred?" With concern, Daphne leaned in closer to her phone.

"Oh, something about believing the colour turquoise is associated with evil or some such nonsense."

"Well, she's right, Mildred. Even as a lower-ranking Elder, I am aware of that. Have you been encountering the colour turquoise, Mildred?" Daphne inquired with genuine worry.

"Yes, in my dreams."

"Mildred, that is deeply troubling!"

"I'm more troubled by the fact that I've been noticing the sudden appearance of turquoise in my right palm, though."

Daphne let out an audible gasp.

"Daphne, are you alright?"

In a state of panic, Daphne coughed and spluttered, "Yes, yes, I have to go," She knew that Suzanna would need to be informed of this development immediately.

✜✜✜✜

Suzanna looked out at the rolling Welsh hills, feeling a sense of familiarity, "Not far to go," she murmured to herself. The journey had been uneventful, but the sensation of the car guiding its own way in auto-drive left her unsettled. With nothing to occupy her, she tapped her fingers on the steering wheel as if she were listening to music. She would have to get used to not having control and relying on technology.

Taking a moment to assess her appearance in the rear-view mirror, Suzanna felt a surge of confidence. She had taken care with her presentation, ensuring she was prepared in case she crossed paths with the enigmatic Curator once more. Her hair was neatly tied back, her makeup understated, her perfume subtle, and she had freshened her breath with mouthwash. Glancing down at her attire, she wore a black waistcoat, a crisp white shirt, a tailored pencil skirt, and sensible shoes *(designer, of course, but they were flats, no heels to slip on). Her tartan jacket was on the seat next to her.*

As her phone buzzed inside her clutch bag. Suzanna retrieved it to see Daphne's name flashing on the screen. "And I was hoping to keep her cat for a while longer," she mused.

Activating the phone's speaker, she placed the phone on the passenger seat. "Hello Daphne."

"My Lady, I hope that you are well," Daphne greeted.

Suzanna detected from Daphne's tone that it was just a pleasantry and not a question. "Yes, I'm fine, and yes, I have your kitten. I've just got to attend to something else, and I'll drop her over to you."

"Yes, my Lady, that's most kind of you. I'm very keen to meet her," Daphne responded.

"I've been entrusted with a Sphinx cat; can you believe it? I'm thrilled."

"Yes, well, that's wonderful, of course…I look forward to seeing mine."

"Is everything okay Daphne? I can sense that something is troubling you. I know you better than you think."

"It's Mildred, my Lady."

Knowing she may well bump into the Curator, having information could only help her good standing. "Please do tell me, Daphne. What about Mildred? What's on your mind?"

"I have just finished talking to her on the phone. Fennaway has been back to see her, about another cat-related problem, or so I assumed,"

Suzanna scratched her head in thought. She really didn't want to get involved in another one of Mildred's cat-related problems. Last time, arranging a cat swap and unexpectedly encountering the civilian vet had been somewhat tricky. "Oh no, so what has happened now?"

"It's almost overwhelming to figure out where to begin. This concerns her new kitten; she's named it Comet."

"Okay, an unusual name, but there you have it."

"If that were the only unusual thing, I wouldn't be calling. Mildred insists the kitten has already gained weight and bears some sort of marking."

"Gained weight already! What on earth has she been feeding her?"

"Fish paste apparently."

Suzanna stuck her tongue out and screwed her face up at the thought of fish paste.

"She claims that when she runs her hand over the marking, she feels some sort of shock."

"A shock! What sort of shock?"

"Well, I don't know, but incredibly it's not that which is worrying me."

"Oh, this had better be good if you're not worried about that, Daphne!"

"She insists she's seeing the colour of the dark realm in her palm."

Suzanna's eyes widened with concern; there were no more light-hearted remarks to be made. "You can't possibly mean…"

"Yes, my Lady, she's a carrier of turquoise."

✤✤✤✤

"It seems so tranquil outside here," Safiya said, looking at Nubia as she pressed the button for the internal privacy screen to be lowered. Their Escarrabin driver leaned over to the entry post and dapped her security pin against the sensor.

"We know what lies beyond these gates, my Lady," Nubia said.

Safiya managed a fleeting smile as the trees started to shake in front of them, a drone hovered above, watching their every move.

"It's still our home, Nubia. We will get the mess cleaned up," Safiya reassured.

"I wasn't referring to the damage, my Lady. Just a small matter of a multi-headed creature below the house and a Gatekeeper flying around," Nubia replied.

Safiya looked out of the car window, the trees parting to reveal the entry gates into Loxley.

"As I say, we'll get this cleaned up," Safiya remained resolute.

Nubia braced herself as the car inched forward. Even from the top end of the driveway, they could see the escalated security measures.

The drone zipped overhead toward the central dome of the house while multiple Escarrabin, armed with their Scatterblades, were stationed around the grounds. The driveway had been cleared, but the extent of the damage was unmistakable. Rubble was strewn across the lawns, windows were shattered, the front doors were beyond repair, and the fractured portcullis hung to the side.

"And to think that most of the damage is inside the house," Safiya observed as Raysmau descended the steps ready to welcome them.

As the car came to a stop at the foot of the steps, Raysmau swiftly opened the car door on Safiya's side and offered her hand, "Do you need assistance, my Lady?"

Overwhelmed by the sight of their ruined home, Safiya accepted, "Thank you, Raysmau. On this occasion, I will."

"I'll get my own door then!" the driver turned around, "Sorry, my Lady, I was just about to do that for you," she apologised as she opened the car door.

Nubia stepped out of the car, "not necessary, I've got it." She grabbed Safiya's cane as she got out and slammed the car door closed.

Safiya turned back to thank their driver. "Thank you so much for driving us and taking care of us, Jazmin. I hope you can finally get some rest," she expressed her gratitude.

"I think I will, thank you, Ma'am," the driver responded.

Raysmau knocked on the roof of the car, and the car pulled away in the direction of the security wing.

"Nubia, she's just driven us for nearly eight hours. You shouldn't be so rude," Safiya scolded.

Nubia glanced down at the floor, handing Safiya her cane as she did.

"Thank you, Nubia," Safiya acknowledged, shaking her head with displeasure at Nubia's impoliteness, then turned towards the head of security. "So, Raysmau, thank you for welcoming us. Is the Reeve here yet?"

"No, Ma'am. She is on her way back as we speak," Raysmau replied.

They ascended the steps slowly, the grand entrance now a shadow of its former self. The stone-tiled floor still bore the marks of dampness from the Escarrabin's successful efforts to extinguish the fire.

"I've heard the architects are on their way," Safiya remarked.

"I've been informed of that as well, Ma'am," Raysmau confirmed.

Safiya scanned the central lobby. The stone and woodwork were scarred from blasts from multiple pulse fires, and many of their precious artworks had succumbed to the flames. Broken chandeliers, shattered vases, and sculptures had simply been brushed to the side.

Safiya looked across at Raysmau's quarters. The broken gate and door were now propped against the wall.

"We will fix this, Ma'am," Raysmau assured her. "We better had, Raysmau, we better had. Talking of which, where is the Armourer? Is she settled in?"

"We've given her a room in the security wing," Raysmau replied, her expression revealing a sense of unease.

"Look, Raysmau, this was not my decision. The decision was made by the Grand Council. I know you will be offended by her being here, but there is not enough communication between the Reeves and us. As the security arm of the Reeves, you and the Escarrabin are part of this."

Raysmau continued to look Lady Safiya in the eyes.

"It's for the good of all of us, Raysmau. We are going to need all the help we can get," Lady Safiya emphasised.

Raysmau nodded in reluctant agreement.

"Good, I'm heading up to my quarters. I'll catch up with the Armourer later."

Raysmau nodded again, maintaining her composure. "Yes, my Lady."

Safiya headed in the direction of the stairs, acknowledging the Clerics with a nod as she passed by, her mind undoubtedly preoccupied with the new developments.

"Well, seeing as we are going to be working more closely from now on, have you got any Scotch, Raysmau?" Nubia inquired.

"No, madam Curator, I do not."

Nubia looked displeased, "see to it you work on that, will you." Nubia turned, heading in the same direction as Safiya, choosing not to acknowledge the Clerics.

Raysmau put her hands on her hips. She sensed that things were about to change, and deep down, she knew she was not going to like it.

✟✟✟✟

Batteries, replacement cat food, and maybe even a doctor wouldn't be such a bad idea. Mildred stared at her happy cat mug. She'd drunk half of its contents; the top half of the smiling cat was beginning to fade. The cat on the mug always vanished without heat. She prodded her finger on the cat transfer, and the heat of her touch started to bring the cat back to life again. "If only everything was that easy." She tried to run her fingers through her hair, but gave up on that idea, her fingers constantly jamming in her knotted mane. *There's only so much tea I can drink; I must do something;* she thought to herself.

She rubbed at her eyes and pushed herself to her feet. Mildred reached for a 'Frank's carrier bag' from the chaotic pile on the sideboard, muttering about always forgetting to grab one before leaving the house. "Not everything in life is progress!" she exclaimed wagging her index finger, mimicking Mr Franks' favourite saying with a wry smile.

"Kitten without a name, come over here for a hug." The kitten was sleeping, her request was duly ignored.

"Well okay then, I'll come to you," Mildred said with a resigned chuckle, making her way over to the tiny ball of fur.

Abruptly woken, the kitten's head bobbed up, feeling Mildred's weight crash on the sofa, scattering the dust everywhere. "Right then," she said picking up the newborn and giving it a gentle hug. "You know, Comet is unnerving me a little, but not you, you're lovely, aren't you now, aren't you now." Mildred started making playful noises as the kitten pawed back at her, "Ok then, it's tickly belly time!" The kitten was placed on her back, and then Mildred's fingers went crazy across the cat's belly. She continued to paw and playfully bite her temporary keeper. "Aww, you're a little so-and-so!" Mildred laughed, the sound filling the room with warmth and light. "Oh, hey Nahla!" she exclaimed as her older cat jumped up on the sofa to inspect the commotion. "She's so cute, isn't she Nahla!" Nahla started playfully jabbing at the kitten. "Nahla, it's going to hurt having to give this one away; I need to do that soon." Mildred drifted away in thought, "What happens if she says no? What if she doesn't want this little fluff ball of fun, Nahla? Does that mean I can keep her?" Nahla stopped pawing and looked at Mildred, "You understood my question then, what do you think?"

Nahla was immediately distracted by Comet strutting into the front room. The kitten stopped playing and pushed as hard as she could against Mildred to get the right way up. Mildred turned around to see what had made the kitten suddenly change behaviour. Her concern grew as she watched the kitten slip behind Nahla to hide in fear. "Are you both scared of Comet?"

There was no reaction. "Nahla, are you scared of Comet?" Nahla looked up, but her eyes were expressionless and difficult to read.

Looking back at Comet, Mildred crossed her arms; Comet was staring at her again, "I never thought I'd say this, but Nahla, what do you think? Shall we give the new lady Comet instead?"

✣✣✣✣

They lingered in the narrow alleyway for as long as they could. As the morning rush hour approached, encountering people would be inevitable. Anticipating the need to leave, they sought refuge from the bright sunlight in a nearby car park. They stayed hidden behind a utility building until most of the working population had settled into their workplaces.

"Sire, I think the magic house will be populated by now."

Duat looked at their surroundings. Despite the busy traffic, there were very few people walking around. "We should avoid drawing attention to ourselves and stay away from the locals as much as possible."

Bellator adjusted his veterinary jacket, the bandages on his midsection showing signs of damp red spots, they would need changing at some point. He could still feel the after effects of being kicked in the ribs by Aazar.

"Sire, the phone indicates that we can take the footbridge ahead," Aazar pointed directly in front of them. "It will lead us over the river, and then there appears to be a passageway we can take to get closer to the magic house, just a couple of roads away."

Their conversation was interrupted by movement to their left. They noticed a couple of men in uniforms nearby, one of them was speaking into a radio. "Are those officials of some sort? Who is he communicating with?" Duat inquired.

Aazar examined their uniforms and explained, "No, they are not officials, I've seen them before, they put tickets on cars. They are traffic wardens and are a nuisance. They are filming everything with body cameras, so we should avoid them."

Duat adjusted his glasses and glanced at the cloudless sky. "Bellator, you will follow behind us. Try not to stare at anyone. We shall enter the magic house and we will get some answers."

☩☩☩☩

"Come on, Nahla, you need to go out and do your business," Mildred said, putting on her shoes and unblocking the cat flap. "Nahla, Nah... oh, there you are!"

Nahla crept across the floor and stopped. "Well, off you go then."

"Wow!" Mildred had never seen her cat move so fast, practically sprinting through the flap. She quickly snatched open the door, but

Nahla had vanished from sight. She stepped onto her overgrown garden path and looked up and down the road. "Oh, hello, Mr Jenkins. Did you see Nahla?"

Her neighbour, bent over weeding his garden, looked up. "Whose Nahla, Mildred?"

"Eh? ... oh, what am I like... sorry, was just talking to a friend who has a cat called Nahla, my mistake. Have you seen my Missy? She just sprinted out of the house."

"Oh yes, I saw her alright, ran straight past me, gave me quite the fright. If you can ask her to stop doing her business in my garden, that would be appreciated."

Mildred froze in an instant and went red in the face with worry. "How do you know I can talk to my cat?"

Mr Jenkins laughed until he saw that Mildred had intended her question. "Well, I, erm; it was just a joke really, Mildred, why can you?"

Mildred put her hands on her hips. "Don't be ridiculous, Mr Jenkins! Honestly."

Mr Jenkins looked somewhat embarrassed. "Well, all the same, Mildred, I'd rather not be picking up cat poo."

"Mmm, I wonder where she went to in such a hurry. Anyway, I'll see you soon, better get my bits and go to the shop."

Mr Jenkins gave a little intended smile.

"Oh, I'll talk to Nahla about her pooping later." With that, the front door was closed.

Mr Jenkins looked reasonably perplexed, shook his head, and carried on weeding.

Mildred grabbed her jacket, put the Franks' carrier bag in her pocket, pulled up her wrinkled stockings, then put on her cloche hat and grabbed her purse off the side. Spinning around, the two kittens were nowhere to be seen. "You two behave yourselves, I won't be long." She checked the cat flap was secured and stepped outside. She stopped pulling the door closed, noticing Mr Jenkins picking up what looked like more cat 'business' from his garden. Closing her front door gently, she ducked and tiptoed to the end of the path. Thinking it best to avoid her neighbour, she stretched for the top of the gate and removed the latch as quietly as she could. Waddling through, she pulled the gate closed behind her and peered over the top of the hedge. Stealth mode had worked so far. She continued to waddle along the hedge line and peered up her neighbour's pathway. When the coast was clear, she ran past the garden out of sight.

In the house opposite, the two Escarrabin behind the net curtain looked at each other. "Did you get that on film as well?" A bemused nod followed.

'That was close,' Mildred thought to herself. She quickly checked behind her to make sure no one else had seen her. Now, walking at a normal pace, her heart sank as she saw the youths up ahead at the bus stop. *I'm not going the long way around. I need to stand up for myself more. I will not be made a fool of;* she kept repeating the words in her head. She took deep breaths the closer she got to them.

"Eh eh, it's Mildred!"

Mildred looked down to avoid eye contact but kept walking.

"The crazy cat lady graces us with her company again," there were sniggers.

Mildred quickly glanced up; there were four of them. One had a foot resting on his skateboard, two were standing, and the other was sitting at the bus stop.

"You want to join us, Mildred?"

Mildred took a deep breath and looked at the one who spoke to her. "No, I'm fine thank you," her words were quietly spoken.

"What was that, was that a yes?"

"Come on, Mildred, what's the matter with you today? Where's that dumb cat at?"

Mildred took a deep breath and stopped walking. "You know, there was a time a few years ago, when you boys were nice to me."

"Oh yeah, Mildred, that's 'cos Sam fancied you. Used to talk about you at school."

There was laughter all around, except for Sam and Mildred. Sam was immediately red-faced. "I never used to do that, stop making stuff up."

Having heard enough, Mildred started to walk again.

"It's a fair point though, Mildred. Yes, we used to let you on the bus first, but you were so, how can I put it…elegant."

John, the one who was speaking, seemed to be the leader of this group. He smiled, the other three cackled to themselves.

"Seriously, you were like…"

"Cute."

"You see, told you what Sam had been saying about you."

"Yeah, yeah…" Sam remained red-faced following his admission.

"It's like, look how your clothes have changed, look at your garden, look at…"

"Have you ever thought that your words might have consequences?"

John was instantly silenced.

Mildred's voice trembled with hurt and frustration as she spoke up. "You boys are mean to me and I will take it no more. I am not a figure of fun; I just want to be left alone."

John, seemingly oblivious to Mildred's distress, reached for his phone. "Say, Mildred, come on, Sam, jump in. A picture with your first love. Need this for my socials."

"Get off, no way!" Sam kicked his skateboard at John. "It's never happening."

Mildred's plea grew more urgent. "Do not take my picture!"

But John persisted, his fingers swiftly tapping the phone's screen. "Come on, Mildred, it's not a problem." He said, trying to unlock the phone.

"I told you NO! Stop mocking me. I'm not taking it from any of you anymore. I just want to be left alone!"

John lifted his phone forward. "Oh, come on, Mildred, it's just a picture." His phone flashed as a picture was taken. "Must have left my flash on." He pulled the phone back to adjust the settings. "Ah, here we go." He lifted the phone again, not noticing that Mildred had stepped forward to him. "Okay, Mildred, let's get one more." He looked up. "Say, what's happened to your eyes?"

Mildred put her right hand up, clutching hold of John's forearm. "I told you no, do not make fun of me."

John instantly froze. Mildred's eyes were bloodshot, her pupils had darkened. The other three continued laughing. "You're being overpowered by the crazy cat lady!" They continued to laugh but seeing John's face, their laughter ceased. "John, you alright, mate?"

John's panic was palpable as he struggled to free himself from Mildred's grasp. His phone slipped from his trembling fingers, crashing to the ground as he was overcome by fear. "What's happening!" he cried out, his body shaking uncontrollably.

Desperation filled the air as the boys tried to intervene. "John, John, what are you doing?"

"I'm burning!!" John started to scream.

"Let go of him!" One of the boys grabbed Mildred's arm. She swiftly turned to face him, her eyes making him feel instantly numb. John, having lost eye contact with Mildred, looked at his arm. The area where Mildred had grabbed him had undergone a startling transformation. It had become bluish-green, and he could see his veins pulsating with the same otherworldly colour. A searing heat overwhelmed him, and he collapsed to the ground with an intense throbbing pain in his head.

"What's happening?" The male voice from behind caused Mildred to release her grip, she stumbled, using the bus shelter to steady herself. John lay on the ground trembling.

"Mate, what's wrong?" Two of the boys gathered around John, the other who had looked into Mildred's eyes looked utterly terrified. John examined his arm, and to his relief, the unusual colour was rapidly fading; his body temperature felt normal again, and he flexed his hand.

"Did you boys not hear me? Now get and leave Mildred alone!"

The two lads helped John to his feet. Mildred glanced down and kicked the phone towards them. She spoke in a low voice that the man behind her couldn't hear, "You listen to me, John, my boy. You and your friends will never mock me again, ever!"

John nodded, looking petrified.

"Go!"

John nodded again. The boys grabbed their terrified friend and headed quickly in the other direction.

"You're forgetting something!" All four turned around as Mildred kicked the skateboard towards them. Sam picked it up, nodded, and they all fled as fast as they could. Mildred leaned against the bus stop, still in shock, needing its support.

"You okay, Mildred?" She didn't know his name, but it was the second time he had come to her aid. The man with the long hair and motorcycle leathers looked at her with some concern. "They didn't hurt you, did they?"

Mildred tried her best to avoid eye contact and shook her head.

"Are you sure you are, okay? It looks like you've got something in your eyes."

Mildred raised her hand, indicating she was fine.

"Well, if you're sure, I don't like these boys picking on you. You know where I am if you ever need any help."

With her eyes watering, Mildred watched as he turned and headed back up his driveway. She glanced at the veins in her right palm, still pulsing with the vivid turquoise colour.

Chapter Thirteen:
DARWIN'S GATE

Mildred gently placed her index finger over the central veins of her left wrist, inhaling deeply as she attempted to steady her racing heart. Gradually, her breathing began to return to its normal rhythm. She had been sitting at the bus stop for some time, she cautiously glanced around, ensuring no one was observing her. The earlier surge of adrenaline had subsided, and she felt a sense of calm returning.

Flexing her fingers and then forming a tight fist with her right hand, she released it. Her palm had returned to normal; the strange discolouration had faded away. Still unsettled by her confrontation with the boys, she found herself replaying them in her mind. The image of John's terror-stricken eyes lingered, she couldn't shake off the unnerving sensation that she could overpower him. It had been an utterly horrible and surreal experience.

Rocke Road was quiet, punctuated only by birdsong. It was a beautiful summer's day, absent of people. The boys who had caused the earlier disturbance had fled and not returned. One of their comments stuck with her; they had mentioned her past. They used to let her get on the bus first, and they remembered doing so. Recalling her former life, she realised how drastically things had changed. She used to work, dress impeccably, and exude confidence. That routine was from a few years ago; since Nahla had arrived, her interest had waned; the person she used to be seemed like a distant memory. The clothes she had once cherished were now donated to charities, and her makeup had either been discarded or lay forgotten, gathering dust.

Reflecting on the time since she lost her job and Daphne's unexpected appearance at her doorstep, she recognised she had lost interest in everything except for her cats. She no longer had a mobile phone and had distanced herself from social media. Save for the occasional Kat Chamber meetings, she had withdrawn from human interaction and found solace in the company of her cats.

Rubbing her temple, she pondered how her life had lost its allure. Something had shifted within her, altering her very core, and it all stemmed from Daphne's arrival. As she allowed her thoughts to wander back to her childhood and her forbidden desire for a pet, she recollected her adoptive mother's words about responsibility, *'the time will come when you are responsible for others,'* it had never made any sense. Now, at the threshold of middle age, she found herself entrusted with the care of Nahla and Comet. As she gradually unclenched her fingers, the foreign colour in her palm had vanished from sight.

Leaning her head against the bus stop, she drew a deep breath and rose to her feet. She decided to take a slow walk to the shop, considering whether she might need to seek medical advice from a conventional doctor, not a doctor who could talk to cats.

✠✠✠✠

In the canteen of the security wing, the Armourer stared at what had just been presented on her dinner plate. "Is this really all you have? I would have thought the food here would have improved over the years!"

The server was unimpressed and responded with disdain. "Perhaps you'd like to speak with our chefs? I'm sure they would be thrilled to hear your culinary viewpoints." The server's smile was somewhat patronising. "I would also like to remind you that you are a guest here."

Word had clearly spread about her arrival. The Armourer turned around; she noticed some off-duty Escarrabin staring at her. It was obvious she was being talked about. She made a point of acknowledging them with a confident smile and headed to where the others were sitting. Vacant chairs were immediately pulled in towards the tables. It wasn't the most hospitable of welcomes. Their unwelcoming behaviour did not come as a surprise. She understood they viewed her with suspicion, almost as if she were a spy. When the time came, she would make her presence felt. With a broad smile across her face, she took a seat at a vacant table.

With deliberate intent, she removed her long jacket, knowing that all eyes were trained on her. As the jacket was placed on the back of a chair, she immediately heard murmurings. Taking her time to remove her leather gloves, there could be no doubt they all caught sight of her webbing and the array of concealed weapons and devices. She carefully laid her firing weapons on the table. The tension in the room was palpable as she seated herself, facing her critical audience with unwavering determination.

Looking around the canteen, eyes were upon her every move. She had their attention. She reached into an inside pocket of her waistcoat and retrieved two short metal objects. The tension in the room heightened as she leaned on her elbows on the table, one metal object in each hand. Every move she made was under scrutiny. Locking eyes one by one with multiple officers of the Escarrabin. It was time to test them. She could see one of the Escarrabin moving her hand towards her Scatterblade.

"Are you ready?" she asked, her voice cutting through the uneasy silence. Nervous glances were exchanged among the officers. The security guards were on edge. The server hurriedly retreated as two chefs emerged from the kitchen door.

"Ready?" she repeated, her tone carrying an air of challenge. A few others discreetly placed their hands on their Scatterblades. "BANG!!!!" The Armourer's voice reverberated through the room as she forcefully smashed the ends of the two bits of metal into the table. Those who had drawn weapons immediately appeared embarrassed upon realising that the two metal objects had transformed into nothing more than a knife and fork.

"Well, it seems we're all a bit jumpy, aren't we!" she said as she forked some food into her mouth and grimaced, "this really is dreadful," she commented pointing her fork at the officers. "You know ladies, I've got specialised equipment with me, unlike anything you've ever seen. I could venture into the grounds and procure something far tastier for us to eat immediately." She pushed the dinner plate across the table.

Her comment was met with stern and perturbed faces.

"Say, is Raysmau not joining you ladies? Or perhaps you're not good enough for her?" she teased with a bright smile.

"Please disregard our guest, soldiers of the Escarrabin," the highest-ranking officer in the canteen, the Sergeant-at-Arms, declared as she rose from her seat. "She'll be on her way soon enough." The Armourer dragged the plate back towards her and continued to chew at her food, waving her fork at the Sergeant, "We'll see."

The act of talking while eating was an unsightly display, some of the Escarrabin wrinkled their noses in distaste at the general lack of etiquette.

Still gesturing with her fork, the Armourer surveyed the canteen, "I'm eagerly anticipating working with you all!"

Her words were met with stony silence.

They tried their best to avoid drawing attention, but it seemed impossible. Despite staying in the shadows of the overhanging buildings, they couldn't escape the curious glances of passing drivers, stares from pedestrians, and the barks from alarmed dogs being pulled to the other side of the street. The three bizarre characters kept their heads lowered, trying to avoid making eye contact.

It wasn't their clothing that drew the most attention, but rather their skeletal appearance and peculiar oversized sunglasses that seemed to intrigue passersby.

"Aazar, how much farther until we reach our destination? I can't stand being so close to these humans."

Aazar studied the navigation readings on his phone, "It looks like we must cut through the passage directly in front of us, and that leads to what looks like a square. Grope Lane is directly in front of the square Sire."

"They stare too much. Look at them."

Bellator and Aazar lifted their heads slightly.

"They drain the resources of this place, colonise and swarm, consuming everything as they do so. Their vulgar pursuit of wealth is foolhardy. There are no monetary riches for them in the afterlife!" Duat grinned and wiped the falling saliva away from his chin.

"Sire! Huddle up," Aazar turned his back to the passing cars, grabbed Bellator unnecessarily hard and pulled him in. Aazar snatched a street map from the free dispenser. "Sire, come next to me. Police are approaching."

Duat quickly glanced over his shoulder and saw a police car slowly moving in their direction. "Please do not stare at them, Sire. It will only draw attention."

Bellator peered as best as he could, enough to see 'West Mercia Police' printed down the side of the car as it passed.

"She looked at me, the driver!" Bellator exclaimed.

"I told you not to stare!" Aazar scolded.

Bellator's patience with Aazar was wearing thin. He'd had enough of the insults and the way he was constantly being spoken to. "I didn't stare!"

Duat gazed straight ahead into a shop window, catching his reflection and the slow-moving cars behind him. He noticed the police officer in the car stealing a glance at him, but the vehicle continued on its way.

They waited until the unwanted car had passed around a bend before releasing from their huddle. Aazar returned the map and looked up at the striking sculpture before him—a three-pronged arch adorned with intricate designs. Duat followed Aazar's gaze and then turned his attention to the accompanying plaque. "It's called Darwin's Gate," he said.

Bellator looked puzzled. "What's that, Master?"

Duat shook his head, "I have no idea. It's unlike any gateway I've ever seen."

"Is it a portal, Sire?" Bellator asked.

Duat examined the hardened glass structure, which also seemed to incorporate steel and copper. "I don't believe so," he responded, prodding at the structure. He glanced at the plaque again, but the engraved text didn't appear to be instructions for use.

"Why is it here, Master, and who is Darwin?" Bellator asked.

"I'm not sure. I've never heard of him. It's probably another form of their idol worship," Duat remarked, glancing across the road. The passageway Aazar had mentioned was just to the left of a bar called The Hole In The Wall.

"Sire, if this is not a portal, I think we should proceed quickly. In this one-way system, the police may come back around again," Aazar said.

Duat nodded, "Bellator, come."

Bellator was keenly aware of his lack of knowledge about this place. He was grateful to be free from incarceration, but he still had no plan. Taking a deep breath, he replied, "Yes, Master."

They waited for a break in the traffic, then crossed the road together. They cut through the narrow passageway and ascended a few steps that brought them into a bustling square. Directly in front of them was a large brick building, a museum to their right, there were people everywhere they looked. It was evidently a central meeting point, teeming with activity.

"Sire, we head there," Aazar indicated ahead.

At the end of the square, a narrow passageway was flanked by overhanging timber-framed buildings. The thick black beams and white surrounding walls were characteristic of many structures in the town.

"It's a short climb up the hill and then…" Aazar immediately stopped speaking, "what is wrong with you?"

Bellator's nostrils were flaring, and his nose twitched.

Duat grew impatient. "What's wrong with you now?"

"I don't know, Master, I've…" Bellator faltered.

"Well, well, well," Aazar stepped into Bellator's space, bringing his face so close that their oversized glasses almost touched. "Maybe he is not so useless after all, Sire,"

Aazar stepped back and turned to Duat. "He can smell them; he can smell those who practice magic."

✜✜✜✜

"Yes, I understand. Thank you, Raysmau. I know you'll need to speak with the Reeve first. Please ask her to come up when she is ready, and I'll let my Cleric know."

Raysmau disconnected the call. Now that the Reeve had arrived, she wanted to speak with her before taking her up to see Lady Safiya. Retying her hair, she walked into the control room and asked, "Where is the Reeve now?"

"The gates have just opened, Ma'am," the security officer replied.

Raysmau nodded and said, "I'll go out to greet her."

By the time she had walked across the central lobby to the entrance doors, the Reeve's car was almost at the bottom of the steps. As the car drew to a halt, Raysmau indicated to the security driver to remain seated. The tinted glass of the rear passenger windows made it nearly impossible to see through. She opened the near side passenger door to see the Reeve sitting there. "Hello, Ma'am," Raysmau greeted the Reeve with a warm smile and a respectful nod.

The Reeve stepped out of the car and offered her hand forward, "It's good to see you, Raysmau."

Raysmau happily shook the Reeve's hand, "It's good to see you as well Ma'am."

Raysmau closed the car door and nodded at the driver, "She'll take your bags up for you."

"Mmm?" The Reeve was studying the damaged façade of the Manor House.

"Your bags. They will be taken to your quarters," Raysmau clarified.

As the car pulled away and disappeared around the corner of the building, the Reeve surveyed the area and took note of the numerous armed Escarrabin on duty.

"I've staggered the security Ma'am, and you'll observe their Scatterblades are secured to their backs. However, I must admit that I've only provided them with minimal information," The Reeve turned to face Raysmau. "To be honest, I'm at a loss for words when it comes time to address them. We know he will return, but how? They are all on edge, only too aware that a great danger lurks below the surface. I may speak to the Escarrabin with authority, but they are not naive. They understand there are unknowns that even I am not privy to. They are understandably apprehensive."

The Reeve acknowledged, "There are many reasons to feel apprehensive, my friend. We need to take decisive action, starting with gathering all the Watchers below. After that, we must inspect the iron wall. Have there been any sounds or movements detected below?"

"No, Ma'am. However, the Lady of the House wishes to speak with you," Raysmau responded.

The Reeve took a deep breath, knowing that meant Nubia would be accompanying her.

"We also have an unwelcome visitor, I'm afraid."

The Reeve immediately locked eyes with Raysmau. "Is she already here? The Armourer?"

"Yes, Ma'am. I wasn't sure if you were aware of her arrival. She has made her presence known. She is a battle-scarred woman who holds a strong contempt for us. Things may become complicated and possibly unpleasant," Raysmau confirmed.

The Reeve nodded, "My Elder anticipated her arrival; she had someone on the inside during the Grand Council meeting."

"I understand, Ma'am. Also, Kalara, one of my senior Escarrabin, whom you haven't met, is here. She would like to discuss her findings from the outside. She believes the Gatekeeper is responsible for Lady Tempest's death."

"I believe that to be the case. Let's meet with Kalara first, then visit Lady Safiya. Unless absolutely necessary, let's avoid the Armourer."

✢✢✢✢✢

The bell on the shop door tinkled, causing Mr Franks to look up from his newspaper in surprise. "Are you okay, Mildred? You're as white as a sheet," he said.

Mildred nodded and closed the shop door behind her. She appreciated his concern. "Thank you for asking, Mr Franks. I'm just not feeling quite like myself today."

"Should you see a doctor?" Mr Franks inquired, showing genuine concern.

Walking from the bus stop to the shop, she'd made her mind up she'd seen enough of 'doctors' for the moment but would keep an eye on things. "I'm sure it's nothing, will probably pass. She couldn't help but notice that he looked genuinely concerned."

"If you are sure Mildred." He adjusted his belt so his belly could overhang more comfortably. He paused as a deeper look of concern worked his way across his face, "say it's not contagious, is it?"

Mildred considered the colour she had seen running through her palm and blood vessels, "No, nothing like that," she replied.

"Well, I'm in the pink of health, but it's always good to be cautious," Mr Franks said, smirking.

Mildred didn't feel the need to explain further. "I think it's just women's things, you know."

"Ah," Mr Franks stammered, pretending to flip through his newspaper, his face turning red. "Well, uh, you know where everything is," his rasping gruff voice had returned as he looked down, pretending to read the newspaper to avoid any further discussion.

Mildred's thoughts were still in a muddle from what happened; she found it difficult to concentrate on the simplest of things. *What did I need?* She placed a hand for support against one of the old humming fridges. She blinked repetitively, almost doing a double take, there was a huge variety of different fish pastes. When she bought her recent supply, they had been on the shelves, not in the fridge, "say, Mr Franks, I've not seen these fish pastes before."

He immediately looked up, "Well, funny story that Mildred." He put his hands on his hips, "You pretty well wiped me out of fish paste, so I spoke to my supplier on the phone. Apparently, it's coming back into fashion, or so he told me." Mr Franks waved his arms in the air; he was obviously clueless as far as fish paste cuisine was concerned. "Sold me a job lot, has to be kept in the fridge apparently."

"Oh right," Mildred leaned forward to inspect them in finer detail, they were the strangest varieties she had ever seen. "These sound a little unusual, Mr Franks," he was still listening to Mildred, who he had often described as 'his favourite customer'. "Aubergine and shrimp surprise! Aubergine surprise! Who's ever heard of such a thing?"

"Even aubergines have their place, Mildred." *I'm sure they do, must be a better place to put them than in fish paste though?* "Okay, if you say so," she said, grabbing a pot along with a 'yams, kale and mackerel surprise' flavour. *That should keep mine happy.* Her thoughts were on Nahla and Comet, as well as the unnamed kitten she was trying her best not to get attached to. In the next couple of days, she would have to travel to Much Wenlock to 'deliver' the new kitten to a complete stranger. She dreaded it recalling how she had initially reacted to Daphne when she first visited Mildred's doorstep. The new girl is going to think I'm a lunatic! It wasn't like dropping off a bunch of flowers. Additionally, how was she going to explain she wasn't a *'girl'* anymore but a Lady of the Kat Chamber? It was almost like an official title, try explaining that! And it was another Daphne! Rubbing at her head momentarily she then grabbed some tea bags, milk and dinner for herself.

Mr Franks' Tardis of a shop had plenty of nooks and crannies. She wandered around casually, glancing at phone leads and adapters, things she no longer had any use for. She smiled and paused, seeing the 'happy gathering' card, the artwork on the front featuring the cat that looked like Nahla. Her smile quickly faded as she recalled how many she still had of them at home and how dismissive the older members of the Kat Chamber had been towards her. She couldn't return them as they had all been written in.

She took her goods to the counter. "Reading anything interesting?"

"Just the usual Mildred, still some rumblings about the missing CCTV footage following the accident outside here and further allegations of cheating at the sheep diving contest."

He picked up her goods one by one and rang them into the till, "I'll have to charge you for a bag Mildred, not everything in…"

He noticed Mildred pulling a Franks carrier bag from her pocket, "I'm prepared this time!"

He smiled, despite losing a sale of yet another carrier bag. He started to bag up the items.

"I've a bone to pick with you Mr Franks,"

He looked up, shocked. "With me Mildred?"

"Mmm, these batteries you keep selling me. I need them for my clocks at home, my clocks have stopped…again!"

Mildred reached into her jacket pocket and placed the batteries on the counter.

"Well now, Mildred, I've had no complaints from anyone else," he said as he adjusted his belt to give his belly room and reached up behind him to lift the clock off the wall above the counter. "I'm very sorry about this, Mildred, but let's try them in my clock. As you can see, it's happily ticking and has been for years."

The years of dust accumulation indicated the clock's long service. He removed two batteries and replaced them with Mildred's ones. "Let's see then." He lifted the clock to his ears and looked at Mildred. "There you go, see, look, the hands are moving."

Mildred frowned and took the clock from him, lifting it to her ears. "Well, I don't know what to say."

"You don't need to look embarrassed, Mildred. These things happen. You probably put the batteries in the wrong way around. Happens all the time, I'm sure."

Mildred was at a loss; she was sure she'd checked for such a simple error.

Suzanna tapped away at the steering wheel, pondering Daphne's words about Mildred. As she peered out of the window, she recognised the familiar surroundings; the journey was drawing to a close as the car arrived at the road with no name. Turning in, the semi-circular dead end lay ahead. The colour turquoise and the Orders' fear of it was known to her. The subject had never been explained to her in detail, but it was known. The notion of one of their own carrying the colour in their bloodstream was exceptional, but what it meant for Mildred and the Order, she wasn't sure. If Nubia were here, she'd broach that subject with caution.

The car came to a halt at the end of the nameless road, and the navigator screen flashed 'destination concluded'. She pressed the button to lower the window. Leaning as far as she could, she attempted to connect her pin badge to the entry post.

As she hung out of the car window, a humming from above caught her attention. There were no rustling trees, no noises from below, and her pin badge had not made contact. The car engine cut off, and in the quiet, she shrunk back into her seat as the drone descended. Suzanna tried to cower behind the steering wheel, but her efforts were futile. The drone drew level with her, and in a panic, she quickly raised the car window as the black and chrome-coloured drone hovered beside her. Her eyes widened in terror as a menacing-looking device emerged from the underside of the drone.

"Car! Can we go somewhere, please? This thing does not look friendly!"

Terrified, Suzanna reached for the navigator for support. "Help me, please, start the car! Let's get out of here!" Peering out of the window, she watched as the weapon-like device retracted back inside the drone. Panting with fear, she pressed her hand against the glass to protect herself as the drone suddenly ascended at an incredible speed and vanished over the treetops. Adrenaline coursed through her as she grappled with her fear and the potentially near-death experience she had just endured. Her hands trembled uncontrollably as she cautiously reopened the window. Gingerly craning her neck outside, she scanned the gently swaying treetops. The drone had vanished and she found herself alone once more. "Thanks for your assistance!" she muttered as she reconnected the unhelpful navigator and cautiously stepped out of the car onto the tarmacked semi-circle. Glancing at the treetops and down the road, she couldn't spot anything further out of the ordinary. With her hands on her hips, she deliberated her next course of action.

She couldn't help but wonder if the drone was somehow connected to Loxley. It hadn't fired at her, at least not yet, and she wasn't even sure if what she had seen was a weapon. Since she was already here, she decided to try to gain entry. She leaned down and connected her pin badge, and immediately the ground started to shake around her. Holding onto the car door for support, she felt as if a mini earthquake was happening. The trees to the side of her started to give way and part, gradually revealing the entrance of Loxley in the distance.

The car engine suddenly sprang to life without her doing anything. *Oh, right, I guess we're going,* she thought as she jumped in and closed the door. She glanced behind, everything appeared to be clear as the car edged forward. Brimming with nerves and excitement, Suzanna tapped her fingers on the steering wheel. The trees had settled on either side, and she could hear the concrete slab lifting from below. There was a loud crash of moving parts as the slab settled, and the entry to Loxley was complete.

A loud bleeping sounded and a light flashed on the dashboard. "Yes, okay, I've got it," she said as she reached around to grab her seatbelt. The bleeping stopped and the car proceeded through the entrance gates and headed down the driveway. Suzanna looked up in shock "What on earth..." she murmured. Leaning out of the window, she could see some distance away that the Mansion House had been damaged. People in uniforms were stationed across the grounds, all looking at her. The drone was now flying around the central dome of the house.

Widening her eyes, it looked like some of the windows were missing, and the entrance doors were open; in fact, it looked like the doors may be missing altogether. Large slabs of stone were scattered all over the lawns, judging by the scorch marks, it looked like there had been a fire. As the car approached the entrance, Suzanna noticed in the rearview mirror someone in uniform appeared on the driveway behind her; whoever she was, she looked intimidating. Now, up close to the mansion, other uniformed women with large metal objects on their backs were watching her. The car pulled to the left and headed down the side of the building, as they moved further from the main entrance, the damage seemed to decrease. The windows were intact, and the grounds were still immaculate. She recognised the doorway up ahead,

Nubia was not standing there this time; that was something to be grateful for. Suddenly, the car stopped. Suzanna disconnected the navigator and placed it in her bag. She went to open the car door when she noticed another lady in uniform staring at her from a distance. This was not a pleasant welcoming party. Looking around, she couldn't see anyone else. Nevertheless, something had happened here, and whoever these women were, they seemed nervous as well as intimidating.

Reaching into her bag, she took out the navigator, the power was still on, "Navigator, who are these women?" The cursor flashed, but there was no response. Suzanna had encountered security at gatherings before, but these women seemed different, dressed as if part of an army. Despite her unease, she decided to proceed and stepped out of the car, only to watch it restart and drive off, leaving her with the realisation that she had no idea how to call it back. The woman in uniform continued to watch as Suzanna headed towards the entrance she had used previously. This time, wearing sensible shoes, she made her way without slipping or tripping on the gravel. Mentally preparing herself, she approached the door, knowing that the room behind it gave her the creeps. Unsure about what had happened at the front of Loxley, the main entrance didn't seem like a place to venture, especially considering her rank. She pressed her lapel against the illuminated button with the Kat Chamber symbol, hoping to attract as little attention as possible and to avoid upsetting the Curator again. Despite being a tradesperson's entrance, it was still quite impressive.

Her pin badge worked. The old, heavy oak doors creaked and started to open, revealing the dimly lit cold room behind. Inside, there was a chill, even at this time of the year. The room was empty, flickering candlelight was the only visual aid. The heavy doors moaned and closed behind her, the thud of heavy wood on stone sent a harrowing echo around the room. It was unnerving, and she didn't enjoy being alone. She walked across the creaking wooden floorboards as quickly as she could. She didn't believe in ghosts; if she did, they would probably reside here. She would be thankful to exit this room and leave the creepiness behind her.

She proceeded onwards, entering the next room, where the air felt damp, and in the candlelight, Suzanna could see dusty and presumably unloved artworks hung for no one to see, an old, dusty-looking fireplace and a viewing balcony overlooked her to the right. This time, she would make a point of getting to see the other rooms and their contents in more detail, especially the long walk; she wanted to visit there again. Fortunately, she remembered the way out and headed towards the far door.

Beyond the carpeted corridor there were brightly lit rooms flooded with natural sunlight or showcasing elaborate electric chandeliers. Continuing, it wasn't long before she stepped into the corridor of clocks. However, something had changed. She stood in silence; the corridor was eerily quiet. What was going on? The last time she was here, this corridor had been alive with ticks and chimes. It was as if the corridor had died. She looked at the pristine carpet edged with gold runners down its length, the wooden panelling lining the sides of the corridor, and the chandeliers that radiated wealth. But in the silence, something was missing. Walking over to one of the unticking grandmother clocks, she stared at its face; something looked familiar. She turned around, the clock on the other side said the same time. Rolling up the sleeve on her left arm, she glanced at her watch and moved further down the corridor to look at other clocks. Two minutes past twelve. They all said the same. The same time her watch had stopped. Suzanna dropped her bag to the floor and started to wind her watch, but nothing happened.

Surely, it couldn't be a coincidence? Suzanna picked up her bag and moved towards a painting of an older lady on the wall. She had only glanced at this artwork when she had visited previously. Nubia had not given her the time to study it in more detail. The inscription on the painting read 'Lady Femi' along with the date 1724 – 1798. As she gently brushed her hand across the cheek of the serious-looking lady in the painting, a sense of familiarity washed over her, feeling as if she recognised her from somewhere, although given the date, that seemed unlikely. Suzanna, who was emotional at the best of times, felt a surprising wave of sadness, upset by the lady in the portrait. Reluctant to turn her back on the painting, Suzanna took a couple of steps back and headed towards the doorway on the right. She remembered glimpsing ancient-looking weapons mounted on the wall in this room before Nubia reprimanded her and all the doors in the corridor had suddenly closed.

This time, the door was closed, and it had been implied to her that some areas were 'off-limits'. Suzanna tapped her pin badge against the illuminated button in anticipation. The Kat Chamber icon changed to green as soon as her pin made contact and she was granted access. Before entering, she surveyed the corridor and, no one else seemed to be present, and she could not detect any CCTV cameras focused on her.

Pressing down upon the antique-looking gold handle, the door opened freely, revealing a room filled with intriguing artefacts. After entering, she pushed the door ajar, just in case she struggled to get back out.

Now able to see the room to its full extent, it was not dissimilar to others she had seen, wooden panelling ran from the floor to the midway point of the walls, and the carpet was thick, immaculate and no doubt expensive. Multiple reading lights and two chandeliers illuminated the space, giving it the appearance of a library. The room also contained old battle weapons mounted on the walls. *Why would you have weapons in a library*, Suzanna thought to herself.

Suzanna approached the wall on her right, where she saw a display of swords, spears, and body armour with a statement underneath that read, 'Here we were clad in skins.' One double-edged sword caught her eye – the gladius – accompanied by a shield called the scutum. The shield looked heavy, covered in leather, and bound with metal, with an unfamiliar symbol in the centre and the date '55 BCE.' Suzanna guessed that these items had Roman origins.

In one corner, a mannequin wore a chainmail suit with a heavily scarred helmet and a nose protector, but there was no information sign explaining its significance. As she walked over to the windows, Suzanna marvelled at the impressive Welsh landscape, with a lake and a prominent boathouse in the distance. The thought of having an office in such a beautiful place brought her joy, but she was interrupted from her thoughts when she noticed a uniformed woman staring at her. Feeling intimidated, Suzanna stepped back from the window out of sight.

The remaining walls of the room were lined with bookshelves. With the abundance of single-seated chairs in the room, it appeared to be a space for study and reflection. The books were old, with delicate-looking bindings. Suzanna ran her fingers across the tops of a couple of them. Although the room was clean, the books were dusty, and she had to wipe her hands together. In the corner, nestled between two bookcases, was a pile of picture frames. The way they were haphazardly piled on top of each other suggested that they were discarded to this corner and not meant for regular viewing.

She placed her bag on the floor and picked up the first picture. It was a portrait of an older lady, presumably an Elder. She blew on the picture, immediately coughing as the dust scattered into the air. Using her hand as a fan, she tried to move the dust out of her airspace and gently put the frame down on the floor. Underneath was another portrait; the woman's face was stern and unnerving, to the point of being intimidating. As with the previous artwork, there was no inscription indicating who they were. *Why were they stored here and not mounted on the wall?* Perhaps they had fallen out of favour in the past and were now discarded to the corner to gather dust. A much larger artwork was buried underneath, it depicted a scene with soldiers. As she studied it, the details immediately caught her attention. Suzanna shook her head, confused, and turned around to study the swords mounted on the wall of the library. They looked very similar to those being carried by soldiers in the artwork. Suzanna frowned in puzzlement at what she was seeing. There were multiple people in the picture; the body armour worn and the contours of the soldiers at the front were definitely women. There was an unusual gold casket being carried by four larger hooded figures, one at each corner. The casket had a flag with a red cross draped over it. It can't be! Behind the four carrying the gold casket were other people wearing full body armour, carrying swords and some with shields bearing a red cross in the centre.

Suzanna shook her head again. They were men! She was positive about it. This picture may well have been hidden away, but what was it doing here and furthermore, what did it mean? Still gripping the picture frame, she glanced at another artwork that had been hidden below it. It was another picture of the gold-looking object, this time without a flag draped over it. Bending down to study the object in more detail, she jumped at the sudden slam of the door.

"What are you doing?" Suzanna recognised the voice in an instant.

"Madam Curator," she turned around, her face conveying her guilt.

"I asked you what you are doing?" Nubia's hands were held together in a ball, her presentation plain but immaculate as always.

"Erm, Madam Nubia, I was just looking around. I am curious about this picture though…"

"Put it down." Suzanna bowed her head, suspecting a reprimand was coming, but what would it be for this time?

Suzanna clumsily put the artwork back into the corner.

"Be careful. People are replaceable, art is not!"

"Yes, sorry, my Lady." Suzanna delicately made sure the picture was back in its corner. She thought it best to leave the pictures of the serious-looking ladies propped against the wooden panelling.

"Why are you here?"

"You mentioned that I could come here, now I'm a level Six Elder."

Nubia's lips twitched a little with acknowledgement, "that I did. However, some areas are off-limits to you."

"My pin badge allowed me in," Suzanna spoke assertively.

Nubia closed her eyes, hearing the tone, and took a deep breath. "Your badge does allow you entry into some parts of the Manor, however, you looked like you were rooting around."

"I'm just trying to learn." Suzanna smiled nervously.

"Far too inquisitive you are. All will be explained in time."

"I also have some information about Mildred. You asked me to keep an eye on her."

This immediately grabbed the Curator's attention. Nubia took a couple of steps forward, "Go on."

"I'm informed of something most terrible, Madam Curator, and if I'm honest, I'm not sure of the full significance of it."

"Go on."

"I've not seen it personally, but I'm told Mildred has the colour of turquoise in her blood." Suzanna double blinked as Nubia simply nodded and bowed her head.

Chapter Fourteen:
GROPE LANE

Duat adjusted his glasses and examined the weathered wall-mounted sign. "So, this is it."

Aazar tucked his phone into his jacket pocket. "Yes, we are at the foot of Grope Lane. I'm certain the entrance to the magic house is concealed somewhere along this pathway."

Duat surveyed the narrow winding hill before him. No doubt built in a time when horse-drawn carts would pass up and down the cobblestones, not like the cars that passed behind him at speed. Glancing up the hill, these days, the passageway suited pedestrians only. The old white buildings, with their black timber beams, overhung the passageway, almost choking out the sunlight.

"Bellator, can you smell their presence?"

Behind his glasses, Bellator shot an irritated glance at the arrogant Watcher. He was growing weary of Aazar's constant mockery. Ignoring the question, he couldn't deny that he could detect traces of magic lingering in the air, confirmation that the magic world was close at hand.

Absent of cars and motorbikes, the lane was frequented by pedestrians making their way to the main road and the bustling shopping district. Infiltrating the elusive 'house of life' belonging to the practitioners of magic would require careful timing and discretion to avoid drawing unwanted attention.

Duat confidently led the way heading up the winding hill.

Halfway up the passageway, they passed by a couple of intriguing shops. The storefronts were visible from the ground level, but the steps inside led to lower levels, giving the impression that the shopkeepers were conducting their trade from underground basements. Aazar and Bellator followed closely behind. If anyone passed by, all three kept their heads bowed or pretended to look elsewhere.

Stumbling upon a particular shop, Bellator was captivated by the peculiar patterns on display in the window. His attention was caught by macabre skeletal designs that were unfamiliar to him, likely belonging to a species other than human. As he peered up, a sign revealed that it was a tattoo studio, a concept entirely foreign to him. Gazing at his reflection in the glass, he moved closer to scrutinise his form. With no reflection devices at Loxley, he assumed his appearance mirrored that of the other Watchers who had been confined for so long. In the dim light of the lane, he adjusted his glasses, tilting his head to observe his large, bloodshot eye and the thin, stretched skin covering his skull. Opening his mouth a few times, he caught a glimpse of his misshapen teeth. He couldn't remember how many teeth he should have, but many were missing. Before he could inspect further, a piercing scream from below startled him, prompting him to hastily lower his glasses. Glancing into the tattoo studio, he saw a woman behind the shop counter, pointing and shouting in another direction. Through the glass, her distressed voice carried, "Come and see this!"

Brushing the drool from his mouth, Bellator swiftly caught up with the others.

Duat abruptly halted his steps and spun around with a look of concern. "What was that?" he exclaimed.

"What, Master? I didn't see anything."

"I thought I heard a scream."

Bellator thought he must have looked guilty of something as Aazar and Duat stared at him. With nothing to add, Bellator shrugged his shoulders, hoping he would not be pressed for drawing attention to them all.

"We must exercise caution out here. There are too many who could disrupt our plans."

Bellator nodded at Duat.

Aazar glanced to his near side, "I think it's here, Sire, somewhere behind this wall."

Still scrutinising Bellator, Duat raised his right hand. "Well?"

Nervously, Bellator nodded, fearing an impending confrontation. "Yes, Master, I can sense their presence."

"Good." Duat acknowledged, gesturing downhill. "Watch behind Bellator. And Aazar, keep a vigilant eye ahead, particularly around that bend, in case anyone approaches us. Both of you, alert me if you spot anyone heading our way."

Bellator anxiously glanced over his shoulder, only to spot the woman who had recently screamed emerging from the entrance of a nearby tattoo studio, accompanied by two men, both wearing vests, their arms covered in strange patterns. The woman pointed directly at him, prompting the men to direct their attention toward Bellator. Desperately, he averted his gaze, pretending to have interest in the display window of a neighbouring shop.

He could feel the weight of their stares bearing down on him, causing panic to well up inside him. He was relieved to hear one of the men speak loudly enough for him to hear.

"It's nothing, just an off-duty vet wearing steampunk glasses!"

The words didn't mean anything to him, but they seemed to have an impact. He watched out of the corner of his eye as the men retreated down the stairs. The woman hesitated for a moment but eventually went back inside the shop. Bellator quickly glanced behind him, thankful his master hadn't noticed anything. Duat remained fixated on the wall directly in front of him.

Bellator decided not to investigate further and moved away from the shop window. Duat trailed his right hand along the unremarkable, white-painted wall and quickly glanced up. Above, was a mounted CCTV camera, serving no purpose other than to observe the wall.

Stepping back, he surveyed the hill, observing pedestrians passing by at the opposite end of the lane but none ascending it. "Both of you, stay alert," Duat instructed, shutting his eye to concentrate and shaking his right hand. "We must proceed with this, and then we'll contact my Master, they will need an update."

Bellator glanced back, surprised by the comment. Duat put him on edge at every turn, and the thought of others like him was not an enticing prospect.

As Duat's right palm started to glow, he turned to Bellator and said, "Everyone has a Master."

Unnerved, Bellator bowed his head slightly, observing Duat's glowing palm. He swallowed and immediately turned away to keep an eye on the high street at the end of the lane.

In the shadows of the overhanging buildings, Duat lifted his glasses to study the wall in more detail. Satisfied he had the right place, he pressed his palm against it. Within a couple of seconds, he removed his palm from the wall and stepped back with concern. He looked up and down the lane, pleased to see that Aazar and Bellator were not watching him. Duat knew something extraordinary was at work. He closed his eye again, placed his palm back on the wall, and concentrated. After a few seconds, he started to move his palm in small circles. Saliva started to run from his mouth as he screwed his eye up in concentration, pushing determinedly against the wall. The turquoise glow spread outwards as Duat's body started to shake. He lifted his left hand and pressed against the wall to stabilise himself. The recoils were intense; the wall was resisting him. He pushed harder, the blood vessels of his eye turning turquoise as more drool fell from his mouth. Yelling noises escaped him from the physical exertion, his knees started to buckle, and his blood vessels became alive with the colour of the dark realm. A moving turquoise circle resembling a cluster of ants immediately spread across the wall, and a faint outline of a doorway emerged.

"Sire…" Aazar called urgently, scanning the hill. "Sire!" he repeated, noting two figures approaching from around the bend. "SIRE!!"

Bellator heard Aazar's frantic calls and spun around, alarmed to see Duat's body convulsing uncontrollably.

Although faint, an outline of a doorway was now visible as the round glow of turquoise extended farther across the wall.

Taking action, Aazar hurried down the slope and put his hand on Duat's shoulder, "Sire!"

"What!" Duat exclaimed as he instantly swung around, his eye wide, bloodshot, and brimming with anger. The central vein supplying his eye was enlarged and pulsating. Duat let out a furious yell, covering Aazar's face with spittle as he seized him by the throat with his left hand and forced him to the ground. Duat placed his glowing palm over Aazar's skull, the turquoise circle and the doorway's outline vanished instantly.

"Please, SIRE, NO! People are coming. I was trying to warn you!"

Duat hissed aggressively and released him. Aazar fell against the floor, scrambling out of arm's reach, and springing to his feet. Terrified and perspiring, he moved away as the two approaching figures came around the bend towards them. Duat swiftly turned in the direction of the wall, thrusting his glowing palm into the veterinary blazer he wore. Bellator made sure he was looking the other way as the couple walked past, the male nodding at Aazar. "Afternoon." Aazar remained silent as the strangers glanced at him and quickly looked away. When they were further down the lane, the couple exchanged words and both turned around. All three strangers appeared to be looking in different directions. Bellator quickly glanced at them as they exited the lane and moved into the high street. Duat removed his hand from his pocket and studied his palm; the colour was fading quickly. He immediately spun around, glaring at Aazar. "Never interrupt me again."

Bowing his head as he spoke, Aazar said, "Sire, I understand it was not my intention, but I did not want you to be caught. We do not want police involvement."

Bellator closed in on them; the fear in Aazar's face was obvious.

Duat looked up and down the lane; they were temporarily alone. "I can't get in. The door is here but it's sealed by one of their protective spells. We need to go to the other place for support. I must communicate with my Master." Duat looked aggressively at Aazar again and started to move back down the hill.

Bellator wiped some drool from his chin and looked at Aazar with a grin across his face.

┼┼┼┼

"Yes, yes, okay." Mildred fumbled with the door key in the lock. "I'm coming." She could hear her phone meowing like a cat. Pushing the door open and slamming it behind her, she dropped her shopping on the kitchen table and quickly grabbed the phone.

"Number one, Rocke Road, Mildred speaking."

"Have you been working out, Mildred?"

Mildred rolled her eyes; she recognised the voice instantly. It was Mildred from Alpine Grove; she was a new addition to the ranks and had been thoroughly unpleasant thus far.

"It sounds like you're out of breath."

Miserable Mildred was correct; she was slightly out of breath, and there was obviously nothing wrong with her hearing.

"I'm fine, just rushed in from doing a little shopping."

"Well, you can't possibly need any more fish paste. You must have loads of those sandwiches left over."

Mildred pulled the phone away from her ear, hearing Mildred's sarcastic laughter at the other end of the phone. "Actually, I'm all out, everyone loved them."

"But you had loads left?"

"Yes, but when you are my rank, you get invited to other events." It was a little white lie; she crossed her fingers so that it didn't count.

There was silence at the end of the phone as rude Mildred considered Mildred's words. "Yes, well, I suppose you are important now, aren't you!"

"Look, Mildred, have I done something to upset you? You are very off with me, and you were also very rude to Daphne the other night as well."

"I don't know what you mean, Mildred. You must be imagining things."

"Mmm... so why did you call Mildred? What's on your mind?"

"I just wondered if you had received your new cat yet, with your promotion and all?"

"Yes, a beautiful cat. I've called her Comet."

"Comet! Weird name for a cat. Anyway, how did you get your promotion?"

Mildred looked surprised by the question. "I'm not sure if I can discuss that with you." *Truth be told, she didn't know why it had been given to her; she had done nothing out of the ordinary to earn it.*

"I see. Do you know what your gift is yet?"

"Gift, gift? I don't know what you mean. I was given Comet, and that's all I need, thank you."

A sharp laugh came out of the cat's bottom into Mildred's ear. "Not your cat, Mildred. We all adore cats, of course. No, what is your personal gift? All Ladies develop a gift. Some develop quickly and some take time. There are no timescales on these things."

"How do you know these things?"

"Mmm, that would suggest you haven't discovered yours yet?"

Mildred holding the cat phone, noticed the other Mildred had avoided the question. Mildred flexed her right hand and extended her arm; all appeared to look normal. If what had happened at the bus stop was a gift, she had no idea what to possibly do with that. It scared her. "So, you called to see if I'd received a new kitten?" Mildred's tone carried a hint of suspicion.

"Yes, and also, I thought it would be nice to catch up. You know, get to know each other better. You can invite the other Mildred, from Merewood Close. I'd be thrilled to be involved in a cake-making afternoon, we all know how good her cakes are."

Mildred pulled the phone away from her ear again. She barely knew this new member of the Kat Chamber. She also knew things she didn't, she was always rude, and she didn't want to spoil an afternoon cake-making by having rude Mildred come along. "Mildred, look, I'll need to check. Now I'm a level Eight Elder, I think I'm only supposed to associate with others of the same rank." Mildred shrugged, having no idea if that was true or not. In any event, she didn't know any other level Eight Elders.

"Oh, I see. So, I'm not good enough for you now then?"

"That's not what I'm saying, Mildred. But also, you've not been a member for very long, so there are processes you need to follow." Mildred had no idea what she was talking about, but the words about formality seemed to be having some effect.

"I see. Well, I think I can learn a lot from you, Mildred. I'm positive of it. In fact, I can feel it in my blood."

✣✣✣✣

The Reeve was grateful to be sitting in Raysmau's office. It provided a temporary escape from the chaos of the central lobby and the fallen balustrades above. It was a moment of tranquillity amid the turmoil.

"Kalara is on her way, Ma'am," Raysmau informed.

The Reeve nodded in acknowledgement.

"Despite the circumstances, did you enjoy meeting with your Elder, my Lady?" Raysmau inquired.

"Meeting with her was necessary due to the circumstances. There was little to be joyous about. Both she and I are deeply concerned. However, I'm pleased to report that she appeared to be in good health," the Reeve replied.

Raysmau nodded, her smile fleeting.

"Mind you, the weather is always better in Spain, of course, Raysmau," remarked the Reeve.

"That's hardly difficult, my Lady, compared to here. Probably why so many British live over there," Raysmau quipped.

Their brief exchange was interrupted by a knock at the door.

"Come in," called out Raysmau.

Kalara entered the room.

"Kalara, may I present the Reeve," Raysmau introduced.

The Reeve stood and shook hands with Kalara.

"It's a pleasure to meet you, Ma'am. Lady Raysmau had already assigned me elsewhere before the start of your tenure here," Kalara said.

The handshake was firm, and the Reeve replied, "It's good to meet you as well. I understand you have some information to share."

"Yes, Ma'am," Kalara responded, turning to Raysmau, "May I, my Lady?" she asked, gesturing towards an empty seat.

Raysmau nodded in approval.

Kalara pulled up a chair next to the Reeve. "My Ladies, Lady Raysmau already knows this, but I have intercepted footage that I believe shows a Watcher murdering Lady Tempest. I have no doubt about this."

"Have you seen this footage, Raysmau?" the Reeve asked, her eyes narrowing in concern.

"Yes, Ma'am", Raysmau's tone was solemn.

Kalara took the phone from her jacket pocket and placed it on Raysmau's desk. "The footage is on there if you would like to see it, Lady Reeve."

Raysmau shook her head. "You don't need to see it, Ma'am unless you particularly want to. I'm afraid it's quite conclusive."

The Reeve shook her head, her expression grave. "No, I don't need to see it. I'll take your word for it."

"Kalara tells me the footage is no longer in the hands of the civilian police, but it is available on the cloudy web."

Hearing this, the Reeve raised her eyebrows and shook her head, not understanding.

"Dark web, my Lady," Kalara interjected.

"Oh," the Reeve nodded. "Now I understand."

Raysmau coughed slightly, her face flushing with embarrassment.

"Kalara, I'm sure you are aware that anything on the dark web can be discovered. It poses an active security risk. We can't have civilians finding out about the Watchers, or us for that matter."

"I know, Ma'am. I've locked it down as best as I can, but I will need your permission either to keep it stored or destroy it."

The Reeve pondered the words, "Leave that with me for twenty-four hours. I'll come back to Raysmau with my thoughts. However, please actively monitor it to see if there are any interceptions."

"Yes, Ma'am, of course."

"What else were you able to glean from this or the area concerned?"

"To be honest, Lady Reeve, strange things were happening in the area. I'm positive that a member of the Grand Council, on occasion, was present. She left a cell phone data trail tying her position to the area of Shrewsbury, in Shropshire. From what I can ascertain, she travelled alone, so her actions were not known to anyone else. After I detected the signal, I monitored her phone. There were no calls that I could detect to anyone else of relevance." Kalara shifted herself in her seat and took a deep breath. "There is something, though, something that I haven't mentioned to you either yet, Lady Raysmau."

The turning of Raysmau's thumbs around each other stopped. "What is it?"

Kalara took it in turn to address both ladies. "I believe this member of the Grand Council was communicating with someone involved in magic."

There was an instant frown across Raysmau's face as she looked at the Reeve with concern.

"That's quite an accusation, Kalara. None of our kind communicates with the world of magic."

"I know, Madam Raysmau, but I'm reasonably positive. I cannot be fully sure, but I believe there may be a magic house hidden within the area, what they call one of their houses of life."

The Reeve rubbed at her temple; she had been told by Lady Berenike that Lady Ebonee had communicated with the magic world. For now, she would keep that to herself.

Raysmau started turning her thumbs again. "I've never heard of something like this; it goes against the grain. My Lady, this is almost unethical, the magic world, really!"

The Reeve stopped rubbing her forehead. "This cannot be a coincidence. Too much is happening and all tied to one area, at the same time." The Reeve looked at Kalara. "Raysmau knows of this, but you do not. I was there a few days ago; I delivered a cat to an Elder in the area."

"You did, Ma'am. In Shrewsbury?"

The Reeve gently nodded, her mind deep with consideration.

"Madam Reeve, I hope I'm not speaking out of turn, but isn't it the Elder's responsibility to present cats to their new protectors?" Kalara asked.

Raysmau swiftly interjected, "Kalara, that does not concern you!"

The Reeve held up a hand. "No, it's okay Raysmau. Kalara is right, and we have plenty to work out." She turned to Kalara, "I did deliver a cat, but this one was a very special cat, possibly associated with the ancient prophecy," the Reeve explained.

"The one that will come?" Kalara inquired.

The Reeve nodded. "We cannot be sure, but it bore the hallmark, along with other recent events. It's not conclusive, but it looks probable."

"Kalara, as you know, we are keeping constant surveillance on the Elder in question," Raysmau added.

"I understand, Ma'am," Kalara acknowledged. "May I ask if there is anything to report as yet?"

Raysmau crossed her arms. "Not unless you consider constantly yelling down the street for her cat, banging tins, and making a racket as news. And then she fell over while chasing her cat around the garden, and her existing cat uses the neighbour's garden as a toilet!"

Kalara and the Reeve looked puzzled. "It concerns me that Mildred has this responsibility," Raysmau concluded.

The three of them sat in contemplation, the weight of their conversation hanging heavily in the air.

"Murder, the prophecy, magic people and the foretold cat all in one area," the Reeve looked at Raysmau, her expression grave "Something of some significance must be about to happen over there. Surveillance on Mildred will not be enough."

Raysmau nodded in agreement as they both turned to Kalara.

"Yes, my Ladies," Kalara rose to her feet, understanding the unspoken urgency. "I shall depart for the area immediately."

"Kalara, listen. Report to me regularly and avoid communicating with any of the other Escarrabin matters we've discussed. We need to avoid panic and keep speculation to a minimum," Raysmau cautioned.

Kalara nodded acknowledgement.

"We still do not fully comprehend Duat's intentions here at Loxley, but his failure, has alerted us to his presence," the Reeve remarked, rising from her seat. "You can be certain the Gatekeeper will now be drawn to that location. If he isn't there already. He'll want to put an end to the prophecy as soon as possible. It's all we have to defend ourselves. He cannot afford to let us defy him. We have resisted the dark realm in the past, and they failed," the Reeve raised her index finger, "If Duat prevails, we will be powerless to stop him. He will need to eliminate the Elder or the cat she is protecting."

✟✟✟✟

"I would have preferred to enter the magic house first before reporting to my Master." They crouched in an alley to the side of an old theatre. The shade was welcome as the temperature of the day was now at its peak. Duat kept his right hand covered in the pocket of his veterinary blazer. "I need to know why one of their so-called Elders has been spending time with the wonder workers."

"Do you have any suspicions why she would have been there, Sire? Although my knowledge is sparse about the magic realm, I am aware that the two organisations do not associate with each other."

"The magic types are meddlers Aazar, much like the Order, or the League of Light, as they call themselves." Duat smiled viciously. "The pathetic power of light over darkness. But you are correct, they do not associate and haven't in a very long time. Although there are numerous magic orders in the world, they all come together as a group when necessary. Although some groups have different perspectives and approaches, they are all in agreement that our reality exists."

"Should we fear them, Master?"

Duat wiped drool away with a smirk. "No, but your question is reasonable to the unwise. Their focus is here, Bellator, in this place. They immerse themselves with their potions, spell making, and wielding wands." Duat wiped his chin as he laughed. "They conceal themselves from the people around them yet seek to exert influence in this world. They live in plain sight but out of media and social influence. For the public, there is a denial they even exist! There is, however, another term for those who live in such a manner."

Bellator glanced at Aazar. Aazar slightly shook his head, not knowing the answer. "Outcasts."

Duat gazed up and down the dimly lit passageway, ensuring that there was no one in sight. "No, Bellator, we do not fear them. The others, however, the Order, are a different story," Duat whispered, leaning in towards Bellator. "They are driven by fear." He rested his head against the cool, ancient bricks of the theatre wall and drew in a deep breath. "The magics do not interfere, but they can sense unusual seismic activities and monitor the stars, water, earth, and the elements. The Order, on the other hand, has no interest in such matters. They were established with a singular purpose: to destroy us. They are soldiers who consider themselves warriors!" A mischievous grin crept back onto Duat's face. "Their origins trace back to a time in ancient Egypt when the region flourished. It was a land of creation, prosperity, and wisdom. The people worshipped diverse gods, and their beliefs were well-founded. They possessed knowledge of the afterlife, the Duat, and the Gatekeepers. They were aware that a time would come when we would cross over. In their afterlife beliefs, those who failed were consigned to what they termed 'damnation'—a realm of anguish and suffering, adorned with lakes of fire and trees of turquoise. This is why the Order fears the colour turquoise so greatly; it thrives within me for that reason. The intellects of ancient Egypt understood the existence of portals and the transition between our realm and theirs. This knowledge is why the Order bides its time; they are aware of my brothers and I, and they know of our desire to reign here and establish a new realm of living souls under our dominion, not just those who have crossed over into our realm."

"Has it always been an army of women, Sire?"

"That you are unaware of this does not surprise me. Many of their own members do not know the full story, something that time has conveniently forgotten," Duat said, turning to Aazar. "Men have always fought amongst themselves and against one another. They battle for ideals and territory. The first alliance of the Order with the male race didn't persist. These women refused to support the petty ideals of men so they created their own army to ensure my kind could never come to rule. They lived a life of service, hidden from everyone else. Cats were their idols, as it is believed that cats have more than one life. Members of the Order desired to live beyond one human life to ensure that they could provide a continuous defence. Do you understand?"

"I think so, Sire. Did they merge bloodlines?"

Duat nodded, "They did. They alternate between two forms of the living, as a feline and in the female form. That is why the cats, from their unique bloodline, are overly independent. They alternate their lives until their time is no more until they cannot live any further."

Bellator rubbed at his wounds to try and soothe his pain. "Master, how many lives do they have?"

"Nine human lives and nine feline lives. They alternate between the two until they are done. They are present in this place for a long time, compared to a standard human life term. Occasionally there is one with tainted blood. That one remains in human form and lives her nine human-length lives in one. Irrespective, they are all female."

Bellator knew that something hadn't been answered. "Master, I must ask, what are we?"

Aazar leaned forward, eager to hear what the Gatekeeper had to say.

"You were the failures."

Aazar and Bellator glanced at each other.

"Don't you see? A very long time ago, bloodlines were tampered with as they strived to perfect their creation. You are the original casts, the unintended results of their scientific meddling. They labelled you as Watchers, but you were never meant to be, merely a byproduct of their interference. They falsely believe that you carry tainted blood when, in fact, you possess purity. United with my kind, your purity will be their downfall. They eventually succeeded in their experiments and gained their nine lives," Duat pointed at them, "you both gained something that was never part of their plans; you have eternal life."

Duat grinned as Aazar and Bellator locked eyes, "that is, until you are struck down, of course. Your bodies are as frail as theirs."

Bellator scratched at his skull, remembering nothing but Loxley and not knowing how long he had lived.

"They had spent hundreds of years trying to establish what they considered to be the ideal bloodline They were so focused on their preparations to fight my kind that they abandoned and imprisoned you. As a result, many of you rebelled, fought back, escaped, and now you roam, yearning to be reunited. For this reason, they hunt you, imprison you, torment you, and attempt to control you. Serving me and my brothers in this new realm is your genuine purpose."

Bellator and Aazar bowed their heads in thought.

"They brought you into existence only to abandon you. Your intelligence surpassed theirs, and as time passed, your very form evolved. That's why you possess an all-seeing eye. But both of you are unaware of how to harness its power. You've wandered for far too long, your memories and principles fading into obscurity."

Aazar turned as the sounds of footsteps echoed down the passageway. They could not stay here for much longer. "Sire, what is the plan?" he inquired.

Duat rose to his feet as a stranger approached them. "Not far from here lies an ancient portal from the last time one of my brothers crossed. The portal cannot open, but we can communicate through it. We must locate it so I can contact my Master. We will request assistance, crush the magic house, and then turn our focus to the Elder that lives in this town."

Chapter Fifteen:
A HOTEL FOR ELDERS

"So, do you know about this Madam Curator?"

Nubia gave the slightest of nods.

"I'm not aware of the full complexities regarding the dark colour, but I know it's something to be alarmed about."

"We are worried, Suzanna, but the matter has already been brought to my attention."

Suzanna was taken aback by Nubia's response and once again felt intimidated by the small but formidable lady.

"I understand you want to learn, but you've arrived at a busy time."

Suzanna nodded, apart from the unformed ladies outside, she hadn't seen anyone else to earn the tag *'a busy time.'*

"Come with me, this room is for contemplation, not questions and answers," Nubia added, suggesting that Suzanna needed to follow. They both stepped into the corridor of unticking clocks, with Nubia a few paces ahead. During her previous visit, Suzanna caught a glimpse of the tapestry she had wanted to study. Nubia stopped abruptly and turned to face Suzanna. The door of the library (come weapons room) slammed shut, followed by two other doors that had been open, causing a resounding echo; Nubia gave a brief smile, turned around and quickened her pace. Suzanna looked around her; her hands shook slightly with adrenaline. *How does she do that?* she considered and quickened up her pace. Without a chance to study the tapestry, they turned into the long walk. Suzanna spotted the central lobby up ahead, where uniformed guards were moving about. The damage was obvious from this point. Struggling to keep up with Nubia, Suzanna found the courage to ask, "Madam, Nubia."

Nubia maintained her pace. "What is it?"

"I'm sorry, my Lady, but I must ask, what has happened here? The lobby and entrance didn't look like this a few days ago."

Nubia stopped abruptly and turned to face Suzanna, making her feel uneasy under her piercing stare. "Why do you avoid eye contact?" Nubia inquired, stepping closer.

"Erm, it's just...I've always been like that. I cannot explain," Suzanna replied nervously.

One of Nubia's eyebrows rose. "That's an unusual gift to have. It must mean something. I suppose we'll find out in time."

Suzanna tried to focus on Nubia but struggled.

"Gas explosion."

"I'm sorry, what was that, my Lady?" Suzanna asked, blinking a few times.

"Gas explosion. You should have seen it, I saw it, quite something. Still, no harm done. Repairs will be underway shortly." With a succinct smile, she turned around and resumed her quick walk. "I have an urgent meeting to get to."

As they passed two intimidating uniformed guards standing next to the lift shaft, both guards nodded at Nubia, who did not reciprocate. Suzanna avoided their eyes but couldn't hide her disbelief upon seeing the damaged gaping lift shaft absent of the lift itself.

Stepping into the central lobby, Suzanna froze and gasped as she saw the full extent of the damage caused by the gas explosion. The balcony on the right-hand side had collapsed, and the walls were covered in black patches where flames had done their worst. Charred picture frames were missing their canvasses, and the beautiful chandeliers she had seen before were gone.

"Suzanna!"

She looked over at Nubia in shock.

"Like I say, a gas blast."

Suzanna nodded; she had no words.

"Go over there and speak to the Clerics; they will point you in the right direction. I need to go," Nubia instructed.

"Madam Curator, before you go, may I ask," Suzanna took a few paces forward to be out of earshot, "who are those, the ones wearing the uniforms?"

"Well, they are security obviously, what else do you think they are doing?"

"I guessed that my Lady, but…they look very intimidating."

"Well of course they do. They are security! Besides, you've seen them before." Nubia nodded, noticing Suzanna's perplexed expression, "At the gatherings, there is always security present."

Suzanna glanced around the central lobby; she counted seven of them. She had seen security at the gatherings before, but they had never dressed like this.

"I would keep an eye on you a little longer, but I must be elsewhere. Go see the Clerics."

Suzanna noticed four white-robed figures sitting at the further side of the lobby.

"Your shoes are more practical this time, I notice," Nubia nodded.

Watching Nubia start to make her way up the steps, Suzanna felt that was about as good a compliment as she was going to get.

Feeling alone she casually turned around and noticed security watching her every move. On the right-hand side, not far from where the entrance doors had been, there was an alcove with a gate resting against a wall. The path of the fire and the deep markings with small craters around them were obvious. Quite perplexed, she turned back to look up the stairs and saw Nubia still heading up, watching as she climbed. Nubia pointed in the direction of the Clerics. Suzanna smiled, nodded, and slowly headed towards their desk.

As Nubia disappeared, Suzanna paused and glanced up the stairs again. The walls on the first floor were adorned with similar markings and, in some areas seemed to have sustained more severe damage. Suzanna placed her hands on her hips, unable to comprehend what she was seeing. It couldn't have been a fire that caused this amount of destruction. It seemed more like the aftermath of a weapons fight.

✣✣✣✣✣

Taking the batteries from her pocket, Mildred grabbed the clock from the wall. "Right then," feeling confident that she had checked this before. Had she really made such a simple mistake? Her clock required two batteries. After removing the plastic cover, the instructions for how to insert the batteries were clear. "Okay, so that's the positive end, and that's the negative end." She placed both batteries into the clock and held it up—nothing! Bringing the clock to her ear, she couldn't hear a thing. Frowning, she shook the clock and double-checked that she had inserted the batteries correctly. She put one hand on her hip, shook the clock one last time, and finally gave up. "I must need a new clock; it's strange that it would stop working like that."

"Oh well, not to worry. Okie dokie then, it's feeding time." Mildred turned the carrier bag of shopping upside down, spilling the contents across the kitchen table. "So, aubergine and shrimp surprise it is! Aren't you all lucky?" Nahla and the unnamed kitten were on the sofa. "It's nearly your last meal here, little one. Tomorrow I'm going to have to deliver you to your new cat mum. Do you fancy some fish paste, Nahla?"

Nahla bowed her head slightly as if trying to hide, and Mildred laughed. "Oh, come on, you know you love fish paste. Speaking of which…" She opened the fridge door quickly, and the strong smell of fish paste instantly hit her. "Cor… blimey…" Mildred flapped her hands to disperse the smell, feeling as if the stale sandwiches were launching a fish paste attack. "Ofttt, honestly," she muttered. Grabbing the plates, she quickly made her way to the front door. Stacking the plates on top of each other, she opened the front door and quickly closed it behind her. "What am I going to do with these? They can't go to waste."

The garden was a tangled mass of overgrown weeds. As she walked through them, she tried to avoid being stung by nettles. Peeking her head over the bushes, she looked to see if Mr Jenkins was in his garden next door. It would be a neighbourly gesture to offer him some sandwiches. However, she couldn't spot him; *he must be at work*, she thought. *Oh well, it's the thought that counts.*

"Oh, hey there!" she said to a woodpigeon perched in her tree. "Are you hungry?" She shuffled down the weed-strewn path toward the gate, placed the plates on the ground, and looked up with a smile. "I've got a treat for you!"

Grabbing four sandwiches, she held them up triumphantly. "Come on then, help yourself—no charge!" Mildred giggled to herself, but the pigeon remained unmoved, just staring at her. "Not to worry, I'll pass them up to you."

The branch above was at least ten feet high. The first sandwich she threw went far too high and got stuck in the tree somewhere. The second didn't fare much better. "Oh, come on," she urged as the pigeon continued to stare while sandwiches flew past its head. "That's odd; birds love pastes, don't they?"

"You need to add this to the report," Ana said as she filmed from behind the net curtains in the house across the street.

Soad yawned. "Why? Seriously, what is she up to this time?"

"It looks like she's throwing sandwiches up a tree!"

"All right, I'll tell you what I'll do. I'll leave them on the wall, and when you and your friends are ready, you can help yourself."

Plates were spread out on the garden wall and she went back to the kitchen, relieved to be free of them. She opened the kitchen windows to address the overwhelming fishy stink.

Mildred clasped her hands together and said, "All right, it's feeding time. Comet! Where are you hiding, Comet?" As she gathered up the feeding bowls and took a tin of cat food from the larder, she attempted to unscrew Mr Franks' innovative new fish paste creations. "Whoa, this is difficult." Mildred's face flushed as she struggled to turn the opening of the glass container with the tight lid between her thighs. She released her grip, took a breath, and started flexing the fingers of her right hand.

"Really, why do they make things so difficult?" Mildred pressed down on the cap, "Oh, come on, will you!" She gritted her teeth as she turned the cap as glass fragments from the bottle's top flew across the kitchen. Her right hand was instantly splintered by the glass, "Aww!" she shook at her hand, but the strength she felt was overwhelming.

Mildred placed the broken jar of fish paste on the table and examined her hand; trickles of blood were running down from five small cuts. "Oh, what have I done now?" she exclaimed. Reaching for the sideboard, she tore off a section of kitchen roll. Gently, she dabbed her fingers, watching the small amount of blood absorb into the paper.

Just then, Comet appeared in the kitchen doorway. "Oh, there you are, Comet! All I wanted to do was feed you and look what I've done. I had some new fish…" As Mildred pulled the kitchen roll away from her hand, she flexed her fingers in shock—the cuts had vanished. Turning her hand over back and forth, she continued to flex her fingers repeatedly. "How can that be?"

She glanced at Comet, who was staring back at her with her tail swaying from side to side.

In the scarred central lobby, the aftermath of the 'gas explosion' was far more devastating than Nubia had led her to believe. She had merely shrugged it off, but even to Suzanna's untrained eyes, this would take a long time to repair, if it was repairable at all.

The Clerics were seated directly in front of her, she had never seen them closely before. The last time she was here, she had felt an instant chill in their presence.

Adjusting her jacket and smoothing out any creases, she gulped and walked toward the white-robed figures. They appeared to be busy with something unseen behind a large oak desk, their movements suggesting they were typing on computers. Six of them were seated in a line, their cloaks immaculate, each adorned with a stark black symbol intricately embroidered at the top of their hoods. If possible, Suzanna wanted to study the symbol to understand its meaning.

Not more than a meter away from the Clerics' desk, a chill ran through her as if she had dipped her toe into a bucket of ice water. She instinctively tried to pull her jacket tighter for warmth, but it made little difference as she reached the desk.

For what seemed like an eternity, she stood there, and not even one of the robed figures acknowledged her or looked up. She looked around uncomfortably for support, but there was none, so she turned around again and saw the palest face she had ever seen staring at her. Suzanna couldn't help but cry out a small scream of shock. The Cleric's eyes and lips were pale; from under the hood, small strands of the whitest hair fell down the sides of the face. The Cleric looked like it had just stepped from a freezer, barely alive at best.

Suzanna's hands trembled with fear, her scream having alerted the others. Six startled pale faces stared at her, and as she glanced around, movements from the top of the stairs drew her attention. Two uniformed guards were looking in her direction, their expressions unreadable.

Coughing slightly under her breath, Suzanna managed to say, "Oh, hi, how are you? Do you speak English?" Anxiety caused her to shake her head, then added, "Or do you speak at all?"

The Cleric she addressed looked at the colleagues on either side, their expressions reflected confusion and disapproval. The Cleric returned her attention to Suzanna, her voice calm yet authoritative, "We speak many languages, Lady Suzanna. Do you have a preferred language?"

Surprised and a bit shaken, Suzanna instinctively took a step back. The Cleric spoke perfectly, and the tone of voice suggested she might be female.

Not wanting to meet their eyes any longer, Suzanna looked down and pretended to kick a stray piece of debris on the floor. "You know my name?" she asked quietly, her voice wavering.

"Of course, my Lady. You were identified upon entry."

Suzanna nodded slowly, piecing together what the drone was for.

"Madam Nubia said you could…"

Suzanna couldn't face them; their presence unsettled her. Instead, she pretended to kick something else on the floor. "…point me in the right direction, thank you."

"Yes, my Lady, I can assist you with that. Will you be staying with us for long?"

"Oh, I hadn't considered that. Is this place like a hotel for Elders? Is there room service or…?"

"No."

Suzanna's words faltered, interrupted mid-sentence.

"It's protocol for us to know, Lady Suzanna."

"I see. By the way, may I ask," Suzanna leaned against the desk, carefully avoiding their eyes. She lowered her voice to a near whisper,

"What happened here? It looks like something serious." She noticed two of the other Clerics look up at her question. The Cleric she was addressing lifted a finger to confer with her colleague beside her. The fingernail was pale and incredibly long, and their conversation remained unheard.

After a moment, the hand withdrew, and the Cleric looked back at Suzanna. "It was a gas explosion—very unfortunate, my Lady."

"A gas explosion…" Suzanna repeated, intrigued.

"The architects are on their way as we speak, my Lady."

Suzanna nodded. "Well, good. Very good. Good job. I'm glad to hear that!"

The Cleric glanced at her colleague again.

Suzanna realised she had no idea what she was talking about, and it was clear the Clerics had figured that out too.

"Other than the direction you need to head, is there anything else, my Lady?"

Suzanna glanced around, aware that security was watching her, but they couldn't hear her words. She casually nodded to her left. "Those marks on the walls and up the stairs don't look like a gas explosion to me. Did something else cause that?"

The Cleric didn't need to confer this time. "Information such as that is for Level Five Elders and above. You are a Level Six, my Lady; therefore, that information is off-limits to you."

The Cleric stood up. "Come, follow me, my Lady. We are to head down the corridor behind us."

Suzanna was itching to ask more questions, including what the symbol on their gowns meant, but she could tell that would have to wait for another time. As the Cleric moved toward the corridor behind the main desk, Suzanna heard voices behind her. She couldn't make out the words but caught sight of a huge woman stepping out from an area to the side, accompanied by a dark-suited lady.

"Excuse me," she said. "I'm sorry, but what should I call you?"

"You don't call us anything, my Lady. We are Clerics."

"Oh, okay. So just 'Cleric' then?"

The Cleric nodded.

"Okay, then Cleric, who are they over there?" Suzanna inquired, nodding toward the right. "She's enormous compared to me."

"That is Lady Raysmau, my Lady. She is speaking with the Reeve."

"The Reeve? Who is that?"

"I suspect you will learn in time, my Lady. But for now, if you would like to follow me..."

Suzanna nodded a couple of times. Both ladies she had seen looked to be very intimidating.

✠✠✠✠

MILDRED'S HOUSE - THE FOLLOWING MORNING

Mildred let out a huge yawn, stretching her arms as she sank back into the softness of her well-worn bed. Blinking repeatedly and dabbing at her eyes, she knew she had to get up. The morning birdsong told her more about the time of day than her clock, with Mr Frank's useless batteries.

Rubbing her forehead, she realised it was the first night in a while that she had slept through without any bad dreams. That was something to be thankful for.

Noticing the absence of cats at the end of her bed reminded her that today was the day she would have one less cat in the house. She needed to visit the new lady. With a sigh, she tucked her legs under the duvet, pulling her knees tightly into her chest. She didn't want to say goodbye to the new kitten, but she sensed there would be problems if she didn't. What on earth was she going to say?

Recalling when Daphne arrived at her home, she remembered it being one of the strangest experiences of her life—well, up until that point. Receiving Nahla was a lovely gift, but being invited (or rather told) to join the 'local cat club' sounded like fun. There was much that went unsaid.

With a tug at her tangled auburn hair, she began to mentally rehearse what she would say to the new lady. What if she didn't want the kitten after all? That would be okay; at least she would have tried. Mildred smiled, hoping for that outcome, even as she worried about how awkward it would be knocking on a stranger's door.

"Nahla… Nahla, where are you?" Mildred called out as she tossed back the covers and slid out of bed and made her way to the top of the stairs. "Nahla?"

Yawning, she descended the stairs and entered the front room. "Anyone around?"

The sofa was empty, the cushions undisturbed, and everything seemed unusually quiet. Moving into the kitchen, she needed to check that the cat flap was securely fastened. It was, but an overpowering fishy smell still lingered in the air. Frowning, she wrestled with the old window latch to allow some fresh air in.

Mildred opened the larder and removed a tin of cat food, yawning as she called out, "Come on, it's feeding time! Where are you all? I guess I don't need to bang the tin for you. You're all in here somewhere. Come on now."

Holding the tin and a fork, she crouched down, searching every nook and cranny of the kitchen. "Mmm…" Without the ticking of the clock in her front room, the house felt peaceful, except for the woodpigeon cooing from the tree at the end of her path. Not a sound could be heard. On her knees in the front room, she set the tin and fork down on the faded carpet.

"Oh, there you are!" A paw was sticking out from under the sofa. Mildred got up. "I don't know why you're ignoring me." She grabbed the sofa and dragged it to the side, revealing both cats. The nameless kitten looked terrified, tightly wrapped against Nahla. Panic was evident in Nahla's eyes, her paws clinging to the kitten.

"Nahla, what's the matter with you both?" Mildred asked, kneeling beside them.

In a state of distress, Mildred stroked Nahla's head. "What's going on, and where is Comet?"

Nahla seemed to appreciate the strokes as Mildred lifted her into her chest. The kitten immediately jumped onto Mildred's knees. "What's wrong, little one? What troubles you?"

As she held Nahla, she could feel her cat shaking. "Tell me, what is it?"

Nahla leaned her head in the direction of the sideboard, where hundreds of bits of paper were strewn across the top. Following Nahla's gaze, Mildred asked, "What is it? What's going on…"

Suddenly, she jumped back in shock, grabbing the kitten and standing up, clutching both cats tightly.

Comet was underneath the sideboard, staring at her, beside a large black rat.

✟✟✟✟

"From what you've shared with me, Sire, it's not far from our current location." Aazar held his phone forward, taking instructions from the navigation app. "May I ask, when we get there, will it be obvious?"

"It's an old portal, long since rendered defunct. There are various closed portals around this planet that can still be used for communication with the right tools, but they are of little use otherwise."

Aazar nodded. "I see. Presumably, people here will be unaware of it; it must be hidden away."

"None of my kind has walked here for hundreds of years. The portal will still be here, but what surrounds it is unknown."

"We are now on Benbow Street, and it should be further up here, Sire."

"Bellator, keep up!"

"Yes, Master." Bellator was not far behind, taking the opportunity to learn more about the people who lived here. A nearby shop window drew him in, displaying posters and cards that caught his attention. He grimaced at the pictures of cats that had misplaced their owners. This shopfront stood apart, cluttered and chaotic, his focus was drawn to a faded sign above the main window: 'Frank's Convenience Store.'

After taking a final look at the cat pictures, he clutched his waist, growled, and quickened his pace to catch up with the others.

"It can't be." Aazar abruptly stopped outside an old building with stained white walls and black beams. While it resembled other properties in the area, this one emanated noise from the inside. Its general appearance was undesirable. "Sire, respectfully, this cannot be correct."

Duat peered through the grimy windows, which were obscured by layers of dust and neglect. Inside, people were gathered in one area, their laughter raucous. A young lady stood behind the counter where most people congregated. Duat scratched his head, his unease growing. "The Futility Public House." He wiped drool away from his mouth after reading the text on the glass.

"Sire, this is one of their drinking establishments. Nothing can be gained from entering here."

"Yes, I am well aware of this."

"However, from what you've described, the indications are that it is somewhere here."

Duat nodded, scanning the grim façade of the building. Its surface was marred with grime and fading paint, a testament to years of neglect. "It is here, I can feel it." He placed his right hand on the wall of the dirty-looking building, closed his eye beneath his glasses, and concentrated.

Aazar turned around. People were passing by on the busy street, and they were attracting attention. Bellator noticed Aazar nodding awkwardly at a few passersby. He followed suit, wiping away his drool between every smile he tried.

Duat angrily removed his hand. "It's no good; the portal is too old. I cannot detect it. We need to be right on top of it for me to have any effect and reopen it."

"Could it be inside or possibly located elsewhere, Master?"

Duat paused to gather his thoughts. "It's possible, Bellator. Over time, landscapes change; humans destroy the natural land and build their monstrosities upon it. This is one such place. We have no choice; we must proceed carefully."

"Sire! Do you really want to go in there? It's incredibly risky!" Aazar exclaimed.

Duat turned to Aazar sharply. Unnerved, Aazar took a couple of steps back and bowed his head. Flexing the fingers of his right hand, Duat waited until he felt the familiar pulse of energy that coursed through his palm. "We have little choice. The portal is not out here, so it must be in there."

As soon as Duat turned away, Aazar glanced at Bellator with concern, knowing this was a dangerous plan. Any attention from others or law enforcement would distract them from their mission.

"Both of you, come. It looks like we can enter through here." Duat took a few steps to his right and grasped the bar of the revolving door. Unsure at first, he let the first compartment of the door turn before stepping inside. He continued pushing until the door had turned 180 degrees, allowing him to enter the Futility. Aazar hastily followed while Bellator, perplexed, turned a full 360 degrees before finally understanding how the door functioned.

As the three of them entered the pub, all conversation ceased. Every pair of eyes turned to stare at them; they were certainly an unusual sight and the music stopped abruptly. Duat took the lead, heading toward the main area where people were gathered. The sight of three skeletal beings wearing strange glasses—two dressed as vets and one in a formal black suit—did not blend well with the local dress sense.

As they approached the bar, the crowd parted, quickly grabbing their drinks to move out of the way. Duat wiped his mouth, acknowledging the young woman behind the bar, she grimaced as he shook saliva from his hand onto the floor. Aazar stood to Duat's right, menacingly focused on anyone who dared to stare at him, while Bellator lingered nervously behind.

The young lady behind the bar smiled at the locals first before addressing the trio of newcomers. "So, I'm guessing you're not from around here."

A roar of laughter erupted from those gathered at the bar. Beneath his breath, Aazar began to growl. Duat stepped closer to the bar to respond to the young lady who had spoken.

She placed her hands on her hips with amusement. "So, would you like me to address you by your name?"

"You know of me?" Duat sneered, feeling a sense of satisfaction at the recognition.

"Well, yes; it says so on your badge," she said with a cheeky smile. "Shall I call you Sarah?"

Laughter erupted once more as Duat glanced at the badge on his uniform. He ripped it off, reading: *'Castle Hollow Veterinary Practice, My Name Is Sarah, How Can I Help?'*

In fury, Duat tossed the badge across the bar. "SILENCE!"

A brief hush fell over the room before sniggers erupted into collective laughter. Duat turned to Aazar in confusion, knowing he had lived among humans for a very long time, he needed an explanation.

"This insolence is unacceptable." Duat began to flex his fingers.

"No, Sire, don't."

"What did that suited guy just call him?" someone chuckled. The locals were clearly entertained by the afternoon's spectacle.

Aazar moved next to the bar. "Where is it?" he demanded.

The lady behind the bar stopped laughing, noticing the state of his teeth. Aazar opened his mouth, gritting his remaining teeth together. The lady grimaced and took a step back, staring at the large, pulsing vein above the strange glasses the suited man wore. Aazar leaned on the bar, his long fingernails coming into view. "Where is it? I will not ask again!"

She shook her head, becoming increasingly nervous. "What... what are you after?"

"Where is the portal?"

The young lady looked toward the locals for support, but no one dared to intervene as the atmosphere shifted from laughter to concern.

"Did you say 'portal'?"

"Yes," Bellator stepped forward, asserting himself.

The lady shrugged nervously. "I've never heard it called that before, but the toilets are over there." She pointed to the far side of the room, "right next to the Sway."

The suited man and the two veterinarians exchanged glances. Duat nodded, "Then that is where we shall head— to the toilets."

Aazar growled under his breath as they walked past the locals toward the restroom.

"Blimey, those guys must really need the loo!" someone laughed, pointing at one of them reading the sign above the rear exit doors.

"Sire, look at this sign," Aazar exclaimed. *"Danger: entering the cobbled area of the Sway has resulted in multiple injuries when under the influence of alcohol. Enter at your own risk; the management takes no responsibility.'* They are referring to a dangerous place; maybe the portal is out there?"

Duat nodded as Aazar pushed against the heavy exit doors.

"Come, Bellator, it's here somewhere."

✣✣✣✣

"Shoo!" Mildred shouted as she aimlessly kicked her leg in the air. Comet and the large rat were unfazed by her frantic antics as she hurried into the kitchen, quickly placing Nahla and the kitten on the kitchen table. "You both stay there; I've got a broom around here somewhere," she declared, hands firmly placed on her hips, spinning in frantic circles.

The broom hadn't been used in a while, so she couldn't remember where she had last put it. Peeking back into the front room, she noticed the rat had moved from under the sideboard and was sniffing around the faded fabric of the couch, its large brown tail swaying back and forth, completely indifferent to her shouts. Mildred tapped her fingers on the wall, "Out, get out!" she shouted, but the rat showed no intention of leaving. "Comet, why aren't you doing something?"

Frantically, she searched behind the kitchen door, shuffled through the pantry clutter, and behind the bin with its tea-stained wall, feeling her frustration mount. Placing her hands on her forehead, she muttered, "Come on, come on, where—oh yes!" Suddenly, she remembered it might be in the old shed.

Snatching the keys from a wall hook, she raced to the back door. Fumbling with the keys, she finally turned the lock and dashed outside into her densely weed-populated backyard. The back wall was choked in trailing weeds, and stinging nettles had sprung up through the cracks in the broken concrete floor. The shed was overrun with wild rose bushes, nettles, and blackberries.

Putting one foot against the side of the shed for balance, she tugged at the stubborn door that hadn't been opened in years. It finally gave, revealing a broom draped in spider webs. Grabbing it, she raced back into the house, charging like a knight heading into battle. "Come on, OUT!" she yelled with determination.

The rat, sensing the chaos about to unfold, instinctively darted away, running in circles around the sofa. Mildred swung the broom across the old carpet in hot pursuit, sending dust and spider webs flying everywhere. However, she quickly realised that she was no match for the quick-footed rodent. Knowing her efforts were futile, she headed for the front door and propped it open, hoping to guide the rat outside.

Mildred closed the kitchen door to keep Nahla and the kitten from running outside. "Comet, you stay there!" she called out. Comet barely moved, watching her *'protector'* creep towards the rat, which was only a fraction of her size. "And, you stay put," Mildred said, pointing at the well-fed rat. She knew that if she blocked the stairs, there would be few places left to escape. Holding the broom at full extension, she crept towards the stairs. "Right, you! I want you to leave now!" She charged at the rat as it sprinted into the hallway, disappearing into the weeds in the front garden. Using the broom to push the front door closed, Mildred let out a sigh of relief and tossed the broom aside. "Comet, you, okay?" The scarred cat watched as Mildred hurriedly opened the kitchen door. Nahla was sitting on the kitchen table while the kitten bolted out of the room in a panic and sprinted up the stairs. "Nahla, come here." Mildred lifted her cat and, with concern, gave her a big hug and carried her into the front room. "I can't believe it! What was a rat doing in here?" The thought sent shivers down her spine. Surprisingly, Comet didn't seem affected by the incident as Mildred headed upstairs. The kitten, whose real name was yet to be discovered, was hiding behind a pillow on Mildred's bed. Mildred gently placed Nahla on the bed and picked the kitten up, running a hand down her side to calm her. "Your heart's beating quickly—oh, you poor dear." Taking a seat on the edge of the bed, she held the kitten close, wishing that time would stretch indefinitely. The looming farewell later that day felt unbearable, but her mind drifted toward the mystery of how and why a rat had got into her house in the first place; also, what was it doing with Comet?

Chapter Sixteen:
AUDIBLE DEMOLITION

The cobbled area, known affectionately by locals as 'the Sway,' was a patchwork of rough, uneven stones. People had traversed these stones for hundreds of years, wearing them smooth and causing some to sink into the soil below.

Two men ceased their conversation abruptly when the three strangers appeared on the cobbles. With drinks in hand, one nudged the other and whispered to him.

As the three spread out, they scanned the rear of the building. There was a parking area with half of the spaces occupied and an old, crumbling wall to the left, but nothing seemed out of the ordinary.

"Hey, mate!" One of the strangers called out, tapping Bellator on the shoulder. Bellator turned in an instant with annoyance on his face.

"Great, I've been meaning to call my vet about my cat…"

Bellator's expression twisted into a snarl as he bared his jagged, misshapen teeth, hissing, he covered the man's face with spittle. The man wobbled in shock, losing his footing on the uneven cobblestones, and crashed to the ground, his glass shattering as he fell. "What the hell…!" he spluttered, bewildered, his friend lunged forward, grasping him by the arm and pulled him back to his feet.

"Let's get out of here!" they yelled, bolting through the door back into the bar.

Duat nodded at Bellator with some admiration. Bellator, who wore a smug expression, ensured Aazar got to see it.

Duat ran his hand along the wall at the back of the pub, but he couldn't feel anything; nothing was coming to him.

Nearby, the clanging of plates could be heard from an open window of an outbuilding. Whilst inside the pub, the music resumed. Hopefully the locals had forgotten about them.

"I'm not sensing anything, but it must be here," Duat murmured. "Bellator, there's an archway over there. Go investigate for anything unusual, then make your way back to the front. Look for crevices in the walls or any signs that could indicate an opening. It may have been intentionally concealed."

"Yes, Master," Bellator replied.

As Bellator stepped into the direct sunlight, he adjusted his glasses and rubbed at his side. "Master, I'm sorry, but my wounds are still incredibly painful…"

Duat abruptly interrupted him, prodding at his shoulder. "You are free because of me! You escaped the Order's clutches because of me. We are about to embark on greatness."

Bellator bowed his head slightly.

"Your pain is irrelevant!" Duat insisted.

Bellator pressed against his side for support. "Yes, Master." He turned from Duat, hesitantly retreating a few steps towards the archway. As he passed, he noticed Aazar had a wry smile of amusement on his face.

Next to the wall on the left, an old green van sat amidst an array of parked cars. Beyond the cars loomed the backs of several buildings, displaying a variety of architectural styles. When Bellator turned around, he noticed Duat and Aazar engaged in deep conversation. He had no idea what he was supposed to be looking for. 'Anything that could lead to an opening'—what did that mean? Everything around him felt foreign after being imprisoned for so many years.

Frustrated and weary, he moved through the carpark, each step a reminder of his need for support for his wounds. Exiting into the narrow road that wound to the side of the pub, he noticed the high street lay beyond. He reflected on the peculiar shop he had seen earlier. Perhaps it held some pain relief he could use.

Unlike most, Nubia didn't bother to knock; she simply let herself in.

Lady Saffiya's Cleric looked up and said, "Good day, Madam Curator."

Nubia stood in front of the Cleric's desk with her hands behind her back. "The place is in bits; there's not much good about it."

Used to Nubia's abruptness, the Cleric didn't take the bait for comment. "Would you like me to inform the lady of the house that you're here?"

"That would be good, thank you. Or shall I let myself in?"

"She's currently with someone. I'll just check, my Lady."

Nubia frowned and nodded; who *could she possibly be with?*

Aside from the self-portrait of Lady Safiya, there was little to look at as Nubia paced up and down the room. She needed to address the fact that Mildred, *'the protector,'* had the colour of darkness in her veins. Nubia chewed on her lower lip, knowing that the prophesied cat could be for better or worse.

"My Lady, she will see you now."

Nubia nodded and walked through the door that the Cleric held open for her. The last time she was in this room, had been when they had realised that the prophecy had been fully fulfilled.

With Alicia, her Siberian and oldest cat, perched on her lap, Safiya sat in her normal chair. At the foot of her chair were two more of her cats. The other woman, a well-known figure from the past, was the one who caught the eye.

"Nubia! You haven't changed a bit!"

"Well, Armourer, I'm approaching my last cycle, so I am feeling my age."

The Armourer stood and offered her hand.

Nubia took the hand and winced at the firm grip of the robotic hand. The Armourer didn't let go as they sized each other up. "You, however, have changed."

The Armourer laughed. "Safiya, some things haven't changed; the Curator can still be counted on for her bluntness."

Nubia looked at Safiya in shock. "Oh, no, I didn't mean that. Well, in terms of age, there appear to have been some, um, changes in your appearance."

"Oh yes, it's nothing. I've blown myself up a couple of times since I last saw you!" The Armourer's grin felt somewhat misplaced, as if she were owning her injuries. "Innovation, Nubia; it's the only way forward." She released Nubia's hand and returned to her seat. "I seem to recall you are not a great supporter of innovation. Has your view on such matters changed?"

Nubia glanced at Lady Safiya. "No, Armourer, Nubia's methods are still traditional," she said. Safiya smiled as she stroked her cat.

"I don't like computers; not everything…"

"I didn't bring any computers, Curator. However, I think you may like what I have brought!"

Safiya and Nubia exchanged worried glances, their private concerns confirmed by the Armourer's grin.

"Well, I suppose we should begin. Nubia, would you like a seat?" Safiya asked.

"No, thank you, my Lady. I'm happy standing."

"As you wish. As you both know, your presence here, Armourer, is at the behest of the Grand Council. I believe I speak for Nubia when I say we have our reservations. We understand you are here to help, but I sense your presence may upset the balance we have with the Reeve and the Escarrabin."

"Respectfully, Safiya, the Reeve who failed didn't inform you about a creature lurking below. This is the same Reeve who allowed a Gatekeeper to enter Loxley and overpower a Cleric to do its bidding. This Reeve," the Armourer replied.

Nubia grinned a little because, despite her concerns about the Armourer's reputation, regaining some control over security matters could only be advantageous to the Order.

"Armourer, the Reeve is on her way here and can speak for herself, so you can speak to her directly about your concerns."

"And that I will do, Safiya."

Nubia frowned, "Armourer, you ought to use the Lady of the House's correct title when addressing her!"

"Should I now? Don't you need to be a member of the Order to ensure such formalities are followed?"

"You are a member of the Order."

"An outcast one."

Safiya held a hand up, "Nubia, honestly, it doesn't matter."

There was a light knock at the door, "Come." Safiya lowered her hand and resumed cat stroking.

"My Ladies, the Reeve is here."

They all glanced at each other, "Very well, show her in, thank you Cleric."

As she walked in, the Curator eyed the Reeve's suit up and down, even with what was going on, she was still dressed as a banker; she kept that thought to herself for now. The Reeve stopped in the centre of the room, nodded at Lady Safiya, acknowledged the Curator and looked with some concern at the battled-scarred guest. "Good afternoon, my Lady."

"Thank you for coming, Reeve. I appreciate that you've just returned from Spain."

The Reeve nodded, "Yes, my Lady."

"Let me introduce you to the Armourer."

With a fixed smile, the Reeve turned to her right to focus on her potential nemesis. "I had heard of your arrival."

"Good news travels fast, Reeve. That's what they say among the other folk," replied the Armourer.

"Why is your presence here considered good news? The Reeve's, along with our warriors of the Escarrabin, take charge of security-related matters."

"Warriors!" The Armourer rose from her seat, smiling. "Come now, Reeve. None of you are true warriors; you are merely the current mantle of weapons carriers. It's high time the Armourers were reinstated."

"Judging by your extensive self-inflicted injuries, I, along with others, do not share that view."

The Armourer's trench coat opened as she placed her hands behind her back, revealing her sidearms. "Pain is progress; progress is pain, Reeve!"

Perplexed by this statement, the Reeve addressed Lady Safiya with concern. "I'm not even sure that makes any sense."

"It makes perfect sense, Reeve. Now, as I understand it, we have some Watchers to round up. Pray tell, how do you plan to do that?" the Armourer smiled broadly.

Concerned but refusing to be intimidated, the Reeve fixed her eyes squarely upon the Armourer. She stepped closer. "I don't need to remind you, I do not discuss matters of security, even with the Lady of the House."

"Reeve!" The single word spoken by Safiya hung in the air.

The Reeve turned to Safiya, "Yes, my Lady?"

"Reeve, I know this will be uncomfortable for you and your soldiers, but we want you to collaborate with the Armourer, even if only for a short time. The Grand Council has requested it. Please do not make them enforce it."

Finally, the Reeve shifted her focus from the Armourer.

"Until this situation passes, you must agree that we need all the help we can get."

The Reeve turned to her left, glancing behind her. The Curator had been unusually quiet, but the grin on her face suggested she was enjoying the dialogue taking place.

"I will, of course, need to consult with my own Lady; she may need to communicate with other members of our Order."

"Of course, Reeve, and I encourage you to do so," Safiya replied, noticing the Reeve's unhappiness. "But first, could you please answer the Armourer's question?"

The Reeve turned to the Armourer; she appeared eager to speak. Taking a deep breath, the Reeve ran a hand through her hair. "You are probably aware of a foreign entity potentially behind a wall of iron…"

"A foreign entity?!" Nubia interjected, her tone relaying her disbelief at the vague description.

"Yes, Nubia!" The Reeve turned towards her; the Reeve's frustration was evident. "None of us have laid eyes on it; we've only heard it, and as I understand, we haven't heard it again."

"It's okay, Nubia," the Armourer interjected gently, her calm demeanour contrasting with the mounting tension. "I know it's suspected to be the Hydra," she added. The Reeve turned sharply to the Armourer, her eyes narrowing in disbelief. "You don't seem concerned in the slightest!"

The Armourer shrugged. "Everything burns sooner or later."

The Reeve ran a frustrated hand through her hair, stepping back in shock. "I can't believe what I'm hearing, my Lady. This cannot be taken seriously! We are not entertaining this!"

If Nubia were honest, she felt a bit uneasy about the Armourer's brash words.

"Sounds like old snakehead has drifted off back to sleep anyway, so we probably won't have to engage it. Yet." The Armourer shrugged her shoulders as she spoke.

Safiya's cat, Alicia, glanced up as if to nudge the Lady of the House to intervene; common ground was not being found. "Armourer, please, pause for a moment and let the Reeve speak. Reeve, what would you do next in the below?"

Rubbing her tired eyes in disbelief at the Armourer's flippant attitude on how to handle security matters, the Reeve wished she could be anywhere but here. She took a deep breath to calm herself, put her hands on her hips, and turned away, unable to face the Armourer any longer. "My Lady, due to the potential presence of a foreign entity below," she directed her focus back to Safiya, "we must take protective measures with full body armour and breathing apparatus. We'll take our Scatterblades…" The Reeve trailed off, hearing the Armourer's disapproving tut.

The Reeve spun around, "What? Why are you tutting?"

"Well, it's simple really. What do the Watchers fear? What can they not fight against?"

The Reeve sighed. "Yes, we have light grenades; I was just getting to that."

"Well, that's no good, is it?" The Armourer's grin was somewhat patronising. "All that will do is make them run. I've been informed there are many tunnels down there, mostly uncharted and untouched by anyone currently alive." The Armourer glanced at Nubia and shrugged, awkwardly asking the question.

Nubia shook her head. "No, despite my age, I was not aware of much of this; it's the Reeve's doing."

The Reeve turned around, shaking her head in displeasure.

"So, Ladies, we don't want them to run. If they do that, we'll all be down there for weeks."

"We?" The Reeve's voice crackled with incredulity.

"I will be joining you, Reeve, and I will not be playing hide-and-seek like the rest of you."

"Oh really, so what do you propose, Armourer, do you have any experience of such matters?" the Reeve said, crossing her arms.

"Well, to start, I'd bring them to me! No need for pulse weapons, no need for exploding lights, sound penetration will do it, disrupt their brain," she said, grinning as she surveyed the room. "Their heightened senses are beyond ours, well, as far as hearing is concerned anyway," the Armourer said, prodding her skull a few times. "So, BANG!" The Armourer clapped her hands together, "High-pitched audible demolition! They won't run, they can't escape it, they will be drawn to the sound to try and counter it, and that's when you round them up!"

The Reeve's folded arms slid down as her hands went into her pockets in thought.

"You have something like this, Armourer—a device that can draw them out?"

"Oh yes, Safiya. It won't hurt them in any way; it's like a magnet. I switch it on, and they follow. While I think of it, it can't be used anywhere near dogs, suppose it's a daft question, but are there any dogs on the grounds?"

Three members of the Order looked shocked by the question; three cats also appeared confused.

"No, I didn't think so. Anyway, I wouldn't worry about all the faff; that's what I'd do."

"Reeve?" Safiya prompted.

The Reeve was still looking down at the floor. "Yes, my Lady," she replied.

"What are your thoughts?"

The Reeve was thinking that if such technology existed, she had just been made to look foolish. "Well, if the Armourer is certain that such a device will work, I think it's worth a try, my Lady." She avoided looking at the Armourer.

"Great!" The Armourer slapped the Reeve on the shoulder. "I'll meet you downstairs in a bit, I need to change my arm and take a pee anyway."

The three of them watched as the innovative weapons scientist, come danger magnet, opened the door and let herself out.

The Reeve and Nubia looked at Safiya, seeking words of support and guidance. Safiya nodded, "I see what the Grand Council meant when they said she was a bit wayward."

-|--|--|--|-

The cold sensation she felt when near the Clerics was uncomfortable, Suzanna kept her distance as she followed the Cleric up the stairs.

"Lady Suzanna, your office is on the first floor. We usually follow the carpet to the right, but as you can see, we had a mishap—the balustrade collapsed, along with that section of the floor. We must take the longer route."

"Oh yes, the gas explosion," Suzanna replied.

The Cleric continued walking, glancing at Suzanna. "Pardon, my Lady?"

"The gas explosion?" Suzanna clarified.

The Cleric picked up her pace. "We have to take the long way around."

"Yes, you mentioned that. I don't mind, it's wonderful to see more of Loxley, it really is a wonderful building and obviously old. On that point, is the gas problem commonplace? Also, just a thought: can I bring my cats here? I haven't seen any others around."

"Lady Suzanna, your role as cat protector is to be carried out in your home; it does not extend to these grounds. Only the Lady of the House keeps her cats here."

"There is a Lady of the House! May I ask who she is?"

"You will see her occasionally now that you are a Level Six Elder and have achieved your status to be here, my Lady. Her name is Lady

Safiya." The Cleric glanced around again. "And no, we do not have gas problems."

"Oh, okay. Well, I have to say, this incident looks like it was a significant issue."

The Cleric understood that Suzanna didn't believe the explanation about the gas explosion. "I will say this, my Lady: the event was unusual. Loxley is usually a place of contemplation and order. Such events are, shall we say, rare."

Suzanna noticed the Cleric's hands were shaking slightly; she seemed nervous about the subject and clearly wasn't telling the truth. Despite the awkwardness of the conversation, they continued at a steady pace through two corridors, passing multiple doors and stairways. A brief pause came as they entered an expansive quadrangle. Intricate arches soared overhead, corridors branching away from every point. "This place is enormous," Suzanna exclaimed, practically gushing. It was overwhelming, a far cry from her home in Shrewsbury. Surrounded by such historic beauty so expertly crafted, it felt elegant, luxurious, and a little bit intimidating. However, her smile faded as her gaze fell upon a desk manned by several Clerics. There were so many questions pressing at the forefront of her mind. "Excuse me, what is your real name, please?"

The Cleric abruptly halted, her back still turned to Suzanna, unaccustomed to being asked such a question. "I've told you, my Lady, my name is Cleric. That is how you address me and my sisters." The Cleric lowered her hood and turned around. "You only just discovered your real name a couple of days ago, my Lady."

Suzanna flinched as the pale lady took a couple of steps closer, a shiver ran throughout her body. Her pulse quickened as the woman with deathly white skin and eyes moved within touching distance. Suzanna felt a chill as if her core temperature had plummeted, she took a few steps backwards, instantly regretting her question.

The Cleric seized the opportunity to observe Suzanna's attire in closer detail. "Do you have any other questions? I can sense that you are cold and look uncomfortable. Not every Elder possesses that gift."

"I'm sorry," Suzanna stammered, unable to bear the Cleric's stare. "What gift is that?"

"You have the ability to feel, but you cannot see."

Suzanna stepped back further. "What on earth does that mean?"

"You are becoming aware of your connection to us. You feel us. It's a gift; it shows that your senses are attuned to the unseen, despite your lack of vision. This heightened awareness explains why you tend to avoid looking people directly in the eye. To be frank, my Lady, I'm uncertain about the implications of this gift or how it might develop in the future." The Cleric pulled her hood back up and stepped backwards, allowing Suzanna the personal space she needed. "Do you feel more comfortable now?"

Suzanna shook her head, still looking at the floor. "I'm not sure. I don't know what is happening."

"Your reaction is entirely normal. Your status as an Elder and your true name have only just been revealed to you, and this is where the nature and development of your abilities begins, it is very rare for an Elder of a lesser rank to be aware of their abilities. For those who do discover them early, the initial enthusiasm often leads to confusion and uncertainty about how to harness their newfound skills. In some instances, this can have disastrous consequences, though such incidents have decreased in frequency over the years."

Suzanna scratched her head. Now that the Cleric had covered her face and stepped back, she began to feel more at ease. "Please don't think I'm being rude, but I must know: what do you do here?"

"I told you, my Lady—I am a Cleric."

Suzanna nodded. "Yes, I know that, but what do you actually do? There are so many of you."

"We manage administrative details for the League of Light."

"Right," Suzanna said, scratching her head. "Um, okay, how do I word this?" She focused on the Cleric's robe to avoid making eye contact. She noticed how immaculate and pressed the robe was. She couldn't see the Cleric's feet, only her hands. Her fingernails had no pigmentation. "Do you go outside at all? It's just... it looks like you—maybe you don't?"

"No, my Lady, the sun poses a significant threat to us, just as it does to the Watchers."

Suzanna's ears pricked up. "I'd like to know more about them!"

"In due time, you will. I believe we all will, and it may be sooner than you think."

Suzanna flinched. "What does that mean?"

The Cleric turned slightly. "That is above your level, my Lady." The Cleric resumed her pace. "This way; your office is not far from here."

✣✣✣✣

It was now early afternoon. Dressed and trying to put the morning's events behind her, Mildred read the card that had been delivered to her home by persons unknown:

'Daphne, 18 Crosshouses Road, Much Wenlock.'

The pet carrier was ready on the kitchen table, complete with a blanket for the kitten's comfort. Mildred estimated the bus journey would take around thirty minutes or so. Shaking her head in disbelief at what she was about to do—or, more accurately, what she had been told to do—she headed into the front room.

The kitten and Nahla were on the sofa while Comet was sprawled out and seemingly asleep in the single-seater armchair. "Something's not right here, Nahla. Why aren't you all getting along?" Sitting down on the sofa, she cradled the tiny kitten in her hands. Looking into the kitten's young eyes broke her heart at the thought of having to say goodbye so soon. "I don't make the rules; I do have room for you here," she murmured. "I know that Nahla likes you." She glanced at the other chair. "I'm not so sure about that one, though."

Holding the kitten with care, Mildred walked into the kitchen and gently placed her in the open pet carrier. "Nahla, come here and say goodbye. She doesn't live here anymore." Her words were full of emotion. Nahla walked into the kitchen and hopped onto one of the chairs, then onto the table. Nahla peered into the carrier behind the grill. The kitten seemed to say goodbye as Nahla pawed at the grill. "Comet, would you like to say goodbye?"

Comet's eyes were open, but she remained motionless.

"Of course, how thoughtless of me, Comet. I don't even know your real name." Mildred apologised. "Do you understand me?" Mildred gently placed the carrier on the floor in front of the chair. Comet straightened up, bowing her head low, her focus unbroken as she stared at the kitten behind the grill. "There we go, Comet. Go on, say your goodbyes." Comet offered no response as the kitten's hackles raised, trying to hide at the back of the carrier.

"Oh, dear, what could have happened between you two?" Comet didn't take her eyes off the kitten as Mildred lifted the carrier from the floor. "You know, I truly think there's something very strange going on with you, Comet."

The scared kitten lay back down, looking as if she would resume sleeping very soon.

"Come on, Nahla! With the young one away, you deserve a little adventure." It seemed Nahla didn't need any more convincing; she dashed out the moment Mildred opened the front door. Watching Nahla bound into Mr Jenkins' garden, Mildred held the crate aloft, feeling sad about saying goodbye to this beautiful cat. "I truly hope this new girl appreciates you. Remember, if things don't work out, you're always welcome here. You can stay anytime you like."

As Mildred gently closed the front door behind her, she made her way down the path and opened the gate. Glancing to her left, she suspected the bus would be arriving soon, what she hadn't counted on was the boys at the bus stop who were staring at her.

✛✛✛✛

Out of sight of Duat and Aazar, Bellator slipped down the passage and made his way to the main road. Since escaping Loxley, it was his first time alone; now, he had the opportunity to think for himself and master his own actions.

The road was busy, with cars passing by in both directions and people walking along the high street carrying their shopping. Dog walkers were common in the area, but unruly hounds didn't bother him, and there were no cats in sight. As people entered and exited the shops, there was one place that appeared mostly undisturbed: the convenience store he had glanced into before. Looking over his shoulder, he saw that the other two hadn't noticed his disappearance and were not searching for him. As he walked down the road, Bellator glanced through the pub window; a group was gathered around the bar again, laughter and awful music filling the air. The screeching sound of instruments was painful to his ears.

There were people having tea in the Tudor House Café but peering through the dirty windows of the convenience store, he saw no one inside except a man reading something. With a quick turn to look back up the road, he was confident he was not being watched and pushed the door open.

A tinkling noise filled the air as he entered, he immediately looked up in panic, unsure of what the sound meant.

"Oh, it's okay; just my security system!" the man behind the counter said, rocking back and forth with laughter as he adjusted his belt to make his belly hang more comfortably over his trousers.

Bellator stared at the man, unsure of what to do next. He stepped inside the shop and let the door close behind him, causing the bell to ring once more. Fascinated by the noise, he stretched out his arm and began prodding the bell of the 'security system.'

Unseen by Bellator, the man reading looked quite perplexed by the stranger's behaviour. "Are you okay?" he asked.

Bellator released his grip on the bell and looked the man up and down. The man behind the counter looked uncomfortable. Bellator wiped some drool away from his mouth onto the floor.

The man grimaced, "Can I help you with something?"

Bellator shook his head; he suddenly felt out of his depth and nervous in this unfamiliar setting.

To his left, he spotted disorganised shelves overflowing with an array of bizarre products that left him bewildered. The man behind the counter was fixed intently on him as Bellator pretended to examine the items on the shelves. Out of the glare of natural sunlight, he lifted his glasses slightly and picked up a strange-looking object from a shelf. The sound of the rustling bag drew further attention to him. *What was this thing, and what was it for?* He held it up to his face.

"Nope, I don't like them either!" the man behind the counter exclaimed.

Bellator quickly covered his eye and focused on the man speaking to him.

"I sold one a few days ago. Though, you never can tell what people are like, not everything in life is progress," the man said.

Bellator ignored him and read the label, *'children's clown mask.'* What could Duat have possibly meant when he told the Reeve, *'We all wear masks?'* Was this what he meant?

Feeling confused, he dropped the plastic bag to the side and wandered through the maze of the shop. He needed medical supplies for his wounds.

Strange mechanical devices were making noises. He placed his hand inside one of the vibrating units and felt an instant chill, snatching his hand away in shock. He started reading the labels of the oddities inside; there were various tins containing fluids and something called fish paste.

Running out of patience, Bellator knew he had to return before the others noticed he was missing.

Bellator strode over and brought his hands down on the counter with a loud thud. He pointed at the man behind the counter, "You—man specimen. Fix me."

Mr Franks' eyes widened in shock, and as he stepped back, he noticed the stranger's hands were grimy and battered, the fingernails were broken, and his teeth were the worst he had ever seen. The man had poor hygiene standards and the glasses he was wearing were somewhat unusual.

"Well!"

"Well, what?"

"What are you doing, what is your purpose?" questioned Bellator.

The man grimaced as saliva fell upon his newspaper, "I was reading about the sheep diving contest, there are lawsuits in progress, apparently."

Bellator frowned, "What's a sheep?"

The rotund man rocked back and forth with laughter, "That's funny, so what can I do for you?"

"What do they call you man creature?"

Shaking his head with some confusion and with a touch of trepidation, "I own this place, I'm Mr Franks, you see." He lifted a carrier bag, "My name is on it, I'll have to charge you for the bag if you want one; not everything in life…"

"I have sustained injuries from pulse bursts. The Hydra is alive, a wave of fire swept over me and now I have escaped. Soon, I will rule over all of you. Now fix me, I'm short of time."

Mr Franks started to perspire in panic, "Do you need a doctor?"

"I need a vet; the last one was killed."

"A vet has been killed! I've not read about that in the paper" Mr Franks was immediately concerned, "was it locally?"

"Cretin, are you a vet?"

"No, I'm a shopkeeper. But you are?"

Bellator growled and ground his teeth, "What do you mean, imbecile?"

"You are wearing veterinary clothing, are you not a vet?"

Bellator looked himself up and down, "This is the dead vet's clothing."

Mr Franks stepped back further, looking around for a means of escape, "What do you want from me? I've done no harm to you!" His body shook all over.

Bellator rolled up the sleeve of his left arm. The dressing the former vet had applied was damp with blood, "and here," he lifted the tunic exposing his very vascular and thin torso. The bandages barely clung to his body.

Mr Franks nodded, "You need First Aid, wait there." Mr Franks dived from behind the counter and moved as fast as he could to some shelving further down the shop. He quickly returned with a green box with a white cross on it. Ripping open the cellophane, breathing heavily from his exertion, he popped open the box and took out some bandages, plasters and some securing pins. "Here, take these, and wait, hang on," he reached behind for some painkillers, "take these too; instructions are on the side." He immediately stepped back out of arm's reach, his hands shaking profusely.

Bellator gathered up the bandages; he had seen how the vet had applied them before, and this would do for now. Clearing the counter, Bellator filled his pockets.

"Would you like some toothpaste as well?"

Bellator stared at the shopkeeper, "what is that?"

"Nothing, it doesn't matter; please take the bandages free of charge; I'm happy to help." Mr Franks trembled all over as the skeletal man stepped away from the counter. Starting to feel some relief, the non-paying customer was leaving; he froze as the man dressed as a vet stopped and turned towards him, "What, what is it?"

There was a huge vein pulsing down the stranger's forehead. He then walked over to the right and stopped at the greeting cards. He snatched at the card with a black cat on the front and growled. Turning to Mr Franks, he shook his head, turned the card around, placed it back and headed towards the door.

As the shop bell tinkled, Mr Franks rushed to the front door, hastily locking it. As he stared through the glass, he could see the vet heading up the road. Falling against the door, his pulse pounding unsteadily, he turned the shop sign around to say 'Closed'. Placing a hand on his chest, he snatched the door blind closed, "Out of towners." He shook his head and, for the first time in years, decided he was going to take the afternoon off.

※※※※

As Mildred approached the bus stop, she noticed the boys seated there immediately standing up. She recognised the usual troublemakers, along with another boy she didn't recall. Taking a deep breath, she prepared herself for their usual taunts. However, to her surprise, the usual jeering was absent.

As she drew closer, she could see their faces more clearly. She glanced nervously to her left, noticing the motorbike parked outside the friendly neighbour's house, but the rider was nowhere in sight. Something felt different this time. John, usually the ringleader, hid behind one of the other boys. There were five of them in total. Clutching her cat carrier tightly with her right hand, Mildred felt determined not to be a victim of their harassment any longer.

The boys moved aside as she secured the carrier on one of the seats at the bus stop.

"Hello, Mildred," one of them said.

With her back to the group, Mildred closed her eyes, bracing for the familiar sting of unkind words. She paused, but to her astonishment, nothing followed.

She turned to face them. It was clear from their body language that they were nervous. One of the boys already had his skateboard in hand, prepared to leave.

"Who just said hello to me?" Mildred asked.

There was silence.

"What happened to the usual taunts you throw at me? Where are they today?" Mildred didn't realise but they noticed her flexing the fingers of her right hand.

"I said hello, Mildred," said one of the boys.

"Really?" she replied, turning to the boy on her left. "You've never said hello to me before. Why would you today?"

The young man shook his head slightly, clearly nervous. "I wasn't here when it happened, but John told me what you did… what you can do."

"I see…," she responded *(though she didn't)*.

Mildred moved closer to John, who had been the most abusive of them all. "Why do you pick on me?"

John stepped back, ensuring he was out of her reach. The cat lady unnerved him. Mildred positioned herself between John and his friend. John nervously scratched his head, his shaking hand visible to all.

"John, isn't it? That's your name?"

Seeking support from the others, John found none. He nodded and quickly glanced into Mildred's eyes; they were not the scary colour from their last encounter.

"Why do you pick on me? I've done nothing to you," she said, her voice steady with a strength of character she hadn't felt in years or perhaps ever. She moved even closer to the not-so-confident boy.

John glanced again at his friends again. Backup was in short supply as the boy with the skateboard put his board on the ground, ready to make a quick exit.

Mildred leaned in toward John, her face only a few feet away from his, causing his body to shake with fear. "What's the matter, John? Cat got your tongue?"

With that, John took off running as fast as he could. "Something's not right with you, Mildred!" he yelled bravely from a distance.

The skateboard boy was gone, quickly followed by the other two. The last one on the left yelled, "Weirdo!" as he disappeared.

Once the boys were out of sight, Mildred took a deep breath and looked down. She had been flexing her right hand for some reason. Relaxing her hand, she immediately looked up with a smile. They had gotten the message, and soon others would too: she was not someone to be mocked any further.

Chapter Seventeen:
MUCH WENLOCK

Mildred was still smiling as the bus drove past her and turned with a gentle curve at the end of the quiet cul-de-sac. With a swell of anticipation, Mildred picked up the cat carrier. "Here we go," she said, raising the carrier to eye level. Peering inside, she felt a rush of affection for the young kitten. "You know, I'm not an expert, but I think you might just turn out to be a Ragdoll cat. And you know something else? I'm genuinely sad to be saying goodbye to you, even though we barely know each other." She paused for thought, "Something unusual is happening. I feel good and strong. I haven't stood up to anyone in years."

She lowered the kitten, considering what she would say to the stranger she'd be meeting in about half an hour. There was also the small matter that a large rat had been in her house. She needed to check for any gaps leading to the outside when she got back. Rats were a rare sight in her neighbourhood, the occasional glimpse might be caught along the banks of the River Severn, but that was a good couple of miles from her home on Rocke Road.

As the bus approached, the door opened automatically as Mildred stepped on board. "Much Wenlock, please, anywhere along the high street."

"Okie dokie," the driver replied, pressing at his terminal as a ticket printed out. He passed it to Mildred. "Cash or card?"

"Oh, cash, please," Mildred replied, peering into her purse, laden with crumpled receipts and loose change. "I don't bother with cards much."

"Good for you! We need to keep cash flowing," the driver grinned, "everyone uses cards these days, and many places don't take cash anymore—honestly, where's the sense in that?"

Mildred fished a note from her purse and handed it to the driver.

"Up to anything nice with your cat then?" he asked as he fiddled with the change. It was evident he'd had cats on his bus before.

Mildred looked down the bus; it was no wonder he wanted to talk—no one else was on board. "Not especially, just visiting someone."

The driver smiled politely. "Well, Much Wenlock is a pretty place, but so is all of Shropshire if you think about it."

"So, what's his name?" the driver asked, nodding at the cat peering through the carrier grill.

Mildred raised her eyebrows. "It's not a him, it's a her!"

"Oh, I apologise; it was just a turn of phrase." The driver handed Mildred her change.

"Well, some phrases could do with updating," Mildred replied.

The driver nodded politely. "So, what's her name?"

"No clue. I haven't been told her real name yet," Mildred shrugged.

The driver's face was reasonably perplexed as Mildred walked to her seat.

In the rearview mirror, the driver watched the cat lady with the unusual dress sense take a seat. The doors closed, and the bus pulled away in the direction of Much Wenlock.

Drumming her fingers on the Cleric's desk with impatience, the Armourer observed the armed Escarrabin eyeing her every move. They were clustered in small groups on the balconies above as well as at ground level.

"So, how's your day?" she asked.

The nearest Cleric lifted her eyes slightly. The Armourer couldn't help but notice an empty chair in the row of meticulously arranged seats. It had been many years since she had been at Loxley, but one thing remained constant, the presence of Clerics. "Where's the other one?" she inquired.

The Cleric covered her mouth and whispered to the colleague beside her. As they conferred, the Armourer's fingers continued their rhythmic tapping. "You need to have permission to speak to me, don't you?" leaning forward, she was unfazed by the Clerics' white eyes and overly pale skin. "I'm an outcast, you see." She flashed a mischievous smile. "Until today, of course, I was surplus to requirements." She grinned. "So, where is the other one?"

After conferring, the closest Cleric finally spoke, "She is currently guiding a new Lady to her offices here at Loxley, Madam Armourer."

"Do you scare easily, Cleric?" the Armourer asked playfully.

The Cleric exchanged a glance with her colleague, but no further words were shared. "I'm not sure what you mean, Lady Armourer," she replied carefully.

"Ah, it may not have been explained to you yet. I'm not to be addressed as 'Lady' because I'm catless, you see. I'm not entrusted as a protector." She leaned in closer, "more of a destroyer, actually." She winked and turned, hearing heavy footsteps approaching from behind. "Ah, good Raysmau, are we ready to get started?"

Turning back to the Clerics, she drummed her ring-laden fingers on the desktop one last time. "This may get a bit noisy," she grinned, then bent down to collect her backpack from the floor.

"So, I take it you've been informed that I'll be accompanying you," she added, making eye contact with Raysmau.

Raysmau nodded stiffly, adjusting her protective face mask and the layers of body armour that encased her frame.

"That getup looks a tad uncomfortable," the Armourer remarked.

"Do you need body armour, Armourer?"

"No, I'm fine. Shall we take the lift?" She playfully elbowed Raysmau's side. "How many are going down below?"

Raysmau was completely unimpressed by the Armourer's antics. "The Reeve will answer that question. She is on her way."

"I see... Say, have you ever used the sword application of your Scatterblade? It's not bad, just a bit cumbersome for quick swings and blocks."

Raysmau slowly shook her head.

"I see... Oh, look, here she is."

The Reeve, armed with her spear and clad in armour, was making her way down the stairs. At the bottom, she nodded at Raysmau, leaned toward the Clerics, exchanged a few words, and ignored the Armourer to address her head of security.

"Raysmau, ask them to come into the lobby."

"Yes, Ma'am." Raysmau pressed her push-to-talk button. "Control, ask the Sergeant-at-Arms to send them in."

In a matter of seconds, sixteen armed Escarrabin entered the lobby, dressed in full battle armour and wearing facial protectors.

"Wow," the Armourer said, studying their armed support and examining the Reeve from head to toe. "Dressed for battle, then!"

"We are taking no chances, Armourer."

"Me neither." She slung her backpack over her shoulder as the Reeve observed how ill-prepared the Armourer looked.

"I don't understand your wit. You do appreciate the gravity of the situation, don't you?"

"Of course, but stress is bad for your health. I don't want to dwell on it. We will do everything we can."

The Reeve stepped into the Armourer's personal space. Although she was significantly shorter than Raysmau, her height was still imposing compared to the Armourer. "A Gatekeeper has crossed!"

"Yes, Reeve, I do understand this, really, I do, but stress is harmful for the ticker. We all deal with things in different ways. I handle it in a manner that works for me, which does not involve getting intimidated by you—if, indeed, that is what you are trying to do right now."

The Reeve flicked her reinforced nose guard down. "Gather them up, Raysmau," she commanded, her voice steady and authoritative.

Raysmau nodded. "Yes, my Lady."

The Reeve and the Armourer locked eyes in a momentary stalemate.

"You will follow my lead, Armourer," the Reeve declared.

A smirk broke across the Armourer's face as she shrugged, "We'll see."

The Reeve turned, leaving the tension behind as she moved toward Raysmau.

"Ma'am, do we need to take her down?" Raysmau asked.

"Raysmau, I would rather we didn't. We have little choice—for now."

"Yes, Ma'am, understand. Everyone, fall in!" Raysmau shouted.

The Reeve continued, "She claims to possess a device that will summon the Watchers to us. If what she says is true, I must concede that it will be a helpful and time-saving tool." The Reeve stopped speaking as the Armourer drew up beside her.

"Do you wish to address them, Ma'am?" Raysmau inquired.

The Reeve nodded and moved to the front. Holding her spear in her left hand, she placed the blunt end on the floor, pointing the spear tip skyward.

"Right, Escarrabin. I know the events of the last few days have been unprecedented. There are still many courses of action we need to take to defeat this Gatekeeper and the dark forces he represents. That starts today with rounding up the remaining Watchers below. I know many of you feel trepidation about going below again, especially after our losses. However, we must take this course of action, and we are still uncertain how many Watchers are below or what they have been doing."

The Reeve began to walk up and down the line. "As most of you know, we believe there is a wall of iron at the base of the below. We have yet to lay eyes on it, so we must confirm its existence and verify its condition. We know that the Gatekeeper, in Watcher form, went by the name Duat and attempted to breach this wall. We believe, although cannot confirm, is that he ultimately failed."

Raysmau studied the faces of her soldiers; they were nervous. An excursion below was long overdue.

"Recently, strange noises reported by members of the Escarrabin have abruptly ceased. You are all aware of what is speculated to hide behind that wall; its silence conveys one of two things: either it remains confined, or it has either died or withdrawn elsewhere. Given our uncertainty, we are taking no chances. That is why you are clad as you are. Readings and movement detectors will be used."

The Reeve paused; her attention drawn by a cough from behind. "Oh yes, you will see that someone else is joining us. Her attire is different."

The Escarrabin studied the trench coat-wearing, battle-scarred lady.

"This is the Armourer. She is supporting us at the behest of the Grand Council. Apparently, she has technology that may assist us." The Reeve halted, anticipating a witty quip from behind. After a few seconds, no such comment came. "Right, all of you, make your way to the doorway that leads down."

The Escarrabin had seen the Armourer in the lobby and at lunch. Gossip about her spread quickly; she was someone to be feared and was considered a loose cannon. Whether she could help remained to be seen.

Mildred nodded at the driver, "Thank you very much."

It had been a while since she had visited Much Wenlock, but she immediately recognised the characteristics of the buildings. The small town was like Shrewsbury, filled with black timber-framed structures from the Tudor and Georgian periods of history.

As the doors opened, Mildred stepped off the bus into the high street.

"Hope you have a good time with your friend," the driver said.

Mildred smiled politely, doubting that would be the case.

As the bus pulled away, she approached a local information map next to the bus stop. 'Much Wenlock Town Council' was marked above the sun-faded map. Running her finger along the map, she realised it wouldn't take long to find Crosshouses Road. From the 'you are here' marker, she calculated it would be only a few minutes' walk.

In a rarity for England, the weather had truly embraced the word 'summer', with consistent heat and cloudless days. While occasional storms were inevitable the sky appeared clear for the foreseeable future. She adjusted her heavy blue coat, feeling the heat, and lifted her cloche hat to expose her forehead.

Mildred drew a short sigh of relief as she arrived at the foot of Crosshouses Road. She studied an information sign to learn the stone for the houses was sourced locally, and the building construction was in the early twentieth century. The older timber-framed structures were behind her now, predominantly in the centre of the small town. One observation was clear about Crosshouses Road: the houses and gardens were immaculate. Every home looked like a show home, the upkeep of which must have been highly time-consuming. No wonder the town attracted so many tourists.

Mildred stopped abruptly halfway down the road as a realisation struck her. Closing her eyes, she suddenly remembered that she had forgotten the house number where Daphne lived.

Oh no, she thought, her mind racing as she tried to gather her thoughts. She had made the effort to get here and didn't want to have to return, saying goodbye to the kitten had been hard enough. Rubbing her chin in contemplation, she recalled the visit from her Elder – it felt like ages ago. Chances are, Daphne hadn't forgotten Mildred's house number at Rocke Road.

It was the middle of the afternoon, so most people would be at work unless they were retired. True, it was the summer holidays, so parents may be home, but every driveway was filled with cars—except one. She had never driven a car, maybe the new Daphne hadn't either. It was worth a try, so this would be the first house she would check.

The car-less driveway and the surrounding garden were pristine, the garden was manicured. Mildred frowned slightly as she compared it to her own garden—it didn't look as good as this one. Perhaps hers could use a little trimming, but it couldn't be that bad, or Mr Jenkins next door would probably have already commented.

Unclipping the gate, Mildred slowly walked up the driveway, thinking about the words she wanted to say. She hadn't rehearsed a speech, but she knew some important things needed to be expressed. Still, it would likely come out as a jumble of gobbledygook in any case.

Outside the stranger's front door, Mildred lifted the carrier to eye level to look at the beautiful, living ball of fluff inside. "I think you might be home, little one." The kitten blinked at her as Mildred took a deep breath, knocked a few times on the door, and stepped back.

This was undoubtedly one of the strangest things she had ever done. Through the large pane of glass set within the door, she caught glimpses of movement heading toward her. Taking another deep breath, she prepared herself.

A well-dressed woman, probably in her late thirties to early forties, opened the door.

"Good afternoon, my name is Mildred. Are you Daphne…" Mildred's voice faded. The woman before her wore makeup, but her eyeliner had run, and her mascara was in tatters as tears flowed down her face.

"Yes, what do you want?" The lady with a blond bob hastily attempted to wipe away the remnants of her tears from her eyes.

"Oh, I'm so sorry." Mildred felt instantly awkward. "Shall I come back another time?"

Tears continued to stream down the lady's face. "No, I have all the time in the world. What is it? What are you selling?"

"Selling? Oh, no," Mildred stammered and tried her best to smile, finding the situation even more awkward than expected. "I, erm, have a cat for you."

Daphne blinked, her eyes red and puffy from tears, her expression utterly confused. "What?"

"Yes, that's what I said when I was handed a cat."

"Look, this is not a good time for me." Daphne rubbed her eyes vigorously, smudging her mascara further. "I've had some bad news. I don't know what charity you're from, but could you please come back another time or leave me some information?" Daphne started to close the front door, but Mildred assertively stepped forward.

"No, tell me, what has happened?"

"Happened?" Daphne echoed, her voice cracking. She rubbed her eyes, her face marked with black streaks from her makeup. "Look, I'm sure you mean well, but I don't know you. Now, if you don't mind, please come back another time."

Seeing the stranger so upset, Mildred moved closer to the door and gently pushed her left hand against it as it began to close, something dawned on her, this was all too familiar. "Look, I know I'm a stranger to you, and I understand that. But I come bearing good news, I promise. Please, tell me what has happened."

"Can you please remove your hand from my door, or I'll call the police!"

"Just tell me, and then I'll leave, I promise."

Daphne sobbed, "I've just lost my job, okay!"

Mildred nodded and removed her hand from the door as it slammed shut. She placed the carrier gently on the ground, took off her hat, and put her hands on her hips. After stepping a few paces down the pathway, she closed her eyes and tilted her head skyward. Feeling the sun on her forehead, she realised what had happened: they were behind this—the society, this organisation of strangeness. She had lost her job only a day or so before her Elder appeared at her door with a cat; it had all been planned, and they must have been responsible for it!

╬╬╬╬

With his veterinary tunic full of bandages, Bellator slipped quietly back into the passageway of the Futility. He peered around the corner to investigate the cobbled area known as the Sway, where Duat and Aazar were still conversing.

"There you are, Bellator. What have you discovered?" Duat asked.

"Nothing, Master. There isn't anything of note down this passageway. I scanned the front of the building, and nothing is obvious," Bellator replied.

Duat exhaled deeply with frustration and nodded. "Keep out of the way of others; we do not want to attract any more attention than we already have."

Bellator looked away, muttering, "Yes, Master."

"Let's study this area where all the cars are parked; it's here somewhere," Duat continued.

As the three of them moved around the cars, surveying the surrounding walls, Bellator slipped behind a large transit vehicle and pulled up his tunic. The bandages the vet had applied practically fell off. Satisfied that he wasn't being watched, he kicked the blood-stained bandages under the transit. He recalled how the vet cared for him and pulled some gauze from his pocket to try to replicate the actions.

Pressing against his side was still incredibly painful as he applied a singular bandage and wrapped another tightly around his ribs for support. The pain was intense, and he grimaced as the sun beat down on him, worsening his discomfort. Rubbing the sweat from under his glasses, he rolled up the sleeve of his right arm. The burns had improved, but his thin skin appeared to be dying or already dead as he pressed at the blisters.

Just then, a black cat with a white-tipped tail sprinted past him. It jumped onto the bonnet of a van, then onto the van's roof, and finally up onto a high wall. Bellator paused his bandaging, watching the feline move with purpose. The cat's tail was ridged as it gracefully traversed the old, crumbling wall.

Wanting to avoid attracting attention, Bellator slid back behind the transit and moved to the other side, trying to catch Duat's attention. "Master, Master," he whispered, but neither Duat nor Aazar heard him. Out of sight from the cat, he waved and eventually caught Duat's attention, pointing at the wall. Duat stepped forward with interest as Aazar joined him, nodding. "Sire, I've seen this cat before; it's one of them, I know it!"

Duat grinned. "Then it is here for a reason."

They both moved closer, neither caring if they were seen. Bellator emerged from behind the transit as they approached.

The cat, about to leap down from the wall, froze with her hackles raised. All three of them stopped moving.

"Yes, Aazar, it's definitely one of theirs!"

The cat, sensing she was being watched, turned around.

"She knows of us."

The black cat flared her teeth and hissed aggressively.

Duat raised a hand. "Come now, vermin, who were you in your former life?"

The cat stepped forward, her hissing becoming more intense with each pace.

"You don't fear us, do you? But I know you are here for a reason."

They were distracted when a man stumbled through the door behind them. He giggled to himself but froze upon seeing three thin men trying to calm a cat on the high wall next to the kitchen. He broke into laughter. The cat immediately jumped down from the wall and sprinted past them, racing down the passageway that led to the main road.

"Well, that was useless, wasn't it?" the man swayed drunkenly. "That cat's always here but never comes when you call her. We've all tried." He took a sip from the bottle he was holding and leaned against the wall.

"What is wrong with that fool?"

"He's inebriated, Sire. They do it to escape reality."

Completely uninterested, Duat surveyed the wall. "It must be behind here, and the cat knows it." There was no way to climb it; Duat stretched but barely reached the top, and it was insufficient for him to pull himself up.

"You need a ladder for that!" They could hear laughter from a drunken man behind them.

"You know of such a place, man cretin?" Duat asked.

The question elicited further laughter. "Why do you want to look over that wall? Everyone just tosses their rubbish over it!"

Aazar took a few steps forward. "That needn't concern you."

Behind them, Duat began flexing the fingers of his right hand.

The man swayed a couple of times before bursting into more laughter. "That's enough fresh air for me. You're funny, you lot," he said, steadying himself before heading back inside.

Aazar turned and walked back to the wall.

"He'll never know how close he was." Duat stopped flexing the fingers of his right hand, "this is why these imbeciles need leading."

Aazar nodded, "Yes, Sire."

"Is there such a thing as a ladder shop?" Bellator shrugged as he pressed against his ribs.

"I think he was making fun of us," Aazar replied, nodding at Bellator.

"Sire, if you get on my shoulders, I can lift you up."

Duat shook his head. "Let's just get on with it."

Duat balanced himself against the wall while Aazar crouched down, taking Duat's weight on his shoulders. Scrambling to the top of the wall, Duat pulled himself up. The wall was crumbling along the top, making it precarious as Duat sat there. "Come," he said, stretching down to pull Aazar up to him. "Grab my foot, Bellator, and push me."

Bellator did as he was asked, and when they both were at the top, they reached down to drag Bellator up as well. Now all three could see what lay on the other side of the wall.

"Are you sure about this, Sire? What a mess!"

"It must be here; this is where the cat was headed. It's aware of something that we are not." Duat leapt down from the ledge, carefully navigating the shards of broken glass that littered the ground. "Watch your step down here," he warned, his voice low and serious.

Aazar and Bellator followed closely behind him. The area was cluttered with debris—aside from a rusted shopping trolley and a handful of discarded beer kegs, it was nothing more than a typical refuse site devoid of anything valuable or unusual. Suddenly, a clattering noise drifted from the nearby kitchen. Duat crouched near the window, peering through the grime-streaked glass. "It's just machinery inside. Hurry, both of you, come here. We might uncover something hidden behind those overgrown weeds."

Following Duat's lead, Aazar and Bellator crouched beneath the window as he began to tug at the thick strands of ivy. Glancing over his shoulder, a faint grin spread across his face in triumph. "There's definitely an entrance behind here."

The two Watchers exchanged sceptical looks before moving swiftly to join Duat, who had already slipped through the dense foliage. "Come quickly! There's no time to waste," he urged, his voice carrying an eerie echo in the damp, shadowy space they entered. As the ivy coiled shut behind them, they could see Duat inspecting a wall to their right, his expression shifting to one of concentration. He drew closer, removed his glasses, flexed his fingers, and paused expectantly.

A familiar colour began to emanate from his palm, illuminating the area around them. He placed his palm against the wall, nodding approvingly. "There is life here; that cat must have sensed it. I suspect it even felt some form of distress."

Removing his hand from the wall, Duat stepped back with purpose. "You'll recognise this image, Bellator. After all, they kept you in chains for far too long."

Bellator put his glasses in his pocket and moved cautiously toward the dim light, squinting at the markings etched into the surface. Though the scratches were old and barely distinguishable, a sudden realisation washed over him, and he hissed in recognition.

Duat grimaced and spat on the ground in contempt, a smug smile spreading across his lips as he gestured toward the ancient symbol of a cat, reminiscent of the Egyptian sphinx. "Behold the mighty Kat Chamber."

✟✟✟✟

Mildred checked to ensure the kitten was okay before placing the carrier in the shade behind the front wall of Daphne's garden. She needed time to think. Sitting on the wall with her hands on her knees, she leaned forward, bobbing her head as she replayed events from a few years ago in her mind. It was true—she didn't miss her former job, and her friends had distanced themselves from her, or perhaps she had distanced herself from them.

She looked down at her scuffed brown shoes and brought her feet together. They were worn and in a state of disrepair. There was a time when she wore heels not unlike those Jessica had worn the night of the gathering. Mildred scratched her head, mentally correcting herself; Jessica was not actually Jessica anymore—her real name was apparently Suzanna.

Away from the traffic on this quiet road, she inhaled the clean air and tapped her fingers on her knees. After Daphne—her Daphne, not the crying lady in the house behind her—had arrived at her door, something had changed within herself. It was only over the past week that she had truly begun to consider it. Looking at the beautiful gardens lining the road, she realised she was no longer bothered with her own. Her old work clothes had been donated to charity shops, and her makeup was either discarded or out of date, something last Friday night would attest to. She didn't take any pride in her appearance anymore; her old mobile phone had been given away, and she used to have a couple of social media profiles, which might still be floating around in cyberspace.

Her transition into solitary nothingness had begun with the loss of her job, and then Daphne arrived with Missy. What she was doing now was precisely the same, just for the devastated lady in the house behind her this time. If Mildred were to advance up the 'ranks,' whatever that meant, would Daphne behind her, then be doing the exact same thing to someone else?

There was menace at work here; she could feel it. The Kat Chamber sinks its claws into you, pays you, and suddenly your life transforms into a near obsession with protecting cats. Her mind had shut off to everything else happening around her. She had no interest in friendships and no ambition to change her life in any way. *'You were meant to join; your membership was predestined a long time ago,'* Daphne had said. It all made little sense, and now, here she was, sitting on a stranger's wall because she had been instructed to do so.

"Why are you still sitting on my wall?"

Miles away, Mildred hadn't heard the door open behind her. She turned around to find Daphne standing on her doorstep. The tears had stopped, but the traces of makeup smudged by crying were still visible. Daphne's question was passive, her body language calm.

Mildred smiled slightly and nodded a couple of times as her mind scrambled for words that might help her connect with this woman. "It's difficult to explain," she began hesitantly, "but I think I may know why you lost your job."

"Why? Do you know my former employers? Are you involved in this?"

Mildred stood up. "I'm not sure, to be honest."

Daphne frowned.

"Would it be possible for me to have a cup of tea? I'd also like to get this little kitten some water and out of this heat."

✢✢✢✢

"Control, we are starting our descent down the stairs."

Gingerly manoeuvring through the large rupture in the wall, the stone stairs were mostly intact, albeit cracked in places where debris had settled. With face masks secured and Scatterblades raised, the Escarrabin descended to the first floor below, kicking away rubble and fragmented stone as they went. The pulse blast discharged by Bellator had demolished the doorway above with such force that twisted metal fragments had been propelled through the front windows, scattering across the lawn.

"Gamila, status update?"

Gamila held her meter in front of her scanning the surroundings meticulously. "Nothing, Ma'am. Readings are within normal parameters," she reported, her eyes shifting to the motion tracker in her hand. "Zero movement, nothing detected."

"Proceed forward."

As the Escarrabin, Raysmau, and the Reeve reached the first floor below, the Armourer casually drifted up behind them, hands in her pockets.

With weapons primed, the soldiers fanned out, checking every crevice and alcove they could find. The air was cold and silent, eerily quiet, creating a sombre atmosphere as they reflected on their losses and contemplated what lay ahead. The air was thick with the smell of decay; charred remnants from the fireball had left the walls scorched and discoloured.

"Gamila, proceed down. The rest of you, follow."

They collectively moved to the second floor. The artificial lighting was dim and flickering, casting shadows on the walls. The Escarrabin spread out, creating a full three-hundred-and-sixty-degree perimeter.

"Gamila, readings?"

"Nothing, Ma'am. All is eerily quiet. The air is breathable."

"Okay, we need to move further." Raysmau paused, hearing a feigned cough from behind.

"So, you want my help, ladies?"

Raysmau shot a sideways glance at the Reeve, unsure how to respond.

The Reeve sighed and gave a reluctant nod of permission.

"Okay, Armourer, show us what you've got, please."

"Very well, I'm happy to, Raysmau." Taking her hands out of her pockets, she gently placed her backpack on the ground and untied it. "Hang on, there's so much stuffed in here, we don't want anything to go bang, do we!"

The Reeve and Raysmau exchanged worried glances. Curiously, the Reeve lowered her spear to get a closer look at the open pack, but it was quickly shut as two white spheres were presented. The Armourer raised them high for everyone to see.

"Ping-pong balls? You're going to use ping-pong balls?" the Reeve asked her voice a mixture of disbelief and irritation.

"Oh, Reevey, you'll recognise the shells," the Armourer replied with a mischievous glint in her eye, "but what lies within them is unknown to you. Now, I'm just going to head down to the next level and wake the Watchers up a bit."

"Wait a second! You don't know what's down there. At the very least, let us check first."

The Armourer smiled. "I'll be just fine, Reeve. Besides, we know what's down there: Watchers. What are they going to do, dribble on me?" With that, the Armourer made her way to the stairs.

"You're being awfully reckless about this." Raysmau interjected, "They may have united and could attack you."

"Well, if that happens, I trust you'll come to my rescue, Raysmau!" The Armourer called back, "Oh, and girls, cover your ears. There's going to be a bit of a bang at the outset."

The Armourer proceeded down the stairs as Raysmau nodded at Gamila and Alian. "Follow her down." They both nodded, holding their Scatterblades forward and stepped into the darkness below.

At the base of the stairs, Alian flicked the switch on her Scatterblade igniting the torch. The beam of light revealing tunnels leading in several directions.

"Any readings, Escarrabin?" The Armourer walked into the centre of the large chamber.

"No, nothing detected at all, Gamila replied."

"They'll be hiding in the tunnels somewhere, lurking like shadows after what happened. Okay, let's fetch them out." The Armourer gripped one of the ping pong balls and, using her mechanical arm, threw it as far as she could down the dimly lit tunnel in front of her. The ball sailed through the air, bouncing off the walls before disappearing into the darkness. She repeated the action with the tunnel behind her. "That should do the trick."

Taking a device from the inside pocket of her trench coat, she smiled and rattled it for the Escarrabin to see. "Aren't you forgetting something?"

The soldiers looked confused.

"Cover your ears." Without hesitation, the Armourer pressed a button on the device. Instantly, a blinding flash illuminated the chamber, followed by two thunderous bangs that reverberated throughout the underground.

The Escarrabin immediately clutched their ears, and the Armourer followed suit. "Told you!" she laughed as the bangs subsided into echoes below. They lowered their hands from their ears.

"Right, give it a few seconds." They stood, listening to the rumbling of the echo. "Mmm, that's a bit embarrassing. Oh wait, here we go." They instinctively covered their ears as an ear-piercing shrill filled the air. The Escarrabin above were yelling in pain. "Oh, wait, wait, wait…" The Armourer adjusted a dial on the device, and gradually the shrill faded away.

Gamila looked at Alian in shock and then turned to the Armourer, "What the hell was that?"

"Audible technology. We can't hear it now, but they can. Call the others down; it won't be long before they appear."

"Ma'am," Gamila pressed her push-to-talk button. "Please come downstairs."

The Escarrabin began to appear as movements became visible in the tunnels in front and behind them. "You see, Reevey, that's how you do it!"

✢✢✢✢

Daphne's house was immaculate. "Would you like me to take my shoes off?"

Daphne couldn't help but look the stranger up and down; her style of dress was older than her years would suggest. "No, don't worry." It was anyone's guess why she was carrying a cat.

Mildred noticed that Daphne was barefoot, her toenails perfectly manicured and painted.

"Come through here," Daphne said, guiding her into the kitchen. It was enormous compared to Mildred's; everything looked new and sparkling, and everything gleamed with freshness. There was a huge Range cooker, a coffee maker, and even a dishwasher.

"This is very impressive, Daphne. I love your kitchen."

"Are you sure you wouldn't prefer a glass of wine?" Daphne swallowed the remainder of her glass and quickly poured herself another.

"Oh, no, thank you. I don't drink wine anymore; those days are behind me." Mildred gently placed the carrier on the floor and headed toward the open folding doors that led to the back garden. The garden was striking. With her back turned, Mildred smiled slightly and nodded upon noticing the garden table with only one chair—no one else lived here.

"So, you used to drink then?" Daphne asked.

Mildred turned around, "I'm sorry?"

"Drink. You used to have a drink?"

"Oh, erm, I hadn't really thought about it for a while. I used to have a social life, but that seems to have dwindled of late." Mildred smiled, trying to think of what to say next.

"So, what do you know about my work? Do you have anything to do with me losing my job?" Daphne took a gulp of wine. "Losing my career, I guess you could say?"

Mildred nervously glanced at the house owner, who held the wine glass in one hand while her other hand rested on her hip, looking far from impressed. "Err, well, no. It's a little complicated."

"Isn't it always?" Daphne set her wine glass down with a thud and switched on the kettle. "Tea, you said. Do you have a preference?"

"No, thank you—unless you have Earl Grey?"

"I do. Earl Grey it is. I'm guessing you don't want milk?" Daphne noticed the frown on her guest's face, which clearly indicated that the answer was no. "Some people add milk, you know. Who are we to judge?"

"Yes, well…"

"So, tell me—why are you here, and what do you know about my former job?"

Mildred was suddenly distracted by the kettle boiling. "Wow! That's quick. The kettle on my hob takes ages. I even have a mug that reveals a smiling cat when you add hot water!"

Daphne didn't seem impressed; she tapped her fingers impatiently on the table.

"So, yes… erm… right."

"Why are you in my house? Let's start with that."

"I told you, I have a kitten for you! You are going to be her new protector!" Mildred grinned as she shared this exciting news.

Daphne did not reciprocate the enthusiasm. She took another large gulp of wine and rubbed her temple. "I really must stop letting strangers into my house."

"Well, we are strangers right now, Daphne, but I'm going to be your new Elder in the cat club!"

Daphne squinted and shook her head several times before picking up the wine bottle to gauge how much she had drunk.

"I sense your trepidation; I felt the same way when my Elder arrived. She's also named Daphne. I thought she'd escaped from an asylum!" Mildred rocked back and forth with laughter, which quickly faded to silence as she tapped her temple for inspiration. "A few years ago, my Daphne arrived at my door and presented me with my Missy. It was a complete shock, but it turned out to be a wonderful day."

Daphne stared, clearly confused. "I have no idea what you are talking about."

"Missy, my Missy—well, that's not her real name, of course. She's called Nahla now."

There was a momentary silence in the kitchen.

"So, this kitten was delivered to me by the sheriff lady, and apparently, I'm to give her to you. This beautiful kitten is now yours!"

Daphne took a deep breath, shook her head, and removed a tea canister from her cupboard, adding a tea bag to a mug.

"Look, I've lost my job—something you may know about—and you show up, a complete stranger and give me a cat." She poured boiling water over the tea bag.

"Well, yes! Isn't that great news?"

Daphne placed the kettle down with a sigh, her hands resting on her hips.

"I think there might be a misunderstanding. I don't know what happened at your work, but all I do know is that when Daphne showed up at my door, I had recently lost my job as well."

Daphne stirred the tea.

"It all seems very familiar; do you see?" Mildred tried to explain.

"Nope, I'm still clueless about what you're talking about."

"For now. I'm sure it will all become clear in time." Mildred had very little understanding of her own words, she realised this was going to be a difficult sell.

"So, you think I'd like a cat? And if I were to take in said cat…" Daphne removed the tea bag and passed the mug to Mildred, shrugging her shoulders.

"Thank you," Mildred said gratefully, taking the mug. "Well, you will be invited to join the cat club. It's called The Kat Chamber, spelled with a K."

Daphne giggled and took another gulp of wine. "I have no interest in a cat club. Doesn't sound like fun to me."

"Well, it's mandatory—you have to join."

Daphne blinked in shock and then burst out laughing. "Oh, I have to join, do I?" Her laughter grew louder. "You're funny, just what I needed on a day like today."

Mildred took a sip of tea, unsure of what to do next.

Daphne's laughter faded, her expression shifting to concern. "Wait a second, how do you know my name? How do you know where I live?"

Mildred swallowed some more tea. "Oh, that's easy. The Kat Chamber knows where everyone lives, especially those who were predetermined to join."

Daphne put down her wine glass with a thud and began tapping her fingernails on the countertop. Her patience with Mildred was stretching thin.

"Look, would you like to see the kitten? It might help change your mind." Mildred set down her mug and picked up the carrier.

"No! Absolutely not, I wasn't allowed to have pets as a child, and I'm not going to start now."

The carrier was gently placed on the countertop. "You weren't allowed to have pets? Mildred's expression shifted to one of concern."

"No," Daphne shrugged. "What of it? Why do you look so concerned?"

"It's just… I wasn't allowed pets, either. My parents—well, my father mostly, wouldn't allow it."

"Really?" Daphne crossed her arms. "That was the same for me."

The two strangers studied each other, intrigued.

"Do you still speak to your parents Daphne, if you don't mind me asking?"

Daphne shook her head, sadness washing over her as she looked down. "No, I lost them when I had just turned eighteen."

Mildred propped a hand against the countertop to support herself as her heart began to race.

Noticing the shock on Mildred's face, Daphne felt compelled to ask, "What is it?"

"Erm," Mildred stammered, she struggled to run a hand through her hair; the conversation had taken a surprising turn. Her words were softly spoken as she wrestled with her thoughts. "I lost mine not long after I turned eighteen as well."

Daphne's concern deepened as the connection between them became apparent.

"I've never met anyone else who has experienced what I did at such a young age." Mildred shared.

"May I ask how you lost your parents? If it's too personal, I completely understand," Daphne gently asked.

Mildred nodded, taking a deep breath as she recalled the painful memories from her late teens. "No, it's okay… I was here in Shropshire while they were abroad, and there was a terrible event—a hurricane. They didn't make it."

Daphne's eyes widened in horror.

"I couldn't find any information about it in the news. Some female officials visited me at home and told me what had happened. Now that I think about it, I never asked them for identification. I'm not even sure what government department they were from." Mildred continued, her voice shaking slightly as she noticed the troubled expression on Daphne's face. "What's wrong?"

"I lost my parents in exactly the same way," Daphne replied.

Chapter Eighteen:
KNIGHTS OF OLD

"Come towards us!" the Reeve commanded, raising her spear high, its blade glinting ominously in the dim light. Her voice echoed off the cavern walls, resonating with authority. "If you comply, you will not be harmed." As she spoke, more Watchers slinked out from their shadowy hiding places within the dark, damp tunnels, hissing as they drew nearer, their skeletal forms moving with disturbing fluidity.

"Armourer, how long does your audible device last?" the Reeve inquired, shifting her attention to the figure beside her.

The Armourer shrugged her shoulders nonchalantly. "No idea, I've never really timed it. I suppose it works until I press the button on my remote to switch it off again."

"You don't know?" The Reeve pressed, disbelief seeping into her tone.

"Honestly? Not really," the Armourer admitted with a wry grin as she gestured vaguely. "Chemistry, physics, astrology, biology, whatever realm you explore, some elements are always guesswork at the beginning. Trial and error leads to discovery." With that, she straightened up, an air of confidence surrounding her despite the tension in the air. "Besides, there aren't many Watchers in my village to practice on."

The Reeve lifted her nose guard and rubbed her brow in exasperation. "I'll take control of the tunnel in front; you'll cover the rear."

"Yes, Ma'am," Raysmau confirmed.

"Escarrabin, divide! Half with me, half with Raysmau," the Reeve instructed, her voice steady.

With her hands casually returned to her pockets, the Armourer seemed amused. "And what role are you assigning to me?"

"I honestly have no idea if you even know what you're doing," the Reeve retorted.

"Oh, come now, Reeve. What kind of gratitude is that? I've brought these creatures to you." Standing confidently in the centre of the chamber, she watched as the Escarrabin divided to cover the two main tunnels, their movements commanding as they waved their arms and shouted directives to herd the Watchers forward.

The skeletal figures, draped in tattered dark robes, appeared in distress, their elongated fingers dirty and grimy, clutching at their ear sockets with urgency.

Recognising their discomfort, the Reeve raised her voice to reach the Armourer. "Are they in pain?"

The Armourer detached herself from her thoughtful stance, her mechanical arm stiffly trying to scratch her head, betraying a hint of awkwardness. "Well…"

"All of you, round them up!" the Reeve ordered the nearby Escarrabin, her voice firm as she motioned. "Bring them into the centre of the room." She then lowered her spear, stepping closer to the Armourer with a look of resolve. "Well?"

"No, not really," the Armourer replied, her tone thoughtful. "It's more a matter of discomfort, I think. They should only feel pain if they remove their hands from their earholes, I suppose."

"Listen, Armourer. They may be our enemies, and I know what they represent. But they are still living beings. I won't have them harmed unless they turn on us."

The Armourer blinked in surprise, momentarily taken aback. "Well, you seem squeamish. From my limited experience with your predecessor, you don't sound like a Reeve at all."

"All the same, we must keep them here to prevent them from venturing outside. I don't want them to suffer," the Reeve asserted, her voice steady with determination.

"Mmm, intriguing," the Armourer mused, her eyes narrowing thoughtfully. "I don't believe in suffering; none of us do. But I do believe in what is right and wrong. I met your counterpart, the former Reeve. She didn't care for me any more than you seem to, but we spoke enough for me to know she would have had a different view."

"Yes, well, that didn't work out for her," the Reeve muttered under her breath, the weight of her predecessor's fate hanging in the air.

"What was that, Reeve?" the Armourer asked, leaning in with curiosity.

The Reeve shook her head, dismissing the thought. "Doesn't matter. Raysmau! Bring all of them forward, and we'll do a headcount. Gamila, give me a reading."

Gamila glanced at her display, eyes flickering with concentration. "Nothing, Ma'am. No further movements detected in this area. Air is breathable."

The Reeve nodded as the two groups of Escarrabin efficiently rounded up the Watchers, forming a tight circle around them. "Escarrabin, remove your masks!" she commanded, a shadow of authority clouding the room as the air thickened with tension.

They complied with the Reeve's command. "Armourer, please switch off your device; I cannot bear to see the Watchers in any further discomfort."

"If you're certain Reeve, I'll give it a try," the Armourer replied. She removed her control device from her pocket and adjusted the volume.

A high-pitched shrill erupted immediately, shocking everyone as they instinctively clutched their ears. The faces of the Escarrabin and Watchers contorted in pain.

"Sorry! Sorry!" the Armourer shouted, visibly embarrassed, as she frantically pressed the volume control again. A wave of relief washed over her as the noise ceased, plunging the area into a welcome silence. The Escarrabin and Watchers glared at her in anger. "My mistake—I pressed the damn button in the wrong direction," she explained.

Once the disgust had faded from the Reeve's face, she nodded at Raysmau to issue her orders. "Watchers, listen up! Due to recent events, you will all be relocated from the below. You will be housed in the Cleric's residence. Make no mistake, we will cleanse this entire area. If there are any more of you down here, they will be found. Alian, what's the headcount?"

With a nod, Alian began to walk around the inner circle of the Escarrabin, their Scatterblades poised in case of revolt. The Watchers appeared incensed, counting the black robes; many drooled and growled, but not one spoke.

"Thirty-eight Watchers accounted for, Ma'am," Alian reported.

Raysmau nodded. "Yara and Kassia, take the lead. Watchers, follow the Escarrabin and proceed up the stairs into the central lobby."

The Watchers did as instructed, they hissed as they walked, but there was no resistance or fight.

"Escarrabin, six of you remain here."

The Reeve beckoned Raysmau to come to her, "What do you make of this? They're showing no signs of resistance whatsoever."

Raysmau nodded thoughtfully. "I must admit Ma'am, I anticipated some form of pushback from them."

The Reeve narrowed her eyes hearing a voice from behind, "I think the situation is quite clear." The two turned to the Armourer.

The Reeve gritted her teeth. "Please, do share your perspective, Armourer."

The Armourer's smile widened, unperturbed by the tension. "Well, here's my take: a Gatekeeper was present, and he communicated with them. Though he may have concealed his true nature, you can bet they know by now."

"And?"

"And Raysmau, they are confident he'll return to free them. Why resist when they believe their freedom is imminent. They likely know that one among them has already escaped. From what I've heard, the Gatekeeper took flight, Watcher in tow, like a bird escaping from its cage."

"That is true; we both saw what happened," the Reeve agreed.

"I understand, Reeve," the Armourer replied, her tone shifting cautiously. "But I still lack a comprehensive description of this Gatekeeper or any updates on who is investigating his identity. Which gate does he guard?"

"We do not know just yet. There are seniors conducting research as we speak, and our own Clerics are also looking into this."

"Let's hope they come up with a solution soon, Reeve. In the meantime, we need to reach the wall of iron below. We must ensure it is intact and that the Hydra is secured behind it. I'm telling you both that creature is there for a reason. Nothing happens by chance; it's guarding something!"

The weight of their similarities was still settling in.

"I honestly don't know what to say to you, Mildred. You show up here, knowing my name, knowing my address, and we've both experienced similar, harrowing traumas." Daphne picked up her wine glass, thought better of it, and put it back down. "This house is my lifeline; it was the only inheritance I had after my parents passed away."

Mildred nodded slowly. "Yes, it was the same for me."

Daphne's hands trembled as they swept across her face. "Now what am I going to do? I will be financially destitute without this place."

"No, no you won't," Mildred shook her head.

"What do you mean? My work is specialised; it's rare to find anything similar nearby. I'll have to uproot my life and sell," Daphne's voice was barely above a whisper.

"No, you won't. I think that's why I'm here. It's all starting to make sense in a very strange way."

Daphne sighed and stared at the kitchen ceiling. "What could that possibly mean?"

"The cat club will pay you."

Daphne's eyes widened in disbelief, locking onto Mildred's face as shock coursed through her. "What? That makes no sense whatsoever!"

"I know it sounds strange, but that's what happened to me. I was at rock bottom, then I was told to join this club, and suddenly, money started appearing in my bank account every month."

"What! That's absurd."

"I can't blame you for thinking that, Daphne, but it's the truth. I never gave the cat club my bank details; the money just materialised. I never thought to question it until recently…"

"And you think this will happen to me? I just join this cat chamber…"

"Spelled with a K," Mildred interjected.

"Uh, yes, whatever. But I join, I adopt the cat, and suddenly all my financial worries disappear?"

Mildred offered a shrug. "I do understand how bizarre all of this sounds."

"Do you? Oh really?" Daphne's voice was laced with scepticism.

If she were honest, Mildred needed some time to think for herself. "Look, I don't know the kitten's real name, but she is meant to be yours."

"What do you mean, real name?"

"Well, every cat has a name."

"Well, of course they do," Daphne replied with frustration.

Mildred smiled softly, a sense of déjà vu washing over her as she observed the scene unfolding before her; "In time, it will all make sense, probably," she said as she unclipped the carrier and removed the kitten in question. "Here, she's for you." Mildred extended her arms, holding the tiny kitten forward.

Daphne stepped forward with some trepidation. "But she's so small! How can she possibly survive without her mother?"

"To be honest, I don't know the answer to that. Just know that it will be okay…as long as you protect her."

"Protect her?" Daphne echoed with shock.

"Well, yes. You are now a protector of cats. It's a very special role."

Completely bemused, Daphne extended her arms, allowing Mildred to gently place the kitten into her embrace. She cradled the kitten against her own chest. "What sex is she?" Daphne asked, scrutinising the tiny face peering up at her.

"Female; they always are."

Daphne's eyebrows shot up in surprise as she stared into the kitten's eyes.

"Yes, I know. I don't have the answer to that one either." Mildred added with a slight chuckle.

"Look, I don't know about…" Daphne faltered as the kitten's eyes locked onto hers; she felt an immediate connection. "You are very beautiful," she whispered, almost to herself.

"She is beautiful," Mildred agreed, "If I'm honest, it's been very hard for me to part with her." Mildred observed how Daphne's body language changed. She appeared momentarily content, "You see, you were meant for this."

Daphne looked up in complete shock. "She's mine?"

"Yes, for you and only you," Mildred affirmed, taking a sip of her tea, her thoughts drifting toward the questions she longed to pose to her own Elder. With the weight of the recent events pressing on her, she felt an urgency to leave. "So, I'll be off then," she said, rising from her seat.

"What? You must go?"

Mildred smiled. "Yes, you need to get acquainted with each other," she nodded towards the kitten nestled in Daphne's arms.

"But I'm clueless about what to do."

"It will come to you naturally," Mildred reassured her, "At least that's what happened to me." Mildred picked up the carrier and headed for the front door.

"Well, I have more questions! You can't just show up like this and then leave."

"Yes, I can." Mildred replied, "Apparently, it's the way things are done."

Daphne shook her head in disbelief. "So, what happens now?" she asked, glancing down at the tiny bundle in her arms.

Mildred shrugged her shoulders. "We'll be in touch, I guess."

"Erm…"

"I'll see myself out." Mildred took one last look around the immaculate house. "I suspect we'll get to know each other very well, Daphne."

Daphne nodded, her focus was entirely on the kitten.

As Mildred opened Daphne's front door, she turned back around. "Daphne, just one more thing."

Daphne looked up.

"Be careful of those who wear strange glasses."

"What does that possibly mean?"

Mildred took a breath. "I really have no idea."

With that, she closed the door and left.

Daphne immediately went into her front room to watch the oddly dressed lady leave. She glanced down at the new addition to her household and gently stroked the kitten's head. "What on earth do I do now?"

✟✟✟✟

The Clerics hastily retreated from their desk in the central lobby; the sight of so many Watchers congregated in one area was unnerving.

"Alian, please escort the Clerics away from here. It's clear they are frightened. Take them to the refectory, where the others are assembled. I assume the Clerics' residence is now unoccupied?"

"Yes, Madam Raysmau, they've all been moved. They've been relocated. I must mention, though, they are quite unhappy about the abrupt change."

"Duly noted. However, their quarters are shielded from natural light; it's the only place we have other than below. We have little choice. We will find them a more suitable accommodation as soon as circumstances allow."

Alian nodded in understanding. "Yes, my Lady."

The Reeve strode purposefully across the central lobby to join Raysmau. "I never imagined I would witness a day like this"

The Escarrabin, with Scatterblades in hand, formed a circle around their hooded detainees.

"It is a day of days, my Lady. Raysmau confirmed."

"Are the Clerics' quarters secure, Raysmau?"

"They are, Ma'am everything is as planned. I've already designated the guards I want to be stationed there. Once the Watchers are confined within the Clerics' residence, their chances of escape will be minimal."

The Reeve nodded appreciatively. "Good. Look, I want you to join me below as soon as the lobby is clear. The Armourer is still down there; she wants to inspect the wall of iron. I think we should join her. We need to keep a vigilant eye on her."

"Yes, Ma'am, I'll be there as quickly as I can."

"Good. I'll meet you down there. I'll do my best to hold her attention for as long as I can; she's a law unto herself." The Reeve glanced upwards, her focus shifting. "Speaking of which…" She nodded toward the second balcony, where Nubia stood, her eyes studying their every move.

"There are a lot of snakes around, Ma'am," Raysmau noted.

The Reeve grinned. "And we know what we think of those! I'll see you below."

Raysmau nodded as the Reeve quickly headed toward the opening leading to the stone stairs below.

✢✢✢✢

"Right, I'm heading down below," the Armourer declared.

"Wait, Armourer. Raysmau will be joining us as soon as the Watchers are secured," replied the Reeve as she assessed the dimly lit stairs.

The Armourer shot the Reeve a disapproving glare with frustration.

"Look, I understand I can't tell you what to do, but we've been paired together despite having different masters."

"And who do you think I answer to, Reeve? Who is my master?"

"I know you will be reporting to the Grand Council."

"As someone who has been discarded, I will act according to my conscience and what I deem necessary for the greater good. I'll share what I must and no more."

"Regardless, you don't know what you're walking into…" The heavy thud of boots echoing towards them interrupted the tension. "Ah, Raysmau, good. Are the areas secured above?"

"Yes, Ma'am. The area is locked down. I'm not sure what fate awaits the Cleric's residence, though. There's saliva all over the floor already."

The Armourer couldn't help but smile at the grim image. "That's nothing compared to what they'll do to the walls. I suspect we'll see evidence of that down here shortly. So, Reeve, are you ready to proceed?"

The Reeve grimaced slightly and lowered her nose protector.

"I really don't think you'll need to wear all that gear; it looks terribly uncomfortable if you ask me."

Raysmau couldn't agree more with the Armourer's words; her suit of armour had been worn on and off for the best part of two days. She kept this thought to herself.

Gently placing her backpack on her shoulder, the Armourer headed towards the stairs leading down from the second floor into the darkness below.

"How do you even know where you're going? There are tunnels branching in every direction," Raysmau asked.

"I don't, really," the Armourer admitted, her voice steady despite the uncertainty. "I'm just counting on the idea that if we keep heading downward, we'll eventually reach somewhere worth going. These stairs must have been constructed for a purpose." She glanced at the Reeve, a hint of determination in her eyes. "Built by her kind if the stories I've heard are true."

The Reeve shook her head as they both followed the Armourer into the gloom. The flickering lights from the floor above quickly faded. "Not exactly a welcoming sight, is it?" The Armourer leaned to her left, peering into the abyss below, where a sheer drop awaited without a railing to offer any reassurance. "I can't even see where it ends." Halting her descent, she unshouldered her bag, crouched low, and began rummaging through its contents. "Let's see what treasures we can find."

"More ping pong balls?" Raysmau quipped.

The Armourer looked far from impressed by Raysmau's comment. The Reeve's smirk didn't help. "I saved you both a lot of time and effort and don't you forget it. Your size doesn't intimidate me, Raysmau, so quit with your petty remarks." In the low light, she gently removed a variety of unrecognisable devices from her bag. "Oh, here we go." She produced a small sphere, holding it up for them to admire. "This little beauty lasts a lot longer than those light grenades you keep tossing around, I can tell you. Here, Reevy, hold this. Be careful; they can be a little unstable at times."

The Reeve's expression turned apprehensive as she delicately took hold of the sphere, giving a sidelong glance at Raysmau.

"Don't call me that; it's condescending," the Reeve said.

"Reevy? I kind of like it."

"Well, I don't. We may have been put together, but you will show me respect. The Reeves have supported the League of Light for generations. And I'll remind you that you are a guest here. It is not I who made you feel discarded, as you put it; that is from your own doing."

The Armourer smirked. "Well, as you put it like that, I guess we can discuss that another time. But for now, let's see what's below. Pass that to me, Reeve." Her tone was patronising as the Reeve handed the sphere back to her. "Right then, if I push this here..." she muttered, her voice trailing off, a sly smile forming across her lips.

She pressed a button as a series of intricate mechanisms whirred to life within the sphere.

"No flashing lights or a countdown clock?" Raysmau asked, raising a sceptical eyebrow as she observed the scene before her.

The Armourer chuckled, "That's just for films and television, it's all for show, with no practical purpose." With a casual flick of her wrist, she tossed the sphere over her shoulder into the dark abyss below.

"So, should we cover our ears?" Raysmau inquired nervously.

"Oh yes, that would be advisable," the Armourer replied with a teasing tone as if relishing the impending spectacle.

An enormous flash erupted from the depths, the explosion was accompanied by a thunderous roar, a sound so powerful that it seemed to reverberate through their very bones. Instinctively, all three clamped their hands over their ears while the Reeve and Raysmau dropped to the ground in shock, their eyes wide with disbelief.

"Ha ha! Amazing what you can create with fireworks and some of the Armourer's magical ingredients!" she cackled to herself, her laughter barely audible over the overwhelming noise. The deafening boom echoed ominously in the distance, a sound that stretched into the void. After several heartbeats, they gradually lowered their hands, their senses slowly returning to them while the unsettling sound of the explosion lingered in the air.

"Well, if the Hydra is still down there, I'm guessing it heard that!" the Reeve said.

Raysmau nodded in agreement with the Reeve's words.

The three of them peered over the edge. "Wow, it's quite a way down," Raysmau remarked, her voice a whisper as they gazed into the dark abyss.

The orb that the Armourer had casually tossed down below pulsed with scintillating white light, flooding the ancient staircase with an ethereal glow.

"Oh, look!" The Armourer beamed, her eyes sparkling with delight as she pointed at her creation. Red, white, and blue flames erupted in vibrant bursts, spiralling and dancing upward six feet into the air like jubilant fireworks. "Roman candles! I wondered where I had put them."

Raysmau and the Reeve exchanged wary glances.

"How long does your light last?" the Reeve inquired.

Still smiling broadly, the Armourer looked at the Reeve and shrugged. "No idea. Come on, let's go down."

The Reeve took a deep breath as the three of them descended. They quickly discovered that getting a good footing was essential; the stairs were worn, ancient, and slippery from the damp.

"What's that?" Raysmau pointed ahead, her curiosity caught by a feature on the wall further down.

In the shimmering light below, carvings and mysterious shapes glistened with moisture. Whatever the images were, they looked to be very damp.

"Volemon, just as I suspected," the Armourer stated, her voice low but filled with intrigue. She turned to the two soldiers, her gaze sharp and knowing. "You don't know what it is, do you?"

The Reeve and Raysmau exchanged glances, their uncertainty evident; it was clear they were on unfamiliar ground.

"Honestly, you really know very little about who you are dealing with here," the Armourer said, shaking her head in mild disbelief. "It's their language. Let's head down and take a closer look."

They carefully navigated the steps, drawing closer to a collection of symbols etched into the wall. Many of the designs appeared to be stuck there as if pressed into the stone by unseen hands. With gloved fingers, Raysmau reached out, delicately touching one of the damp symbols. "Wouldn't do that if I were you," the Armourer cautioned, her voice tinged with urgency.

The Armourer noticed Raysmau's curiosity as she ignored her previous comments and dabbed a finger at an unfamiliar symbol.

"Raysmau, they secrete it," the Armourer said, her voice tinged with caution.

Raysmau continued to probe, unsure of what the language meant. "Secrete it from what?"

"Secrete it from where, is the question," replied the Armourer, a sly smile forming at the corners of her lips."

Raysmau glanced at the Armourer catching a quirked eyebrow of warning. "Trust me, you don't want to know."

Immediately, Raysmau flinched and pulled her hand away from the wall. The Armourer watched with an amused expression as Raysmau vigorously rubbed her gloved hand against her armour in clear distaste.

"That will need a deep clean afterwards!" The Armourer grinned.

"Disgusting creatures!" Raysmau retorted.

"Are they now, Raysmau? Look at their ingenuity and resourcefulness—an ancient language with depths of meaning, along with much to say."

"How do you possess such knowledge?" The Reeve interjected.

"Well, when you're put to the wayside, you become a hermit and immerse yourself in study. I still have access to certain records, you see. I suspect what I know was not included in your training." The Armourer replied and moved closer to both of them. "The Order and the Reeves keep many secrets from you, you know."

"That's enough, Armourer. Can you decipher it? Do you know what this language says?" Raysmau pressed.

The Armourer peered intently at the wall, shaking her head slowly. "No, no one does." She caught sight of Raysmau sniffing at her glove. "You've heard of the Rosetta Stone, I presume?"

The Reeve nodded, her surprise evident. "Yes, of course."

"Then you understand that before that discovery, Egyptian hieroglyphics were an enigma—an ancient language lost to time. The Rosetta Stone, with its inscriptions in ancient Greek alongside the hieroglyphics, proved vital. It became the key to deciphering a long-forgotten code."

"I'm aware of this," she said.

"But what you don't realise is that the Watchers are remnants from a distant past. They flourished in a time of unrivalled power, yet their existence was never meant to persist."

"Their bloodline is poison!" Raysmau exclaimed.

"Their bloodline was crafted, Raysmau. I don't know much more than that, there are no surviving records to shed light on this mystery, at least that I'm aware of. However, I can tell you this: Egypt once stood as a beacon of greatness. Cats were revered and treated as divine beings. It's likely that someone, or perhaps a coalition of minds, sought to manipulate the very fabric of the nine lives belief. I can't substantiate this theory, but my instincts tell me that the ancient notion of cats possessing nine lives was taken literally. In their primitive attempts at chemistry, scientists and magicians tampered with the essence of life, merging bloodlines, and not all those experiments ended favourably."

"We all know that those of us in our respective Orders have the rare gift of resurrection. That's what sets our bloodlines apart, empowering us to fulfil our duty—to safeguard the realm."

"Yes, Reeve, I understand. But have you never pondered why our bloodlines differ from those around us? While I can't provide evidence, I have a haunting belief that we were also conceived in that ancient cradle of civilisation, akin to the Watchers. The crucial distinction lies in our fate—we perish only to be reborn, transitioning between feline and human forms until we exhaust our nine lives!"

Raysmau and the Reeve exchanged glances.

"You both look surprised. Are you aware of how you return?" The Armourer's voice was steady.

Raysmau nodded.

"But do you know what cycle you are on?" The Armourer continued, "I suspect not, and neither do I. That's why our memories of past lives elude us. Only one among us retains her human form for a full nine life cycles. I'm sure you know who I mean, Reeve?"

The Reeve's mouth opened, partially in surprise. "She talks about memories of old."

The Armourer nodded, a gleam of acknowledgement in her eyes.

Raysmau looked surprised. "Are you talking about Nubia?"

The Reeve confirmed with a slight nod, the dawning realisation evident in her expression. "Yes, I believe we are. I had no idea."

"There is plenty you do not know, Reeve. She is very old; you should show her more respect. Her experiences far exceed your own" The Armourer glanced at the unreadable language. "It's utterly captivating. There's much to admire. It's a shame the Rosetta Stone didn't decipher this language as well." With a sudden shift in focus, she turned to the Reeve. "Say, Reeve, could I have some one-on-one time with a Watcher? We need to learn from them."

The Reeve shook her head firmly. "I don't think that's a good idea. They won't talk to you anyway."

The Armourer shrugged dismissively. "Oh, I can surely encourage them..."

"I'm not comfortable with the idea of you pushing them."

The Armourer's expression shifted to one of incredulity. "I never suggested such a thing! It's the only path to understanding. If we don't grasp our enemy's nature, we'll never conquer them."

"That might be true, but the thought unsettles me."

"Unsettled? Do you know that outside these walls, in the world outside, they experiment on animals and devastate lands in the name of knowledge and power?"

"I don't agree with that either. But for now, the answer is no. Let's focus on checking the wall and see if it's sealed. Raysmau, how are your readings?"

"The air is breathable, Ma'am, nothing untoward."

"Armourer, let's proceed down."

The Armourer, still grappling with her unresolved questions and frustrations, let out a reluctant sigh as she began the descent.

As they moved closer to the bottom, the inscriptions on the walls started to fade. In the centre of the floor, they noticed an old, discarded torch that had long since extinguished. "There's a chamber ahead. I have a feeling we're getting close," the Armourer declared, her voice echoing faintly in the stillness.

Upon reaching the bottom, the Armourer shielded her eyes and hurled a glowing sphere into the chamber. It soared through the air before crashing against the iron surface with a resounding bang, illuminating the space around them with a brilliant flash.

"Wow!" the Armourer exclaimed, genuine awe lighting up her features as she stepped into the chamber. "I must say, Reeve; your predecessors certainly knew how to construct impressive structures."

The Reeve and Raysmau followed cautiously, the air thick with anticipation. Just as they entered, the Reeve reached out taking a firm grip on Raysmau's shoulder. "Wait! Look at that!" she exclaimed, pointing with her spear toward the right wall. There, intricately carved into the stone, was a formidable serpent, its jaws wide open in a silent hiss. "Check the readings!"

Raysmau shook her head. "Readings are clear, Ma'am."

Releasing her grip, the Reeve stepped closer to the serpent, an air of reverence surrounding her. "This is here for a reason. It's the Uraeus."

"So it is," the Armourer mused, her eyes narrowing as she tried to fathom its importance.

"Snakes everywhere," Raysmau muttered under her breath.

The Armourer knelt to examine the serpent more intently, tracing the intricate details with her fingertips. "This is truly fascinating. The serpent is both feared and revered, entwined with the Order and the Reeve's legacy. I suspect this could be a mechanism; look at how unnaturally wide its mouth gapes—it's almost grotesque. I wonder if our friend, the Gatekeeper, disturbed it, which might explain why he failed to enter. Speaking of which, let's assess the integrity of this iron wall."

The Reeve crouched down and noticed a key in a slot. "Raysmau, I suspect this is one of the missing keys."

"There's another one here, Ma'am. It looks like force has been applied to it; it's bent. Should I try and extract it from the keyhole?"

"No, leave it, Raysmau," she cautioned, her stare still fixed on the damaged key. "We now know for sure that he didn't open it."

"Mmm, that's interesting. The damage to the key suggests the Gatekeeper was in a rush; something must have made him panic," the Armourer said, "and I think I know why."

The Reeve had already noticed a circle indentation set into the wall; she knew that the final key was meant to be used there. She instinctively pressed her fingers to her neck, reassuring herself that the final key was still secured on the chain that rested there.

As the Armourer joined her, she lowered herself to inspect the circle more closely. "Something was intended for this spot," she declared, brushing her fingers delicately over the outline of the circle. A gleam of realisation sparked in her eyes. "Yes, I'm certain—there is another key. Look," she exclaimed, rising with renewed energy. "Two keys are inserted, yet there is nothing here. It appears to be a safety mechanism."

The Armourer crossed her arms and nodded, a proud smile spreading across her face. "This mechanism is quite clever. It guarantees that no single person can unlock this wall on their own." She gave the Reeve a hearty clap on the shoulder. "Not bad at all! Pretty clever, right?"

With an air of determination, the Reeve commanded, "Raysmau, channel some of your strength into the area next to the serpent on the right. I'll push against the left side. We need to confirm the integrity of this wall." They parted ways, the Armourer remaining at the centre of the chamber, her eyes scanning the surroundings. "Is that all it takes? If the wall is sturdy, everything is fine?"

"Of course it's not fine, Armourer!" the Reeve retorted, urgency lacing her voice. "There's a Gatekeeper out there, who knows what he's scheming?"

The Armourer raised an eyebrow, a smirk playing on her lips. "I think you may be missing my point, Reeve."

Raysmau and the Reeve propped their weapons against the wall and began pushing and probing in various places.

"What do you mean by that, Armourer?" Raysmau asked.

"Well, both of you must consider the question at hand: why is this structure here in the first place? What did your predecessors foresee that required such fortification, or what secrets are they attempting to keep us from unearthing?"

"I was wondering if there's a beast hidden somewhere beyond this wall. How did it come to be there, and why is it so eerily quiet now? That's what I was thinking," Raysmau responded.

"That's an astute observation, Raysmau. Reeve, do you have anything to add?"

"I know as much as you," she answered, though her voice betrayed a hidden truth; the missing key was still in her possession.

"Well, it's safe to conclude that the Watchers have been effectively rounded up, the Gatekeeper hasn't breached the wall's defences, and the beast that lies beyond it is still subdued. Well done, considering the circumstances," the Armourer said placing her backpack gently on the ground. "Leave that, both of you. You'll be there all day. I came prepared; I have something in my bag."

They both retrieved their weapons and approached the Armourer with interest.

"I hope I have brought enough," she admitted, her eyes scanning the towering wall. "I didn't anticipate it would be this formidable."

"What do you have to ensure the wall's integrity?" the Reeve inquired.

"Oh, here we go, Raysmau," she said, removing a large tube and pulling a plunger from her pack. "It's similar to the device that decorators use, except I created the contents to effectively bind to anything."

The Armourer stood up. "This will take a while. If you both want to wait upstairs, I need to apply my paste along the top of the wall and down the sides. I believe there will be a small gap somewhere, as that serpent statue was intentionally placed there. I think it released something into the air, and if that's the case, it has evaporated or moved through a gap somewhere. We need to seal it. Honestly, both of you should head upstairs; I've got this."

She then removed a tiny detonator from her pack and started tying wires around two prongs attached to the top of the device.

It was obvious that Raysmau and the Reeve were staying put as they exchanged glances before turning back to face the Armourer.

"As you like, but it might take some time, and there will be a loud bang as the putty sets after I light it."

"What is the purpose of the bang?"

"Nothing, I just like it," said the Armourer, shrugging her shoulders.

✟✟✟✟

"Why would someone have taken the time to scratch this onto the wall?" Aazar asked.

"It's a warning," Duat acknowledged.

Aazar pressed, "A warning to whom, Sire?"

Duat's attention shifted to the crude markings, a frown etching his features. "It's difficult to say. The roughness of the scratching suggests it wasn't crafted by human hands. I suspect the local feline creatures can sense the significance of this place. Perhaps one of their blood cats is always nearby to this area." He flexed the fingers of his right hand, the movement deliberate and urgent. "You both take cover in that corner behind me. Stay out of sight. If I can connect with my Master or my kin, I don't want them to see you."

They followed his instructions as the dark room started to glow with a turquoise light.

Using his palm as a torch, Duat held his hand up, scanning every brick and misplaced stone. This wall, he realised, wasn't as old as the one bearing the scratchings. Someone from the past had known of this old portal and attempted to seal it away. Duat took his time, focusing intently, looking for an indentation or any clue from which he could start. Saliva dripped between his misshapen teeth, resembling the closest thing to a smile that a Gatekeeper could manage. "Someone has been busy," he murmured, almost to himself.

"Have you found something, Master?" Bellator asked, his voice full of anticipation.

Duat ignored the question entirely, extending the index finger of his left hand. His elongated fingernail brushed against a tiny red cross etched into the stone. At the touch, the stone shifted, and a deep thud resonated throughout the room. Instinctively, Duat withdrew his finger and took a couple of steps back. The three of them stood in silence for a few seconds, exchanging glances. Duat chose not to look at them, feeling embarrassed that nothing significant had happened. Just as he was about to place his hands on his hips, a thunderous bang echoed from beyond the wall. He stepped back further, hearing the noise of shifting bricks and a creaking pulley system at work. A rumble emanated from above, spraying them with dust and shards of stone. Bellator, startled, staggered backwards toward the fraying streams of ivy while Aazar steadied himself against the side wall as larger pieces of stone fell.

Abruptly, the rumbling ceased. A red glow began to pulse ominously from behind the fractured stone where Duat had pressed. With cautious determination, he edged closer, lifting his left hand in a gesture of command. In response, the wall erupted forward with a cataclysmic crash, sending a plume of dust spiralling into the air. Duat instinctively covered his face, his throat filled with grit as the disturbance emitted a massive cloud that engulfed the small cavern. He waved his hand furiously, desperate to clear the suffocating haze.

As moments stretched into what felt like an eternity, the dust gradually settled. Aazar emerged from beneath the makeshift shelter of his suit jacket, spitting out remnants of debris, while Bellator anxiously adjusted his glasses, peering through the ivy veils to shield his eyes from the harsh sunlight that poured in.

Duat continued to brush away the lingering particles with his left hand, his right hand secure beneath his veterinary tunic. The distant red glow pulsed softly, shrouded in mystery and difficult to judge in proximity. "We have found it!" Duat exclaimed, his voice a mix of exhilaration and disbelief as he swiped at the air, coughing again as he ventured deeper onto the strewn bricks and stones. He revealed his right palm, lifting it toward the passageway that now lay before them. The turquoise light illuminated a circular threshold, its rough edges hinting that it had been excavated long ago. Reluctantly, Duat lowered his palm, allowing the only illumination in the passage to emanate from the distant red glow.

"Sire, is everything okay?" Aazar's voice echoed softly in the dark room.

Duat shook his head. "Something is not right here."

Bellator stepped back into the cavern, wiping at his eye. "What's happening?" he whispered.

"I'm not sure," Aazar responded.

Duat's focus sharpened as he stared down the elongated passageway. A stark red light bathed the walls. He knew he had to act. He raised his palm to light the passage and took a couple of steps forward. Suddenly, he froze, the unmistakable sound of clicking reverberating ominously from both his left and right. Taking a deep breath, he was acutely aware that he didn't want to move a muscle. With his palm still glowing softly, he sprang backwards, barely escaping the wrath of multiple spearheads that erupted from hidden slots in the walls. They shot forth with lethal precision, whizzing past him and narrowly missing his right hand. In a frenzy, Duat stumbled over a crumbled stone, collapsing heavily onto the floor.

"Master!" Bellator and Aazar rushed to assist him, surprised to find him practically laughing. They helped him to his feet, brushing the dust from his clothing.

"What is it, Sire?" Aazar asked, a mix of worry and curiosity in his voice.

Duat shook his head, partially amused but annoyed with himself. "That was just a crude trap," he said. He stepped forward, noticing that there were about thirty spearheads either embedded in the walls or scattered across the floor. With newfound determination, he kicked the tips of the spears aside. "I should have known that I would trigger this device," he continued, his tone now a mixture of irritation as well as realisation as he turned to face the others. "Before the wall collapsed, I heard noises from behind; those were the mechanisms of this ancient weapons system activating. The red cross wasn't just a marker for an entrance, it also served as a trap, and I think I know who is behind this."

Bellator and Aazar exchanged bewildered glances, the identities of the designers of this defensive contraption eluding them.

"They were architects of their time," Duat elaborated, "in fact, it wouldn't surprise me if they still exist in some form, even now. They considered themselves warriors, bankers, and protectors and were in possession of very powerful artefacts." He turned again toward the dark tunnel as the red light slowly faded, plunging the passageway into an eerie pitch black.

Aazar nodded, his expression shifting from confusion to recognition. "I recall them, Sire. They held significant influence in this realm a long time ago."

Duat nodded back at Aazar. "Yes, my friend. The Knights Templar."

Chapter Nineteen:
LAPIS LAZULI

"Well, she's back. I guess she must have just gotten off the bus," Ana said, craning her neck from her vantage point at the window opposite Mildred's house. "I can't quite see the bus stop from here."

"Well, her cat sprinted home some time ago. I don't think I've ever seen a cat move that fast," Ana said as Soad joined her surveillance partner at the net curtain.

"She doesn't look so happy, does she?" Soad observed.

"I think it's obvious why. Just look at the way she's swinging the cat carrier," Ana pointed out.

"Mmm, she must have delivered the newborn. I guess we'll just wait here for the next level of craziness," Soad said.

They both studied the fairly new member of the Kat Chamber, who was dressed in a long coat, a cloche hat, and wrinkled stockings that were visible even from their distance.

"She must be boiling in all that get-up," Soad remarked.

Ana nodded in agreement.

Minus a cat, Mildred meandered back to her modest, somewhat weathered home at number one Rocke Road. Placing the empty cat carrier on her wall, she removed her hat and took a moment to inhale deeply, trying to ground herself after the eventful day. A couple of stray fish paste sandwiches lay scattered under her tree, as well as some caught in its branches. A woodpigeon broke from its melodic cooing to regard Mildred with some curiosity, quickly recalling the last chaotic encounter where she had bombarded it with her culinary rejects.

"Not keen on my offerings, then?" she quipped to the indifferent bird. The woodpigeon remained mute. "Guess not," she conceded with a light chuckle.

With a creak, Mildred pushed open her gate, gathered the empty cat carrier, and kicked the gate shut behind her. A deep, heavy sigh escaped her lips as she opened her front door and was immediately hit with an overwhelming feeling of sadness. With the front door firmly shut, her house had downsized from three cats to two. The loss of the nameless kitten weighed heavily on her heart.

"Come on, where are you, Comet, Nahla?"

With a resigned thump, she dropped the carrier unceremoniously on the worn floor, she tossed her hat aside, kicked her shoes towards the cluttered corner of the room and flopped onto the couch with such force that a cloud of dust shot up into the air.

"Nahla, Comet!" she called again, but the house remained completely silent. "Oh, come on, I've had a long day and probably made a fool of myself in the process. Don't make me get up and start banging the tin for your attention."

Just then, Nahla appeared at the front room window. "Oh, there you are!" Mildred exclaimed, barely able to see her through the dirt-stained glass. "I guess I'll get up then."

She moved towards the front door, checking the cat flap as she went. The old phone book was still propped against it; Comet must be lurking somewhere inside the house. As she opened the front door, Nahla tore past her into the living room.

"Wow, you're eager to get in! What's got you all worked up?" Mildred chuckled, closed the door, and dropped back onto the couch. "What's the matter? Come over here, why do you look so nervous?"

Nahla sprung onto Mildred's lap. "Oh, ha ha, that's a warm welcome! Never seen you do that before. Come on, it's hug time…" Mildred paused, noticing Nahla's expression, her amusement faded. "What's the matter? You look like you've seen a ghost!"

Nahla burrowed into Mildred's coat. "Are you cold, or what are you hiding from?" Mildred wrapped her arms snugly around Nahla. "This isn't good," she murmured, running her hand gently over Nahla's head. Her cat was shaking. "You don't feel cold. What's troubling you?"

Mildred rose from her chair and crouched low, peering beneath the sideboards to locate her missing cat, not to mention the scurrying rat she had spotted earlier.

"Comet, where are you?"

She rechecked the cat flap. "Nahla, have you seen Comet? Is she giving you trouble?" Clutching Nahla tightly, she headed upstairs. "Comet, where are you?"

Upon entering her bedroom, Mildred screamed as a rat dashed out and bolted down the stairs. The sight sent her heart racing, yet a relief washed over her as she spotted Comet perched gracefully on her bed. Mildred trembled, feeling Nahla tense in her grip. "What's going on with you, Comet? Making friends with rats! I'll take care of that in just a moment. Did you somehow invite that little intruder into the house? Come on."

With Nahla cradled in one arm, she reached out and scooped up Comet with the other. "Alright, let's…" Suddenly, a jolt of pain shot through her as her hand brushed against Comet's scar. Her eyes rolled, and she found herself overwhelmed by vivid imagery that shook her mind. This wasn't the same old nightmare; this felt different.

She continued to shake, holding both Comet and Nahla as an unsettling vision unfolded. Three figures hovered in her mind, wearing peculiar glasses; two appeared to be veterinarians, while the third was garbed in a dark suit. Their bodies were unnaturally thin, and their skin nearly translucent. One of them stepped forward, locking eyes with her, yet he didn't reach out or speak. Instead, he was merely a part of a memory that had etched itself into her mind.

The view looked to be from the top of a wall, with surroundings familiar. The name 'The Sway' emerged into focus, a place Mildred hadn't set foot in for years, but she knew it was located at the back of the Futility pub. Suddenly, the viewpoint dropped down, pulling away from the wall at incredible speed, distancing her from the three figures and heading out of the archway of the Futility.

Just as abruptly as it had started, the vision ceased, jarring Mildred back to reality. With wide eyes, she let go of both cats, her heart racing and her breath quickening. As she wiped away the tears that had begun to well, she saw Comet retreat a few steps, her whiskers twitching in confusion. Meanwhile, Nahla, with an unsettling intensity, focused her eyes on Mildred and gave a slow, knowing nod. Anxiety gripped Mildred as she stood there, fraught with apprehension about touching either cat. At that moment, she recognised the glimmer of distress in Nahla's expression, her cat nodding, telling her. It dawned on her that she had just witnessed something through Nahla's eyes.

✤✤✤✤

"Sire, I'm surprised to find any reference to the Templars here,"

Duat nodded.

Aazar stepped forward, studying the fallen arrowheads. "I remember them, but I had no involvement with them. I've never seen or read anything suggesting an association with the League of Light."

Duat nodded again. "A man-based army; it's certainly an enigma."

"They were famed for safeguarding treasures deeply entrenched in their faith, albeit their history is marred with fighting over many years. In later times, they faced persecution and fled to the shadows, a handful survived, yet I've not encountered tales of their presence in this area."

"It's strange, we must be missing something, but we shall set it aside for a moment. Bellator, step forward," Duat commanded, lifting his palm as he focused; the tunnel was relit in shades of turquoise.

Bellator stepped over the arrowheads that littered the ground. "Master, will there be any more of these defensive devices?"

"I don't know, but we must proceed carefully. Aazar, remain vigilant and scan the walls; we can't afford to be caught off guard again."

They ventured cautiously down the narrow tunnel, the faint, flickering light from the cavern behind them gradually dimming with every hesitant step. Bellator tightened his tunic around him, a futile attempt to shield his wounds from the biting chill that seeped through the air. As they descended deeper, the earthy scent of damp stone filled the remnants of their nostrils, and a faint glow began to emerge from an opening further ahead, beckoning them forward.

"I believe we've found it," Duat murmured, "Both of you, exercise extreme caution as we enter this room. There may be traps waiting for us." Aazar reached out, his fingers brushing against the rough, moisture-laden surface of the wall on his left. It felt uneven and cold, yet he could discern no obvious signs of concealed dangers.

At the end of the dimly lit tunnel, Duat extended his hand, casting a glow that illuminated the shadowy chamber ahead. In the centre stood a stone plinth, its surface was astonishingly smooth, almost polished, contrasting sharply with the rugged walls that surrounded it. The walls were unadorned, without any inscriptions or markings, evoking an eerie sense of emptiness.

With cautious steps, Duat ventured into the room, fully aware that the plinth served as the communication device. To his right, an ancient torch hung from an iron ring, its surface coated in layers of dust. Carefully, he held his hand near the torch. With his left hand, he thoroughly examined the area around the torch for any concealed traps. Satisfied that it was safe, he lifted the torch free from its decaying ring.

As he blew gently on his palm, a spark ignited, bringing the torch to life and filling the cavern with a golden light.

"Bellator, take this," he instructed, passing the lit torch to the Watcher, the flickering turquoise energy in Duat's palm dissipating into the air.

With the torch in Bellator's hands, the cavern came into sharper focus, revealing nothing of particular interest, just a barren expanse of stone.

Aazar stood in the centre of the room, observing Duat intently. Although he hesitated to speak, it was clear that Duat was grappling with uncertainty, seemingly unsure of what to do next.

"Bellator, hold the torch higher," Duat commanded, hoping to illuminate their next course of action.

"Yes, Master." He followed the instructions as Duat examined the expansive ceiling of the cavern, with puzzlement across his face, he shook his head. The stone above offered no clues, just an endless expanse of rough-hewn rock and shadow.

He approached the stone plinth in the centre of the cavern. Measuring about one foot square and rising to a height of four feet, there were no markings at its base, nor any engravings or carvings adorning its sides, just a flawless slab. However, it was here for a reason. Drawing in a deep breath, Duat closed his eye, seeking a connection with the stone plinth. As he concentrated, a vibrant flash of turquoise ignited in the palm of his right hand. This was no ordinary hue; it was a rich, deep shade, far more intense than anything he had encountered before, pulsating with energy.

As his body shook, his palm became stuck to the top of the plinth, he snarled, grinding his mishappen teeth together. His palm began to turn red as the bones in his hand became visible. His body shook throughout as drool fell onto the plinth and sizzled as if it were hitting a hot surface. Turquoise spread from his palm, engulfing the top of the plinth, and spilt over the sides, covering the entire length of the plinth.

Duat was yelling in pain as a circular pattern appeared on the wall in front of them; the circle rotated faster and faster as their bodies felt like they were being dragged towards it. There was a flash and the entire cavern began to shake as the turquoise from his palm pooled at the base of the plinth. Bellator and Aazar grabbed at the walls for support as the three of them were lifted into the air.

Bellator dropped the torch as he and Aazar grasped at the stone walls as their bodies rose until they were vertically in line with the whirling vortex. Duat's body lifted while his palm remained glued to the plinth.

Duat's yelling grew louder as he writhed in agony until there was a deafening sound of a crack, and the room ceased to move. The three of them instantly fell to the ground.

Duat whipped his right hand away from the plinth, and shuffled backwards on his behind, each movement deliberate as he gradually regained his composure. The vivid redness in his hand began to fade, he dabbed at his watering eye and pushed himself up to his feet with effort. Unsteady, he wobbled slightly, his body struggling for balance as he pressed against the sturdy plinth for support. He glanced over at Aazar, who was brushing down his suit. Bellator was clutching the wall tightly, his face a picture of fear. "Pick the torch back up," Duat commanded, his voice breaking through the tension in the air. Bellator, still shaken, nodded repeatedly and without hesitation, bent down and retrieved the torch. He quickly returned to the wall, gripping it once more with a sense of urgency.

The vortex on the wall before them had decelerated, yet it continued to spiral in a relentless clockwise motion. At its core, a grainy, colourless image materialised, revealing a shadowy realm dominated by a central throne shrouded in serpents with grotesque multiple heads.

Duat's discomfort was palpable as a colossal figure with a crown of horns emerged, his formidable back presented to them as he disdainfully pushed the serpents away from his throne.

For Bellator, the very presence of this entity was enough to evoke profound terror. The figure's body language radiated an uncompromising authority as he settled heavily into his seat. His long, bony fingernails rhythmically tapping against the throne's arms. Each sound was punctuated by a simmering rage that seemed to permeate the air around him. Aazar nodded in reverence, a gesture mirrored hesitantly by Duat.

"Gatekeeper, I do not take kindly to being summoned, particularly for a discourse with the one who was chosen, the one meant to instigate change, the one who has ultimately failed." Duat kept his head bowed, shadows cloaking his expression. "My Lord, there was a failsafe established by the Reeves," he growled, lifting his eye to meet that of the fearsome figure. "We were unaware of its existence."

Serpents writhed around the torso of Apophis, the Master of the Underworld. "You were selected and bestowed with special powers unlike those you have in this realm. Your presence before me now, side by side with those vile creatures they call Watchers, fills me with disgust." Aazar and Bellator exchanged glances laced with fear.

Duat extended his hand forward. "My Lord, I executed the plan with precision. I infiltrated their heavily fortified headquarters and uncovered the imposing wall that guards the gateway portal. The Cleric whose mind I manipulated remained ignorant of an additional key needed to breach this wall alongside the former Reeve."

Apophis shook his head, a serpent coiling around his neck. He practically spat with rage, "Those bloodline experiments they term Clerics are as utterly inept as their counterparts, the Watchers, like the pathetic two standing behind you." His voice was laced with contempt.

Duat cast a fleeting glance over his shoulder at the two Watchers, their faces pale and their eyes wide with trepidation. "My Lord and Master, I must inform you that those involved with the League of Light have undergone significant evolution since our last encounter. They possess advanced weaponry and defences, unlike anything we've faced before. My form is just as fragile as theirs, and they wield technologies capable of unleashing pulsations of pure light potent enough to destroy. If I am struck, survival is unlikely. I needed to retreat, to gather my strength and devise a new strategy for what lies ahead."

The figure leaned forward, "Gatekeeper, we are worshipped and feared in equal measure. We command the power over the afterlife for those who pass through this realm."

Duat's expression remained resolute as he replied, "Respectfully my Lord, beliefs have changed. Many now wander in ignorance of our existence. That is why so few come to us now, unlike in the times of old."

"Do you honestly believe I am unaware of this? We all recognise the truth of it! That is precisely why you are there! We will reclaim our worship and reign in fear once more; we shall ascend to dominance across the realms and the mortal world. We will flourish amidst the ashes of their crumbling existence, and we shall wield ultimate judgment over the afterlife again." His words hung in the air, commanding Duat's attention.

"My Lord, their prophecy has come to pass; they are fearful. I suspect, as before, that a guardian will arise to protect them. From this very place where I commune with you, I can feel the pulse of someone bearing their bloodline. I have also sensed a cat with abilities nearby. Furthermore, there is a dwelling of the so-called magic world that resides right in this very town. Aazar, who is behind me, suspects one of their senior Elders has been visiting there. This cannot be a coincidence, for these two worlds typically remain apart. I suspect something is converging between them. I tried to penetrate the magic sanctuary, but there is a formidable magic seal that envelopes its walls."

The Master of the Underworld tapped his long fingernails against his throne. "They know you are there, but the magic users are powerless against our might."

"I agree, my Lord. Yet should they manage to open the portal by the wall of iron, they could traverse to our domain, just as we can to theirs."

"Good, bring them to us, and we'll exterminate them all. Apophis started laughing and chatting his long teeth together. "They would be too terrified to even take the journey. They'll be slaughtered, judged, their souls cast for eternity to the fires."

Duat gave a nod.

"Gatekeeper, is this all you have to say, or is this what you wanted to tell me?"

"No, my Lord, I respectfully require some assistance," Duat said, bowing his head slightly.

With a look of disgust, Apophis collapsed back into his seat.

"My Lord, I fully recognise of what I am asking, but their arsenal is formidable enough to vanquish me easily. The one-way portal I travelled through, whose opening was in Paris may not open again for centuries, and we remain unaware of when it will open next time."

"You presume, Gatekeeper, that it will open again."

"Yes, my Lord."

"What is your request? Speak plainly and without hesitation!"

"My Lord, what I seek is armour to shield me from the threats I face. I possess the ability to control and convert and bend them to my will. I can conjure a searing white light so blinding and disorienting that it can incapacitate even the most fearsome adversaries. But I understand that despite this might, it only takes one calculated strike from an enemy to slip past my defences."

Duat's master narrowed his eyes, observing the Gatekeeper closely. "You sound scared, Gatekeeper,"

"No, I assure you, I am not scared, my Lord," he countered earnestly, holding his focus steady. "What I feel is awareness of the challenges ahead. This armour is not just for me; it is crucial for all of us to bring about significant change. I am prepared to confront the enemy, but I must be adequately equipped to ensure my protection. Additionally, I respectively ask for others to join my side. We can defeat them, identify their guardian, and put her to death."

Apophis shook his head. "You know the portal you travelled through is sealed."

"I understand, my Lord, but you can transfer remnants and power while this vortex is open."

Fingernails began tapping again as Apophis gritted his teeth. "So be it!" His right hand formed a fist and slammed down against his throne, the sound reverberating like a crack of thunder. He tilted his head back, steam curling from his mouth. Serpents wrapped around his torso, arms, and neck as he unclenched his fist and lifted his arm.

Bellator and Aazar instinctively stepped back, their faces reflecting a mix of fear and disbelief as Duat was abruptly pulled toward the ancient plinth. With a forceful motion, his right palm struck the surface, a sound echoing in the still air as if metal had met metal. Instantly, Duat's hand turned a fiery red, and he let out a piercing yell. Before they could react, he was lifted off his feet, suspended in an otherworldly grip. A thick mist began to coalesce around the plinth, swirling ominously and engulfing Duat, obscuring him from view.

Bellator looked around, but there was nowhere to flee to. Duat's torso trembled, and he spluttered as though something had entered his body; the sound of his anguish was deafening. The redness of his palm subsided as he collapsed to the ground, gripping his sides in pain.

As Apophis slowly lowered his arm, serpents descended from him to the feet of the throne. The creatures hissed softly as Apophis tilted his neck side to side, the sound of cracking bones echoing in the stillness, unsettling Aazar enough to make him instinctively take several further steps back.

"Get up, Gatekeeper!" the Master of the Underworld commanded.

Duat struggled against his pain as he gradually pulled himself to his feet, relying heavily on the sturdy plinth for support. His bloodshot eye, red and swollen, streamed with tears.

"You now possess a shield that can protect you," Apophis declared. "You will know how to wield it when the moment arrives." Without hesitation, Apophis reached down, grasping a serpent that coiled around the base of his throne, and threw it into the swirling vortex.

In that instant, a brilliant flash erupted, and as the light dimmed, the serpent materialised on the ground before Duat.

Breathing heavily and leaning against the plinth for support, Duat focused on the serpent as it slithered toward him. He glanced upward at the vortex, surprise etched across his face, as his Master slammed his right hand against the armrest of the throne. The serpent reared up on its tail, hissing wildly, and crumbled to reveal seven stones. The two Watchers stood mesmerised at what had just transpired in front of them.

Leaning back in his throne, Apophis observed them. "You have your assistance. Take the stones and plant them carefully. Ensure that no one sees you. They may be unruly at first, but they are yours to command."

Duat nodded slowly with determination, "Yes, my Lord, I will do that."

"Forget about the magic place for now. Concentrate exclusively on the one that carries their bloodline. If necessary, concern yourself with the magic realm afterwards. Your objective remains clear: breach the wall of iron and open the portal so that I, along with others, can traverse the distance to join you."

"Yes, I understand my Lord."

"Now, go!"

With those final words, the grainy image before him began to dissolve as the vortex started to turn again. Duat hurriedly extended his hand to grab the ancient stones, carefully tucking them into the pockets of his veterinary tunic. As his right palm connected with the plinth, the very air around him began to tremble. He could feel the forces at play shifting; their return to Shropshire was imminent.

✠✠✠✠

"Cleric, do you have any updates on when the architects will arrive?"

"My Lady Reeve, we've received notification that they are now in the country; it should be just a matter of hours."

"Thank you." The Reeve propped her spear against the Cleric's desk and removed her helmet. Running a hand through her hair, she placed her helmet on the desk and moved to the centre to ensure all of the Clerics could hear her.

"I hope you are all feeling more comfortable now. I know the sight of so many Watchers grouped together is unsettling, it is for all of us. I assure you that housing them in your residence will only be a temporary measure until we can find a more secure location for them."

A couple of the Clerics nodded, and the one whom the Reeve had spoken to replied, "We understand, my Lady, but this is our home."

"We know. It's the only place here that can be secured without access to sunlight. We will do everything we can."

The Cleric nodded briefly, but the Reeve understood that the arrival of the Watchers in her quarters of Loxley would not sit well with her.

"Thank you for all the support you give to us," the Reeve said.

"Thank you, my Lady." The Clerics bowed their heads and resumed their work.

"Oh good, Armourer, I'm glad I've caught you." The Reeve walked across the lobby toward the stairs.

"Yes, Reeve?"

"I wanted to inform you that the Watchers have been securely contained in the Cleric's wing."

The Armourer shrugged nonchalantly, "I was already aware of that, Reeve. Was there something else?"

The Reeve shook her head. "Not especially, although I know you have reports to prepare."

The Armourer's smile broadened a sparkle of mischief in her eyes. "That I do, but not about you. Not just yet."

The Reeve nodded slightly, a small smile on her face.

"Well, if that's it, I'll be off. I have work to do."

"Such as?" The Reeve questioned.

"Well, now I've successfully put some of my devices to good use. I have some exciting new ideas brewing, especially now that I've seen the Watchers up close and personal again."

The Reeve didn't comment, pondering the implications of the Armourer's words.

"You know," the Armourer continued, "this situation we find ourselves in might get a lot more uncomfortable before it gets any better."

The Reeve nodded slowly as the Armourer headed up the stairs. "Armourer, if you are conducting any of your experiments, please do them in the building on the other side of the lake, not in the main house."

"I'll bear that in mind, Reevy," the Armourer winked as she continued up the stairs, leaving the Reeve to her own thoughts.

✣✣✣✣

With her knees drawn tightly to her chest, Mildred rocked gently back and forth on her bed. Her two cats, Comet and Nahla, watched her with wide eyes, though the two seemed indifferent to one another.

Mildred buried her face in her hands and rubbed her tired eyes. Sleep would be nice, but it felt unlikely.

"Oh, my days, what am I to do with you both?" she exclaimed, her voice a mixture of weariness and confusion as she leaned against her headboard, her fingers tangling in her hair.

She gestured dramatically towards Comet. "You," she said, "give me a jolt like an electric shock, and sometimes, I can see a woman trying to speak to me. And you, Nahla," she continued, turning to her other cat, "have taken it up a notch with these visions." She shook her head, a weary smile creeping across her lips. "I think that about sums it up. Can you imagine me calling the doctors to explain all of this? They'd be whisking me away in an ambulance, and you'd be left without your cat mum."

Nahla, sensing her distress, nudged Mildred's leg with her paw. "It's like you're trying to tell me something," Mildred scratched at her head. "That vision I had... it was definitely linked to the Futility. I used to pop in there from time to time, back when I had a 'normal' job, like normal people do!"

Crossing her arms, Mildred pondered, "Is this what it's like for Dr Fennaway? She can talk to cats, but can she see through their eyes? Is this what my Elder Daphne meant when she spoke of special powers?" She flailed her arms in a mixture of frustration and fascination. "That's my Elder Daphne, mind you, not the new one from Much Wenlock," she added, shaking her head to try and clear her thoughts. "It's all just too much!" Leaning forward, she tenderly stroked Nahla's soft fur with one hand while gently brushing the top of Comet's head with the other, careful to avoid the scar that marred her flank. "You know, these dreams I've been having lately... they're filled with scrawny pale figures. One keeps inching closer and closer." Suddenly, a wave of apprehension washed over her, and she released both cats in shock, falling back against the headboard, her heart racing as her eyes locked onto Nahla. "Nahla?" Mildred whispered, her voice trembling as panic flitted across her features. "Nahla?" In a slow, almost deliberate manner, Mildred got up and shuffled backwards against the bedroom wall, one hand pressed tightly against her heart, her breath hitching in her throat. "The figures I've been seeing in my dreams Nahla, are these the same ones you've seen at the Futility?"

Nahla, her beloved cat, responded with a slow, deliberate nod.

✟✟✟✟

Duat studied the stones resting in his palms, their surfaces smooth yet cool to the touch. All seven were an intense shade of blue.

"The stones are the colour of lapis lazuli, Sire. What do you think it signifies?" Aazar inquired.

"I'm well aware of what colour they are, but what puzzles me is why he has sent me these."

"I'm not sure I understand, Sire."

"I requested assistance; my intention was to receive another Gatekeeper, I'm not sure what will evolve from them. We must determine a suitable location to bury them, somewhere where stone does not lie beneath."

"I will do my best to think of an appropriate place nearby, Sire."

Duat returned the stones to his pocket, casting a look at Bellator. "Bellator, you are as pale as a Cleric."

Aazar managed a grin, although the memory of their unsettling experience at the vortex still lingered in his mind.

Bellator frowned. "I don't understand how you can smile. You heard what the Lord said about our kind!"

Aazar's smile quickly faded.

"I'm alright, Master. The burns still trouble me."

"A long time ago, your bloodline's power of immortality would have healed those wounds more swiftly. Your blood vessels would have been reborn. Your skin would have renewed itself seamlessly, leaving no scars behind."

Bellator lowered his head in acknowledgement. "Yes, Master. I understand."

Duat pulled his glasses from the pocket of his tunic, and with a grunt of amusement, he kicked aside some of the fallen arrowheads and stepped over the fallen wall. Back in the shadows of the dim chamber, he lingered for a moment, casting a final glance at the scratched symbol of the Kat Chamber. He put on his glasses, pushed aside the lines of ivy and stepped into the sunlight.

✢✢✢✢

With her hamstrings taut from inactivity, Soad hunched over. "Look, I'm going crazy, Mildred is safe in the house."

"What of it, this is our job. We are assigned to this."

"Well aware, but when was the last time any of us did surveillance?" Soad extended her back and put her hands on the wall.

"When was the last time we did anything?" Ana said with a wry smile.

"Yeah, you got me there, okay," Soad said, turning away from the wall and laughing. "We've been cooped up here for a few days now, and our supplies are running short. I noticed a convenience store is located right around the corner."

"We've got enough to last until we're relieved."

Soad let out a huge puff of air. "Cover for me, will you? I'm going for a jog. I need to do something."

"What! You can't leave, what if something happens?"

"Oh, come on, all that's going to happen is her chasing her cat around the garden again."

"You are aware there is a Gatekeeper out there, and this woman on the other side is somehow connected to it!"

"Seriously, how can she be? She throws sandwiches up trees and cat turds into the guy next door's garden."

Ana couldn't help but laugh.

"You've got my number, call me. I can run fast."

"Our phones are tracked. If they check, they'll know you left."

Soad chewed on her lips. "Mmm, that's true. Okay, I'll leave the phone here."

"That's not what I meant; you can't risk her seeing you."

Soad shrugged. "No chance. I'm going out the back door and cutting through the garden to the street behind. She'll never see me. Hang on, wait a second. Do you hear that?"

Soad smiled. "I recognise that sound!" She left the room and went into the rear bedroom. From the first-floor rear window, Soad watched as the motorbike rider stepped off her bike and turned off the engine.

Soad hurried back to the surveillance room, "It's Kalara. Now you have backup. I'm definitely going for a jog."

Ana rubbed her temples. "Look, just be quick, okay?"

"Sure! I'll catch you in a bit. If there are any problems, stick a drone up. I won't miss it." Soad grabbed her trainers and sprinted down the stairs.

Ana turned back to the net curtain, hearing the back door close downstairs. "I really hope nothing happens," she murmured to herself.

✣✣✣✣✣

For what felt like an eternity, Suzanna sat in her new office, the hours slipping by as she aimlessly twirled a pen between her fingers. She felt a cautious sense of relief at being away from the unnerving presence of the Clerics, whose blank, inscrutable faces haunted her thoughts. In what Nubia often dubbed 'contemplation,' her mind wandered, but her body remained still, never quite knowing what to do next.

Her office, positioned on the first floor of Loxley Manor, was just a corridor away from where three white-robed figures sat. She didn't know what they did or why they appeared so pale, but an unsettling chill surrounded them. Sitting at her grand oak desk, barefoot after tossing her shoes aside, she had no clue what to do next. She left her door open, but no one knocked. The surrounding doors, identical to her own, remained eerily silent, their doors steadfastly closed.

Peering out of her window, she took in the landscape that stretched endlessly before her, its beauty marred only by the presence of the imposing security personnel. The tranquil scenery lacked any sign of life; not a single bird flitted through the air, nor did she glimpse any cats roaming the hallways. It felt as though the whole place was ensnared in a heavy silence.

As Daphne's Elder, she had always strived to impart wisdom and articulate her thoughts when conversing with her. But in this moment of introspection, she realised the daunting truth: she felt utterly unprepared, even ignorant. On her desk lay unmarked sheets of paper—smooth, white, devoid of any insignias, not one item bore the name of 'Loxley Manor.' There was no nameplate at her desk stating 'Lady Suzanna,' just an assortment of pens and a solitary green reading light. There was no computer, although that was technology she hadn't used in some years.

The walls were lined with picture frames, yet each one hung empty, lacking any canvasses or artwork. It was as if the office had been recently vacated.

Pulling one knee up onto her chair, she rubbed her foot absentmindedly, lost in a haze of thoughts. Where was she supposed to find something to eat? What about her car? How would she retrieve it? Questions spiralled endlessly in her mind; each one leading to another. This place, said to be a sanctuary for contemplation, offered little else. Not particularly eager to approach the Clerics with her queries, she rested her hands on the desk, using them as a makeshift pillow, and allowed her head to follow suit.

Chapter Twenty:
TAME THE REJECTS

Mildred sat in her kitchen, holding a cup of tea. The sound of a motorbike close by interrupted her daydreaming. With a resigned sigh, she placed the cup down and rubbed her temple for what felt like the umpteenth time. *What to do, what to do,* she thought, her right foot tapping anxiously against the floor as she wrestled with the idea of calling Fennaway, the peculiar cat doctor. *How can I even start to explain what's going on? It's like both cats are trying to communicate something important,* she pondered, her thoughts spiralling wildly and proving less than fruitful.

Her hand paused mid-rub as a flicker of inspiration ignited in her mind. Nahla lay curled up at her feet. "Nahla," she called softly, her cat raised her head. "The Kat Chamber warned me to be careful around those who wear strange glasses!" Mildred exclaimed, her voice laced with urgency. "The figures from that vision, whatever it was, they were all wearing weird glasses!" Nahla blinked slowly, her tail flicking back and forth.

"But what do they mean?" Mildred wondered aloud.

Having cut through the back garden, exchanging a few words with Kalara, Soad hopped over the low brick wall onto Darwin Street. She paused briefly, scanning the street to ensure no prying eyes had seen her. Walking quickly to warm up her muscles, she proceeded down the road, fully aware of a shortcut that lay ahead. This route would guide her back onto Rocke Road, just beyond the bus stop and out of view of their surveillance post, hopefully avoiding detection by Mildred.

As she stepped onto Rocke Road, Soad cast a glance down the street towards the wild, overgrown garden at the bottom. There were no signs of movement. Satisfied, she picked up her pace and began jogging towards the high street. For members of the Escarrabin, to be away from some form of duty, even in retirement from active service, they were still bound by commitment. They were expected to go to selected homes to study for the betterment of the Order and its ideals. Interacting with anyone outside of their Order was not just infrequent; it was utterly unconventional.

As she ran up the hill at the lower end of Benbow Street, her pulse quickened, not from the physical exertion but from the acute awareness that she was breaking the rules of the very principles she'd vowed to uphold her entire life. The street buzzed with activity and was busier than she had hoped, dog walkers strolled leisurely, and older individuals manoeuvred with the help of mobility aids. Groups of teenagers congregated, their laughter loud, while many were glued to their phones.

Her eyes darted across the street, landing on the convenience shop. Today, its door was firmly shut, and a blind was pulled down tightly behind the front door. Soad decided to pause for a moment to people-watch. She stood there, captivated by the diverse lifestyles unfolding before her. Everyone was carving out their own path with a sense of freedom, free from the tight confines of her own commitments.

A man appeared next to the shop door, adjusting his waistband as he fished keys from his pocket to let himself in. From across the road, she spotted a jumble of adverts and postcards in the window. Her curiosity getting the better of her, she glanced both ways to avoid traffic and made her way across the street. *What do people here do for fun?* she wondered to herself.

As she drew closer, her eyes read over flyers about missing pets, a forthcoming church fete, and a mysterious event labelled *'karaoke,'* she wasn't sure if she pronounced that word correctly in her mind. The state of the window was appalling; layers of dust and grime cloaked the glass. She chuckled softly, picturing what Raysmau would say if their own quarters resembled this chaotic display.

Peering intently through the smudged glass, she observed the disorganised interior of the shop, items scattered haphazardly, a reflection of disarray. Shaking her head in disbelief at the scene, she glanced to her right and immediately froze in fear. Without warning, a wave of adrenaline surged through her body. Swallowing hard, she instinctively took a cautious step backwards, her breath quickening. In a panic, she pushed against the shop door, relieved to find it unlocked. She stepped inside, slamming the door behind her, causing a bell to jangle above her head as she crouched low, desperately trying to hide.

"I'm sorry, but we are closed. I'm having a rare day off, and by God, I need it!" called out the shopkeeper, his voice a mix of irritation and exhaustion. The young woman, likely in her mid-twenties, seemed oblivious to him, shuffling along the dusty floor with wide, terrified eyes. "Excuse me, what do you think you're doing? I just came in because I forgot my wallet! We are closed!" he protested, his frustration palpable.

"Ssshhh, get down! Get out of sight!" she implored, waving her arms frantically for him to duck behind the counter. The shopkeeper scratched his head, bewildered. "I've just about had enough of today. I'm telling you…"

"Get down! Don't make a sound!" she insisted.

The shopkeeper snorted, "I'm not going to hide in my own shop! I've had enough weirdness here today, and you're only adding to it! Honestly, someone died outside recently, there's missing CCTV footage, people wearing dead veterinarian's clothing, and confirmed cheating in the sheep diving contest. What is the world coming to?"

He froze, heart pounding, as he spotted the skeletal figure lurking just outside his shop, the same one who had visited earlier, wearing those strange, unsettling glasses. Without a moment's hesitation, he dove behind the counter, his pulse quickening as two more figures materialised beside the first.

Duat and Aazar halted in their tracks, Bellator slightly ahead. Bellator turned back with concern on his face. "Master, what is it? Are you all right?"

Duat lifted his head cautiously while Aazar rubbed the nub of his nose. They exchanged a heavy glance, and in that instant, Duat's fury simmered to the surface. "One of them is nearby."

Aazar nodded, "The scent is distinct, Sire, but this blood carries a different essence." Duat flexed the fingers of his right hand, his muscles coiling with tension. "I recognise it well; it belongs to one of the captors, one who held you against your will, Bellator."

Bellator's glanced down the hill, where a mix of men and women ambled by, unperturbed. None resembled the ones who had confined him.

"Sire, what should we do?" Aazar's voice was laced with urgency. "I can sense their presence, but we're exposed here, out in the open."

As people walked past, they received curious stares and growls from nearby dogs.

"The captors are here for a reason, Aazar, and you can be sure it revolves around the one in this vicinity."

Soad squeezed into the corner of the shop, crouching behind dusty, discoloured teddy bears. She glanced back and saw that the shopkeeper had hidden out of sight; he had listened to her. Perspiring, she had seen three of them, but only two had escaped Loxley. One of them had to be the Gatekeeper in Watcher form. He must have united with another. Knowing his powers and realising she was unarmed, she closed her eyes in terror, flinching as saliva splattered against the glass right in front of her.

"Sire?"

Duat turned around, watching every movement around him. He shook his head, wiped his lips, and shook the saliva onto the adjacent shop window.

Bellator craned his neck, scrutinising the windows above, his senses were unable to tell the presence of the Escarrabin.

Duat reached into his pocket, feeling the stones his Master had given him. "We have work to do. Ignore the fool; we need to create growth, and we shall do so after dark. I sense that we don't have much time before more of them arrive."

Holding a teddy bear in front of her face, Soad inhaled deeply, a wave of relief washing over her as she saw the three Watchers move away. She peered through the glass; the Watchers were heading down the hill. Leaning against the wall, once they were out of sight, she gasped for breath, her heart beating wildly in her chest. "Man type, you can come up now."

The shopkeeper's head bobbed up over the counter, his face a picture of concern. "Do you know them?"

Soad could hear the tension in his voice. "Oh yes, but..." she paused, realising she was speaking to someone who wouldn't understand. Standing up, Soad placed the teddy bear back on the shelf and headed toward the front door. The bell tinkled as she opened the door. Peering out, she watched the three Watchers heading down the hill. They were anything but discreet, their unusual appearance causing heads to turn in their direction.

"So?" the shopkeeper pressed.

She spun around, pointing at him. "You never saw me!" Then she darted out the door and disappeared.

Mr Franks rushed to the door and immediately locked it. He squeezed his eyes shut for a moment, muttering under his breath about the strange world around him, "That's it, I'm going for a drink!"

✢✢✢✢

"So, should we investigate?"

Nahla's tail continued to dart back and forth.

"Look, I don't know what is going on here," she admitted, wagging her finger. "Where's your sister at?" She abruptly stood up and started searching the cluttered front room. "Comet, come on!" Returning to the kitchen, she took a generous gulp of tea. "Nahla, something is happening. These dreams are relentless and Comet keeps giving me the fright of my life. Weird colours appear on my fingers, and the boys at the bus stop are now scared of me..." She paused, considering that point. "And then there's you, communicating whatever it is to me. It's potentially the same people from the dreams. It has to be, right? Enough is enough. Time for decisive action. I'll grab my shoes."

Nahla pawed at Mildred's stockings, adding another ladder to the already worn fabric. "What is it, Nahla? We need to go to the Futility; something significant is happening!"

Nahla started to shake her head. Mildred sat down, puzzled and cradled her black cat with the distinctive, white-tipped tail. "What do you mean, no?"

Nahla continued to shake her head.

"Are these things still out there? Are they dangerous?"

The cat's head stopped shaking.

"Why am I asking you questions? It's not like you're going to give me clear answers," Mildred said, gazing towards the front room at the certificate hung on the wall. She chewed her lip, weighing her options. "I'll ask you one more time: shall we go and investigate?"

Nahla placed a paw on Mildred's hand and shook her head.

✢✢✢✢

Soad glanced apprehensively over her shoulder as she crossed to the opposite side of the road, maintaining as much distance as she could. The three Watchers were dressed strangely, their glasses were a strange design unlike any she had seen before; they differed from the ones worn at Loxley.

As she saw them turn to the right, she quickened her pace. By the time she reached the base of the hill, the Watchers had vanished from view, and without a moment's hesitation, she broke into a sprint, heart racing in her chest.

"Soad was really desperate to get away!" Ana remarked, nodding at Kalara.

Kalara, her arms crossed and a slight smirk on her lips, replied, "I don't think she's quite equipped for the demands of surveillance. You've only been here a couple of days; you've hardly started," Kalara said as she placed her helmet, gloves, and leather jacket on the bed and sat down.

"I know. She was just looking for something to do to relieve her boredom."

"Boredom is part and parcel of the surveillance game," Kalara chuckled. "So, what are you seeing? What's going on with the subject person?"

"Mildred. To be honest, not much to report," Ana admitted, shrugging her shoulders. "The truth is, we don't have a clear grasp of why we're even keeping an eye on her. Do you happen to have any insights? I suspect you're holding back."

"I can tell you this: she's of great interest to the Order, especially for a lower-ranked Elder. Just stay vigilant, will you? And no more jogging excursions!"

"You're not going to report Soad, are you?"

Kalara shook her head, "I wouldn't do that. I'm here to observe the area. A more senior Elder was murdered here recently. We suspect the Gatekeeper was responsible and may return to this area. And..."

Before she could finish, Ana raised her hand and blinked rapidly, her eyes widening. "What on earth is she doing now?"

Kalara sprang to her feet, a sense of urgency in her voice. "What? Mildred?"

"No, Soad! She's sprinting towards us."

Kalara frowned in disbelief. "What? Out front? In full view of everyone?" Her voice was laced with concern, eyes darting toward the window.

"Exactly that. It's not good; she looks nervous. Something's off. Kalara, can you keep an eye out? I'm going to let her in," Ana said, urgency in her tone as she hurried down the staircase. She flung open the front door just as Soad burst through, her chest heaving.

"What are you thinking?" Ana's voice rang out as she swiftly shut the door behind her.

Soad leaned heavily against the wall, her complexion ghostly white, all colour drained from her face. Taking a moment to catch her breath, Soad pressed a trembling hand to her forehead. "Watchers...three of them! They are right here!"

✣✣✣✣

Kalara sprinted down the stairs. "What is it? What's going on?"

Soad, still gasping for breath, leaned against the wall, trying to regain her composure.

"She says she has seen Watchers!" Ana exclaimed, her eyes wide with alarm.

"What? Where?"

Soad took a deep breath. "Three of them, just around the corner. They were at the top of Benbow Street."

"Are they coming this way?" Kalara pressed.

Soad coughed. "No, they moved away on foot in the other direction."

"Are you positive about this?"

Soad frowned. "Seriously?"

"Okay, okay. Do you think one of them is the Gatekeeper?" Kalara's mind raced through the implications of that possibility.

"Well, I can't be sure, but I definitely saw three of them out in broad daylight! They were wearing protective glasses; I've never seen anything like it before."

They momentarily paused for breath. Ana bit at her lip with concern, "Kalara, what do you think?"

Kalara nodded. "I do have a view on this. If it is him, and we suspected he might return here, that means he has recruited another. Only one escaped with him, so the other will be acclimatised to life out here, making him exceptionally dangerous."

"We need to go back upstairs to keep an eye on Mildred," Ana suggested.

They headed back upstairs. They gathered at the window, peering out at Mildred's house across the road. Everything seemed calm; there wasn't a sound to be heard.

"Kalara, we need to report this to control."

Kalara nodded in agreement with Ana and pulled her encrypted phone from her leather trousers.

Her call was answered immediately. "Control, this is Kalara. Put me through to Raysmau urgently."

Soad and Ana exchanged anxious glances as muffled remarks emerged from the receiver.

"I don't care, disturb her," Kalara insisted, as she tapped her fingers rhythmically at her side. She nodded at the other two as the call was answered. "My Lady, we have a situation... Watchers spotted...three of them... No, not from the observation post. Soad left to do some external reconnaissance." She glanced at Soad, covering for her. "I'm not sure; I didn't see them. Hold on, my Lady? Soad, how did they look? What were they wearing?"

Kalara's eyebrows shot up in surprise as she listened. "My Lady, two of them were dressed like animal doctors... Yes, I know, it's very odd. The other was wearing a black suit; the nature of his attire suggests he's a roamer and not known to us, which makes his presence extremely worrying... Yes... Soad suspects one could be the Gatekeeper... I understand; I'll await your call."

Kalara put the phone away. "She's coming straight back to us; she sounds very concerned. I guess she needs to speak with the Reeve."

The three of them returned to the window. Nothing was happening around Mildred's house; the street was quiet, but it would be dark soon.

✛✛✛✛

"I appreciated your promptness in contacting me, Raysmau, despite the news."

"Yes, my Lady. The situation sounds quite serious. Soad has reported sightings of three Watchers not far from the house in Shrewsbury that you previously visited."

"They were actually in that very street?"

"No, my Lady, but alarmingly close."

"Soad left the surveillance point?"

"I understand, my Lady. I will investigate it. However, on this occasion, it may have been helpful."

Standing outside Lady Safiya's office, they took a moment to check their appearance.

"Come in," the Cleric said in response to the Reeve's knock. Lady Safiya stood in the centre of the room. "Come through, Reeve, and you too, Raysmau."

As they stepped into Lady Safiya's main quarters, the Reeve's heart sank at the sight of Nubia and the Armourer sitting in the room. There was immediate tension in the air. "I took the liberty of calling the Curator. I understand you're acquainted with the Armourer; she is here at the behest of the Grand Council."

The Reeve nodded solemnly. "Yes, we've met."

"So, what news do you bring us, Reeve?"

"If I'm honest, Curator, I'm here as a courtesy to inform the Lady of the House that we are initiating action."

"I see, and…"

"Nubia, let me address this matter, please."

Nubia puffed her cheeks. "Yes, my Lady," and fell silent.

"So, what has happened now? You are obviously concerned about something?"

"Yes, my Lady." She glanced over her shoulder at Raysmau. "Raysmau received an urgent call from our team conducting surveillance in Shrewsbury in Shropshire. You will, of course, recall the area, given the recent events linked to a lower member of the Order there."

Safiya took a deep breath as she settled into her chair, her cat, Alicia, immediately jumped onto her lap. "Yes, Mildred, the one with the prophesied cat. What has happened?"

"We have reason to believe that three Watchers are in the area. One is potentially the Gatekeeper."

Safiya and Nubia exchanged worried glances. Safiya shook her head and rubbed her temple. She rubbed her eyes. "Wait, you said three Watchers; one escaped from here. Who's the other one?"

"We don't know, my Lady."

"How was he dressed, Reeve? This other one you mentioned?"

The Reeve turned to Raysmau to continue. "I was informed he wore a dark suit. Furthermore, all three of them wore glasses that are different to the ones they wear here."

"He's recruited," the Armourer said, her fingers scratching thoughtfully at her chin as her attention shifted to Safiya. "If that's the case, he could be highly unpredictable. If he has never been contained here or at any other headquarters around the world, he will have evolved significantly, amassing knowledge and skills we might underestimate. As for the one snatched from here by the Gatekeeper, he'll pose no threat at all."

"That is also our thoughts."

Safiya nodded at Raysmau to acknowledge her viewpoint. "So, what do you intend to do? I thought he might return here."

Before anyone else could respond, the Armourer rose from her seat. "No, no, he's not coming back here for a while. Isn't it obvious? He knows that we are aware of his presence and we are now prepared. He would never get in as easily as he did before," she said, giving a patronising smile at the Reeve. "The full extent of why he came to Loxley still eludes us, but the prophecy has unfolded, and he knows it. It's obvious he's going after the one who is aligned to protect us first."

"Do you interpret that as Mildred or her new kitten, the one that bears the mark?"

"I can't say for certain, Nubia; I suspect he'll go for both." She looked around the room, making eye contact with everyone. "Strike them both down, no more mistakes, take no more chances. He'll be heading to Mildred's home imminently; we must assume he knows where she is."

Safiya's attention drifted downward as two of her other cats started weaving around her chair legs. She stroked Alicia, her Siberian cat and exchanged glances with her other two cats. "You look concerned, all three of you," she remarked.

"I'm not surprised, my Lady. Cats are intuitive, especially ones with their bloodline."

"I know, Nubia, I know, my friend." Safiya looked up. "So, what is your plan, Reeve?"

"Yes, my Lady. I intend to leave a skeleton crew of Escarrabin here to monitor the Watchers and stay alert for any signs from below. The rest I intend to take with me to Shrewsbury, along with Raysmau. We will take no chances. It's an all-out offensive."

The Armourer smiled and clapped her hands together. "Now, I'm liking the sound of that!"

Nubia looked in horror, "What are you talking about? An assault out there, in full view of the public! It will expose our world and our Order; there will be no way to cover something like that up!"

"Nubia is right, Reeve. I understand your views, but it's highly risky."

"Respectfully, my Lady, it will be far riskier to do nothing. We cannot afford to leave Mildred and her kitten at the mercy of the Gatekeeper. It stands to reason that if he gets to them, he will turn his attention back here."

Nubia swallowed; the mere thought of him returning made her shiver.

"You know, Reeve, I really should consult with the Grand Council. When are you hoping to do this?"

"My Lady, with every respect, time is not on our side! Security is entrusted to the Order of the Reeves. I'm informing you of the situation to let you know that we will have reduced numbers of Escarrabin here. Giving time to regroup and prepare, I anticipate we'll be leaving before first light. My aim is to reach our destination in daylight and try to locate them when they are at their weakest."

Lady Safiya nodded, considering the implications. "Reeve, I hear you. But Nubia is right; imagine a battle with Scatterblades outside, nothing good will come from it."

The Reeve nodded. "All the same, it needs to be done, my Lady."

"I can help!" the Armourer volunteered enthusiastically.

The Reeve glanced at Raysmau with concern and raised her hand. "Thank you, Armourer, but the task is already in capable hands."

"Are you sure about that? This room seems rather unconvinced. Look, I've developed certain devices that can disable powered cameras and even reduce an area to complete silence. I can effectively provide you with a security blanket." The Armourer nodded, proud of her own ingenuity.

"Is this true, Armourer?"

"Well yes, Safiya, this is what my kind excels at. It's not always about destroying everything, as exhilarating as that can be at times," the Armourer said with a shrug.

Nubia approached Safiya's chair, leaning to whisper in her ear. "Mmm, yes, I think you have a point, Nubia. Ladies, Nubia raises an important observation. The Armourer is here at the request of the Grand Council. Reeve, you believe we don't have time to inform the Council and hear their viewpoints before acting. However, if you were to take the Armourer with you, it could serve as a compromise."

Nubia grinned at both the Armourer and the Reeve, her disdain for the new Reeve still apparent.

"If you agree to this, Reeve, then proceed. However, I must inform the Council regardless. We need to maintain an open line of communication. Do you agree to these terms?"

The Reeve looked at the smiling Armourer, took a deep breath, and nodded.

"Excellent!" the Armourer clapped her hands together. "I'd better go grab my large suitcase. I'll meet you downstairs!"

A FEW HOURS AFTER NIGHTFALL...

"I believe this will be ideal, Sire." Aazar pressed the power button on his phone, closing the screen's glow. "Just a little farther, there's a circular church named St. Chad's. According to my research, there's an old graveyard in its grounds. If we can find a secluded spot away from the tombstones, it should provide a quiet place to bury your stones."

At a brisk pace, they moved along a quiet one-way road called Town Walls. There were no shops or attractions, so interaction with others was unlikely. It was a welcome relief that all three of them could finally remove their glasses.

The chiming of bells in the distance suggested they were heading in the right direction. To their left, beyond a sturdy stone wall, lay a sprawling, meticulously maintained area adjacent to the River Severn.

"Sire, if the church is not suitable, there might be potential over there, Aazar suggested, gesturing towards the grassed area next to the river."

Duat nodded, recognising it as a possible backup plan. However, the sight of people, even at the late hour walking their dogs along the river left him unsettled. There was no telling what might happen once the stones were planted.

"Is this the place, Master?" Bellator pointed at a church on the right. Duat turned to Aazar. "No, this is a different one. Look ahead; that's the circular church."

They crossed the road and headed further up the hill, where the temperature dipped, and a light mist began to rise from the river. They came to a carpark outside St. Chad's Church, with the graveyard located to the right.

A few cars were parked near the church's entrance. "Bellator, check the vehicles and ensure no one is inside them," Duat instructed.

"Yes, Master." Bellator moved ahead of them and into the carpark.

"There's a small gate just ahead, Sire. The entrance to the graveyard must be through there," Aazar observed.

Duat nodded as they passed by Bellator, who diligently scrutinised the parked cars.

The gate was unlocked and it swung open with a creak. The graveyard was smaller than they had hoped. Aazar inspected some of the headstones, many had been here for hundreds of years, their inscriptions barely decipherable.

"Sire, there's a clearer patch over there," Aazar said gesturing to a narrow clearing on the left as they made their way around the back of the circular church. Bellator caught up behind them, "The cars are vacant, Master; no one else is here."

"Good, we do not wish to be disturbed." Duat approached the only area devoid of headstones, a small, roughly twenty-foot square patch of packed earth. He prodded the ground with his foot, searching for any remnants of shattered gravestones, placing his precious stones in a potential grave could lead to complications. Satisfied the area was clear, he removed the stones from his pocket. Just then, he noticed Aazar standing still, his focus fixed on a nearby headstone.

"What is it?" Duat asked.

"It's the name, Sire. It seems familiar," Aazar replied, turning around to face Duat.

"Who is it? Someone worth bringing back to life?" Duat inquired.

"Ebenezer Scrooge, Sire. I know the name from somewhere," Aazar said as he shook his head.

Duat held on tightly to his precious stones, "I've never heard of him. Was he a warrior?"

Aazar's head shook negatively. "It doesn't say, just the name."

"Other headstones mention the year of death," Duat noted as he gazed across the moss-covered headstones.

Aazar nodded in agreement and pulled out his phone. "Let me check."

"Be careful of the light that phone gives off; we don't want to be seen!" Duat cautioned.

"Yes, Sire. I just want to remember why this name is familiar." Aazar closed his eye in frustration before exclaiming, "It's a film prop, they must have made one of their entertainment pictures here. Forget it. I remember the name now, it's from a story." He switched his phone off with annoyance.

"Then let's proceed." Duat crouched down, fingers brushing against the earth as he began to pry and lift the grass and stones, the ground yielding easily.

"How deep do you have to dig, Master?" Bellator asked.

"I've never done this before, so I don't know Bellator, but I anticipate a few inches. We need seven holes with equal spacing. Both of you begin pulling the grass up,"

Despite his aversion to kneeling on the wet ground while wearing his suit, Aazar followed instructions as the three of them clawed seven circular holes of varying diameters. Duat was pleased with what he saw and inserted a stone into each hole, pushing it as deeply as he could with his index finger. "Both of you, seal the holes immediately as I plant the stone," he said.

They continued until all seven stones were buried. The three of them stepped back to wait. The graveyard mists were spreading, and the temperature had dropped sharply as Bellator rubbed at his wounds. He was feeling better; the pain was beginning to fade. They stood in silence as the clock overhead chimed once again. The chime rang eleven times, and in the stillness of the graveyard, the echo seemed to travel for miles.

"How long do you think we should wait?" Bellator whispered to Aazar.

Aazar gave a headshake.

Duat scratched his head.

"Do we need to water them, Master?"

Duat frowned as he turned to face Bellator.

Bellator gave a shrug. "We had to water things at Loxley because it gave them life."

Duat ignored the remark and rubbed his chin.

"Sire, get down."

Three vehicles drove by on the road behind them. The graveyard offered some shelter, but it was limited.

They slowly rose back to their feet, Duat placing his hands firmly on his hips. "I think we..." he started to speak, his words cut short as they heard the faintest sound from one of the mounds, the earth beneath it beginning to tremble and shift. Duat nodded as the grass began to part.

From within the depths of the hole, muffled noises rose upwards, followed by scratches and a spine-chilling screech that shattered the silence. Duat flexed the fingers of his right hand, he knew that whichever Gatekeeper was about to emerge, he would need to assert his authority and control.

As a turquoise glow began to appear, Duat turned to the two Watchers with pride. "My Master has..." Without warning, he abruptly halted mid-sentence, horror washing over his face. "No, no..." The realisation that something was wrong gripped him.

"No! It can't be!" Duat exclaimed, his voice echoing his disbelief.

"What is it, Sire?"

Fuming, Duat swept his arms through the air, sending the turquoise glow in every direction. He pressed his left hand to his temple and shook his head in frustration.

"What troubles you, Sire?" Aazar asked witnessing a paw rising from the ground.

With a heavy sigh, Duat dropped his hands to his sides, the turquoise glow extinguishing abruptly. "My Master is angry," he declared, his voice laced with despair. "This is not the outcome I desired!" The dirt mounds trembled ominously, the earth parting to reveal a flurry of paws clawing their way to the surface.

"Sire, did you mention another Gatekeeper?" Aazar inquired, his eye widening at the sight.

"And they are indeed here," Duat replied, his voice laced with tension, as an eerie, drooling skull emerged from one of the burrows, releasing a chilling howl that pierced through the air. "I should have anticipated this; he shook his head - seven stones. We have the unwelcome representatives from Gatekeeper number seven. My Master has sent me his wretched mutts."

The first of the jackals that clawed its way out narrowed its eyes and growled lowly, its tail draped in spikes, arched in defiance.

"They will need to be tamed. I suggest both of you stand behind me for your own safety." Duat clenched his fists, the muscles in his arms taut with barely contained rage as he glared at the jackals "Rejects!" he shouted as seven jackals stared back at him.

Chapter Twenty-One:
ILLUMINATED WOLVES

Incensed and gritting his teeth, Duat held his palm forward, swinging it from left to right. The black-backed jackal's eyes followed the turquoise glow emanating from him, their grotesque, jagged teeth glistening in the faint light. This sight alone was enough to make Bellator and Aazar step further back.

"Both of you, hold your ground," Duat commanded, "Don't let them see fear; do not let them smell it." The noise was intense, uncontrollable, and escalating. In the dark of the night, the sounds of howling, growling, and vicious hissing confirmed their menace as the creatures advanced from where they had risen.

"Come to me, all of you!" One of the jackals behind the leader stepped forward but was immediately sent sprawling backwards by the leader, the one who rose first. Duat observed this display of dominance, "So, mutt, you must be the alpha," The jackal sat under Duat's palm; its fur was matted and damp, its malnourished body a testament to their scavenging existence. Its deep black eyes seemed devoid of life. A mark, more like a brand, was inscribed on the crown of the jackal's skull. Duat recognised the circle containing a five-pointed star as a reference to the underworld.

Duat placed his palm on the jackal's head, and an immediate flash sparked above the creature's eyes as turquoise veins spread throughout its body. Away from the streetlights, the outline of the jackal in the mists of the graveyard transformed; it became luminous and haunting. Duat crouched down and removed his hand from the jackal's skull. "You are not what I asked for. I needed power, not vicious scavengers. You will do as I command. Now, communicate with the others!"

The jackal slowly turned to the rest of the pack, its filthy coat now pulsating with illuminated veins. Duat stood up, ensuring that Aazar and Bellator were close behind him. Both were clearly nervous; the sight of seven sets of teeth, drooling and poised to attack unsettled them. Duat glanced back towards the alpha, now confronted with its own pack members, all vying for dominance and leadership. The cacophony of snarls and growls that filled the air was deafening.

"Sire!"

Duat turned sharply.

"There are house lights coming on." Aazar pointed to the rear of the graveyard.

In the darkness, the line of houses had been unseen. Now, multiple bedroom lights had been switched on. In the still of the night, the volume of the jackal's infighting was travelling far and wide.

"Alpha. Come to me!" Duat commanded, raising his palm urgently. The alpha, however, was lost in the chaotic squabbling of the in-jackals, its focus scattered among the writhing pack.

"Alpha! I command you!" There was an immediate turquoise flash throughout the torso of the Alpha, and he was immediately subdued. Observing this, the other six wolf-like creatures moved forward, bowing their heads. Duat placed his palm atop each one until he established control.

"Bellator, Aazar, they are safe now, come forward. The seven illuminated jackals had begun to sniff around the graves and the church. "They will do as I command now," Duat declared.

They turned, hearing a sound; one of the jackals had cocked his leg against an old headstone.

Duat growled, "Disgusting creatures!"

Suzanna was startled awake, jumping from her desk as a heavy door slammed shut downstairs. She blinked a few times, hearing other sounds coming from her floor.

Disoriented in the dark, she reached across the desk and switched on the reading light. Yawning, she peered out the window, but the beautiful landscape had vanished into the darkness. Scratching her head, she glanced at her watch, which still read two minutes past twelve. She must have slept for hours.

Panic set in as she realised she had no idea what time it was; she needed to get home to her cats. Unsure how to retrieve her car, she suddenly covered her ears as an alarm blared throughout the building. In a fit of absolute panic and recalling the gas issues reported in the place, she grabbed her bag and sprinted out of her room, running barefoot and rushing past the Clerics.

"Lady Suzanna where are you going?" a voice called out from behind her, no doubt one of the white-robed figures. She ignored it and kept running but froze in a panic when she reached the top of the stairs. Not one for calm situations, she began to shake, took a couple of steps back, and hid behind a pillar. "What on earth is going on here?!" she thought, her heart racing.

Wearing her full armour, the Sergeant-at-Arms pressed the push-to-talk button on her comms device. "Control, we are all present; silence the alarm." She scanned the ranks of the Escarrabin, ensuring they were ready for battle. "Form up!"

In swift unison, The Escarrabin moved to create two orderly lines ready for equipment and armour inspection. "The Reeve and Raysmau will be joining us shortly." With a curt nod, she called upon her scribe, "Add fifteen to the headcount in the record."

"Yes, Ma'am," the scribe replied.

The Sergeant-at-Arms noticed the Reeve and Raysmau entering the central lobby from security control. A frown appeared across her face seeing the Armourer accompanying them.

"Thank you," Raysmau said to the Sergeant-at-Arms with a nod. "How many do we have?"

"Fifteen, Ma'am, it's as many as we can spare, with having to leave a skeleton crew here," the Sergeant-at-Arms replied. She stepped closer to whisper to Raysmau, "Ma'am, may I ask why she is with us?"

Raysmau shook her head, her face expressing what she really felt. "Don't. It's not my decision, nor the Reeve's."

"Understood, Ma'am."

"Look, I need you to stay, to manage the other Escarrabin here. No one knows the armoury like you do, and we need someone of your calibre to ensure its safety and maintain order while we are away."

The Sergeant-at-Arms nodded reluctantly. "I must say, I'm disappointed Ma'am. I'd rather be in the field facing the enemy head-on."

"I understand, but if this goes wrong, there will be many more opportunities for that."

"Yes, Ma'am."

Raysmau then turned to the Reeve. "Would you like me to proceed?"

The Reeve nodded in response. "Escarrabin, pay close attention to what I'm about to say. We have received intelligence confirming that three Watchers have been sighted in Shropshire, which is approximately a ninety-minute drive from Loxley. While we cannot ascertain their identities with absolute certainty, there is a strong possibility that one of them is the Gatekeeper. If that wasn't unsettling enough, we have reason to believe he may not be operating alone. Many of you witnessed the incident a few nights ago; he departed with only one Watcher. This leads us to suspect that he is now joined by a second Watcher, who is described as wearing a black suit, a sign that indicates he may have evaded capture for an extended period. He may have been at large forever."

Despite standing resolutely at attention, the body language of several Escarrabin subtly shifted. It was evident to them that the mission ahead would pose significant challenges. Raysmau continued, her tone growing more serious. "If this is indeed the case, this Watcher will likely be a formidable adversary. We cannot afford to take any risks. Our objective is clear: we need to locate them, and we are NOT on a retrieval mission. This is a search-and-execute operation. If the opportunity presents itself, the Watcher who escaped with the Gatekeeper will be brought back here. Should that not be possible, however, he will meet the same fate as the other two."

As Raysmau paced deliberately between the two lines of soldiers, her eyes scanned their faces, gauging their readiness. "Understand this: we are venturing into public territory. Exposure of our kind is a danger we must avoid at all costs. The mere appearance of us could incite panic and draw unwanted attention. Your Scatterblades are technology that is unknown outside our Order. Secure them to your backs and refrain from drawing them unless absolutely necessary. I doubt the Watchers will surrender peacefully upon our approach. Be sure to set your pulse fire to its minimum setting; we do NOT want to inflict any damage in populated areas."

Raysmau paused for a moment, allowing the gravity of the situation to sink in. "Our destination is a town named Shrewsbury, where a lower-ranked Elder resides. We believe the Gatekeeper will target her life. Have I made myself clear? Are there any questions?" Raysmau anticipated there would be many, yet an unsettling silence engulfed the group as none of the soldiers voiced their thoughts. "Very well then," she declared. "Your vehicles are prepared and waiting outside. Move out now!"

On the flight of stairs above, Suzanna crouched tightly in a ball, her body trembling. Thoughts whirled chaotically in her mind: *'Gatekeeper, Shrewsbury, weapons...'* "Oh no. An Elder in Shrewsbury; they must mean Mildred!" Panicking, she turned around and peered over the balcony. The intimidating figures in armour had disappeared. She spotted Clerics seated at their heavy oak desk: their expressions unreadable beneath the layers of their robes.

Her hands quivered, and an instinctive need to act surged within her. Just as she made her decision, a voice sliced through her racing thoughts, making her jump.

"What are you doing?"

She turned to find Lady Nubia, her presence striking and authoritative. "Um, well…"

"And why aren't you wearing shoes?"

"Um, Lady Nubia, I… I'm not sure what is happening." The words stumbled out, a mixture of confusion and fear.

"You're just curious, Suzanna. You've always been full of curiosity. It's a good trait, but it can also lead to your downfall."

Suzanna swallowed hard, her mouth dry as sandpaper, each breath feeling heavy in her chest. "Your car is outside." To her astonishment, a faint smile appeared at the corners of the Curator's lips. "Off you go, curious Suzanna. And don't forget your shoes."

Nodding, Suzanna found her voice, "It's okay, I have more." With renewed determination, she dashed down the crumbling stairs, manoeuvring carefully around the falling debris. Once in the central lobby, she hesitated. Should she exit the way she came in or through the ruined main doors?

She edged toward the flame-scarred entrance and spotted her car outside, its engine running. "How does she do that!"

Turning back, she saw Nubia at the top of the staircase, nodding with her hands clasped behind her back as she walked away.

✜✜✜✜

Crouched in the shadowy corner beside the church, Duat pushed another persistent jackal away with a grimace, his patience wearing thin. "This is becoming intolerable!"

The jackals, either sniffing him or baring their teeth at Aazar and Bellator, had made for a long night. "Aazar, how long until sunrise?"

Aazar straightened, glancing up at the church's clock tower. "Not long now, Sire, perhaps thirty or forty minutes at most."

Duat inhaled deeply. "We need to devise a plan. Come closer." He gestured for Bellator and Aazar to crouch down beside him, attempting to keep a distance from the unruly pack of wolf-like creatures milling about.

"My Master has bestowed upon me a power; he said it was a shield." Duat held up his palm waving it as if he could summon an unseen force. Yet, despite his efforts, nothing changed. The truth hung heavily in his chest; he had no idea how to wield the power intended to protect him. "What do you recall about the cat we encountered at the old portal? You mentioned you had seen her before?"

"Yes, Sire, once on the main street and again in a small place known as Rocke Road. I suspect the protector resides there."

"Do you know which house she inhabits?"

Aazar nodded, the memory vivid in his mind. "Recently, in the dead of night, I spotted her at a window at the far end of the road. I could sense she was one of them, part of the League of Light."

Duat's stare sharpened, his voice tinged with disbelief. "And you did not act upon it?"

Aazar hesitated, his shoulders tensing. "Well, no, Sire. It seemed futile without a leader to guide us. But now that you are here, it is different."

Duat nodded thoughtfully. "What about the magic house? You saw another Elder visiting there?"

"I suspect so, Sire. I've spotted her a couple of times; she seems older. The way she was dressed and adorned with jewels suggested to me that she holds a significant rank among them."

"But you've never seen this Elder visit the other in Rocke Road?"

"No, Sire. She would slip into Grope Lane, disappear for a short while, then reappear making her way to the train station. She always used public transport, which caught my attention. Typically, someone of her status is chauffeur-driven. This discrete behaviour tells me she was probably here without anyone from their Order knowing. The only other member I've encountered in this area was the one you dealt with, the one they called Tempest. All the other Elders I've met were from a different era and place entirely."

Duat continued waving his hand and nodded. "Why was the Tempest woman in this area?"

Bellator glanced at Aazar for direction, as he had little to contribute to the conversation.

"Well, I suspect it's all interconnected, Sire. The senior Elder, the magic house, the Elder you killed, and the cat whose bloodline we sensed from a distance, along with another protector in the area. It's highly likely that the cat protector is one to be feared, or maybe it's just the cat itself."

"Their prophecy has come to pass, and it foretells of one who will arrive. But the cat we encountered, you've seen it before! Their prophecy has only just taken place, so that particular cat cannot be the one foretold. However, if this protector, the one you think resides on Rocke Road, has just acquired another cat…" His voice trailed off as he processed the implications.

Duat's expression hardened, "If she is indeed the prophesied one, we must eliminate her. How far is her road from here?"

"It's merely a matter of…"

"Enough!" Duat interjected sharply; his frustration palpable as he shoved away a jackal that had lunged menacingly at Aazar.

Aazar nodded in acknowledgement. "Thank you, Sire. It's only about a mile from here."

Duat said with determination. "Then that's where we are heading. We'll need to find rope or chains to secure these mutts."

✛✛✛✛

Suzanna snatched the navigator from her bag and placed it into the console. "Okay, right, where are we going?" She glanced toward the far end of the drive and noticed that the main gates had opened. In the low light, she couldn't see any vehicles, but the dust trail suggested that the soldiers from the lobby had passed through. "Right, follow those cars." She began rubbing her feet, trying to remove small shards of stone. "That really wasn't very clever of me, was it? Car, can we move please!" The engine was still running, but there was no movement in any direction. Frustrated, she shook the steering wheel. "Disengage auto-drive!" To her surprise, the auto-drive button disappeared from the display. Instantly, pressure was released from the brake pedal. "Woo!" Suzanna clapped her hands together. "Okay then!" She floored the accelerator, causing a massive wheel spin that sent dust and stones flying from the wheels behind her. "Whoops," she ducked down, glancing at the windows to see if Nubia was watching.

The car tore down the driveway, she could see the gates were starting to close ahead. "Come on, come on, come on…" It was tight, but she made it through. Due to her speed, she swerved up onto the semi-circular grass verge. Hooking the steering wheel to the left, she regained control of the car and headed down the road of no name.

Three black cars of a make that Suzanna didn't recognise were ahead of her. She kept her distance, following their lights in the dark. As they turned a bend in formation, the vehicles looked identical, all featuring tinted windows. Having visited Loxley a couple of times before, she was becoming familiar with the route. They had only travelled a short distance, but they were headed in the right direction toward her hometown of Shrewsbury. She took a deep breath. "What are you all up to?"

"Ma'am,"

Raysmau turned around, "what is it."

"I believe we may be being followed."

With the exception of the driver, who used her rearview mirror, everyone in the car glanced behind them.

There were three rows of seats in their car. The Reeve sat next to Raysmau while three Escarrabin occupied the seats behind them. One Escarrabin was positioned up front next to the driver.

"Suma, get a lock on that car," Raysmau ordered.

"Yes, Ma'am," Suma replied, unzipping a compartment beneath her left arm's body armour. She retrieved a small telescope-like device from a hidden pouch and extended it, bringing it to her eyes. Pressing a button, she locked onto the car, recording its number plate. After taking a picture of the driver, she paired the device with her radio. "Control, receiving?"

The response was immediate. "Send."

"I'm sending images now. Can you check if it's friendlies? Yes, I understand." Suma released the button to talk. "Control is searching now, Ma'am."

Raysmau glanced at the Reeve as they waited. "Look at that car, Ma'am. It doesn't seem like a threat."

The Reeve shook her head. "Hang on. I think I've seen that car before. Escarrabin, pass me your spotter, please."

Suma complied, and the Reeve brought the device up to her eye.

"Yes, understood. Thank you. Information has come through, Ma'am. No threat detected. It's an Elder named Suzanna."

A wry smile appeared on the Reeve's face. "So, it is. I've seen her from a distance before. She's been associating with the Curator and is new to Loxley. She was recently promoted."

Raysmau nodded. "We recently made modifications to a new Elder's car. I didn't personally see the work done, but it could be that one."

The Reeve passed the spotter back to Suma. "She was involved in a cat swap a few days ago."

Everyone looked confused by the Reeve's words. "Honestly, don't ask. It's odd that she would pop up now. If I recall correctly, she lives in the area we're heading to. Keep an eye on her."

✥✥✥✥

Bellator stood near the church, watching as the first light of dawn began to break. Though the sun had not yet fully risen, he didn't require his glasses in the dim light. In front of him were large, imposing blue gates that, if opened, would allow him entry into the park beyond. Within the park, he could see multiple tents and marquees surrounded by neatly trimmed grass and well-maintained flowerbeds.

He checked his surroundings; even at this early hour, he could see people walking their dogs in the distance by the river. The area outside the park, where he stood, was blissfully free of any irritating human distractions. As he headed through the gates, he glanced back before making his way to the nearest marquee. A simple tug on the awning revealed that it was tightly secured by several large iron pegs. He attempted to pull one of the tent pegs out, but it wouldn't budge. Similarly, tugging at the ropes yielded no results.

Frustrated, he peered inside the marquee and was immediately struck by a sensory overload. Hundreds of different types of flowers greeted him, many of which he had never seen at Loxley before. As he studied the central display, he noticed the variety of colours, noting the distinct absence of turquoise.

Hearing voices in the distance, he quickly sprinted around the displays in search of a cutting tool. He found a pair of scissors behind one of the displays, but they were too weak to cut through the ropes.

Rummaging further, he came across a damp green substance with a sign next to it labelled 'oasis.' Unsure of its purpose, he cast it aside and continued his search until he discovered a small cutting knife with a retractable blade.

With the knife clenched between his teeth, he jumped onto the central display, supporting his waist as he stretched. Despite what Duat had said about his origins and the healing of his wounds, he still felt pain with every step he took. In the centre of the display stood a large wooden pole that extended to the roof of the marquee. Gritting his teeth, he began to shimmy up the pole, grunting in pain as he ascended.

He reeled in agony from his wounds as he reached out to cut the rope overhead. He had to hurry as there were approaching voices. He began slicing through one of the four ropes in the middle of the marquee, ignoring his pain. Each of his four cuts caused the rope to fray before finally giving way.

He grabbed one of the ends and let himself down as the rope began to droop from the middle of the tent. As he dragged the rope outside, he noticed that workers were beginning to move about the site. He wound the rope around his shoulder and continued till he was satisfied. Using the knife, he cut the rope again, put the blade into his pocket and started to run back to the church.

"Oi! Who are you?"

Bellator didn't turn around; he kept moving toward the blue gates. Behind him, there was a loud crack, followed by multiple screams and the chaotic sounds of people in a panic.

Bellator ran through the blue gates and turned around to see the huge marquee collapse. He heard glass shattering, along with other noises of objects being crushed. In the distance, he spotted a dozen or so people with their heads in their hands, completely overwhelmed by the chaos.

Gripping his rope, Bellator glanced up at the sign above the blue gates, that read, 'Welcome to Shrewsbury Flower Show.' He shrugged his shoulders and turned back toward the church.

Chapter Twenty-Two:
SWALLOWS HAVE FLOWN

Time had slipped away, accompanied by the consumption of numerous cups of tea. "I can't handle any more tea, Nahla; my bladder is about to explode! I can't keep pacing around this house indefinitely," Mildred complained, rubbing her tired eyes as she rose from the couch. Sleep had eluded her for most of the night, interrupted only by brief naps plagued by unsettling dreams. Peering through the dusty kitchen windows, she realised it was early morning, signalled by the birdsong and the stillness of her neighbours' homes. Mildred yawned and stretched, feeling the weight of exhaustion that had never been an issue until recently. Her bedtime used to be consistent, and she had always been an early riser.

As she stretched, a cat's tail brushing against her legs caught her attention. "Well, there you are, madam. You've been quite absent for most of the night. What have you been up to?" Mildred murmured as she scooped up Comet, automatically showering her with affectionate strokes. The weight of Comet came as a surprise, she extended her arms and held her up in front of her face. Strange, she thought, along with everything else happening at the moment. "You've definitely grown. How can that be?" Bringing Comet close to her chest, she went to check the, still full, food bowls. Neither cat had eaten. "How are you gaining weight without eating? This isn't natural at all. If this continues, I'll have to call the vet!" The unnaturally sized kitten remained expressionless. *Questions, questions. If I call the vet, do I call the nice lady or their vet, Fennaway, the cat whisperer?* She kept her thoughts to herself. The thought of Fennaway unsettled her, and she quickly decided. "Listen to me," she called out to Nahla in the front room, "if you both keep refusing to eat and not spending time together, I'll be calling Dr Belloch. You hear me?" Pointing at Nahla, who was listening from the couch, Mildred ran her hand inadvertently across Comet's scar, causing a sharp pain. Comet leapt from her arms and bolted upstairs. Mildred inspected her hand, only to see a flash of turquoise running along her index finger. She shook her hand in shock until the colour dissipated. "Right, that's it. I'm doing something! I'm going to the Futility to find out what's going on!"

✤✤✤✤

Duat was initially pleased to see Bellator return with an armful of rope. However, a sense of unease lingered nearby, prompting him to rise to his feet. "What have you done? What's all that noise in the distance?"

Bellator turned around, noticing a crowd of men shouting from the tented area across the road. He shook his head. "Nothing of note, Master. Here, will this do?" He handed the coiled rope to Duat.

"I'm not sure; let's give it a try."

"Respectfully, Sire, it might be better if you handle the death dogs."

"Are you afraid of the mutts?"

"No, Sire," he lied, although the tremor in his voice betrayed him. "They respond better to you."

Duat murmured under his breath as he began to uncoil the thick coarse rope. "You, alpha, come to me!" In the morning light, the black-backed jackal's illuminated coat had faded from view. Duat tied a loop at the end of the rope. The jackal obeyed, lowering its head in submission. Crouching down to meet the creature's eyes, Duat spoke with conviction, "Listen to me." He held his palm over the jackal's skull. "You will control your unruly pack."

The jackal flashed its dirt-stained teeth, the odour from its matted fur was of decay. "Today, we will be fighting an old enemy, and you will show no mercy." The alpha growled, it turned to face the others in the pack and howled. The six other dirt and blood-stained jackals joined together in a collective howl.

Bellator flinched, turned and glanced nervously towards the workers across the road. They were all staring in their direction. "Master, silence them! It's attracting attention!"

Duat placed the loop around the alpha's neck. "Silence! All of you!" The howls gradually faded into snarls and aggressive gestures. "Aazar, these beasts are on edge. I don't think we can just walk to the Rocke Road you mentioned; they will attack anyone on sight."

"Yes, leave it with me, Sire." Aazar put his glasses on and entered the church carpark.

"Here, Bellator, hold this," Duat commanded, passing him the rope with the alpha attached to it. Bellator looked terrified as the jackal charged at him. "Sit down, mutt!" The alpha ignored his instruction and bundled into his midsection, knocking him to the ground. "Master, Master!"

"Take him under control, Bellator!"

Bellator howled in agony as the jackal bit his arm, and he began to wrestle with the death dog.

Duat grabbed the rope again and dragged the alpha away. "Sit down right now!" As Duat frantically tied loops in the rope about six feet apart, the alpha did as it was told.

Bellator, whose injured arm from the pulse blast had been beginning to heal, shuffled on his backside to the church wall. His arm was bleeding once more, and the deep teeth marks were all the way down to the bone. Glaring at the alpha, he pressed a bandage from his pocket firmly against the fresh wound. With its tail up and slobber streaming from its broken, blood-covered fangs, it stared at him.

"Right, all of you, come to me!" There was obvious dissent in the pack, none of them wanted to be controlled. He quickly threw loops around three of the jackals, pulling the rope tight to hold them in place, but the others were not so forthcoming. "You all come to me now, or I'll send you back to where you came from!" He raised his palm, and their eyes focused on the swirling colour within, the same shade as the trees that resided next to the lakes of fire from which they had originated.

One jackal moved forward to attack but was silenced by the alpha. Duat could hear voices from the other side of the road drawing closer; the collective growls of the unruly canines wouldn't go unnoticed. He swiftly secured the last of the three, and soon all seven jackals were roped in a chaotic parade of aggression.

Bellator finished bandaging his injured arm, cradling it close as he pushed himself upright. "Master, what do we do now?" Two of the jackals lunged at him instantly. Duat tugged at the rope, preventing them from getting closer, while the other five rabid-looking jackals turned on the two attackers.

"We don't have long before the mutts turn on each other or us," Duat warned.

Bellator nodded but was clueless about what kind of plan they could possibly devise. At that moment, a car pulled up in front of them with Aazar at the wheel. He poked his head out of the window. "Sire, get in!"

The car was tiny and old compared to the others in the carpark.

"Here, Bellator, hold this," Duat said, passing the rope to him. Bellator, terrified, reluctantly accepted it.

Duat approached the car, "Aazar, we'll never get in here."

"It's all I could find, Sire," Aazar replied.

"Well, what about that one?" Duat pointed to a large transit van.

"No, Sire, it won't work with the time we have. Look, people are coming toward us," he warned, gesturing to a group of men in high-visibility vests approaching from the other side of the road. Duat nodded in acknowledgement.

"Good dog, good dog..." Bellator said, raising his trembling palm up. Without the control that Duat possessed, his colourless palm held little significance.

The alpha tore off, quickly followed by the others, pulling Bellator straight off his feet. Duat turned to see Bellator being dragged across the car park on his backside.

"Bellator, get a grip!" Duat shouted in frustration and held his palm forward, "That's enough!" The alpha stopped and howled at the others. The canine group halted as Bellator got up, grimacing and rubbing his rear.

"Bellator, no time to lose! Get them in the car!"

The Watcher froze, not wanting to touch any of them.

Cursing under his breath, Duat flung open the back door of the car, gesturing emphatically at the alpha. "Dog, get in there!"

Aazar looked quite impressed as the alpha bolted toward the open door, dragging the rest of the jackals along with it. The jackals bundled into the car, their paws sending fur and drool flying everywhere. Aazar barely had time to brace himself before a jackal collided with him, claws scratching the skin beneath his glasses. Duat hurried around to the passenger seat. "Bellator, push them in! You'll need to get in the backseat as well!"

Bellator shielded his eye as best as he could with his glasses.

"There he is!" a voice yelled from the other side of the road. Bellator blinked a few times to adjust his vision as he glanced at the men running toward them. "You let the marquee down!"

Determined, Bellator lunged for the last jackal hanging at the rear, giving it a firm shove into the car.

"Make way!" Duat shouted at the chaotic pack. With an almighty shove, Bellator managed to squeeze his way into the cramped vehicle.

Duat shook his head, a mixture of disbelief and irritation on his face. "It would have been much easier if you had taken that large van over there," he said, nodding at the transit in the carpark.

"It would have, Sire, however, this is an older model. I broke the glass and hotwired it. It's not as easy with newer vehicles."

Duat looked at him, confused.

"It's amazing what you can read online, Sire."

In his rearview mirror, he could see the angry group waving their arms frantically. Without hesitation, Aazar slammed his foot on the accelerator and the car's wheels spun away in the direction of Rocke Road.

✢✢✢✢

To avoid being seen, Suzanna kept a safe distance from the cars in front of her. Confident that they had not spotted her, she estimated there was about an hour before they would arrive in Shrewsbury. She needed to use this time wisely to think and plan. Mildred's image loomed largely in her mind: who were the soldiers, and what purpose lay behind the high-tech weaponry they carried?

Suzanna shook her head in worry. A Gatekeeper? The very term sent chills down her spine. What could this title possibly signify? Apparently, this Gatekeeper was planning to make an attempt on Mildred's life. Why would anyone want to hurt Mildred?

Completely in the dark and feeling alone, she was grateful that Nubia had given her the nod – *(whatever that meant)*, but she had no idea of what she was about to walk into. Furthermore, these were events she suspected she shouldn't be witnessing. Her mind continued to chatter away to itself as she did her best to maintain a cool demeanour as well as focus on the cars in front. Each vehicle moved in perfect unison, their tinted windows concealing their occupants and they never deviated from the speed limit. If the intention was to remain inconspicuous, their deliberate and striking presence achieved the exact opposite.

Suzanna tapped her meticulously polished fingernails on the steering wheel, acutely aware that she needed help. Someone else had to witness what was happening—or potentially what was about to happen. According to the rules of the Order, any issues, no matter how small, should be escalated up the ranks. In her case, her Elder was Lady Abrielle. She paused for a moment, thinking about Abrielle, she must have had an office at Loxley for some time. Abrielle would likely be more informed about matters, perhaps even aware of what Suzanna was currently witnessing.

Suzanna considered calling her but hesitated, concerned that some may perceive her as meddling in affairs that did not concern her—someone who reported everything, thus untrustworthy. That wouldn't work. Only one other person came to mind: the one she was the Elder for, the one who was meant to be keeping an eye on Mildred. Suzanna nodded to herself, wondering if Daphne would be awake at this early hour.

"Phone! Call Daphne!" she instructed. Her phone connected to the in-car speaker; Daphne, a Level Seven Elder, did not own a mobile phone, so the call was answered at home after four rings.

"Good morning," came a yawn from the other end. "Daphne speaking…"

"Daphne, good! I'm glad you're up. I need to be quick; I'm driving, and you're on speaker. Are you busy?"

"Well, Aziza woke me, she keeps pawing me in my sleep, so I'm…"

"Great! How long would it take you to get to Shrewsbury?"

"Um, I'd need to check the bus timetable. I'm not sure they're running at this hour, and honestly, I have no idea what time it is. My clocks have stopped working. Why?"

"No time for that. I know you don't have a car. You need to grab a taxi. I can't pick you up since I'm coming from the other direction."

"I don't remember the last time I called a taxi."

"Don't worry about that. How long will it take? I'll be at Mildred's in just under an hour."

"Mildred's? Why are you heading there, my Lady?"

"No time to explain. Can you get there in around an hour?"

"It'll be tight, to be honest. The roads need to be good. What's going on? Is there a problem with her cat again?"

"The roads will be fine at this hour. No, she's in trouble, and she has a problem with a Gatekeeper."

There was a moment of silence. "Did you say a Gatekeeper, my Lady? What's one of those?"

"Honestly, I have no idea, but it doesn't sound good."

✥✥✥✥

Bellator's head was pinned by seven unruly jackals, and his teeth were clenched against the glass of the tiny car's back seat. Duat put his hands to his forehead with frustration, the volume of barks, howls and snarls was driving him to distraction. "Aazar, wind the rear windows down, I can't think!"

Aazar pressed the window controls, a rush of fresh air brought welcome relief to Bellator. "Get off! Get off me!" he shouted, doing his best to push the jackals away.

Duat covered his head as one of the pack jumped onto the back of his seat, scratching his face. "Get back!" he yelled, lashing out with his hand. "Alpha, CONTROL THEM!"

With six other jackals and a Watcher crowded onto a backseat intended for three people, the alpha snarled at his counterparts and made a weak attempt to establish his dominance, but it was ineffective and mayhem continued as they battled among themselves. Bellator howled from the backseat, clutching his wounds, while Duat and Aazar were coated with fur, salvia, bloody splatter, and a random tooth.

"Enough! Pull over, Aazar, I can't stand this any longer!"

"Gratefully Master," Aazar swung the car to the side of the road and swiped at a jackal that was gnawing his shoulder. The vehicle had stopped on one of the main roads used by people travelling to work. The moment the vehicle came to a halt, Aazar lashed out repeatedly at the canine onslaught. The small car shaking back and forth with what appeared to be three adults defending themselves against a pack of dogs gathered some attention.

"Please, Master, take action!" Bellator's arm was bleeding as he tried to cover his face.

"ENOUGH!" Duat spun around, his temper changing the colour of his palm as he held it out. The eyes of the death dogs followed his movements. "You will listen to me, you will take orders from me, you will fear me!"

With that, one of the jackals slipped out of its loop on the rope and jumped through the open window. Duat turned, hearing car horns blaring and brakes screeching as the jackal sprinted across the road, fixated on a person wearing a high-visibility jacket.

Aazar leaned out from the broken window as the traffic warden started to run away, the death dog in hot pursuit. "That may cause attention, Sire," he said.

"Who is that person in the luminous vest? Are they of any importance?" Duat asked.

"No, sire, just another traffic warden. A human irritant," Aazar replied.

Duat turned to face the alpha and seized the dog with his left hand while hearing distant screams. "Listen to me!" he said. "Enough of this, show order right now!" he said, placing his right palm over the jackal's head. Bellator shielded his face from the glow of power while Duat waved his palm across the skulls of the six remaining dogs. "Aazar, how far now? I can't take this any longer."

"Only a matter of minutes, Sire."

"All right, hurry up and get us there before I really lose my temper."

"Yes, Sire."

The car pulled away.

Crys of terror continued in the distance.

Lifting her right hand towards her face, Mildred flexed her fingers back and forth, studying them intently. The strange colour she had seen earlier was now absent. Dressed and ready to go out, she called both of her cats into the kitchen, where their food was already prepared.

"Look, you two, I'm just popping up the road to look at the area I saw in my vision," she exclaimed, waving her arms in the air in frustration. "Something unnatural is happening here, and both of you"— she pointed at each cat in turn — "you know something more than you're letting on. Comet, who is this lady I see occasionally when I brush that mark on your side?"

She tapped her right foot on the floor with her hands on her hips. "Don't think I'm daft! These dreams, or visions, or whatever they are, started just before you appeared, Comet, and just before Nahla went through whatever that experience was. I don't want to call a vet, and I'm not keen on seeing a doctor because I know something is happening to me, something is changing. Yes, I feel stronger, but this colour in my hands and whatever happened with the boys at the bus stop is unnerving. I can't exactly call a doctor and explain that, can I?"

With her foot, she slid the full cat bowls towards them. "For now, Nahla, the cat flap needs to stay closed. I'm worried about you going outside. I can feel that something is going on in this area."

Grabbing her cloche hat and putting on her scuffed brown shoes, she secured the cat flap before heading to the front door. As she opened it, she turned around to see both cats staring at her, neither of them touching their food.

"I just need to find something, something to explain what's going on. I hope you understand," she said with a smile before stepping outside.

It was a beautiful morning filled with birdsong. Curiosity got the better of Mildred, she rubbed at the dirt sheen on her window and peeped into the kitchen. Both cats were sizing each other up but not interacting. Adjusting her duffle coat, she shook her head. This was most unnatural.

"Kalara, she's out in front of the house."

Kalara joined the two Escarrabin at the window overlooking Mildred's house. "Where do you think she's going at this hour? We can't let her outside with Watchers in the area! Ana, check in with the others and find out how long they'll be."

Ana pulled her mobile phone from her pocket, and her call was answered immediately. "Control, where is the procession? What's the ETA at Rocke Road?" Ana nodded as she listened. "Understood, yes, received. Out." She disconnected the call. "Control has a lock on the vehicles. They're still a minimum of thirty minutes away, and that's really the earliest; it could be longer."

Kalara kept her eyes on Mildred. "Look at how she's dressed. She's going somewhere; not about to do anything with that overgrown garden."

Kalara rubbed her head and said, "We have no choice; we need to intervene. We can't let her leave the street until the others arrive. Both of you, get your Scatterblades ready." She walked over to the bed, where she retrieved her tactical shoulder holster from under her leather jacket. As she secured the velcro adjustments around her back, she made sure the straps were tight. She then took out two power packs and a firing weapon from her bag.

Soad and Ana exchanged glances, intrigued. "What's that? I haven't seen one of those before," Soad asked.

"No, you won't have seen it before Soad; it's still in development. It's a short-burst pulse weapon: not as powerful as the Scatterblades, but it can still inflict significant damage. I'm currently field-testing it." She held the pistol-sized weapon up for them to see. "You can see the laser sights on top, but unlike a conventional nine-millimetre bullet firearm, the magazine compartment takes these," she said, holding up one of the power packs. "Each power pack is only good for around twenty bursts, which makes it a bit impractical. That's why I must carry spares. You two have never seen this before, okay?"

The two Escarrabin nodded, though they looked on with curiosity as Kalara loaded the weapon and pressed the safety release. An immediate sound followed, and a red light above the trigger switched from red to green. "Okay, we are loaded." She placed the weapon in her sling, along with the other power pack.

"What are you going to do? She can't know we are here."

Kalara nodded as she put her leather jacket on and half-zipped it to conceal the weapon, "I'm not sure, I'm making this up as I go. But look, we can't let her out of the street and that's that, so I must take direct action." Kalara headed to the stairs, "Both of you keep an eye on me, keep the camera rolling just in case we need evidence. Let's hope things don't get out of hand."

Kalara headed down the stairs and exited into the back garden. As she hopped over the wall and started running down the street, she knew the next junction would take her into Rocke Road; what she didn't know was what on earth she was going to do next.

✛✛✛✛

"How far away are we?"

"The navigation system says about twenty-three minutes, Armourer."

In the lead car of three, the Armourer opened her backpack.

"What do you have in there?"

The member of the Escarrabin, sitting to the right of the Armourer, hadn't spoken a word during the journey until now.

"Well, aren't you the inquisitive one," the Armourer replied, looking the elite security team member up and down. "And what should I call you?"

"I'm Masika, and I know your name. Everyone has talked about you since you arrived."

"All positive things, I'm sure!"

Masika shook her head. "No, not exactly."

The Armourer smiled. "That's okay; it takes a lot more than that to offend me."

"I wasn't trying to offend you; I was just stating the truth. I'm uncomfortable sitting next to you. I've heard you can be wayward."

The Armourer leaned closer and whispered in Masika's ear, "You heard right!"

"I noticed you didn't answer my question. What's in the bag?"

"Oh yes, I didn't, did I? But since I'm not a member of your Order, I suppose I don't have to." She playfully nudged Masika's body armour with her elbow. "However, I will share just to satisfy your curiosity." The Armourer opened her backpack wider. "So, these are exploding golf balls. Now, this device is quite spectacular." She pulled out a tennis ball-sized sphere. "Now, you insert this into a specialist throwing device."

Masika turned to the Escarrabin sitting next to her. "I've seen those throwing things on television."

Her colleague nodded. "So have I. They're designed for dogs"

"Yes, that's correct. It's a throwing device for dogs. You place a tennis ball in the top, hurl it as hard as you can, and the fluffy mutt brings the ball back, and so on and so forth. However! This is no ordinary tennis ball, as you can see. I designed its original purpose for something else. So, ladies, you load the sphere into the throwing device and launch it—hoping you're a good shot. It can be a bit of a problem if you hit the wrong person." The Armourer paused, recalling an event from her past. "So, that's that…"

Masika shrugged her shoulders, "you didn't say what it does?"

"Hum? Oh, if you hit the target with it, it sends a cold shock through the body and freezes the urine in the bladder."

The two Escarrabin exchanged glances.

"Yes, it's crazy, isn't it? Extremely uncomfortable; not advised."

When the Armourer giggled, Jazmin, the car's driver, turned around and raised her eyebrows. "And you created this with that goal in mind?"

"Please keep your eyes on the road driver, that's how accidents can happen."

The driver shook her head and returned her focus to the road.

"And no, I didn't design it for that purpose. It was meant to send a cold shock to the brain, temporarily disabling your opponent." The Armourer nodded to herself a few times, "But it just freezes the urine, but then you know the saying about people being full of it. I tried it out on a man in my village. I was hiding behind a bush and smack! Hit him right in the chest, he had a look of shock on his face for a bit, I can tell you." The Armourer giggled to herself, "Thinking about it I've never seen him again."

Jazmin glanced around again.

"Come on, driver, road, road, if you please." The Armourer pointed forward and clapped her hands together. "But there you go, that's chemistry, that's science. You will all want to see what I have in my trunk, ha ha, it's in the back of the car!"

The occupants of the vehicle exchanged worried glances.

"Anyway, it's a nice day for this; enjoy it while it lasts. The weather is changing, autumn is coming, the swallows have flown."

"What on earth are you talking about?" Jazmin exclaimed.

"What? What do you mean, Driver?" The Armourer replied.

"There is a Gatekeeper out there! Our prophecy has played out. This is not a joke; today, some of us may lose our lives!"

"Well, I'm not laughing."

Masika was incensed and took over, "You were! How can you be so casual and carefree about this?"

"Masika, I feel the fear just like all of you. But if we lose our lives today, we always come back. You know that as well as I do."

The Escarrabin were dumbfounded. Jazmin took the initiative to break the silence. "Ladies, we are now on the outskirts of Shrewsbury. I'll inform the other cars to get ready."

The two Escarrabin in the backseat glanced at the Armourer. She offered them the tiniest of smiles in return. "Don't worry; we'll be fine."

✢✢✢✢

Kalara slowed her pace as she turned onto Rocke Road. Glancing to her left, she noticed Mildred closing her gate. A little out of breath from her unplanned excursion, Kalara checked to ensure her weapon was secured and pulled her leather jacket up high enough to cover it. Mildred was making her way toward her, Kalara knew she needed to intercept and delay her for as long as possible.

Crossing to the other side of the road, Kalara realised she had to think quickly and get her story straight; whatever that might be. Mildred glanced in her direction but appeared to be looking right past her. Kalara scanned her surroundings and spotted a bus stop, but nothing else of significance caught her eye.

Closing her gate, Mildred began to walk up the road. She knew she would have to go out to the back of the Futility, the area the locals called 'The Sway.' The pub would be closed at this time of the morning, but she should be able to get to the back. If she were honest, she had absolutely no idea what she was looking for, and the subject matter was hardly something she could discuss with anyone. Lately, her dreams felt more like visions—specifically, the connection she had between Nahla and Comet. All the strange happenings felt interlinked somehow.

As she walked, she noticed a lady approaching her, dressed as a biker. Mildred looked further ahead, the boys were not at the bus stop; in fact, no one was around. The only other person she could think of speaking to was the local oracle, Mr Franks. He knew everything about the area, a true local who was aware of all that was going on, along with everyone's business.

"Hi, good morning," the biker lady said, interrupting Mildred's thoughts.

"Good morning to you," Mildred replied, nodding as she tried to walk past the lady.

"Say, I'm a politician."

Mildred, not one for politics, noticed the lady's attire. Most politicians typically wore a tie or something formal when they were canvassing for votes. Mildred offered the slightest smile and said, "Good for you. Excuse me, I need to be somewhere."

"Oh, I won't take much of your time. It's good to speak to the community. Politics is all about the people!" Kalara smiled, knowing she had no idea what she was talking about.

"Well, I don't vote, so if you don't mind…"

"You don't! That's such a waste. What can I do to encourage you to change your mind?"

"It's complicated."

"Isn't it always?" Kalara smiled. "Man troubles?"

Mildred shook her head. "No, cat troubles."

"Ahh, I understand. I had a cat once." She hadn't, but maintaining a vested interest might keep the conversation going.

"Well, I have two, and they have unique personalities."

"And that's what makes cats… cats."

"Yes, um, I guess you're right. I'm sorry; I really need to be somewhere."

"I'm very interested in keeping cats safe and creating a new haven for them, it'll be part of my manifesto."

"Haven?" Mildred looked confused.

"Yes, well, a shelter is probably the correct term."

"Well, that's really good to hear! What party are you with? I'll keep it in mind for the future."

"Party? Oh, I see, um, I'm from the No More Watchers Party."

Mildred blinked; she'd heard the term 'Watchers' before. "That's an odd name. Sounds a bit strange if you ask me. Anyway, if you have any literature, just drop it through my door. I live over there at number one."

Kalara smiled. "I don't have any with me. Actually, I was thinking of moving into the area. What's it like? It seems very quiet."

"It's okay, yes, thank you." Mildred's voice trailed off as a small, worn-out car rolled into view at the end of the road. The way it rocked slightly caught her attention. "Anyway, I must go. Have a nice day."

Mildred walked off in the direction of the bus stop.

"STOP RIGHT THERE, MILDRED!" The authoritative tone from behind made her turn around. "What did you just say to me, and how do you know my name?"

Kalara stiffened, a palpable tension radiating from her. Mildred noticed the alarm flickering across her features. "Mildred, you need to get behind me right now," Kalara instructed. She pulled out her phone and began waving towards the windows of the house across the street. "Control, full compromise. Targets in sight; we need immediate support."

The upstairs windows of the house opposite opened, and a net curtain was pulled back. Mildred could see two women dressed in some form of armour standing behind the curtain.

"What the hell is going on? Who are they, and how do you know my name?"

The engine of the car at the end of the road was switched off, and its occupants began to emerge. One opened a rear door and dragged six wildly thrashing dogs from the back.

"I'm asking you again, what is going on?" Mildred's voice was full of fear and confusion.

Kalara shook her head. There were three Watchers accompanied by a pack of wolf-like beasts. She turned to the windows opposite. "Both of you, get changed, get out here with your Scatters right now!"

"Scatters? What on Earth?"

Kalara turned back to Mildred. "You must trust me, Mildred. I'm from the Order. Get into your house, take cover, and lock everything!"

"What? This bloody cat club is out of control! What's happening now?"

Kalara placed a hand on Mildred's shoulder. "You have to trust me." She unzipped her leather jacket revealing a firearm.

"Oh my God!" Terror surged through Mildred and she sprinted away, pushing her gate open with such force that it nearly broke. Hands shaking, she fumbled with her door key, glancing back at Kalara, the leather-clad gunslinger. Just then, two women in armour that she had never seen before appeared in front of the opposite house, holding large chrome-looking weapons. They immediately put on helmets.

In a complete panic, Mildred shook at the door key, "Come on, come on!"

Finally, the key turned, and Mildred kicked the front door open, slamming it shut behind her. Her heart racing, she skidded into the front room, eyes glued on the unfolding scene outside. "Nahla! Nahla!! Come to me! Comet! Come here, both of you, now!" She shouted as loudly as she could.

Outside, the three strangers stood in a line, looking prepared for a gunfight.

Chapter Twenty-Three:
THE HOUSE IN THE CORNER

"That's her, Sire; I'm certain of it," he said, pointing with conviction. "That's the one I've seen before. She lives in that house at the corner of the road."

"Which one?"

"The one dressed in an unusual manner."

The three Watchers saw a lady run off toward the house at the corner.

"They're armed, Master," Bellator noted, he recognised the distinctive Scatterblades that two of them were carrying.

Distracted, the group turned as the sound of a lawnmower suddenly interrupted their conversation. A man, clad in a faded T-shirt and cargo shorts, began pushing it along his meticulously kept lawn. His eyes widened in shock at seeing three strangers accompanied by a pack of fierce-looking dogs.

"Come, friends, let's meet the old enemy in battle," Duat whispered into the alpha's ear, struggling to contain the pack on the length of rope. "Jackals, listen to me, when the time is right, you will attack without hesitation and show no mercy. We will see this through to the end, no matter the cost."

"But Master," Bellator interjected, "they've got firearms. This could end badly for us."

"I'm aware, Bellator, but we are armed too."

The jackals flashed their sharp canines, drool dripping from their bared teeth as they eyed the three armed, Escarrabin at the end of the road. "Remember, my Master told me he provided me with armour. Very soon, we will find out exactly what that means."

The jackals strained against the leashes, desperate to be released as they headed towards a fight that had been a long time coming.

"Remember, unless absolutely necessary, we cannot use Scatterblades out here."

"Kalara, we must protect ourselves!"

"The others won't be far away Ana, so ensure your pulse dials are as low as possible. We must minimise the damage, everything will need to be concealed."

Ana saw a woman observing them from a bedroom window on the right. "Any cover-up will be challenging because we are being watched."

Soad looked with shock towards the bottom of the road, "What are those dogs? They don't seem like they belong there. They look like killers."

Although she didn't know what they were, Kalara nodded. "He's bound to let them loose on us. Let's peel round, keeping our backs to Mildred's house. We must protect her at all costs. He doesn't want us. He is after her or her cats."

"Looks like they are forming a defensive position, Sire."

Duat nodded, "Indeed, they seem intent on protecting the house in the corner."

The jackals pulled them down the road, closer to the Escarrabin.

"Shall we let the dogs loose, Master?"

"Bellator, I sense your nerves, but I want to see them up close. I want to witness the fear in their eyes as the inevitable unfolds around them."

"But what if they open fire? They could destroy us at close range."

"They won't. The three of them are no match for us."

Bellator cast a wary glance to his left; the lawnmower was still running, but the man who had been pushing it stood still in shock. Even with Bellator's limited knowledge of the outside world, this was clearly not a normal day for the man with the mower.

As the two groups drew closer, Duat halted, his left hand firmly restraining the attack dogs while his right flexed with concealed power.

Soad was the first to speak, "A Gatekeeper dressed as an animal doctor. Those beasts you're struggling to control do not look like they belong here."

Duat nodded. "You will meet them momentarily."

"We are armed, one who calls himself Duat," was the brash retort from Kalara.

"You dress oddly compared to your companions. No armour. Either you are exceptionally brave or hopelessly foolhardy," Duat added.

Kalara stepped forward as the jackals writhed in their eagerness to reach her. "Give it up, Watchers; there is nowhere for you to go."

"We're heading to that house in the corner, so you need to 'give it up.' You might survive if you take a step back. You die if you resist. Poor little mishaps, you're alone out here."

"Are you certain of that?" Kalara gestured at Duat with her weapon.

Aazar turned around to witness three unusual-looking black cars pulling into the top of the road. "It's them, Sire, they have found us!"

"Fascinating," Duat remarked, "I can spot twelve of their soldiers among them, plus one who is dressed differently. And look who it is, Raysmau and the Reeve, making their grand entrance." A sly grin spread across his face. "This will be a day etched in memory, the day you all unravel into nothingness."

"Ma'am, our three have weapons drawn on them, but what exactly are those creatures accompanying them?" Raysmau questioned.

The Armourer stepped forward, her eyes narrowing as she studied the scene. "Jackals by the looks of it, I wouldn't underestimate them; very dangerous. So, what's your plan Reeve? You know you're not supposed to use weapons out here."

The Reeve squared her shoulders, determination flickering in her eyes. "I believe the situation has just escalated. Everyone present, draw your weapons and fall into attack formation!"

Nearby, the loud hum of a lawnmower came to an abrupt halt as the man operating it froze in shock upon witnessing a group of absurdly dressed women prepared to defend themselves.

"Do you want my assistance?"

"Get ready!" Raysmau yelled.

"Wait, wait, wait!" The Armourer opened the rear of the vehicle and dragged her trunk forward. "Let's give this a shot."

"Stop, Armourer, what is it?"

"Reeve, this is very impressive, when I dial in the appropriate distance, this produces an electromagnetic pulse blast that takes out everything electrical in the vicinity. Additionally, it creates a barrier behind us to prevent anyone from entering this location without passing out. It causes a brain shock to everyone and everything inside the security bubble I'm about to construct."

"Wait, hold on, is it harmful to people?"

"No, it simply knocks them unconscious; they won't be aware of it and will quickly regain consciousness once I turn it off. We certainly don't want to be on CCTV, do we now? Oh, I should point out that it has no bearing on our bloodlines, and I suspect it will have no effect on the Watchers there."

As the Armourer rushed past them, Raysmau cast a worried glance at the Reeve. With two antennae on top and a visible electrical charge passing between them, the Armourer began to turn a dial and held the contraption up. "All right let's get started. One, two, three." She held her arms aloft as if she were conducting an orchestra, "Boom!" the Armourer yelled. Instantly a pulse blast spread out in front of them, the current flowing down the street was visible by its effects.

A car's windscreen shattered and the man who had been mowing his lawn collapsed to the ground. A vehicle was turning onto the road behind them. As it passed the parked cars of the Escarrabin, the driver lost consciousness and the car gently rolled into a garden wall.

A wave of instability swept through the Watchers and the Escarrabin, their minds reeling as if experiencing vertigo. Aazar looked up and saw a woman who had been watching from the window collapse to the floor. The jackals fell to the ground but quickly revived themselves.

Watching from her kitchen window, Mildred instinctively clutched her stomach as an unsettling wave of nausea washed over her as she fell against the sink. Shocked, she watched a woodpigeon fall from the tree next to her gate. Steadying herself, she rubbed her eyes; something had happened all around her.

It was eerily peaceful, dogs barking in the distance had ceased, and birdsong faded to an unsettling silence. The familiar hum of her kitchen fridge was abruptly silenced, it looked as if all power to the house had stopped.

"Comet! Nahla, where are you? Are you okay? Something's going on!" she called out with worry.

The Armourer shook her head, "Mmm, you know, I think I may have dialled it a little too far," she looked up as the powerlines in the distance swayed back and forth.

"Oh really? You think?" the Reeve retorted, gripping her spear tightly. "Let's proceed. Try to spare the Watcher who was once at Loxley; the other two and the beasts can be taken down."

Suzanna didn't follow the Escarrabin's cars into Rocke Road. Parked slightly to the side, she could see events unfolding. Unsure of what to do, she scratched her head, hoping that Daphne would arrive soon.

As the wave of unease passed, Duat raised his palm and roared in a fit of rage. A blinding white light erupted from his palm, the heat was so great that Kalara covered her eyes and fell to the ground, and the other two helmeted Escarrabin fell backwards. Ana reached forward with her back turned and began dragging Kalara away.

"Get behind me, both of you." Even with their glasses, Bellator and Aazar had to turn away from the explosion of white light. Duat began to shake as he handed Aazar the rope.

Duat collapsed to his knees, the jackals swung at one another in exasperation, trying to get to the momentarily downed Escarrabin. The Gatekeeper let out a grotesque howl of pain, ripping away his glasses as a snout protruded from his head. The blinding white light from his palm was erratic as his body twisted, his clothing falling away in shreds. The gruesome sounds of the cracking of multiple bones made Aazar flinch as Duat's one eye split into two.

"He's transforming! Escarrabin, quickly take them out and cover your eyes from the white light as best you can!" The Reeve led the charge, one hand shielding her eyes while Escarrabin ran at her command, with Raysmau following at the rear. "Remember, use pulse fire only if you're sure of a direct hit." The Armourer stood with her hands in her pockets, happy to observe the unfolding events at the rear.

Vast, powerful wings unfurled from Duat's back and positioned themselves with a resounding crack. Jagged claws scraped against the road's surface, sending up a shower of sparks as the brilliant white light flickered out. The Gatekeeper's red eyes gradually adjusted to daylight, and he grunted loudly as Kalara pushed herself to her feet. The former white light in his palm morphed to turquoise pulsing with energy as he felt an exhilarating rush of power coursing through him, experiencing the sensation of armour for the first time. The

Escarrabin at the end of the road were charging toward them; it was only a matter of time before they opened fire.

"Aazar, release the Jackals!" Duat yelled.

Having never witnessed the Gatekeeper's transformation before, Aazar's heart raced, and he nodded in fear. The air around him thickened with tension as he began to unloop the death dogs, their growls menacing. With a thunderous flap of his wings, Duat ascended, towering over both Aazar and Bellator. He lifted his right claw, the sharp talons extended like daggers as he roared.

Aazar and Bellator felt a rush of wind as Duat directed his palm toward them, unleashing a brilliant pulse of turquoise light that surged forward. The energy struck them with a force that made the ground tremble. "Now fight!" Duat roared. A shimmering turquoise shield of protective light instantly manifested around them, encasing Aazar and Bellator in a luminescent barrier alive with energy.

The death dogs transformed, their frothy mouths curling into menacing snarls as their black eyes ignited with a fiery red glow. They swiftly formed a disciplined line, howling in unison. From deep within their bodies, protective scales began to erupt. The scales sprouted with impressive speed down their flanks, glimmering and reflecting light, covering their limbs and skulls in protective armour.

"ATTACK!" bellowed Duat, his wings flapping powerfully as he launched himself into the air. In response, Aazar and Bellator instinctively separated, running to either side of the road to avoid the initial onslaught of blinding pulse fire that erupted around them. The ground shook with energy, sending shockwaves rippling through the air.

The Reeve lifted her spear as an armoured jackal charged towards her, froth flying wildly from the corners of its mouth as it bared its razor-sharp teeth. Kalara, now steady on her feet, fired at the jackal running directly for her. The pulse blast ricocheted off its back with a loud crack, deflecting away with a burst of sparks and causing the shot to veer off, slamming into a nearby house shattering its front windows. The impact made the jackal stumble, momentarily dazed, but it quickly regained its footing, lunging forward with renewed ferocity. "Blimey! They're shielded!" she exclaimed in panic.

Standing beside her, Soad and Ana opened fire, their blasts of energy connecting solidly with the jackal, knocking it off balance and sending it tumbling backwards with a pained yelp. The Reeve released the button on her spear to make the trigger battle-ready and raised it to her chin. Using the sights, she zeroed it. With a precise pulse, she struck it across the back. The jackal howled and shook itself, its red eyes furious with rage.

Ana was the first to make a move sprinting toward the tree at the front of Mildred's garden. Leaping onto the garden wall, she scrambled up the tree, calling out to the other two. "Here, both of you! Get up here!" she shouted.

As the jackals ran through the gardens of Rocke Road, Bellator took cover behind some bushes. He peered cautiously at the turquoise glow in front of him, he hoped it would provide some protection; it hadn't been tested yet. Without a weapon, he decided hiding behind the bushes was the safest option.

Overhead, Duat descended and landed solidly on the roof of the house opposite Mildred's. He roared and slid on the roof, causing roof slates to crash to the ground.

"My God!" Mildred screamed and dived for cover having seen some form of flying creature on the roof of the house opposite. Outside, there were so many bangs that it sounded as though sections of her road were being torn apart. "Nahla! Comet! Both of you, come to me!" She peeped over the kitchen sink. The winged monster was being hit by some form of light fire; it appeared to have some kind of protective shield. Every time it was hit, there were flashes of the same colour she had been seeing in her palm. In the tree at the end of her front garden, two oddly clad women were dragging up the woman in leather she had spoken to earlier. Mildred pressed a hand to her chest in panic as the woman in leather was finally hoisted up just as a rabid looking dog hurled itself at the trunk of the tree, scratching and digging its claws in, trying to climb up. "Nahla, Comet! We are getting out of here!"

While searching through her trunk, the Armourer weighed up her options, "Nope, don't need that, oh, they might be useful." She glanced to the left and noticed a barefooted woman rushing past her towards a taxi that had arrived just to the side of Rocke Road.

"I'm so happy you're here, Daphne." With a horrified expression on her face, Daphne exited the taxi. The sounds of small explosions and howling dogs were emanating from Mildred's Road.

"What is going on?" the taxi driver asked, stunned by what he was witnessing.

Thinking fast, Suzanna said, "Oh, it's a movie set, a huge movie is being made. Look, you must leave; being caught on film will ruin the authenticity!"

"I can't see any cameras!"

"No, they're further down the street. How much does Daphne owe for the journey?"

"I didn't see anything advertised about making a film. Call it forty pounds."

Suzanna shrugged, "You know what these Hollywood types are like; they like to keep these things quiet to avoid any fuss." Her hands were shaking as a loud bang echoed from behind, followed by screams. Suzanna quickly took her purse from her pocket and thrust a bunch of notes into the driver's hand. "That well covers it, thank you. Off you go!"

Suzanna wrapped an arm around Daphne and pulled her aside to take cover behind some trees.

"Lady Suzanna, what on earth have you gotten me into?"

Suzanna glanced behind her to ensure the taxi was heading in the opposite direction. Relieved to see him leave, she turned to Daphne,

"I'm glad he didn't drive into the road. Something happens if you go in there, I saw it happen; a car crashed into the wall over there!"

"What is going on?" Daphne asked, peering into the road from behind the cover of the trees. She froze as she saw a huge winged creature roaring in the distance as if it were directing something. "What on earth is that?"

"I'm not an expert, my friend, but I think that might be what they call a Gatekeeper."

They both glanced to the right and noticed they were being watched. Suzanna looked the observer up and down; she wore a heavy trench coat and was dressed differently from the others.

One of the death dogs had pinned a member of the Escarrabin to the ground, she screamed as she released a pulse blast that missed her target entirely; the pulse of light, sailed over the houses in the street, hitting something in the distance. Another Escarrabin focused on the jackal, discharged her weapon and a blast of white light struck it across the back.

Another jackal lunged and caught one of the Escarrabin by the throat and began dragging her across the tarmac, two of her colleagues rushed to her aid using the end of their Scatterblades, hitting the creature repeatedly across its armoured scales.

Raysmau tried to focus on the words that were being said into her ear during the commotion, "Yes, go ahead, control!"

"We have a redline indicator on an Escarrabin, Ma'am; it looks like Karima."

Raysmau saw two Escarrabin fall during the medley. One was wrestling with a jackal on the ground, the other not offering any resistance as she was dragged across the tarmac. Her two fellow team members hit the jackal repeatedly across its back.

"I'm on it. Over!"

Raysmau ran towards the lifeless Escarrabin, "Both of you, get out of my way!" The other Escarrabin stopped hitting the jackal with their Scatterblades and stepped aside as Raysmau turned the dial on her pulse rifle, there was a huge blast as the jackal was split into two and blown across the ground. Looking at the other Escarrabin wrestling with the death dog, Raysmau shouted, "Sana, let go of the jackal, I don't want to hit you." Sana stopped wrestling with the dog. "You, mutt! Look at me," the jackal looked up, its red eyes full of rage as it let go of the Escarrabin and ran at Raysmau. It was immediately hit, the Escarrabin to its side instantly covered in dog hair, skin and scales.

Aazar walked casually across the road, pointing and shouting at the Escarrabin while his turquoise shield absorbed the relentless barrage of pulse fire. The Gatekeeper observed from above, satisfied that Aazar was drawing fire away from him. He noticed frantic movements behind the dirty windows of the house across the street, where their prophesied cat resided. Outside, a jackal struggled to climb a tree.

He searched for Bellator but couldn't see him. "Aazar, assist the jackal outside of the house!" the Gatekeeper bellowed, gesturing urgently towards the corner house as he soared into the air. He spotted one of the Escarrabin lying motionless on the ground; the discarded Scatterblade next to her body would be useful for Aazar.

With a terrifying roar, the Gatekeeper spread his wings and flew directly at the Escarrabin, who were frantically aiming their weapons in a desperate attempt to defend themselves. Their blasts ricocheted harmlessly off his turquoise shield. As he landed with a powerful thud beside the lifeless body of the fallen soldier, he swiped at two of the Escarrabin, hitting one across the head and sending her reeling backwards. Her helmet bounced across the ground as she shielded her face in pain.

Terrified, the other soldier stumbled backwards, firing multiple blasts at the Gatekeeper's shield. The sheer force of the impacts caused him to stumble back as he temporarily lost footing. The Gatekeeper snatched the Scatterblade from the ground and took flight.

"Jazmin, keep shooting; he was shaken by those final volleys!" With a shout, Raysmau sprinted beside the Reeve. They both reflexively dove as a blast rang out to their sides, "Ma'am, our blades are having little effect. We have little choice, we have to use more pulse power."

A jackal ran at them as the Reeve and Raysmau shot the death dog across the skull and back. The dog fell, wounded, its legs twitching as it tried to regain its feet and get upright. "Ma'am, we have no choice."

The Reeve had to shout her reply over the noise, "Raysmau!" A flash lit up to their left, prompting them to duck once again. "I understand, but we need to consider the damage we are causing to this road. We are never going to get away with this!"

"Yes, Ma'am, but we must finish this first. We can worry about the consequences later."

"Aazar!" The Gatekeeper screamed as it flew over Mildred's house, dropping the Scatterblade into the long grass of the front garden. Without hesitation, Aazar sprinted towards the weapon. Just as his fingers were inches away, twin pulses of energy slammed into his back, discharged from the tree.

"Both of you, keep firing at him! That shield cannot last forever!" Kalara shouted from the lower branches of the tree, discharging her sidearm at the agile jackal below.

"So, who are you two, and what are you doing here?" The words were shouted from the top of the street by a woman standing by the security vehicles. She waved them over with urgency.

"I guess we better do as she says," Suzanna said, glancing at Daphne.

"Do you really think so, my Lady?" Daphne replied, her voice trembling in fear.

"We need to figure out what's going on and why they are here on Mildred's Road."

Suzanna sprinted towards the stranger. "I'm Suzanna!" She ducked behind one of the cars for cover. "Come on, Daphne!"

"Are you one of us?" the woman with extensive facial scars asked.

"Yes, I think so." Suzanna pulled back the lapel of her jacket to reveal her pin badge.

"What level are you?"

"I'm Lady Suzanna, degree Level Six. Daphne come on!" Suzanna waved her arms. Daphne reluctantly ran over and hid behind her.

"What Level are you, Daphne?"

Daphne hesitated, shielding her ears from the sound of pulse blasts, her breath quickening with panic. "Daphne, Degree Level Seven."

"Seven! This is well above your pay grade," the woman exclaimed.

Daphne's shaking hands brushed strands of hair away from her eyes. "And who are you?"

"I'm the Armourer!"

Suzanna and Daphne exchanged worried glances.

"Right, hold these, will you?" The Armourer said, her voice steady but urgent as she passed them what looked like a ping-pong ball. Daphne, her hands trembling slightly took hold of one. The Armourer raised a cautionary finger. "Careful! These are quite unstable in the wrong hands," the Armourer warned. She removed her large coat and laid it gently on the floor. Then, she took a device from one of the pockets and placed it into a trouser pocket. Rolling up her sleeve, she exposed what appeared to be a robotic arm.

"Suzanna, pass me that!" She pointed at the ball. Suzanna complied, handing it over as the Armourer clenched the white ball and took aim. "I need to be cautious, you see. Don't want to hurt any of our own. Both of you stay there, I'll be back in a moment," she instructed. The two Ladies of the Order nodded, relieved to cower behind the vehicles.

Stepping into the fray, the Armourer took in the sight of three armoured dogs running through the street, attacking the Escarrabin.

She noticed one dog struggling to climb a tree at the end of the street, taking multiple hits from above.

Clutching the ball, she put her fingers to her lips and let out an ear-piercing whistle. The two women behind her covered their ears in pain. "Come on, doggy!" she whistled again, capturing the attention of the nearest dog, which had been viciously attacking the arm of a pinned Escarrabin.

"Come here now, I have a little surprise for you!" The dog captivated by her call, released its grip and sprinted toward the Armourer at incredible speed. The Armourer retrieved a switch from her trouser pocket. "I better not miss; this could get tricky!"

With careful aim, she launched the ball toward the dog. "Come on, come on, here, little doggy!" As the jackal ran in the direction of the ball, the Armourer pressed a button on her controller. An enormous explosion erupted, the sound was deafening as the dog was thrown skyward. The shockwave shattered a window in a nearby house, glass raining down as the jackal crashed back to the ground.

"Boom!" The Armourer exclaimed, her laughter ringing out as she raised her hands in triumph. "That was way more powerful than I thought! Ha, ha-ha!" Daphne and Suzanna exchanged worried glances as bits of dog hair drifted through the air.

Aazar snatched the Scatterblade from the grass as he was hit repeatedly by a reign of pulse fire from the Escarrabin perched in the tree. Having never held a Scatterblade before, he ran into the well-maintained garden next door to Mildred's house and disappeared around the side of the house. The jackal could distract those up in the tree while he tried to master how to wield the complicated weapon.

"Ma'am, can you see the other one?" Raysmau's voice cut through the chaos. Herself and the Reeve were training their fire on the Gatekeeper.

"What other one are you talking about, Raysmau?"

"The Watcher. I saw one run around the back over there, the one in the suit. I haven't seen a trace of the other one."

"Let's keep our focus on Duat, we can't let him get away!"

"Right. It's probably best if you two stay here," the Armourer instructed Daphne and Suzanna. "Do not touch anything in this trunk, one wrong move and we'll all go up in bits. I may need to come back and use some of my creations if this gets more intense." She grabbed another ball from the trunk. Now armed with two explosive balls, she strode purposefully down the road.

Bellator, nestled deep within a bush, watched closely, he had witnessed three of the dog's fall. Aazar had run for cover but was now armed. Bellator contemplated his next move, he was still unarmed, so felt content to let events unfold before him, waiting to choose his moment.

From the safety of cover behind the cars, Suzanna and Daphne peered out, their breaths shallow, hearts racing. Before them, two wounded Escarrabin staggered, supporting one another and headed towards them. One soldier had a significant leg wound, blood seeping steadily from beneath her battered armour, the other appeared to be in serious pain, clutching an injured arm.

"We should help them," Suzanna urged.

Daphne shot her a bewildered look, "My Lady, we don't even know who they are."

"I think they're security for us; I've seen them at Loxley, her eyes were fixated on the approaching figures"

"What's Loxley?"

Suzanna placed a reassuring hand on Daphne's shoulder. "I'll explain later. Let's get them to safety."

"Are you sure?" Daphne questioned.

Without hesitation, Suzanna, barefoot, ran toward the wounded soldiers. They froze, startled, as she winced in pain, stopping to remove stone shards embedded in her left foot.

"Who are you?" shouted the soldier with the leg wound, raising a chrome-coloured weapon. They noticed a second woman emerge from behind the vehicles.

"Come on, let me help you!" Suzanna urged. "I'm Suzanna, Degree Level Six. That's Daphne, Degree Level Seven. Come on, over here, Daphne!"

The Escarrabin, grimacing in pain, lowered her weapon. Suzanna rushed forward and wrapped her arms around the injured fighter. Daphne joined them, and together they supported the soldiers back to the cover of the vehicles. Once shielded, they all collapsed onto the ground.

"Here, hold this," one of the soldiers passed Suzanna her Scatterblade. Terrified and with trembling hands, Suzanna took the weapon examining its elaborate and heavy construction.

Gritting her teeth, the soldier undid her body armour, tearing at her clothing beneath. Using her torn vest, she hurriedly fashioned a makeshift tourniquet for the bleeding wound on her leg. "Where is your blade?" she asked her fellow Escarrabin.

The soldier shook her head, her face pale. "I lost it back there when one of those dogs took a chunk out of my shoulder." She gestured weakly down the road; they could see her fallen Scatterblade in the wreckage further down. "If this gets worse," she pointed at Daphne, "you'll need to go and retrieve that." Daphne's face twisted in anxiety.

With the other Watcher out of sight, the horde in the tree focused on the jackal prowling below. With the pulse dial set to a minimum, their efforts were having little impact on its protective shield. "Here, someone pass me your blade!" Kalara shouted up to the tree as she swiftly holstered her sidearm.

"Kalara, what do you have in mind?" Soad shouted from above.

The jackal had secured its claws in the bark and was making progress up the tree, its piercing red eyes fixated now only a few feet away.

"We can't turn the dial any further," Soad exclaimed. "At such close range, firing at the mutt could blowback on us."

"Give it to me, Soad; we'll need to go old school."

With a quick nod, Soad leaned down and passed the weapon to her. Kalara snatched it and pressed the button for sword release. A shard of steel, about three feet long, automatically slid out from underneath the main discharge barrel of the weapon.

"Here, Soad, support me! Hold my back!"

Soad steadied herself and complied as Kalara leaned down to strike at the jackal with the sword. The awkward weight of the weapon made any flailing next to impossible from her precarious angle. With both hands gripping the hilt, she launched a determined thrust, but the blade merely clanged against the creature's armoured scales with little effect.

Raysmau pressed the push-to-talk button. "Escarrabin, keep moving forward. Focus your fire on the remaining jackals. The Reeve and I will focus on the Gatekeeper."

Brickwork and debris from people's gardens were strewn all over the road from the number of ricocheting blasts from the jackals' and Gatekeeper's shields, as well as direct hits on neighbouring properties. Inside one of the houses, a minor fire had started.

As the Gatekeeper awkwardly manoeuvred across the rooftops, he spotted Aazar moving around the side of the house next to Number One. Constantly battered by pulse fire, he had no idea how long his protective arch of turquoise would hold. He needed to pick off the attackers. Roaring as he took flight, the Gatekeeper saw three Escarrabin firing at one of the jackals. The jackal's armour held for now as it leapt, ripping a Scatterblade from one soldier's grasp and throwing the weapon aside. The Gatekeeper swooped down, snatching two of the Escarrabin in his talons before taking off into the sky.

The remaining member of the three Escarrabin was pinned to the ground, wrestling with the jackal as it tried to bite her throat. As she grabbed the jackal by its skull, her helmet was covered with drool falling from its mouth. In the distance, she heard yells, and out of the corner of her eye, she watched two of her colleagues plummet to the ground as the Gatekeeper released them. A pulse blast hit the jackal across its back, causing a ricochet that struck her thigh. Although the pulse blast sent the dog tumbling, it remained unharmed.

"Escarrabin, get out of the way!" the Reeve yelled, watching as the wounded soldier howled in pain and crawled across the ground. The jackal regained its footing and turned, only to be hit again. "Get out of the way, now!" the Reeve commanded to the wounded soldier. Adjusting the pulse dial on her spear and lifting the sights to her eye, she fired a heavier pulse blast, sending the jackal into a ball of flames.

"Team Leader, this is Control, receiving?"

"Go ahead," Raysmau replied.

"We've got multiple redlines, multiple redlines."

"We are aware, Control, but there is nothing you can do from there. Over."

Raysmau gathered her thoughts, "Ma'am! Ma'am!" Raysmau shouted and waved frantically at the Reeve. "We are taking heavy losses. We must maximize our firepower."

The Reeve dragged the fallen Escarrabin to her feet. "Can you walk?"

"I think so, Ma'am."

"Good. Keep fighting. If not, take cover at the end of the road."

"Oh, there you are!" Mildred breathed a huge sigh of relief when she found Nahla hiding underneath the sofa. The noise from outside had scared her. "Come on, we need to get out of here." Mildred stretched out her arm, but Nahla was somewhat reluctant to move. "Please, we need to leave." Finally, Nahla relented, and Mildred pulled her beloved cat into her arms.

"Right, where is…" Comet was sitting upright on the stairs as Mildred instinctively ducked hearing an almighty bang outside. "Comet, I think we're at war! There's an alien outside; it must be from that crashed satellite a few days ago. Come on!" But it was no use; Comet, whose real name Mildred didn't know, wouldn't budge.

Feeling Nahla shaking in her arms, Mildred dashed to the stairs and picked up her oversized kitten. "How are you not scared? I'm terrified!" Comet sat peacefully in her arms and yawned. "Oh, come on, that's not normal!"

"Alright, here we go. Out the back door. Hold on tight, my babies!"

"Armourer, glad you could join us! Remaining Escarrabin, concentrate your fire on that jackal!"

With one jackal battling against a sword from the tree, only one remained as it tore through the gardens on Rocke Road.

"No need for that, Raysmau. You're one dog less thanks to me."

The Gatekeeper flew overhead, landing on the roof in front of them.

"Quickly, before he sweeps again!" The Reeve pointed her spear ahead and fired. Raysmau followed suit as the Armourer casually walked forward. "Here, let me try." The beast was some distance away, but with the strength in her mechanical arm, she was confident she could make the distance. The Armourer held her arm up, took a short run-up, and launched the ball into the air. It hit the Gatekeeper's shield and rolled along the roof of the house, dropping into the gutter.

Raysmau and the Reeve ceased fire as the Armourer held her trigger forward and pressed it. A huge explosion erupted as flames engulfed the ball-shaped shield around the Gatekeeper, causing him to roar as the turquoise shield that surrounded him flickered.

"His shield is weakening!" The Reeve pointed as the Gatekeeper lost stability, and the roof of the house partially collapsed, sending a cloud of dust into the air. The three of them stared as the first floor caved in.

"That's going to take some explaining. We weren't supposed to cause any damage, Armourer!"

"Take a look around, Raysmau. It's a bit late for that."

The Gatekeeper took flight, landing on the roof of number one. There were multiple pulse blasts to their left, sending the jackal tumbling onto its back. It was hit again and ceased to move.

"All of you!" The Reeve waved her arms. "He's on the roof of Mildred's house. Come on!"

Mildred pulled the back door open, immediately looking up as something struck the roof. "Come on, you two! We are going!" She clutched her cats tightly, edging her way along the side of the house toward the front garden. As she stepped away from the wall, an almighty roar echoed above. She looked up and froze in horror as the huge, winged creature spotted her, its talons sending roof tiles raining down around her.

Pulses of light hit the creature, but they bounced away, striking Mr Jenkins' house next door, showering Mildred in stone shards. "What's happening?" Mildred screamed as her hand brushed the side of Comet. Instantly, she felt a surge of heat pass through her body and saw the face of the lady from her visions, gesturing and encouraging her to act.

Mildred's eyes rolled briefly as turquoise flashed throughout her right palm. Focusing on the creature, she felt an unprecedented strength as she thrust her glowing palm forward. The Gatekeeper lifted an arm to swipe his talons at Mildred but stopped in shock as he recognised the colour he knew all too well.

"NO!" She shouted as a pulse blast hit the Gatekeeper's shield. He roared, the power of the blast making Mildred's hair fly back as he lifted his claws and went to swipe down. Mildred ducked for cover as another blast hit the side of her house just above her, the proximity knocking her from her feet. Scrambling on the floor, she ensured her cats were okay and quickly looked to the right, a man wearing a suit and strange glasses was pointing a weapon at her.

"Quickly, come on!" she shouted to her cats as she lunged for the back door. Another blast hit the doorframe, sending hundreds of splinters into her back and hair. She kicked the remaining door closed and rushed upstairs.

From the elevation in the tree, Kalara had yet to pierce the skin of the jackal. "Lady Raysmau!" she screamed. "Please hit this thing from the side!"

Raysmau lifted her weapon, and as the pulse struck the side of the armoured dog, it opened its mouth in fury. Kalara jumped from the tree and drove her sword into its mouth. With a firm grip, she pushed hard against the sword until it couldn't move any further. The jackal twitched for a few seconds before its eyes rolled back.

As Soad jumped down from the tree, she spotted the suited Watcher at the front of the house next door. "Ana, look out!" she screamed to her friend above her in the tree.

A pulse was discharged into the tree, catching it aflame and causing Ana to flail as she fell to the ground in a heap.

"Get him!" an unarmed Soad shouted as multiple bursts hit the front of Mr Jenkins' house, forcing the Watcher to retreat to the rear.

Mildred ran to the top of her stairs. From the window, she saw part of her neighbour's house being struck by what looked like heavy weaponry; the suited man was fleeing out the back. "Are you both okay?" she called out, studying her cats as she heard heavy movements on the roof above. In shock, she wasn't sure what to do next.

With the Escarrabin's backs turned, Bellator seized his chance. He slipped out of the bushes and ran to the rear of the nearby house, entering the back garden. The house the Gatekeeper was targeting was only four gardens away. Making sure he remained unseen, he crossed two gardens, pausing to look up at the roof to his left that had collapsed from the pulse fire. A thin trail of smoke was rising from the gap. He knew Aazar was somewhere nearby and was determined to find him.

With the last of the jackals destroyed, the remaining Escarrabin gathered at the front of Mildred's house. They saw her horrified expression through the window as she ran into the bedroom, clutching her cats tightly.

The Reeve pointed at her, gesturing for her to take cover by moving her hand up and down.

The Gatekeeper had stopped moving across the roof. Aside from his heavy breathing, he was silent, focusing intently on the soldiers in front of him. Their weapons were aimed at him, but they had paused in a temporary standoff.

Ana regained consciousness and let out a howl of pain after falling from the tree. The sound made the Gatekeeper roar in response as he took flight, lashing out at two Escarrabin and carrying Jazmin away in his claws.

Wrapped in talons but still alive, Jazmin fired into the underside of the Gatekeeper, the ricochet killing her instantly as she fell behind one of the houses.

At the end of the road, Daphne and Suzanna put their hands to their mouths in shock as the two wounded Escarrabin shook their heads with sorrow.

Soad pointed with urgency, "Look, he's circling again, but that shield is wavering,"

The turquoise ball that had been shielding him flickered repeatedly as the Gatekeeper swung around. They all turned to look at him as he landed on a roof a few doors down from Mildred's.

Bellator entered the garden, which was just two houses from Mildred's. He heard a roar and peered up; the Gatekeeper was on the roof above him. He could see that two gardens away overgrown nettles and six-foot-tall weeds were rolling back and forth as a heavy rustling sound approached him. Soon after, he caught sight of Aazar's thin-skinned skull. Aazar was instantly drawn by Bellator's wave as the Scatterblade he was wielding was aimed at him. Bellator called "The Master is over here, hurry, this way."

The rotten fence panel disintegrated instantaneously when Aazar pushed at it. "Coward, where were you?"

"What do you mean? I was at the front! I took down one of the Escarrabin and managed the jackals. They're down in numbers because of me."

"I never saw you. You're lying. I'll be discussing this with the Gatekeeper later." Aazar pushed Bellator to the side, seeing the tail of the Gatekeeper swinging from one of the roofs above.

"Ma'am, we need to hit him with maximum pulse; that shield is on the verge of collapsing," Raysmau urged.

The Reeve contemplated Raysmau's point. "Instruct one of our team to strike at three-quarters power, Raysmau, we can't wait any longer."

"Yes, Ma'am. Soad, reclaim your weapon. Move up front, three-quarters power, and strike that beast now! The rest of you, take cover."

Soad quickly retrieved her Scatterblade from Kalara, with determination etched on her face, she sprinted into the open road while the others shielded themselves behind walls and trees in the nearby gardens.

"Hopefully, as the blast isn't in a concealed space, it won't cause too much damage," the Reeve said, covering herself behind a garden wall. The Armourer joined her and whispered to her, "I wouldn't be so sure!"

Soad knelt on one knee, grounding herself as she lifted her weapon. She took a moment to steady herself and turned the pulse dial, she waited for the sound notification that the weapon was primed. The Gatekeeper extended his wings and let out a bone-chilling roar, preparing to take flight as the weapon indicated it was ready. Soad released the charge, the force of the blast jolting her backwards.

A powerful burst of white light struck the Gatekeeper's shield. As the Gatekeeper roared and fell backwards, a huge explosion tore through the roofs of three buildings, sending turquoise flecks flying into the air. As the rooftops collapsed and chimneys sank, the last sight of the Gatekeeper was its tail thrashing as it disappeared behind the houses.

The explosion wave swept overhead, lifting Bellator and Aazar from their feet and sending them falling to the ground. The roofs of the houses surrounding them crumbled, and glass showered down from the windows above, cutting their skin in multiple places. As Aazar fell, he lost grip of the Scatterblade. Protecting his face, he attempted to stand up to retrieve the weapon; he glanced across, seeing the Gatekeeper fall into the garden next to them. Suddenly, a huge crash echoed above him, accompanied by the sound of splitting wood. Aazar looked up in horror as the chimney breast of the house leaned dangerously towards him, the crumbling brickwork unable to support its weight. He raised his fists to shield his face just as the chimney gave way and collapsed onto him, breaking multiple bones in the process.

Bellator, struck by splintered brickwork and shards of glass, rubbed his head as he rolled onto his back, quickly adjusting his dislodged glasses. He could see the Gatekeeper's tail thrashing in the neighbouring garden, and muffled sounds of pain were coming from beneath the fallen chimney in front of him. Having witnessed the chimney fall, he suspected that Aazar would not recover from the weight of the debris on top of him. Getting to his feet, he picked up the Scatterblade and glanced across to see the Gatekeeper beginning to rise.

With rocks and flaming debris occasionally falling from above, Bellator scrambled through the rubble. He spotted an arm in a dust-stained suit flailing directly in front of him. "Aazar! Aazar!" he shouted, desperately trying to lift the bricks to free the Watcher. As he uncovered Aazar's face, Bellator saw his lips moving; a bubble of spittle formed as Aazar attempted to speak. Bellator wiped the dirt from his glasses and exclaimed, "You're still alive! That's a huge weight on you!"

"Our bodies are just as weak as everyone else's." Knowing that his ribs were broken, Aazar grimaced as he inhaled.

Bellator pushed against the chimney stack and the masonry attached to it, but he lacked the strength to remove it from the Watcher's pinned body.

"Can you do anything, can you move your legs?"

Aazar tried and yelled but the pain was too much.

Bellator shrugged nonchalantly, "I guess you'll have to stay here then," his voice a mixture of amusement and defiance.

There was a huge roar from behind as the Gatekeeper rose and unfurled its wings.

Through the protective glasses, Bellator could see Aazar's eye widen with concern.

Aazar's words came out in a fractured gasp, a small trickle of blood ran from his mouth as he spoke, "Bellator, what are you doing? You need to fetch the Gatekeeper!"

"Why, he doesn't care about you. You heard what his master thinks of us."

"But he is our Master…"

Bellator's smile widened, a spark of defiance in his words, "he's not my Master,"

Aazar was able to move his left arm as he tried to reach out at Bellator's skull, "Bellator, what are you talking about?"

The Gatekeeper launched himself into the air, soaring over the houses. "My name is not Bellator. He called me that, but I have no idea why. Perhaps he simply fails to comprehend the depths of our existence."

Aazar began to wave his hand in panic. "Who are you? What is your real name?"

Bellator leaned down and snatched the protective glasses from Aazar's eyes. "I'll be taking these. You won't need them anymore; the one you call Sire will need them when he transforms again."

Aazar's eye narrowed painfully as the piercing sunlight flooded in, causing it to turn bloodshot immediately. He gasped, struggling to catch his breath.

"As I said, you really should have treated me with more respect. For my true name is Heka!"

Aazar's arm thrashed wildly, his motion desperate and uncoordinated. "That is... the carrier of serpents...the name of a magic meddler, one who can be traitorous. You'll betray us all!"

Heka nodded and leaned closer to Aazar's face. "And I remember everything. I know exactly how old I am."

"Sire... Sire..." Aazar spluttered, his voice weak and unheard by the Gatekeeper as his body shook. He had lived for thousands of years, and as life drained from him, the last thing his all-seeing eye saw was treachery.

"His shields are down! We can't risk a pulse burst into the sky around here; wait until he lands again."

Gliding in circular patterns over Rocke Road, the Gatekeeper had lost sight of Bellator and Aazar. Weakened and without his protective shield, he knew he couldn't withstand another blast from their pulse technology. Gathering his talons against his midsection, the Gatekeeper slowed and flapped his wings, hovering over the residential area that was now crumbled and ablaze. He realised they wouldn't fire at him from this height.

As he scanned the debris-littered ground below, a movement amidst the rubble of a garden caught his attention, he saw Bellator frantically waving his arms, holding one of their Scatterblades. Descending quickly, the Gatekeeper crashed onto the remnants of a roof, he swayed for a moment, struggling to stabilise himself. "Where is Aazar?" he demanded.

Bellator shook his head with despair. "He's gone, Master," he yelled. "That's it. Soad hit him again!"

As the enormous claw descended from above and gathered him up, Bellator held his arms up, still holding the Scatterblade.

Soad released the trigger as the pulse of light at three-quarters' power headed towards the Gatekeeper. As Bellator was lifted, the pulse burst went straight through the left wing of the Gatekeeper, piercing veins in the skin webbing between bones. The Escarrabin in the road covered their ears from the deafening roar of pain as there was an enormous explosion in the distance.

"Okay, that may also take some explaining." The Armourer muttered, squinting into the distance, "I'm guessing that's the fuel garage that's just gone up in flames."

The remaining Escarrabin shook their heads with worry as they witnessed the huge fireball lift into the sky far behind the Gatekeeper.

Bellator gripped at the underside of the Gatekeeper and held on for dear life. Seething in pain, supporting a Watcher with a Scatterblade, the Gatekeeper took to the air, gliding away erratically until he vanished from view.

The Escarrabin lowered their weapons, taking a moment to assess what had just transpired. Those remaining removed their helmets, with a couple immediately rushing to aid Ana, who had been jettisoned from the tree.

The Reeve took off her helmet, surveying the devastation along the once peaceful road. She turned to look at the house at number one. Mildred was at the upstairs window holding her two cats. "Raysmau, we have a lot of explaining to do," she said. The remaining Escarrabin gathered around Raysmau and the Reeve, all staring at the cat-holding lady, whose body was trembling, her face bore an expression of sheer terror.

The Armourer walked into the centre of the road. Behind her stood two lower-ranked Elders beside the cars while two wounded Escarrabin struggled to get to their feet. Even from a distance, the shock on their faces was evident. Surrounding her were crumbling houses with several others ablaze. Glancing to her right, a frown crossed her face as a random fish paste sandwich fell from the tree in front of number one. She turned to the Reeve and said, "You know, Reevy, I'm not sure whether this was a victory or not."

Chapter Twenty-Four:
RECOVER THE FALLEN

"I'm not sure how long we can hold out for; you can hear the sirens in the distance are heading this way."

Raysmau nodded. "Ma'am, this whole area will be flooded with police and firefighters in no time. There are also civilians living along this road who will need assistance."

The Reeve nodded in response. "Control, can you track the redlines of the fallen Escarrabin?" After receiving instructions, she continued, "Raysmau, we can't leave anyone behind. Some bodies may have fallen outside the protective zone the Armourer created. We need to repatriate and clear out as soon as possible."

"Yes, Ma'am," a hint of frustration creeping into her voice, "but how can we explain all of this?"

The Reeve closed her eyes and sighed. "There is only one who can help us cover this up."

Raysmau let out a heavy sigh. "Nubia?"

"Yes, the Curator and the Clerics. It pains me to ask her for help, but what other option do we have?"

Raysmau nodded reluctantly. "Armourer, can you come to us?"

With her hands in her trouser pockets, the Armourer casually drifted over. "Yes, Raysmau?"

"How quickly can you lower your protective shield?"

The Armourer shrugged. "It's just the press of a button, really. But the civilians in this zone will need a bit of convincing; they need to forget what they've seen."

"Do you have something for that?" Raysmau asked.

"I always have a plan, Raysmau."

Raysmau nodded, giving a brief smile as a sign of appreciation. "Escarrabin! Everyone, go to the cars, secure your Scatterblades, and change into civilian clothing. Those injured wait in the cars, we'll be taking you back to Loxley shortly. We need to conduct a quick house-to-house sweep, Ma'am. We must ensure no one else has been harmed."

"Agreed. Hopefully, at this time of the morning, most people are at work. Armourer, when you deactivate this shield device, will everyone affected in this zone, um, just return to normal?"

The Armourer looked surprised by the question. "Well, yes, Reeve," she replied, "it was just a simple disruption to the brain; they won't need to be institutionalised or anything."

The Reeve bit her lower lip, deep in thought, weighing her options. "Raysmau, we'll need to get changed as well. This isn't exactly suitable for public appearances."

"Yes, Ma'am. I'll take care of that right away."

"Good. Let's head to the cars."

The Armourer glanced down at her attire, practical yet grimy from earlier. "I guess I'll just stay here then!"

"If you have nothing to do, Armourer, you're welcome to clean up the dog mess!"

The Armourer glanced at the fallen jackal carcasses strewn along the road. "I'll keep that in mind, Reeve!"

✥✥✥✥

With everyone now changed and uniforms and weapons secured in the cars, it was essential to move quickly. Kalara and Soad swept through the houses on the left while Ana, now recovered with only bruises and scratches, searched the houses on the right alongside Yara.

"I heard there was a woman spotted at the upstairs window of that house over there," the Reeve instructed, "make sure she's all right. Kassia and Alian, I need you both to inspect the houses at the bottom of the road. Take your helmets and stay alert for any falling debris, those homes with gaping, missing roofs are likely to be condemned. Keep your guard up and try to conceal your helmets as best as you can if you encounter civilians. Also…" The Reeve paused, pulling a phone from the pocket of her black suit. A heavy sigh escaped her lips before she answered, "Nubia, please hold…"

"WHAT THE HELL HAVE YOU REEVES DONE NOW?" rang out a voice of fury and disbelief.

Those were the only words heard as the Reeve lowered her phone, "Raysmau, please recover the fallen and assign whoever you need to take with you. We can only hope they haven't been discovered by civilians outside of this area. If you tell whoever goes with you to say they are from an emergency service, just encourage them to think on their feet and improvise. Track the redlines on their phones. Take one of the cars with you and place the bodies inside. Also, deal with those lower-ranked Elders loitering at the end of the road."

"Yes, Ma'am, right away," Raysmau replied.

The Reeve took a deep breath and brought the phone back to her ear. "Yes, Nubia, you have my full attention."

"Attention! Attention you say, how the hell are we going to cover this up? Property destruction, the use of Scatterblades in the public domain. I'm not one of those magic types who can just wave a wand and the world is just fine, you know!"

"Curator, the situation is what it is. The Gatekeeper was poised to act against Mildred and her cats; we had a unique opportunity to resolve the issue before it escalated further."

"From what I've heard, you've caused chaos throughout the entire street, destroying a residential area. You have no idea of the trouble you've created! And while I'm at it, I believe the flying beast got away!"

"It did, but it's wounded. It took the same Watcher with it. The other one, the one that has been at large for centuries, hasn't been seen. We suspect it has been neutralised."

"You suspect? Heavens above, if anyone else finds him, just a simple blood check could lead to an avalanche of unforeseen complications."

The Reeve could hear tapping at the other end of the phone as Nubia contemplated her options.

"Look, we can't risk it. The entire street will have to be off-limits. We'll need to either buy up the properties or something, I don't know. I need to speak with the Clerics to minimise media exposure and reach out to important contacts, and I'm not just talking about the Grand Council!"

"I understand, Curator. We've also lost Escarrabin; we are still in the process of retrieving those."

"What a mess, what an absolute mess! I'll be in touch; we need to take immediate action. And Reeve, I want to see you when you return."

The call abruptly disconnected. Despite her understanding of the Curator's urgency, at some point it would be worth reminding Nubia that the Reeves did not work for her. Her thoughts drifted as she noticed movement outside the house at number one. Mildred was outside, cradling her cats, an air of determination etched on her face.

✜✜✜✜

It didn't take long for a stream of cars to wind their way past Rocke Road due to the unusual scenes that had taken place in the typically quiet cul-de-sac. The air was thick with smoke curling ominously from rooftops. The earlier sounds of heavy pulse fire explosions had shattered the once peaceful atmosphere.

As Raysmau manoeuvred her vehicle onto the road, she felt the power drain from the engine as it crossed the barrier of the protective shield. She spotted the Reeve rushing toward her, there was no time to waste, and they needed to evacuate urgently.

"How did it go?" the Reeve asked, her voice full of concern.

"Escarrabin are all accounted for, Ma'am," Raysmau swallowed at the memory, "I must admit, it was a very troubling sight."

The Reeve leaned closer, her eyes scanning the interior of the car, clearly pained by the weight of what had transpired. she nodded slowly as Raysmau stepped out of the car.

"Thank you for retrieving them. I know it couldn't have been easy."

"Yes, Ma'am," Raysmau replied.

"Did you encounter any problems with the locals?"

"Yes, a couple of men were around one of the fallen."

"What was the outcome?"

"They did as I instructed. After all, I was much bigger than they were, and I told them I was a paralegal."

The Reeve looked momentarily confused, realising that Raysmau should have said paramedic. At least it seemed to do the trick. "We need to clear out. We should keep a skeleton crew here; Mildred has been on the prowl."

"This is going to take some explaining."

"Well, we can help with that!"

They both turned around. The barefooted Elder was staring at them but avoiding eye contact. "Sorry, I couldn't help but overhear."

"Who exactly are you?"

Suzanna quickly assessed the imposing stature of the lady who had spoken. "I'm Suzanna, Degree Level Six, and this is Daphne, Degree Level Seven."

Raysmau glanced at the Reeve. "This is way above your level, members of the Order or not,"

The lady who towered over Suzanna did not look impressed.

"Well, since I'm not completely daft, I had kinda figured that out," Suzanna took a deep breath before continuing. "However, I'm Daphne's Elder, and Daphne is Mildred's Elder. She will listen to us, and let's face it, you two are kinda intimidating."

The two soldiers conversed quietly. "I know who you are, Lady Suzanna. You've been speaking with the Curator. Listen, both of you, my name is the Reeve. I'm in charge here. You two need to stay put, don't touch anything, and never speak about what you've seen here to anyone else. If I need you, I will let you know."

Suzanna placed a comforting hand on Daphne's shoulder. The look of concern on Daphne's face was clear. Judging by the Reeve's tone, it was obvious that she wasn't fond of Nubia either!

"Armourer, as soon as the Escarrabin finish their house checks, we need to leave. You mentioned something about memory loss for those who may have seen something in the area."

"Yes, that's correct, Reeve. I'll need my bag."

"Look, this is really important. You can see CCTV cameras outside a couple of the houses. Are you absolutely sure your device disabled them? Is there any chance they could be backed up elsewhere or recovered?"

"I'm positive."

The Reeve stepped into the Armourer's personal space, looking intently at her scarred face as she sought further clarification.

"I'm sure, Reeve."

"If this ever gets out, there will be all sorts of complications."

"I'm inclined to agree with you. Just let me know when you want the protective grid switched off. I'll start with lawnmower man over there after I've been to my bag, of course."

The Reeve signalled the Escarrabin search team to come closer. "Were there any civilian casualties?"

The six Escarrabin shook their heads, having swept through the dwellings as fast as they could. "We found a lady upstairs in the house over there," Ana said on their behalf. "A man who lives in the house with the motorcycle outside was also present. There were a few others in other properties, but they were all unconscious and showed no visible symptoms of harm. They ought to revive if the Armourer's claims are accurate. But it's important to note, Ma'am, that the search was hardly exhaustive."

"It will have to do with the narrow timeframe we have. Raysmau, are the injured Escarrabin already in the cars?"

"Yes, Ma'am, all are accounted for."

"Thank you. I need all of you to return to Loxley as quickly as possible. Raysmau and I will stay here, and Kalara, you should remain as well. Once the shield is down, we can move the cars. We'll keep one car parked outside Mildred's; we need to visit her. Now, everyone else, please proceed to the cars. We'll have a full debrief later."

The remaining Escarrabin got into their cars while a few members of the public gathered at the end of the road.

"I think I've earned my place here, Reeve," the Armourer said sternly. "I would also like to be present when you speak with Mildred." The Reeve contemplated her comment. Understanding that the Armourer would report to the Grand Council, it was prudent not to exclude her. The Reeve nodded, "So be it."

"And what about us? We need to be there, too. Remember, we are her Elders," Suzanna insisted.

The Reeve shook her head. "I don't believe that would be wise."

"I'm a Lady of the Order!" Suzanna declared, her voice resolute.

The Reeve looked the lower-ranked, barefooted but otherwise well-dressed lady up and down. "Do you even know what you're saying?"

"Well, um, yes."

"Do you even comprehend what you've just witnessed here today?"

"Well, um… no."

"As I thought," the Reeve muttered, shaking her head slightly.

Suzanna interjected, "But she will listen to us."

The Reeve rubbed her temple and glanced upwards. "Fine, we don't have time for this. There's no space in the car, though, so you'll have to make your own way back afterwards."

Suzanna shrugged nonchalantly. "No worries, mine is just parked over there," she said casually, gesturing towards the corner just outside Rocke Road.

The Reeve shook her head, "Armourer, please release the shield."

"Sure, let me go over to lawnmower man first. Raysmau, would you mind taking care of the driver of that car? Just make something up. There was also a lady at a house further down who may have seen us at the start. I'll visit her next."

Raysmau glanced at the Reeve. "Seems like the right thing to do, Raysmau, if you don't mind."

Raysmau nodded and walked over to the car that had gently crashed into the garden wall.

Standing behind the man with the lawnmower, the Armourer held her device forward, ensuring the electrical prongs were facing skyward. "Here we go!" she exclaimed, pressing the button. An immediate bang erupted from one of the houses with a collapsed roof and sparks shot into the air. Next to Raysmau, the car started immediately as a wave of energy surged down the road as sounds of life returned; dogs began barking from adjacent streets. A woodpigeon outside number one stood up, wobbling unsteadily on its legs. With a startled flap, it ascended into the air. Briefly, it paused mid-flight, shocked by the scorch marks marring the top of its favourite tree. Confused by the chaos below, wings beating furiously it took refuge elsewhere.

The Armourer tucked her device into her pocket as the man in front of her clumsily got to his feet. Rubbing his head, he switched the lawnmower back on, continuing for a few brief seconds until his gaze shifted to the scene before him. The mower was switched off as he stared in horror at the devastation wrought upon the road he called home. Overwhelmed, he pressed his hands to his head, his voice rising in a frantic yell, "What has happened? I can't... what...?"

He was distracted as a voice cut through his panic.

"Are you okay?"

The man spun around, eyes wide in panic, struggling to comprehend what had happened.

"Here, you look like you're in desperate need of some water; the colour has completely drained from your face." The Armourer handed him a small, clear plastic bottle.

He took a shaky sip before turning away again, his head sinking into his hands. "Do you know what happened? Just look at the houses over there!"

"Yes, I'm aware. It's an incredibly strange turn of events, funny old do really. Here, have some more water." The Armourer gestured with her non-bionic arm. As he took a sip, she put a surgical face mask on. "Oh, look, there's hardly any left; you may as well finish it."

He nodded absentmindedly, his face awash with confusion. "It's just so bizarre. I came outside to mow the lawn, and there were people at the top of the road dressed in the most peculiar attire, you know?" His hands gripped his head tightly as he spun around to survey his own home, which seemed untouched amidst the chaos. "I can't believe what I'm witnessing!" He turned back to her, "Do you know anything about this because...say, why are you wearing a mask?"

"Oh, no reason," came the muffled response. "But if you look over there," she pointed toward the end of the road, where the main devastation had taken place. As he glanced away, she discreetly rolled a small, metallic ball next to his foot.

"It's impossible!" he exclaimed, his voice rising in disbelief as he stepped forward, the small ball crushing under his feet. A cloud of dust erupted around him, "what's that smell?" He scratched his head, but the gesture quickly ceased as he felt something shift within him as the water bottle fell to the floor and he stopped moving.

The Armourer stepped closer. "Listen to me carefully. You've never seen me; you didn't see anyone on this road today. Nothing extraordinary occurred. You will come to your senses once I clap my hands three times, and all memories of today will vanish. Do you understand?"

He nodded, a distant look in his eyes.

"Alright then, just stay right there and don't move a muscle until I clap three times."

"I wouldn't worry about the lawn," the Armourer said, glancing around the neighbourhood. "I have a feeling property values in this area may have just taken a hit."

As the Armourer walked over to Raysmau and removed her mask, the driver who had lost consciousness was now inspecting the front of his car, a look of confusion crossing his face as he noted the absence of any damage.

"A gas leak, you say?" he asked the large-framed woman dressed in ill-fitting sports clothing.

"Yes, we're part of the clean-up team. It's important that you leave immediately; there may be a secondary blast." The man looked her up and down, nodded, and quickly reversed out of the road.

On the other side of the street, a man with long hair appeared at the end of his driveway, an air of confusion evident on his face. Kalara went over to calm him and talk about his motorcycle.

"What's up with the lawnmower man over there?" Raysmau asked.

"Oh, that's just my special dust," the Armourer explained with a wry smile. "His mind will forget the events of today. It doesn't harm him otherwise; he'll be fine," the Armourer paused. "As long as I remember to clap three times before we disappear. It could get a bit awkward if I don't."

For the few remaining residents on the street, those who emerged from their houses were encouraged to pack a small bag and leave immediately.

"Raysmau, drive the car down to number one, will you? We need to wrap this up as quickly as possible, the authorities will be here any minute."

"Yes, Ma'am," she replied to the Reeve.

Kalara and the Armourer worked together clearing as much debris from the road as possible while the Reeve signalled for Raysmau to drive down towards Mildred's. When they parked, Daphne and Suzanna stepped out, with Suzanna still shoeless, Raysmau had allowed them both to travel the short distance in the car.

"That's a posh car, isn't it?" Daphne whispered.

Suzanna nodded in agreement, carefully brushing the small stones and dirt from her feet as they stood at the entrance of Mildred's unruly garden.

The Reeve and the Armourer caught up with them as they all stood at the end of Mildred's path.

It was of little surprise that Mildred was watching them from the window. She soon disappeared, only to reappear without her cats at the front door. "I suppose you're all going to explain this!"

The Reeve approached the path first.

"What has happened to my tree, not to mention the roof tiles scattered everywhere?"

"We'll take care of that, Mildred. Please do not worry," the Reeve reassured her.

"Oh really? I wonder what Mr Jenkins next door will say. But then again, I guess his roof looks reasonably intact; I can't say the same for his side wall though." Mildred placed her hands on her hips, contemplating how much her life had changed over the last few days. "Well, come in, come in. I suppose you all better come inside," she stood to the side and gestured for them to enter.

The small group of ladies stepped inside one at a time. The Reeve, having been here recently, was mentally prepared for what awaited them inside Mildred's house; the others were not. Instinctively, they clutched their noses, their expressions contorting in surprise.

"What is that smell?"

The Reeve shot a glare at the Armourer, who shrugged defensively.

"Well, that's a bit rude," Mildred remarked as she gathered her cats and settled onto the couch. Dust swirled into the air as she sank heavily into the seat. She looked at the Armourer, "You're dressed strangely compared to the others."

The Armourer raised an eyebrow, her scars lifting on her face as she studied Mildred's eccentric dress sense, "well, that's a bit pot and kettle isn't it!"

The Reeve cleared her throat. "Yes, well, anyway. Mildred, allow me to introduce you. This is Raysmau, this is Kalara, and of course, you recognise your Elders."

Daphne rushed towards Mildred and gave her a big hug. "I'm so pleased you're safe, my friend. We've been so worried about you." Mildred's attention was briefly distracted by the imposing figure of Raysmau, but she gently returned the hug. Despite everything she had just witnessed, she was happy to see a familiar face, even though it was evident they were somehow connected to the chaos that had unfolded on her once-quiet road.

"Hello, Lady Jessica," Mildred greeted.

"It's Suzanna now, Mildred. Remember?"

"Oh yes, the sword-waving ceremony."

"I would offer you all a cup of tea and a fish paste sandwich," Mildred said, scratching her head, "but my hands are shaking too much to prepare anything."

The Armourer nodded, finally understanding the source of the strange smell.

"Mildred, may I sit down? There are a few important matters I need to discuss with you," The Reeve requested.

Mildred nodded as the Reeve went into the kitchen to fetch a chair. "Firstly, what I'm about to tell you is completely confidential. You must never reveal this to anyone, especially those of lower rank. This information is beyond your level, but given the circumstances, I need to be honest with you. I don't wish to insult your intelligence. I can only offer the truth about what you've witnessed here today. I need to…hang on, sorry," she interrupted herself as her phone vibrated in her pocket. "Yes, Curator, hold on a moment, I'm just in a meeting. Sorry, Mildred, I must take this. Could someone else please take over for me?" The Reeve left the room and stepped into the hallway.

As Mildred sat waiting for explanations, all she received was a small group of ladies staring at her. After a minute of silence, the Armourer broke the tension. "So, you must be the chosen one, then?"

Mildred rocked back in her chair, momentarily stunned.

"Armourer, that's enough."

"Why, Raysmau, she needs to know!"

Mildred, still disoriented, turned to the Armourer, "Wait, you are called; what was it, the Armourer? I noticed that you were not introduced."

"Yes, Mildred, that is correct," her tone was one of pride.

"And you provide… armour?" Mildred shrugged her shoulders as she stroked the side of Nahla.

"Of sorts. I prefer to describe myself as a scientist, a pioneer, an innovator, an…"

At that moment, the Reeve came back into the room and sat down. "Okay, everyone, this is what is happening. The web is being corrected as effectively as possible, and rumours are being shut down, social media accounts deactivated. A colleague at the Geological Service is, shall we say, tampering with measurements."

"What does that mean?"

"It means, Lady Suzanna, that what happened here was an earthquake that led to a series of gas explosions."

Suzanna raised her eyebrows—this wasn't the first time she'd heard of gas-related problems.

"An earthquake in Shropshire!" Mildred remarked.

"Yes, Mildred. Apparently, earthquakes have happened here before, usually only mild tremors. It's the best that could be done in a short timeframe. And…" The Reeve stopped talking as sirens were heard outside. "Kalara, check that, will you?"

Looking out of the window, Kalara couldn't see any emergency services from where she stood, she left the room to investigate.

"Mildred, we do not have a lot of time. But I know you must have seen the winged creature."

Mildred felt a shiver run down her spine as she nodded. "I did. Why were you all trying to destroy it? Was it something to do with that comet that hit Wales the other night? Were you trying to kill an alien species?"

The Armourer balked. "That was a satellite collision, Mildred."

Mildred sat upright, clutching her cats tightly. "So, what was it? Or what is it?"

"That creature is from another realm; it has no purpose here other than to cause havoc, and we need to stop it."

"By destroying half the road! I saw it fly away; it grabbed someone else as it went. Poor person, whoever that was, I hope they'll be okay."

The Reeve scanned the room; this was another issue that needed to be addressed. "The individual you mentioned is no longer what we once called a man; he is something called a Watcher. He equally has no place here."

"Oh!" Mildred pointed. "You spoke of this before, Daphne. Remember when we talked about going Watcher catching?"

Collective frowns spread across the room as Daphne rubbed her temple. "I didn't call it that, Mildred; those were your words. But you were warned, you must understand that not everything in this world stands for good."

"And that's where we come in," Suzanna added.

Mildred, despite their efforts so far, looked nonplussed.

"We are the light in times of darkness."

Mildred frowned at Suzanna. "That sounds more like lyrics from a song or a play."

"Well, it's all I can offer at this time; you need to place your trust in us."

The Reeve was reasonably impressed with Suzanna's words, considering she had no idea what she had just witnessed or was talking about.

The Reeve raised her hand toward Mildred. "Look, this is difficult, but I need to explain something. By now, I'm sure you've realised that the Kat Chamber is no ordinary cat club; in fact, it's extraordinary in countless ways. Everyone gathered here possesses a remarkable bloodline and that includes you, Mildred."

"What?" Mildred's face broke into a smile, more from shock than joy. She immediately glanced at Daphne, who nodded in agreement.

"Much of what I'm telling you may be beyond the understanding of Lady Suzanna and Lady Daphne."

The two Ladies turned to each other in surprise.

"You see, they are both Ladies, just as you are, Mildred. Your bloodline dates back thousands of years to an era when cats were revered not just as pets but as deities. Raysmau, Kalara, the Armourer, and I all have slightly different bloodlines, pure, yes, but different. We are not the protectors of cats; we are the protectors of you, along with the other ladies who are members of the Kat Chamber. The real name for the Kat Chamber is the League of Light."

Feeling overwhelmed, Mildred began to rise from her seat. "You know what, I think I need a cup of tea."

"Mildred, please, let's not get distracted. Time is of the essence. You can have tea later once we reach Loxley."

"What is Loxley?" Mildred inquired.

The Reeve rubbed her chin thoughtfully, weighing her words carefully. "Loxley is the headquarters for the League of Light in the United Kingdom and Ireland. There are other headquarters around the world, but Loxley is our home, our sanctuary, a truly special place. From now on, you cannot continue living here. You must come with us. You and your cats are not safe here. Now that he knows where you live..."

"Whoa, whoa, whoa! Wait a second, this is my home!"

"Mildred, what you witnessed came from a very dark place. You must try to see reason, as there is something I must tell you." The Reeve straightened her back. "The beast, the flying creature you saw, was drawn to this area for a purpose. This will be difficult for you to accept, but he was here for you or perhaps for that cat, we're uncertain which."

Mildred's mouth fell open in disbelief. Avoiding Comet's mark, she pulled the cat close, clutching her tightly to her chest. "Comet, he was here for Comet or for me!"

Suzanna and Daphne exchanged worried glances at each other.

"What do you mean he was here for Mildred or that cat?"

"Lady Daphne, all I can tell you is what I know. Please, let me finish."

"Mildred, throughout history, that creature you saw, be it he or one of his kind, has been here before..."

Mildred's eyes widened in alarm, "In this road?"

"No, no, Mildred." The Reeve raised her hand gently as she inhaled deeply, "I mean, in this world as we understand it." She pressed her fingers to her temple. "It's difficult to articulate, but occasionally, one of them crosses over from a very dark realm; the underworld is one interpretation. It's a place of pain where darkness prevails. He is here to bring his dark world into our realm. Do you understand?"

Mildred shook her head vigorously, dread pooling in her stomach. "No, not a word. That sounds truly terrifying."

"Well, all I can tell you is that when one crosses over into this realm, something is brought to us, some vital gift to our defence. It's a crucial aspect of life's balance."

Mildred's hands trembled as she nodded although still confused. "Okay, and what does that mean for me?"

"At the time of his arrival, that remarkable cat came into being as well. I wasn't truthful with you, Mildred. That mark on Comet's flank is no birthmark; it's a sign of power. You have been entrusted to protect her, and that is why he was here, in your road."

Mildred's heart raced as she cradled Comet, her eyes widening in panic as she examined the distinct mark within the cat's fur.

"As you can see, Mildred, she is no ordinary cat. Look how much she's grown already."

"Well, yes, I had noticed, but…" Mildred's voice faltered as she looked at Daphne's eyes, seeking reassurance. However, Daphne looked just as concerned.

"Have you felt anything peculiar lately? Has anything changed within you, Mildred? It's important we know if Comet is here to protect us or if you are."

Mildred placed Comet gently into her lap. "Protect you? What do you mean?" She shook her head in bewilderment, her hands still trembling. "Look, just a few days ago, my life was all about going to the shop, feeding Nahla, and so on. Nothing extraordinary, you understand."

"We understand completely. And when Lady Daphne visited you a few years ago, your life was undoubtedly different then. Now you live in solitude, as all our early Elders do. It's part of the necessary process as your mind adjusts to your new life with us. You are empowered to do great things, and in time you will be told what Comet's real name is."

"Ma'am, civilian firefighters are in the road dousing some of the houses. Fortunately, most of the fires have burnt themselves out, but the police are conducting house-to-house checks. They've already spotted our car; it won't be long before they make their way here."

"Right, thank you, Kalara. Mildred, listen closely: they cannot know we are here. They will be performing a welfare check and nothing more. You must get rid of them. I know you are in shock, but you need to stay calm. They must not find out about us, do you understand?"

"I... I honestly don't know what to think," Mildred replied, her voice quivering with anxiety.

"Here they come. Two police officers are approaching the path."

"Thank you, Kalara. No one must make a sound. Mildred, if you please, take care of this. Do not let them inside, even if they insist."

The Armourer began patting herself down. "I should have something with me in case we need to take care of them."

"What on earth does that mean?" Mildred gasped, horror washing over her as she sprang to her feet. "Daphne, please keep a close watch on my cats."

A loud knock echoed through the hallway. Taking a deep breath, Mildred brushed herself down, quickly scanning the room, rubbing her eyes before shaking her head and heading toward the hallway.

"Mildred, keep the door open at all times. We will be listening to everything you say."

Mildred swallowed hard; the large-framed lady they called Raysmau was very intimidating.

With a flap of her arms, she opened the front door, trying to look calm, even as her heart raced.

"Good morning," she managed to say, leaning against the doorframe for support as she offered a cordial nod to the two police officers who stood before her.

"Are you okay? You look as white as a sheet," one officer remarked.

Mildred could feel the tremors in her hands as she braced herself against the door. "How, um, can I help?" she stammered, her voice cracking under the pressure.

"No, madam, we're here to help you," one of the officers said, "What is your name, please? Our records indicate that no one is officially registered at this house."

"Erm, it's Mildred," she replied, noticing them both scanning her clothing.

"Look, this is highly unusual, but we've received reports about an earthquake. As you can see, it caused an incredible amount of damage. Although your home seems to be relatively intact, I can see you've lost a few roof tiles. And that's quite a fine-looking car you have at the front, I don't recognise that, it was lucky not to get damaged."

"Yes, I'm fine, just fine, everything's fine... thank you."

One of the officers exchanged a glance with his partner. "Are you certain, madam? If you don't mind me saying, you don't look okay."

"Well, I... erm, guess that's to be expected," she stammered, "you know, with my neighbour's houses collapsing and all that."

"We're a bit perplexed, though. From what we can gather, while several roofs have collapsed, the foundational structures seem surprisingly stable. Also, there are what appear to be some form of blast marks on various properties."

"That must have been caused by the gas explosions; that sent debris flying everywhere."

"Gas explosions? Do you know about that? We've only just been informed about it."

Mildred scratched her head. "Well, yes, it seems obvious, doesn't it?"

The officers exchanged bemused glances. "Not really, madam," one commented while making notes.

"The gas board is on their way. This road must be declared safe before anyone can reside here again. I fear those houses over there might be beyond saving."

"Was anyone hurt?" Mildred interjected.

"No, it's quite incredible. Miraculously, hardly anyone was at home at the time. A couple further down sustained minor cuts, and a man over the road is so overwhelmed with shock he's completely immobilised; we are getting help for him."

From her position in the front room, having overheard every word, the Armourer's eyes widened with realisation. She banged her temple with her hand in frustration. She'd need to get outside quickly to release the lawnmower man before things spiralled any further.

"But interestingly, Mildred," the first officer continued, "no one we've talked to seems to remember what happened except you. Can you tell us what you saw?"

Mildred rubbed her weary eyes, unsure how to respond to the question. "Well, I was, yes, asleep with my cats when suddenly I heard a loud bang, then another one, and I guess that's when the roofs collapsed."

The officer raised an eyebrow, scepticism etched on his face. "They simply fell in on their own?"

Mildred shrugged, her heart racing. "I guess so."

"Did the earth tremble? Did you feel anything? We are still waiting for a reading on the quake's strength."

Completely straight faced, Mildred shook her head vigorously.

"I see. Here's my card. Please call me if you remember anything significant. Mildred, we may need to speak with you again, you may have to come into the station."

"Good heavens! Am I in trouble?"

The two officers exchanged glances, the one who handed her the card easing her worries. "No, why would you think that?"

"Well, I'm just a little in shock."

"That's hardly surprising. Please keep my card. We'll be in touch. And you should pack a bag. Do you have a friend you can stay with?"

"Oh yes, that's not a problem; I have many friends."

The officer nodded, satisfied. "Well, that's all for now. Thank you, Mildred."

With a faint smile, she turned to close the door.

"Oh, don't forget to take your cats; it's dangerous out here. Are they alright?"

Mildred shook her head. "To be honest, I have no idea." She closed the door and returned to the front room.

Raysmau nodded. "You did well, Lady Mildred. Kalara, keep an eye on things, will you? Make sure they don't come back."

"Yes, Ma'am."

Mildred scratched at her head, a look of both relief and confusion etched on her face. "I'm glad that's over," she murmured, feeling her pulse race beneath her skin.

"Are you alright, Mildred?" Daphne asked gently, she rose from the sofa to allow Mildred to retake her seat.

"I don't know Daphne, thank you for keeping an eye on my cats." As she settled back, she gathered Comet into her arms, her fingers gently brushing her scar. "Aww… Comet!" Mildred waved her right hand in the air, shaking her fingers. "Honestly, why do you keep doing that?"

The Reeve shot up from her seat as Raysmau stepped forward.

"Well, well, well, that's highly interesting, wouldn't you all say? How fascinating!" The Armourer crouched down in front of Mildred. "Show me the palm of your right hand, Mildred."

"Why? What is it?"

"Just hold it forward. I don't want to touch it."

Reluctantly, Mildred did as she asked, extending her arm before her.

"Wow," the Armourer said, her eyes lighting up as she rubbed the scars on her face. "It's unmistakable, Reeve. She has it. This changes everything."

"Why? What is it? What's happening?" Not as thrilled as the Armourer, the Reeve came forward to inspect Mildred's palm. The Reeve looked away in shock, "Oh my, I can hardly believe it."

"What? What is it?" Mildred's heart raced, anxiety spiking as she searched their faces for answers.

"How long have you had that colour in your hand, Mildred?" the Reeve asked her facial expression intently serious.

"I don't really know. I've been having bad dreams for a little while, and when you brought Comet to me, it was just after that. It's weird; this colour comes and goes. It doesn't hurt. Only when I touch that mark on Comet it feels like an electric shock of some kind."

The Reeve exchanged a concerned glance with Raysmau.

"Ma'am, what do you want to do?"

The Reeve sat down again. "To be honest, Raysmau, I've never seen anything like this before."

"I don't believe any of us have, Ma'am."

Mildred clasped her hands together, trembling. "What? What is it?"

"Right, okay," the Reeve said, running a hand through her hair. "That colour means something serious. It's associated with power, but not our kind of power."

Struggling for breath, Mildred panted, "What does that mean? Someone, please tell me what is happening to me!"

"I will attempt to explain Mildred, although it can be a little complicated. However, what you are seeing is the colour associated with the dark realm, which is where the creature you saw came from." The Reeve stopped tugging at her hair. "As you know, our organisation was established a long time ago. But I don't believe you know that it was formed in the times of ancient Egypt. In their beliefs, in the afterlife, if you have a good heart or a good soul, you pass into a realm of eternal peace. However, if you have a bad heart and a corrupted soul, you are condemned to a world of eternal torment."

The Reeve reclined slightly in her chair. "If that happens, you are sent to a place filled with lakes of fire and trees of turquoise. That is the simplest way I can put it."

Mildred sank into her seat, looking distressed. "So, does that mean I'm bad?"

"No, no, not at all," the Reeve reassured her gently. "From what I understand, that colour you're seeing is foreign to your blood, but nevertheless, it flows within you. It has been passed to you by Comet.

You've never seen this colour before she came into your life?"

"No, well... no," Mildred admitted.

"Okay," the Reeve paused to gather her thoughts. "We have an ancient prophecy. I mentioned that if one crosses from the dark realm, another will emerge among us, one who is destined to protect us."

Mildred's frown deepened. "Whoa, now wait a second..."

"What time does your clock tell you, Mildred?" Raysmau asked.

"I don't know; it hasn't worked for a couple of days."

Raysmau nodded at the Reeve.

"Mildred, none of our clocks function anymore. Our timepieces show nothing. Our time has stopped, and potentially, our time is over. The beast you witnessed is trying to make that happen. He wants our time to end because only we understand and can fight him and his kind."

"What is he? You haven't said," Mildred asked.

"He's a Gatekeeper, Mildred," came the grave response. "We know we wounded him today, but he will return. He cannot fulfil his purpose unless either you, Comet or both of you are gone."

Daphne swallowed hard, a knot of fear tightening in her stomach, she reached out and placed a hand on Suzanna's shoulder.

"I think that's enough for now." The Reeve rose to her feet. "Kalara, is the road clear outside?"

Kalara returned to the room, "It's clear of police, Ma'am, but the fire services are still here."

"Alright, we need to leave. Mildred, pack a bag and make sure you have carriers for your cats. We don't usually have cats at Loxley, except for the Lady of the House. I suspect she'll be keen to meet you."

Mildred set her cats aside. "Wait a second, what are you talking about? I'm not going anywhere with you!"

The Reeve shrugged as Raysmau stepped closer. "I'm sorry, Mildred, but you must. Your new home will be Loxley."

Mildred moved behind her sofa, her voice shaking. "I'm not going anywhere with you. You cannot force me. I'll call the police!"

"You'll do no such thing!" Raysmau's stepped closer.

Mildred stamped her feet. "This is my home!"

"This changes everything, Mildred. I'm sorry. Look around you; this is not safe. This whole road will probably be condemned. You are too important to us; we cannot leave you behind."

"You cannot force me!" Mildred cried.

Raysmau stepped even closer, her presence undeniable. Mildred's watery eyes pleaded with the Reeve. "And you can call your dog off as well!" she demanded.

"Don't make us force you, Mildred. It's for your own good, we must do all we can," the Reeve said.

"You can't force her if she doesn't want to go!" Daphne shouted.

"Keep out of this, Lady Daphne," the Reeve commanded.

Mildred locked eyes with Raysmau, feeling anger at being told what to do and being ordered to leave her home. This would not stand; she wouldn't be pushed around any longer as a wave of heat surged through her, changing the colour of the blood vessels in her eyes.

Startled, the Reeve stumbled back a step, her expression tense with alarm. "Raysmau, move back! Look at her eyes!"

Raysmau glanced at Mildred's eyes and, without hesitation, started stepping backwards. The Armourer looked incredulous at what she was witnessing as Mildred dramatically extended her right palm towards the Reeve. The Reeve swallowed, her body language instantly becoming uncomfortable at the sight of Mildred's palm alive with the colour of turquoise.

The Reeve's throat tightened with concern. "Now, be careful, Mildred. You have a power there that you do not understand; you need to remain calm," the Reeve cautioned.

Slowly, Mildred lowered her hand, the glow faded, her eyes returning to their natural brown.

"Now you listen to me, sheriff. You do what you need to do, take whatever measures you feel are appropriate, but I am not coming with you."

"Mildred, I understand your concerns, truly I do, but the Gatekeeper will be back…"

"Then prepare for that! Do what you need to do!"

"We cannot leave you here alone."

"But she won't be alone!"

Hearing Suzanna's voice, the Reeve closed her eyes in annoyance.

"She won't be alone; she has us. I live nearby. Mildred can stay with me if she likes, or I can stay right on this road. If Mildred agrees, I'll keep an eye on her along with Daphne."

With her hands firmly planted on her hips, the Reeve let out a resigned sigh and glanced at Mildred, who remained steadfast.

"You can leave me with one of those chrome blasting things if you want," Suzanna added.

Raysmau frowned deeply, the Armourer's laughter didn't help the tension. "You are not a soldier; you are a Lady of the Order, Suzanna."

Suzanna shrugged. "We can all adapt, Raysmau."

"Definitely not." The Reeve retorted, rubbing her temple as she wrestled with the dilemma before her. "Raysmau, Kalara, Armourer, can I speak with you all outside? I'll be back in a moment, Mildred."

There was a heavy silence as they followed the Reeve outside.

"As you can see, Ma'am, there are still firefighters in the road."

She nodded. "I suspect they'll be here for a while, Kalara."

"Do you think the police will return, Ma'am?" Raysmau asked.

"Possibly," the Reeve replied, rubbing her temple as if to alleviate the tension. "I realise I need to make a decision about this, but Mildred is right; we cannot force her to leave with us against her will."

"What exactly are you proposing Ma'am?" Raysmau probed.

"To be truthful, I'm not sure," the Reeve admitted. "The Gatekeeper knows she is here."

"I have a view on this," the Armourer declared. "If she's not here, he'll automatically suspect that we've taken her to Loxley. He knows the location of Loxley as well; all it does is buy time. We can't place her in a headquarters in another country because she needs to remain here, in this country as part of the prophecy. She, or Comet, or a combination of the two, are a crucial part of our defence."

"Or our downfall," Kalara interjected.

Kalara turned to the Reeve, "Respectfully, Ma'am, I heard you tell Mildred that she may be our protector, but I didn't hear you mention to her that she could also lead to our undoing."

"No, I thought it was for the best," the Reeve said, glancing down the heavily damaged road. The properties where they had parked the cars earlier stood relatively unscathed, but the rest of the area was a chaotic mess. "Look at the state of this place. Securing her here will be almost impossible. In fact…" She paused, lifting a finger as a thought struck her. "Wait a second."

With a sense of urgency, the Reeve pulled out her phone from her pocket and called the Curator. "Nubia, yes. Well, I'll explain more when I get back, but Mildred doesn't want to leave this location. Can you start the process to condemn this entire road so we can acquire the properties?" She pulled the phone away from her ear, the onslaught of complaints from the other end was inevitable. "Nubia, just a yes or no will suffice at this time. We have little choice in the matter. Yes, I know. I'm going to implement appropriate security measures. Right, thanks. I'll be back later."

She hung up the call and sighed. "She's always such a joy to speak with." The Reeve turned her attention back to the matter in hand, "Alright, here are my thoughts: the Clerics are handling the internet, and others are addressing what happened here. Hopefully, the earthquake story will hold. Kalara, how do you feel about remaining here for the time being? The property opposite is damaged but probably liveable. I'll ensure supplies and everything you need is provided, including small arms and heavy weapons."

"Of course, Ma'am."

"What about me? Where do you want me in all of this?"

"I'm not in a position to order you, Armourer."

"No, but you certainly have the ability to ask."

"Would you like to remain here?"

"To be honest, I think I need to stay. It's imperative that we locate the deceased Watcher; the matter is of utmost importance."

"If he is dead" Raysmau added, "after all, no one saw what happened to him."

The Reeve nodded thoughtfully. "At the moment, we are assuming that's the case. It stands to reason that if he were still alive, the Gatekeeper would have surely taken him along with the other Watcher. Kalara, how do you feel about working with the Armourer? I'm also going to summon more support and arrange for more Escarrabin to be flown in, so I can provide you with additional cover."

Kalara nodded. "I'm okay with that."

"And you, Armourer? Are you on board with this plan?"

She nodded. "I am, count me in."

"Okay then, let's head inside and brief Mildred about what's happening."

Before they went inside, the Armourer interjected, "I just need to pop down to the other end of the road," the Armourer received curious stares from her colleagues. "I need to release a man with a lawnmower, oh, and a lady in the house on the other side of the road."

When they returned to the front room, Daphne was sitting on the couch next to Mildred while Suzanna held both of Mildred's cats.

The Reeve stood in front of the sofa and looked directly at Mildred, "Mildred, I'm going to ask you one last time: will you come with us?"

Mildred shook her head slowly, her shoulders slumping. "Look, I'm really confused and scared. I just want to be at home, here with my cats."

The Reeve raised her arms to reassure. "Okay, okay. Here's what's happening: we are going to leave, but Kalara and the Armourer will stay here."

"In this house?" Mildred asked.

"No," the Reeve replied with a slight smile. "They will remain on this road. We have a property across the way…"

Mildred looked surprised. "You do?"

"Yes, we do. However, we're looking to acquire more properties in the area, and we will be implementing security measures. That includes having more of us living on this very road. We must do everything we can to protect you and your cats, and that is non-negotiable."

Mildred raised her arms towards Suzanna. "Please, pass them both to me."

Suzanna gently passed Nahla and Comet to Mildred, she hugged her cats tightly, feeling less fearful of Comet. Mildred realised she was changing; there was a lot to learn, a lot to take in. But at that moment, being home with her cats was exactly where she wanted to be.

Appendix One:
LATE FOR SURGERY

THE MORNING BEFORE THE EVENTS IN ROCKE ROAD.

Dr Sarah Belloch shook her head as she studied the small dent on the wing of her car. Slamming the door shut outside Castle Hollow Veterinary Practice, she noticed only one car parked, the one belonging to Samanatha, their receptionist. David, the senior partner at the practice, should have arrived by now. It wasn't like him to be late, especially on a day when they had surgery scheduled.

"Morning!" Sarah exclaimed when she saw Samantha at the reception desk.

"Morning, Sarah! How's it going?" Samantha replied with a warm smile.

"Pretty good, thankfully," Sarah answered, stretching her shoulders as she approached the desk. "I didn't receive any messages from my ex-boyfriend last night. Maybe that private investigator he hired finally had a word with him," Sarah replied.

Samantha took a sip of her coffee. "I can't believe he did that. It sounds like something out of a bad drama."

"Well, you never really know someone, do you?"

"Guess not. The kettle is still hot if you fancy a brew."

Sarah nodded, her mind still partially distracted as she glanced at the notes that Samantha handed to her, which detailed her busy schedule for the day. "I'll grab one in a moment. I noticed David's car isn't here, and we have surgery this morning."

"I noticed that too. I'm planning to call him soon. There's something strange, though. You remember the cat Mr Muddles? He's still here."

A frown creased Sarah's forehead as worry set in. "But he was supposed to go home last night, his owner was coming to collect him."

"I know, but Mr Muddles is still out back in the kennel."

"Didn't the owner call the emergency number?"

"I don't know. David was the emergency call-out last night. Tell you what, I'll have the owner's details here; I'll give them a call."

"Okay." Sarah grabbed the clipboard and walked behind reception. "I'll get a brew. Can you come through when David gets here, please? I'll need some help prepping the room before surgery."

"Sure, no worries."

Sarah let herself into the secured area of the veterinary practice, entered the kitchen, dropped a teabag into a mug, added water, and then went into her office. She placed the clipboard on her desk, tossed her bag onto the chair, removed her shoes, and walked over to the sink. Turning on the hot water, she added soap and started to wash her hands. As steam rose, lost in thought, she glanced at her reflection in the mirror above the sink and suddenly spun around. After turning off the tap, she dried her hands and walked over to the coat rail. She noticed her veterinary uniform was missing. She was certain she had left her tunic on the hanger, but now the hanger was empty, her protective bottoms had also disappeared. Frustrated, she started spinning in circles, surveying the room, feeling completely at a loss.

Returning to the kitchen, Sarah removed the teabag from her cup, added milk, grabbed the mug, and opened the door to reception.

"Samantha, was the cleaner in last night? I can't find my vet's gown or bottoms."

"I don't think so, but she usually doesn't take the washing anyway."

"I know, I was just thinking out loud, that's odd."

"Do you want to hear something else strange? I just called the owners of Mr Muddles to let them know he was ready for collection and let's just say they are not very happy. Apparently, they arrived as planned last night, but David wasn't here. I asked if they noticed his car outside, and they said they didn't see it. Also, I found the security compound unlocked when I got here this morning. David should have locked it on his way out. They tried calling him repeatedly last night, but his phone rang out every time."

Sarah nodded, "That sounds very unlike him."

They both looked up as Julia, the third partner in the practice, arrived. "Morning," she greeted cheerfully.

"Morning, Julia. Have you spoken to David at all?" Sarah queried.

She shook her head. "Why, should I have?"

"No reason, just a couple of strange things happening. I'll check his office." Sarah set her mug down and headed through the security door, walking down the corridor to David's office. As she approached, she could see his door was wide open.

Stepping inside, she immediately put her hand to her mouth. "Come here quickly!" she shouted, urgency in her voice. David's love for the paranormal was well known among them, and as she looked at the poster on the wall and the assorted alien-themed merchandise, everything seemed to be in order. However, the blood-soaked bandages littered across the floor made her stomach lurch. Sarah swallowed hard; David's office was not a place for surgery, yet the inspection bed was covered in stains, indicating that something had bled there for some time. There was also a disturbing amount of a repulsive, sticky substance, perhaps phlegm, coating parts of the floor. Used and discarded surgical instruments lay haphazardly around the room. It was painfully clear that something serious had occurred here.

Within moments, Julia and Samantha rushed into the office, their faces twisting in shock.

"Oh my God, what has happened here?" Julia exclaimed, her hands flying to her head as if trying to grasp the gravity of the situation. She turned to Samantha, her voice rising in urgency. "Are all the overnight animals accounted for?"

"I checked the records this morning. There are no entries indicating any emergencies. No animals have been checked in or out," Samantha replied.

"Regardless, I think it's best you check the back just to ensure that every animal is definitely accounted for."

Samantha nodded. "Of course," and she quickly left the room.

"Sarah, do you have any thoughts about this?" Julia asked, looking concerned.

She shook her head. "I'll call him." Sarah took her phone from her pocket and dialled David's number. They immediately froze when they heard a phone ringing inside the room. Panic set in as Sarah followed the sound; it was coming from underneath his desk. She bent down to pick it up and saw her name displayed on the screen. Quickly, she switched her phone off. David's phone showed multiple missed calls, most from the same number. "Loads of missed calls, presumably from the owners of Mr Muddles."

"Sarah, I think it would be a good idea to check the CCTV. Let's not panic just yet," Julia suggested.

Sarah nodded, her concern evident, just as Samantha returned to David's office. "All animals are accounted for. Nothing has come in or gone out," she reported.

"Samantha, you know how to operate the CCTV system, don't you?" Julia asked.

"I do. Do you want to take a look?" she replied.

"I think that would be a good idea. Something is seriously not right here,"

They moved to the reception area. Samantha took her seat behind the front desk and began navigating the CCTV monitor. The three of them focused intently on the screen while Samantha selected various hours to playback from the previous night. For the most part, the car park appeared empty, and the compound gates were open.

"Oh look, there's someone at the door," Samantha exclaimed.

"Those are the owners of Mr Muddles; I've spoken to them before," Julia clarified.

They watched as the owners of Mr Muddles pressed the front doorbell multiple times.

"They do not look happy at all!" Samantha said, shaking her head, clearly worried about the practice's reputation.

Sarah nodded in agreement. "I would feel the same way if it were my cat. Samantha, can you keep flicking back?"

Only minutes before the very upset cat owners left, they caught sight of David's car rolling away.

"Hey! What the hell happened there? Keep going back, keep going back!"

Samantha did as Julia instructed. Sarah placed her head in her hands as she witnessed three extremely gaunt figures emerge from the practice, their movements deliberate as they approached David's car. One of them turned slightly allowing the camera to capture a clear side profile. In shock, Sarah shook her head and cried out, "What on earth is that? Hang on. Wait, pause the recording. Look, is he wearing my vet's uniform?"

"What did you say?" Julia asked, her face filled with confusion.

In a complete fluster, Sarah began to pace nervously. "I came in this morning, and my veterinary clothing is missing. He's wearing it, Julia!" She pointed at the screen.

Julia and Samantha turned to look at Sarah with concern.

"I think I should keep playing the recording," Sarah insisted, her heart racing.

All three of them leaned in, completely absorbed by the events on screen. They watched in horror as the three strangers got into David's car.

"They have his car keys, look!" Samantha exclaimed as she paused the recording. When she released the pause button, it looked like the strangers sat in the car for a while.

"What are they doing in there? Oh wait, do you see that?" Sarah's voice trembled as she pointed, her eyes wide with disbelief. "The car just shook a little. I think they just started it." Panic quickly rose in her throat as her hands instinctively shot up to cover her forehead.

They looked on in shock as the car lurched forward. It swerved quickly to the left and rolled straight down the steep bank.

Julia covered her mouth with her hands. "Oh my God!" All three of them stood in stunned silence as the gravity of what they had just witnessed sank in.

"Oh no!" Julia yelled as the three of them sprinted for the front door. They raced across the car park to the steep grass verge. Their worst fears were confirmed: David's car lay on its roof at the bottom of the bank.

"DAVID!!!" Julia shouted as she sprinted down the grass bank. The ground was slick with the early morning dew, and suddenly, Julia lost her footing. Sarah buried her face in her hands while Samantha ran down the bank to help Julia. Frantically, Sarah grabbed her phone from her pocket. "Samantha, tell me what you see. I'll call for help."

As Samantha and Julia reached the car, it was immediately obvious that no one was inside. David's small car was covered in dents.

"Oh my God! What is that?" Samantha cried, pointing at the windscreen. There was a strange mucus or saliva stuck to the glass.

"There was stuff like that on the floor in David's office as well." Julia turned around and shouted up the bank, "No one in here! Sarah, call the police."

Sarah nodded. "I will. I'm going to recheck his office."

She ran to the front doors as she dialled. The call was answered quickly, "What service do you require?"

"Police, please! We have a missing person and a car crash to report." She let herself through the security doors and sprinted to David's office, looking for anything that might help. She knew he wasn't there, but any clues would be useful.

"This is the police. What would you like to report?"

"I'm calling from Castle Hollow Veterinary Practice just outside Shrewsbury in Shropshire. We've had an accident; a car has gone down a grass bank and is on its roof, and the owner of the practice is missing."

Sarah listened to the lady on the other end of the phone taking notes as she studied David's desk. Something scrawled on his notepad caught her attention. She lifted the pad to read it. "Yes, thank you. Please send someone as soon as you can." She ended the call and put the phone back in her pocket.

What was written on the notepad was barely legible. Sarah shook her head, trying to make out the scrawl. It seemed to say something like *'cat 2 arts b.'* She scratched her head, puzzled. *Cat, 2, art...* What could that mean? *Cat with 2 hearts?* It made little sense, but then something came to mind. Cat with two hearts!

She ran into her office, grabbed her bag, and emptied its contents onto her desk.

She picked up the Polaroid she had snatched from the private investigator. Cat with two heartbeats! She nodded to herself, Mildred!

Taking her phone from her pocket, she scrolled through her list of recent calls. It was still early morning; she hoped her colleague would answer. In a panic, she turned and hurried back into David's office. Relieved when her call was answered, she took a deep breath, "It's Sarah from Castle Hollow. Have you had a chance to run the results for the cat called Missy? I know I'm following up quickly, but it's really urgent."

The results were ready. As they were read to her, she gasped and covered her mouth in shock.

Appendix Two:
CABINET OFFICE BRIEFING ROOM ALPHA

"Alison, I'm really sorry to pull you away," she said.

Alison dropped her bag onto the solid oak table. "It's no problem, honestly. My feet are killing me." Wincing slightly, she kicked off her shoes, sat down, and put her feet up on the table. "Another cheese and wine party; it was fine until someone wheeled in a wine cooler. Then it turned into the usual chaos, with staff falling out over petty issues. One person even tried to DJ, it was dreadful. So, I'm glad you called. So, is this about what happened earlier in Shropshire?"

"Yes, it's exactly that. I'm afraid things are not necessarily as they seem, or rather, not as they are being reported to the public."

A frown crossed Alison's face. She instinctively removed her feet from the green leather-topped table and leaned forward in her chair. "What do you mean?"

"Well, you know about the earthquake in Shrewsbury, Shropshire, earlier today? I don't believe it was an earthquake."

"What?!" Alison fell back in her chair. "But that's what I've been told."

Jody, Alison's assistant, nodded. "I know. I received an encrypted call from a contact at Box earlier, and she has expressed serious concerns."

"Did someone within the security service contact you?"

"Yes, a contact in MI5. As you know, they monitor the dark web and other related information sources, and the initial concern was that there was no evidence of an earthquake."

Alison shook her head. "I saw a news report claiming that the tremor registered a 2.4 on the Richter scale. How can that be dismissed?"

"Yes, we've all seen that, and that's the problem. First, it's exceptionally rare for that area to experience seismic activity, and second, substantial damage was reported for a 2.4 magnitude quake. The only area affected was a small cul-de-sac called Rocke Road. No other locations were damaged except for a fuel garage behind that road, which was completely destroyed. It's only by chance that no one was injured. The employee reported in sick that morning, and the garage was closed. If circumstances had been different, it could have resulted in fatalities."

Alison nodded. "A close call, then."

"No, it's far more troubling than that. My contact dug a little deeper. Although the incident has been officially classified as an earthquake event, we are struggling to get confirmation from the British Geological Society. Their seismology team is very quiet about it. The report that was released came from an external source, and we believe that report to be false. Whoever is behind this has been careless; they are trying to cover their tracks very quickly."

"You don't believe this was a terrorist incident, do you? Do we need to discuss this in room A?"

"No, most definitely not. This is definitely not a terrorist incident."

"How can you be so certain?" Alison pressed as she shifted uncomfortably in her chair.

"My contact in the security service has informed me that critical databases have been systematically wiped just as questions were beginning to surface. It was inevitable that someone would start connecting the dots."

Alison's eyes widened in shock. "Destruction of evidence? That could be crucial to our understanding of what really happened!"

"Ordinarily, I would agree with you, but not in this case." Jody took a phone from her blazer pocket. "We know there was a complete power outage affecting Rocke Road and some of the surrounding streets. However, it was not a grid failure; I believe it was an intentional act targeting a carefully chosen location. Furthermore, no one witnessed anything. Other than minor injuries, no one was hurt, yet a few houses on Rocke Road are likely to be condemned. Those who have been interviewed report no memories of the event itself; they recall what they were doing before and after, but not during the main incident."

"That's absurd, Jody! You're talking about the complete shutdown of an entire area and everything within it."

"To be honest, Alison, I think that's exactly what happened. And you and I both know who has the ability to do this."

Alison rubbed her chin and shook her head. "That's not possible. They've been inactive for generations, nestled quietly away from the rest of us." Her voice was laced with doubt as she cast a glance at Jody.

"Then this may convince you," Jody said, passing her phone to Alison. "The picture quality isn't very good. There was an electrical power outage in the area, but this footage was captured by a battery-powered doorbell camera, but you'll see enough. This is just a short excerpt of what actually happened on that road."

Worried, Alison took the phone in her hands. "You need to press the play button," Jody instructed.

Alison brought the phone closer to her eyes and pressed play. Panic immediately washed over her face as Jody stood beside her. "What on earth is that? It looks like a rabid dog!" she exclaimed.

Jody looked at Alison with concern. "We actually don't know what it is, but look closely, there are people in the tree above it. You can see a woman holding a strange-looking sword; she's trying to kill it. Frankly, that's the least of our problems. Just speed up the footage a little. There's an overgrown garden behind and to the right of the frame; you'll see someone come into view."

Alison studied the footage, shaking her head. "The way she's dressed, she looks like an old woman. She's holding something." Alison paused and asked, "Are those cats?"

"Yes, we think so, and you know what that implies. But you need to keep watching."

"Oh my God! What the hell is that thing?" Alison gasped, her hands trembling uncontrollably as a huge winged creature came into view on the roof of a house. Tiles fell crashing around the woman clutching the cats, and she suddenly disappeared back into the house. The footage then stopped.

Alison slumped back in her chair and passed the phone back to Jody. "Who else has seen this?" she asked, her voice barely above a whisper.

"I can't be certain. There were some men from Box digging around as well. As I understand it, the footage has been purged from the camera's servers. Of course, everyone is bound by the Official Secrets Act, and let's just say the men involved have been reminded of that. I suspect they'll be monitored, possibly moved out of the department, and perhaps out of office altogether."

Alison buried her head in her hands. Without lifting her head, she muttered, "What was that thing? Does anyone know?"

"If they do, we don't, but suffice it to say, it isn't from this place. You could see the creature was being fired upon by technology that I don't think we even possess. You know who is behind this."

Alison shook her head slowly, got up, and walked over to a decanter on the side. As she poured herself a drink, she thought deeply about the complexities of the situation.

"Look, Alison, I know this is something you rejected. You confided in me a long time ago, just in case something happened to you."

Alison raised the glass to her lips before setting it down with a heavy sigh. "Yes, they had other ideas for me. They thought I could be more useful out here."

Jody's expression grew more serious. "It has to be them."

"It seems that way, doesn't it."

"What are you thinking, what do you want to do?" Jody pressed.

Alison took another mouthful and shook her head. "Truthfully, Jody, I don't know. I'm going to need some time to think about this. My relationship with them and my subsequent departure wasn't welcomed by everyone. I haven't had any communication with them in many years."

"But Alison, we need to take action, we need to do something."

Alison returned to her seat and nodded. "Just give me a little time, please."

"Ok, I'll leave you in peace." As Jody headed toward the door, she glanced back at Alison, her face was a clear picture of worry. "Let me know what course of action you want to take."

Without looking up, Alison nodded.

As Jody closed the door, her last words were, "Thank you, Prime Minister."

UNITED KINGDOM
KAT CHAMBER

KATCHAMBER.COM

United Kingdom & Ireland Kat Chamber Sectors

Scottish Sector
- Ballater
- Dundee

Northern & Northern Ireland Sector

Irish Sector

Wales & Middle Sector
- Loxley?
- Shrewsbury
- Welshpool
- Much Wenlock

Lowlands Sector